"You have nerve,"  cool and jumping to read all the lette already—"

"I rarely read my c

"Well, that's just too ......g out the words, throwing down the file. "Maybe when you've come to your senses, you'll read that through properly."

"What for?" he goaded her, crossing his arms, looking her arrogantly up and down. "I have no intention of changing my mind. I plan on ignoring the whole thing."

"Mr Gallagher," Meredith said through gritted teeth, "I am not to blame for the manner in which your grandmother chose to bequeath her fortune. I have no pleasure in being here, I assure you. But I have a responsibility to act on behalf of the beneficiary, and a legal duty to act in managing and administering the estate."

"Bravo. An impressive speech." He clapped his hands and looked her over, amused. "I guess law school is good for something, after all."

Meredith took a deep breath. "In case I used too many big words," she said sweetly, "it means that, like it or not, I now represent your best interest. I need you to co-operate. Do you understand?"

"Perfectly. Now, if you'll excuse me, I'm very busy this morning. Goodbye, Miss Hunter." The door snapped shut behind him, leaving Meredith openmouthed in the middle of the room.

Also by *Fiona Hood-Stewart*

EVER AFTER
SILENT WISHES
THE LOST DREAMS
THE STOLEN YEARS
THE JOURNEY HOME

FIONA
HOOD-STEWART

SOONER
OR LATER

MIRA

*First published in Great Britain 2006.
MIRA Books, Eton House, 18-24 Paradise Road,
Richmond, Surrey, TW9 1SR*

© Fiona Hood-Stewart 2005

ISBN 0 7783 0115 X

63-0106

*Printed and bound in Spain
by Litografia Rosés S.A., Barcelona*

To my goddaughter
Annabel Freya
with love

Prologue

"So. This is finally it, Bill?" Rowena Carstairs murmured in her deep, tobacco-riddled voice, her eyes never leaving the doctor's face.

The gray-haired, athletic-looking Bill Maguire let go of her pulse and straightened next to the large four-poster. "I'm afraid so," he said, looking at her with a wry, sad smile. He knew it would be futile to pretend.

"That's all right," she said, her creased features breaking into a smile that still sparkled with mischief. "I've had a good inning. Better than most."

"You're sure you won't consider the treatment? There's a small chance it would buy you another year or two."

"Ha! You have to be joking! I'm ninety-three, Bill. If I don't die of one thing, it'll be of another. And to tell you the truth, maybe it's time."

She lay back in the huge canopied bed and closed her eyes, her head propped against a sea of white lace pillows.

"All right, then. I'd best be off now," the doctor murmured with a touch of regret, patting her wrinkled, veined hand, as it lay so motionless on the coverlet it could already be lifeless. "I'll be back in the morning."

"You come," Rowena said, opening her eyes and winking, "but I don't guarantee I'll be here. Depends on how the mood strikes me. So I'll say goodbye just in case. You're a good man, Bill. Thanks for everything."

"Don't talk rubbish," he replied, his tone bracing. "You'll be here harassing the hell out of everyone for a while yet." He laughed and their hands met once more.

Rowena nodded, then suddenly looking very tired, she waved him away. "You be off now. I need a rest. Tell Miss Mabella to come in, will you? She may have some good advice for the upcoming journey." She let out a low, husky cackle that ended in a hacking cough.

"Okay." The doctor smiled and nodded. "Good night, Rowena. Sleep well."

"You bet I will."

Once she was sure she was entirely alone, Rowena sagged against the pillows and sighed. So this was the end. She accepted it philosophically as she did most things. Part of her regretted leaving. But, as she'd remarked to Bill, she'd had one hell of a good run. It was time to go. All that increasingly mattered now were the regrets, those niggling mistakes made years ago that couldn't be changed but might, if things went according to plan, be set on track.

Shifting her position to accommodate her stiff back, Rowena heaved another sigh. She should have listened to her daughter all those years ago. Isabel had tried to tell her the truth, but she hadn't wanted to believe her child's claims. Allowing pride and her own agenda to get in the way, she had paid the price.

"Miss Rowena?"

Opening her eyes, she turned her head on the pillow. "Miss Mabella, you sit yourself down on that chair right here next to me." The formidable figure of Miss Mabella was clad in her usual long white dress under a purple silk cape with rows of beads and amulets hanging loosely around her neck. She swayed as she lowered her bulk onto the proffered chair. The pupils of her eyes shone in sharp contrast to the whites, illuminating her black face. Her complexion looked surprisingly young for a woman her age. On her head she wore an extravagant turban tied in the fashion of the African tribe she descended from and whose language she still favored over the English she spoke only when necessary.

"Time's a gettin' close," she murmured, placing her hand on Rowena's withered forehead. "But I know you're ready to go, Miss Rowena. Ain't nothin' left you can do on this side no more. Gotta leave it up to the boy now."

"You're sure I've made the right decision?" Rowena's eyes closed as she drifted. Already the room and the earthly space around her seemed distant.

"Ain't no saying for sure. The boy, he's a son of Ogun, a strong God. Ogun, he likes justice. The gods is on his side, all right. Ain't no doubt about that." Miss Mabella nodded wisely.

"God bless him," Rowena whispered. "He's my only hope."

"Now don't you worry nomore, Miss Ro. You travel easy. I'm watchin' out for you and yours. Just you let go and let Miss Mabella take care of things." She placed both her hands inches from Rowena's head and began a low incantation in her native Gullah dialect.

"You always have been a good friend, Miss Mabella," Rowena managed with considerable effort. She felt tired. Exceedingly tired. She could sense the end of her earthly journey closing upon her, yet she didn't repine.

As the sun set over the trees in her beloved garden, Rowena thought one last time of the sealed envelopes lying in wait in Meredith Hunter's office. She'd cast her bets and had set the dice rolling in an attempt to salvage the situation. She'd set up the rules by which the game would be played as she thought best. The future lay in the hands of others.

A crumpled, enigmatic smile hovered on Rowena's thin, cracked lips as Miss Mabella chanted softly. She'd be willing to wager that once she was gone, all hell would break loose, big time. Would things sort themselves out as she hoped? It was a wild hope and perhaps a vain one, but it was her best try.

As she sank back and allowed her mind to drift to the gentle sound of Miss Mabella's voice, weariness overwhelmed her. Her eyes closed for the last time. She had only one final regret.

What a pity she wouldn't be here to see who would walk with the winnings.

1

Meredith Hunter skimmed through the thick sheaf of legal documents and, for the second time that day, exclaimed, "This can't be real. Surely Rowena must have been mad to leave such a will!"

She was bewildered. Rowena Carstairs, her favorite client, had been one of the savviest people she'd ever met—and also one of the most loyal. When more than a year ago, after some serious soul-searching, Meredith had decided to leave Rollins, Hunter & Mills, the famous Savannah law firm where she'd gotten her start, in order to launch her own firm, Rowena had insisted on transferring her business. Even when Meredith had advised against it, admitting that her firm would never be able to match the resources of the firm that had ably served Rowena's interests for more than fifty years, the old lady hadn't balked. "After all," Meredith recalled her saying imperiously, "if you don't trust those old windbags anymore, why the hell should I?"

She smiled at the memory, suspecting Rowena

knew that her new firm, Hunter & Maxwell, would never have gotten off the ground without her support. Ro had always looked after those she cared about. And that, Meredith admitted with a sigh, is what made her will all the more incomprehensible.

Slipping her reading glasses down her small, straight nose, Meredith gazed at the piles of legal files strewn around the small office. The Carstairs relations would be furious—probably go straight over to Ross Rollins and hire him to contest. And there was Dallas Thornton, Rowena's estranged granddaughter. The girl would not be a problem in that she'd already stated clearly she wanted nothing to do with her late grandmother's estate. But telling these people that they would receive nothing of the inheritance they'd long expected and that everything—including Rowena's dyed poodles—had been left to a complete stranger would be a daunting task indeed.

Until now Meredith had managed to avoid a confrontation with her old senior partner. But if the Carstairs hired Ross as they inevitably would, she was sure he would take pleasure in trying to bring her down to size. Oh, well. It had to happen some day, she figured. The hard part was she liked him. A lot. An old friend of her dad's, he had written her a glowing recommendation for Yale, hired her and then had been implicated—even if it hadn't been proved—in a political scandal that had brought down Congressman Harlan MacBride, the now former husband of her best friend, Elm Hathaway. Although Elm had never blamed her, and was now happily married to Johnny Graney, she'd felt ashamed to be a part of a firm that valued the old-boy network above its own ethics. And so, with Rowena's help, she'd set out on her own.

Meredith laid the documents back on her desk and tweaked her thick pageboy-style chestnut hair behind her ears. She would first contact James G. Gallagher, Rowena's presumptive heir, whom Rowena's detectives had tracked to London. She'd never even heard of the man—and doubted any of the Carstairs had, either. Did he even know that he was adopted? "None of this makes any sense," she murmured. "Why would Rowena settle a one-hundred-million-dollar estate on a complete stranger?"

"Because it appears he's her grandson."

Meredith turned abruptly and sat up. "Tracy. I didn't hear you come in." She twiddled her pen thoughtfully. "I'm still reeling in shock." Her partner, Tracy Maxwell, stepped farther into the office. "As far as we know, Rowena never even met this guy. She seems to have made a conscious decision to exclude this supposed grandson from her life, but now has left him everything. I just don't get it."

Tracy shrugged, setting her coffee mug down on Meredith's teak desk. "I know about as much as you do, Mer," she replied, leaning back in the creaking leather chair. "But I guess it all boils down to this— blood's thicker than water. By the way—" she grimaced as she glanced down doubtfully "—couldn't we at least afford a new chair? This one's going to collapse any day now, and probably with some valued client in it. We'll be sued for negligence." She crossed her well-shaped legs under her pencil-gray skirt and eyed Meredith. "So?" she queried. "What do you think made the old bird do it? Weird that she never asked you to look over her will or that she never disclosed the extent of her holdings."

Meredith shrugged, shook her head. "I once asked

her about it but she clammed up. Said she had it all sorted out years ago. I figured it was none of my business, that she'd used other counsel for her own reasons, but that doesn't explain why she left her fortune to a stranger. Could it be out of remorse?"

"Perhaps."

"Maybe she wanted to make up for the past. She obviously felt a duty to her bloodline despite the child being given up for adoption." Meredith knew she was desperately seeking a rational motive for her late client's actions, since she was now left to deal with the outcome. "It just seems totally unlike Ro to react like this. I mean, she was one tough cookie and not one given to sentiment, or to mishandling her affairs."

"All I can figure is that certain things come back to haunt you when you know the end is nigh," Tracy answered. "And who would have thought Rowena could be worth so much? All those relatives will be positively nauseous when they realize exactly how much they've lost—and to whom. Which reminds me," she added, a mischievous smile dawning on her dimpled cheeks, "I was talking to Uncle Fairfax this morning and guess what he told me?"

"What?" Meredith's large gray eyes filled with new interest. Tracy was an expert at wheedling casual bits of information out of people.

"We had a most enlightening conversation."

She rolled her eyes. "Tracy, spill it. I'm not in the mood to mess around. I have to take immediate action. I'm already dreading Joanna Carstairs's face when she learns the news."

"Rather you than me, babe," Tracy admitted. "Anyway, Uncle Fairfax remembers Isabel, Rowena's daughter, well. Said they hung out in the same crowd, and that she was very pretty and vivacious, always flirting and acting much older than her age. She also used to hang around with older men, some of them Rowena's own friends."

"That must have been almost forty years ago. And?"

"According to Uncle Fairfax, there was talk about whether she might have let things go a little too far."

"Oh, you mean she had an affair?"

"Nobody seems to know and, as she's dead, no one ever will."

"I guess not. What else did he say?"

"Only that the summer after her sixteenth birthday, Isabel suddenly disappeared for a year or so—supposedly to a finishing school in Europe. She was a bright girl with career ambitions, so everyone was surprised. People naturally assumed she'd gotten pregnant, though it was never mentioned outright. Such things were never discussed in those days."

"Had he heard that she'd given birth to a son?" Meredith asked, attentive.

"No. Like everyone else, he assumed that she'd had an abortion."

"Ethics aside, that certainly would have been the easiest route," Meredith said, brow furrowed, "but she didn't take that course. Instead, she gave the baby up for adoption."

"Right."

"But why give the baby away? She could easily afford to keep it," Meredith argued.

"You talk as if you don't know Savannah, Mer." Tracy laughed, a thin, ironic smile touching her full lips. "If things are bad now, imagine what it must have been like thirty-eight years ago! I doubt Rowena would have tolerated her daughter keeping an illegitimate baby. It just wasn't done. Particularly if the father wasn't suitable husband material, which I presume must have been the case."

"How absurd," Meredith exclaimed, disgusted by such hypocrisy and wondering what sort of woman would have let society and a strong-willed mother force her to give up a child if she'd wanted to keep it.

"Absurd maybe, but let's face it, that's the way it was. Young society ladies who found themselves in a fix went abroad, had an abortion somewhere discreet or gave the child up for adoption. They spent the year away and then returned home with no one the wiser." Tracy raised an elegantly etched brow and reached for the coffee mug.

"Carrying the child for nine months, giving birth to it at this Swiss convent," Meredith said, pointing to a file, "and then simply leaving it behind so she could head back home and party seems so cruel, so unfeeling."

Tracy shrugged. "I doubt Rowena gave Isabel much choice. If it makes you feel any better, Uncle Fairfax did say that Isabel was different when she returned, much more subdued. Nobody talked about it. But obviously," she added, gesturing to the paperwork lying on the desk between them, "there was a child. As for the father's identity, well, presumably Isabel took that secret with her to the grave. And now Rowena—for whatever weird reason—has named the child her heir."

"But doesn't it all seem too simple? I mean, think about it, Trace." Meredith tapped her fingers on the serviceable teak desk, then leaned back and swung in the sagging office chair, crumpling her suit jacket. "Rowena had a complex personality. We know she liked to control things. She didn't leave anything to chance. So why fork over a fortune to a total stranger? And then there are the Carstairs relations to consider, not to mention Dallas. I can't believe Rowena left her at nineteen without a dime when she knows all the problems the poor kid is going through with that property of hers up in Beaufort. The bank's about to foreclose."

"I didn't realize it was that bad. Is there nothing we can do?" Tracy asked anxiously, horrified by the thought of Dallas Thornton, whom she'd known since she was a kid, being thrown out of Providence, the beautiful stud farm that for years had been in her family.

"I don't know yet." Meredith sat straighter. "I'll take all this home tonight and dig my teeth into it once the boys are in bed." She glanced at her watch. "Oh, Lord, it's almost five. Mick's ball game is this afternoon." When she dragged her fingers through her hair and took off her glasses she suddenly looked much younger and more vulnerable and very pretty. She stared at her partner. "You realize what's going to happen, right?"

"Yep. Pretty much. It seems a given that Rowena's relatives will contest the will."

"And guess who they'll hire—if they haven't already?"

The two women's eyes locked. "Ross."

"Right. You know I loved Ro dearly, but I wish she hadn't left me with such a mess." She groaned, "Even if it does make for a dramatic parting gesture. She never liked all her greedy Carstairs relatives, said they reminded her of buzzards at the roadside, waiting ravenously for the morsels her eventual death would bring."

"Looks like she's had the last word. We'll miss her, you know," Tracy said as she got up to leave.

"Yeah, we will. See you tomorrow," Meredith said, a soft smile touching her lips as the door closed behind Tracy.

As she gathered the files she'd sort through later that evening, Meredith recalled that stormy afternoon twelve years earlier when she'd first met Rowena Carstairs. She had been a summer intern at Rollins, Hunter & Mills and Rowena had been holding court in the firm's walnut-paneled lobby, dressed in a flowing purple caftan and a remarkable jeweled pink turban. Her legendary toy poodles—always dyed to match Rowena's headdress of the day—were yapping hysterically at her heels and gnawing on the knotted fringe of the floor's antique Oriental carpet.

The poodles, Meredith recalled, were noted for their ill humor. Neither of the junior partners hovering anxiously beside one of the firm's most prestigious clients had dared to censure the dogs, which by this time were happily chewing their way through a delicately carved chair leg.

Raised to respect the value of things, and too new to the firm to know whom she was messing with, Meredith marched right up to Rowena's dogs and told them firmly to heel. To everyone's astonishment the dogs stopped their destructive activity and settled obediently at Meredith's feet, giving her patent pumps a cautiously friendly lick.

And to everyone's equally stunned amazement, Rowena had burst out laughing and grasped Meredith's hand. "About time someone had the guts to stand up to these little pests," she barked. "Beastly little dogs, aren't they? Touched in the head, I think."

"Must be all that hair dye," Meredith noted wryly.

After an audible gasp, one of the junior partners,

clearly bent on damage control, stepped forward and, muttering apologies, grabbed Meredith by the arm, intent on propelling her back to the copy room. But Rowena stayed his hand. "You know, I bet you're right. That dye probably makes 'em antsy," she said, addressing Meredith, her keen bright eyes narrowing. "Damn, why didn't I think of that? What's your name, gal? It's good to see that *someone* around this mausoleum has some spunk."

Before she'd left the firm that summer, Ross Rollins had told her there'd be a position waiting for her as soon as she finished law school. Surprised, she'd thanked him profusely, but he told her to save her thanks for Rowena Carstairs. "Claimed you're the only one with any sense around here, and threatened to take her business to another law firm unless we hired you. As you've probably gathered," he'd added dryly, "she's one of our biggest clients."

Without a doubt, Rowena Carstairs had been one of Savannah's most flamboyant and original characters. She'd also been a true friend. It was no exaggeration to say that without Rowena's patronage, Meredith would never have been able to start her own small independent practice. So no matter how mysterious and convoluted the will—or how many of her own questions went unanswered—she must do her best to see that Rowena's wishes were fulfilled.

Meredith shoved the documents in her briefcase and, grabbing her coat, moved toward the door. She'd think about all this later tonight, once homework was done and the boys were fast asleep.

Opening the door of her office, she smiled at Ali, her faithful secretary who'd taken a substantial pay cut to follow her on her path of independence. That was loyalty,

Meredith realized. "Have to get to the game but I'll be in early tomorrow. I'm taking the Carstairs files with me, Ali."

"Don't worry, Meredith, I'll be here awhile. Tracy's up to her eyeballs in the *Martin v. Fairbairn* case so we'll be busy. I just put on a new pot of coffee." Ali's slim figure and good posture made her seem always ready for action.

"I don't know how you guys survive. You know, I read somewhere that women can get depressed from too much caffeine. You and Trace should seriously consider cutting down on—"

"You have precisely ten minutes to get to the game and traffic's bad," Ali said, dismissing her. "So long. See you in the morning." She waved her thin fingers and grinned before heading into the tiny kitchen.

Stepping out onto the street, Meredith glanced back fondly at the small redbrick house she'd leased for the office. It wasn't pretentious, but it served its purpose. During the past most difficult months of her life, she and Tracy had built up a growing practice by accepting lower fees than most firms of their caliber. Some simply didn't want to pay the horrendously costly fees of the better-known firms. Other, more humble clients had heard through the grapevine that Meredith Hunter had left a junior partnership at Rollins, Hunter & Mills to begin her own practice because she'd become disenchanted with the way her former firm did business. This, and the fact that she always had time to spare for a lost or ailing cause, was beginning to pay off.

Getting into her old Jeep Cherokee, Meredith prepared to go into Mom mode. It wasn't easy juggling home and the office, especially now that Tom was gone.

She swallowed and gunned the engine, reminding herself that her ten- and eight-year-old sons, Mick and Zack, were her priority. This was no time for tears. The kids needed her. And she needed them.

It was all they had left.

After she'd read the boys a good-night story, turned off the lights and walked down the staircase of the lovely antebellum home she and Tom had dreamed of, saved for, then bought, depression set in. During the day Meredith had so much to do that she barely allowed herself time to think. Work at the office was all-consuming and the kids' schedule was packed with extracurricular activities that had her running from Little League practices to soccer games. She always had dinner to prepare and homework to finish, and although she'd never thought she'd enjoy math, she'd found herself delving into the intricacies of multiplication and long division with zeal, dreading the moment when it would be time to say "bedtime," and she'd find herself wandering around the house alone with only her memories for company.

Turning on the TV in the den, she glanced absently at the time. Nine-thirty. It was still too early to sleep. Maybe she should call her mother. But then she remembered it was bridge night and Clarice and John Rowland would be out. It was too late to call Elm in Ireland and everyone else was busy, watching TV with their husbands, discussing the day's activities. They didn't need to listen to her whining on the phone, or worse, weeping.

She flopped onto the aged moss-green sofa next to Macbeth, the family's golden Lab. Actually he'd been Tom's. Swallowing the knot in her throat again, Meredith stroked the dog between its ears, determined to keep her emotions under control. Faithful old Mac was getting really ancient now. She simply couldn't bear it if he went, too.

Meredith flipped the channels on the remote, unable to concentrate on any of the programs. She'd always followed current affairs and both local and international politics, but now she didn't care what was happening in the Middle East or in Washington, or even here in Savannah. All she now knew was the loneliness of the empty space on the couch next to her.

For the thousandth time since learning of the freak boating accident off the coast of Georgia the year before, Meredith railed at the injustice of his death. Why him? Why them? With so many unhappy people about, why did such tragedy have to befall her Tom?

She took a deep breath and willed herself to stop this railing at fate that served no purpose.

After several more minutes she switched off the television impatiently and went to the kitchen to make herself a cup of herbal tea. Maybe she should go over Rowena's will again and compile some notes for her conference call tomorrow with the New York detective agency so she'd be sure to gather all the information she could on James G. Gallagher, presumptive heir.

Taking a sip of the hot brew, she sat at the old pine table she and Tom had picked up by chance at a yard sale. However hard she tried, it was impossible not to feel his presence everywhere, to make believe that if she closed her eyes then opened them she'd find that it was all a bad dream, that Tom was right here, calling to her from the top of the stairs for something he'd forgotten.

A slim, sad, yet determined figure in her ancient sweats and Tom's old sweatshirt, she opened her briefcase and donned her glasses. Handling Rowena's bequests would help fill some of the emptiness.

An hour later, she closed the file and stretched. Then, after thoroughly checking all the doors and windows and switching off the downstairs lights, she made her way up to check on the kids. She scooped up a fallen duvet, and tucked Zack's dangling leg back under the covers. Then she entered her bedroom and undressed, catching a glimpse of herself in the long cheval mirror that had belonged to her grandmother.

Looking thin and tired, her eyes stared dully back at her. Her skin needed a treatment and her hair looked terrible. She dragged her fingers through it and grimaced, realizing she must make time to go to the salon. She had to appear presentable at the office and for the kids, even if she really didn't give a damn.

Pulling on a pair of Tom's old pajamas, Meredith got into bed and huddled under the covers. Maybe she'd try to read awhile. She flipped through the *Savannah News*, but after ten minutes she gave up and, turning off the bedside lamp, sank wearily into the pillows. And then, despite every effort not to, she did what she did every night and gave way to the unshed tears that had haunted her all day.

A few minutes later she fell into a deep, exhausted sleep.

Thank God she was too tired to dream.

So Rowena Carstairs was finally dead.

On the one hand, the news filled him with relief. On the other, her passing encapsulated the passage of time, a reminder of just how many years had gone by since that long-ago night when…

Better not remember that.

The problem was, he'd never known if Rowena knew or had guessed what had happened. Had Isabel kept quiet all those years? Rowena had never asked him about it. Not in so many words. But sometimes he'd wondered. Rowena had been a strange old woman. There was no telling what she knew. One thing was certain, though. She'd always made him feel uncomfortable.

It wasn't anything she did or said, rather an indefinable uneasiness that crept over him whenever she was present. Then again, that might just be his conscience pricking him. At least now he could finally breathe easy, knowing she was six feet under. Well, would be in a few days, he corrected.

Somehow the idea that Rowena still lay in the morgue sent shivers down his back. All at once he thought of Miss Mabella, the famous voodoo priestess whom Rowena made no secret of visiting.

He shifted in the deck chair, telling himself not to be ridiculous, then deliberately turned the page of the *Savannah News* where they'd dedicated two full pages to her obituary.

Instead, he chose to read the sports page.

2

"So what do we know about our heir?" Meredith asked Detective Garcia on the other end of the line.

"Actually, quite a lot. The guy's in all the papers."

"Oh?" She tilted her head curiously.

"Yeah, he's Grant Gallagher."

"I thought his name was James," she answered impatiently.

"James Grant. He goes by his second name. And what I meant, ma'am, is that he is *the* Grant Gallagher, you know, the corporate raider who took over Bronstern's last year? Remember all that fuss in the news? From what I read, he made a killing."

"Good Lord." Meredith's brows flew up. "But the man's a thief and a bloodhound." She sat up straighter and, in her usual fashion, tipped her glasses.

"Well, I guess that's one way of looking at it. Others might say he's a mighty smart businessman who knows how to make a buck."

"With absolutely no regard for those he bulldozes along the way," Meredith replied witheringly. "Somebody should haul him to jail for what he does. Now, you're absolutely certain you've got the right man?"

"Yes, ma'am. No doubt at all."

"I'll want DNA samples."

"We already got 'em. Our fellow in London got a hair off Gallagher's coat when he was dining in some fancy restaurant. Slipped some dough to the coat-check gal."

"Oh." Meredith blinked, taken aback. By any measure, without the man's consent, that constituted a major invasion of privacy. "I see. Well, maybe we should have a second *authorized* sample. Anyway, send me the complete file and I'll deal with contacting him."

"Sure will. Anything else we can do, just give me a call."

"Thanks, Detective, I will."

Meredith hung up, dazed by this latest news. *Grant Gallagher.* The press usually fawned over him, writing about his meteoric rise to fame and fortune, skipping over the fact that he'd damaged the lives of countless employees. He was the worst sort of corporate raider, buying up companies only to destroy them as he sold off their parts for a profit. And now one hundred million dollars was about to fall into his sleazy, undeserving lap.

"I can't let this happen," she muttered, a picture of Dallas biting her nails over the foreclosure papers forming in her mind. "It's just not fair."

She reread a letter from the convent in Switzerland where the adoption had taken place thirty-eight years earlier. It was dated about ten years ago, which must have been about the time Rowena had hired the detective agency to track down her grandson. She had no doubt of the letter's authenticity. Now, as she perused it again, she wondered why it had taken Rowena so long to initiate the search.

Even as she asked herself the question, she realized it wasn't her place to query her client's motives. But what about Dallas? Somehow she had to do something for the girl. She would come up with a plan, she vowed. But first, despite her natural reluctance, she must follow the will's directives, contact Gallagher and inform him of this windfall. She shuddered.

The next morning, after shuttling the kids off to school, Meredith got to the office as early as possible, hoping something in the files on her desk would present a solution for Dallas.

"Good morning." Tracy poked her head around the door and smiled. "May I?"

"Please, come on in. You'll never believe who the Carstairs heir is," she said with a huff.

"You told me. James G. Gallagher, whoever he is." Tracy sat down opposite. "Coffee?"

"No, thanks. And by the way, he goes by the name of Grant Gallagher. Mean anything?"

"Sounds familiar." Tracy's brow creased.

"Of course it does. Remember at the beginning of last year, that Bronstern takeover up east? All those families put out of work?" she inquired, brows drawn together in a distressed frown. "It was Grant Gallagher who put the whole thing together. Just marched in there, cleaned shop and sent all the jobs overseas. Claimed outsourcing was in the shareholders' best interests. He couldn't have cared less about the people who'd given their lives to the company. He just wanted to fill his goddamn pocketbook. It made me sick."

"Wow! And you mean to tell me that he's the heir to

Rowena's hundred million?" Tracy's eyes popped and she let out a huff. "Jeez, it's not like he even needs the money."

"Exactly. Now you understand why I'm not too thrilled at having to contact the guy about his windfall. Which, by the way, brings me to what I wanted to ask you. I really can't leave town right now. The kids are involved in so many activities. Zack has that dental treatment coming up. I was wondering whether you wouldn't—"

"Don't even think about it." Tracy raised her hand like a vigilant traffic cop. "I'm tied up to the gills in the Fairbairn affair."

Meredith was about to protest, then let out a sigh. It was true that Tracy was carrying an impossibly heavy load. Plus, deep down, she knew the duty was hers. "Okay," she said, a sigh escaping her as she scooped up the papers. "I guess I'll have to get on with it. Maybe I can avoid a trip. I'll write him first and pave the way. There are a couple addresses in the file."

"That's a good start. Send Mr. Gallagher a registered letter requesting a conference call. Don't go into too much detail in writing." Tracy rose and paused at the door. "By the way, have you told the others?"

"Not yet," Meredith answered in a hollow voice.

"And what about Dallas? She still refusing to leave Providence?"

"Yep. She's refusing to come to the reading of the will. She's playing the proud princess, saying she doesn't care. She's already told me that she wouldn't touch Rowena's money, anyway—not that she knows what kind of money we're talking about, of course. It's unfair that she stands to lose so much and that such a creature will inherit what he can't possibly need. I can't fathom why Rowena would do this, I really can't," she insisted, shaking her head. "I just wish I wasn't the executor of the will and could advise Dallas to contest."

"Hardly appropriate," Tracy murmured, sucking in her cheeks, as she was prone to do. "Dallas is a strong-willed young woman. She'll live. It's a pity her father left quite a bit of debt when he died several months ago. Or so I've heard."

"Doug Thornton did indeed leave her that," Meredith said, nodding. "Which makes this decision of Rowena's even more unacceptable."

"Honey, I haven't the faintest idea why she did this, but knowing your client I'd bet big money there's a good reason. Maybe you should visit Dallas and see Doug's stud farm in the process. Beautiful place, apparently," she added. Then, glancing at the file in her hand, she murmured, "Thought at all about what approach you'll take with Gallagher?"

"No, I have not." Meredith bristled. "I'll wait for him to reply to my letter first. Until then I'll concentrate on the Carstairs gang." She grimaced. "The meeting's set up for this afternoon."

"Good luck."

"I'll need it. Don't be surprised if I end up in Intensive Care."

"Because of Joanna, you mean?" Tracy wiggled a brow expressively. "Don't worry. If Rowena's niece acts up, I'll be down the hallway."

"Nice thought, old buddy," Meredith grinned, "but you don't really believe the Carstairs crowd would lower themselves to coming to this modest office, do you?"

"No, probably not." She chuckled. "So where is the meeting?"

"Rowena's town house. She wanted it that way."

"Jesus. Talk about turning the knife in the wound," Tracy exclaimed. "Hasn't Joanna believed for years that she was going to inherit that place?"

"Don't remind me." Meredith gave a hollow laugh.

"Well, call if you need me to send in the National Guard."

"I'll be fine." Meredith gave a thumbs-up. Trace really could be counted on. But right now what she needed was someone to take Zack to the dentist later today. First braces, she thought with a sigh, lifting the phone and dialing her mother in the hopes that Clarice Rowland would be able to help her out. Only God knew how long the meeting might last.

"What do you mean we're to get nothing?!" Joanna Carstairs Lamont blanched, her surgically lifted features tightening with rage. "*We* are the rightful heirs. Each and every one of us is owed a share of that money," she insisted, waving her index finger wildly. "Surely you've got it wrong, Meredith."

"Look, I had nothing to do with this, okay? I'm sorry you're all disappointed. I really can't tell you why Rowena structured her will as she has, since I didn't draft it. But it's all here, and her wishes are quite clear."

She glanced round the exquisitely appointed drawing room, knowing as she glimpsed at their pale, stunned faces what a blow this must be.

"But we have rights," Joanna spluttered. "Charles, say something, for Christ's sake, don't just sit there like a beached whale. My God. This is a disaster." She sank heavily into a deep chintz armchair and muttered under her breath.

"I'm sure something can be done about it." Charles,

a middle-aged well-to-do doctor, swallowed uneasily. He hoped he sounded convincing—he was still absorbing the shock of the announcement and its implications. In a few short sentences Meredith had blighted his most cherished dream.

"Surely the will could be contested?" Patricia, Rowena's youngest half sister, a pious, soberly attired widow of seventy, replied, eyeing her son Ward, who was humming quietly to himself, oblivious to the tension in the room.

"That's certainly within your rights," Meredith responded carefully, "but I must caution you that there would be serious consequences if your challenge failed. There is a clause here to the effect that anyone who sees fit to contest the will loses his or her right to the income of the trust she set up for you a few years ago."

"The bitch!" Joanna screeched. "The goddamn bitch! I should have guessed that she would double-cross us and done something about it while she was still alive."

"You certainly tried." Charles eyed her coldly. "In fact, I distinctly remember you asking me to be part of the team that would certify her insanity."

"You did what?" Meredith asked, looking from one to the other. It was her turn to be shocked. "Rowena may have been eccentric but she was anything but crazy. Anyway," she continued, flipping through the paperwork and pointing to several documents, "she seems to have planned for that contingency. She had several medical examinations certifying the state of her health before she wrote this final will."

"But it's outrageous." Joanna rounded on Charles, her chin jutting out defiantly. "And so what if I did try to have her certified? I'll bet in view of this you all wish you'd agreed to it instead of being so fucking squeamish. My God, if we'd had her locked up, it sure as hell would have solved our present little problem, wouldn't it?"

Controlling her temper, Meredith realized it was probably better to let Joanna have her say. As the woman continued her rant, Meredith took stock of the other members of the family. Ward, Rowena's half nephew, looked vacant as usual. Mary Chris, his sister, had her hands clasped piously in her lap and wore her customary saintly expression. Their mother's face was blank. Charles had gone gray at the gills. The only missing relative was Craig, Rowena's third nephew, who still had to fly in from London.

"This is fucking ridiculous," Joanna was saying. "What the hell did she plan to do with the money, then?" She turned to glare at Meredith. "If we're not going to get it, who is? Surely Dallas doesn't get it all?"

"I'm afraid Dallas doesn't get anything, either," Meredith said slowly, pausing to take a deep breath. She looked up. All eyes were upon her. The room seethed with pressure, as though each and every one there guessed there was more bad news to come. And boy, was there, Meredith thought grimly. Straightening her shoulders, she said quietly, her tone neutral, "The sole heir to Rowena's estate, excepting some personal bequests, is her grandson."

"What?" Joanna exclaimed in a high-pitched squeak.

"Her grandson?" Charles exclaimed, frowning, his jaw tense. "There must be some mistake. She had no grandson."

"Actually, she did," Meredith countered, outwardly calm. "Isabel, Rowena's daughter, had a child out of wedlock."

A general gasp echoed throughout the drawing room. Charles's pallor increased. Joanna sat dumbstruck. Mary Chris blushed and murmured something incomprehensible under her breath, while her mother's set features took on an inscrutable cold expression. Ward just sat there, smiling politely, quite unaware of the true meaning of Meredith's words.

"This grandson," Meredith continued warily, "was given up for adoption at birth. But it appears Rowena tracked him down some ten years ago and made him the sole beneficiary of the bulk of her will."

"Good God," Charles exclaimed, dabbing a white handkerchief to his lips.

"But if he was legally adopted, then he has no rights," Joanna interrupted, her eyes narrowed in bitter anger as she tossed her perfectly colored strawberry-blond hair back.

"He's still her lineal descendent. Rowena established his birth connection. Anyway, the point's moot, because she made him her heir. She had the legal right to leave her fortune to anyone she chose."

"You said *everything*?" Charles interrupted, his voice strained. "You mean the properties, the furniture, all her personal assets?"

"I'm afraid so."

"How much money are we talking about?" Joanna asked, her voice shaking with loathing.

"One hundred million dollars, give or take."

Gasps erupted from all corners of the room.

"A hundred million dollars? But we never knew Rowena had that kind of money." Joanna's manicured hands were shaking now. "How is this possible? How could she have done this? It's not fair."

"I understand how upset you are," Meredith countered, shifting her legs under the desk and wishing that the meeting were over, "but actually it's even more unfair for Dallas. After all, she's a grandchild, too. And Rowena has left her nothing. Except for a string of pearls."

"Not her black pearls?" Joanna hissed.

"Uh, yes. I believe those are the ones." Meredith quickly checked the file.

"But she promised those to me. Why, the old bitch has done nothing but lie and pretend all these years! When I think of the time and attention I lavished on her," Joanna screeched, rising abruptly and turning on Meredith. "It was all a waste!"

"Well," Meredith countered, "you aren't without resources. You will, of course, continue to receive the income from the trust she established for you. Subject to certain conditions."

"The income," she threw scathingly. "As if I cared about the goddamn income. It's the capital I'm interested in—that's what I've been waiting for all these years."

"Naturally," Meredith said dryly, discomfort fast changing to disdain as Joanna's performance evolved, "you will have to continue fulfilling the requirements—"

"Requirements," Joanna spat, prowling the Aubusson carpet of Rowena's stately drawing room, hands clenched. "How dare she do this to us? How dare she?"

"As I was saying," Meredith continued, ignoring the outburst, "the trust's requirements will still need to be met." She swallowed, knowing what would come next. "As the heir to her affairs, Rowena's grandson, Mr. Grant Gallagher, has been named cotrustee with me. We will be the ones to determine if the requirements are met."

Joanna erupted. "You mean to tell me that not only has she named some godforsaken bastard of Isabel's her heir, but that she's made him a trustee to what's rightfully ours?"

"Oh, Joanna, shut up," Charles said tightly. "Meredith, what do we know about this Gallagher person?"

"Well, it's not the best news, I'm afraid. Grant Gallagher is a well-known corporate raider. Remember the Bronstern affair last year?" She glanced up.

"Of course. What has that got to do with it?"

"Everything," she replied, trying to keep the bitterness from her tone. "He was responsible for breaking up the company. I don't know how many people lost their jobs."

"My God," he muttered, "then there's no hope of his declining the inheritance, I guess." His hands fell in his lap and he looked suddenly years older. And very sad, Meredith realized, feeling rather sorry for him, but also wondering why he seemed so devastated. Married to a wealthy Bostonian wife, Marcia, he was probably in a far better position financially than the rest of them.

"This is just so unfair," Joanna continued, her voice shaking as she paced the room.

"Hardly unfair, Joanna. She didn't need to make that trust in the first place. Basically, it all goes on the same," she pointed out reasonably.

"You actually expect me to go groveling to some bastard child of Isabel's for my share?" Joanna stared at Meredith, shocked.

"I'm afraid you won't have a choice. Mr. Gallagher and I will have sole discretion as to the disbursement of funds. In other words, you will have to receive our approval."

"The bitch," Joanna whispered again hoarsely, staring

out of the bay window onto the luscious garden she'd been so certain would one day be hers. "The fucking hypocrite."

"Joanna," Charles reprimanded, "this is hardly the time to be criticizing our benefactress."

"Benefactress my ass," she hissed, her mouth twisting hideously. "She's manipulated us, forced us to kowtow to Isabel's droppings. It's disgusting. Don't you see, Charles? She did it on purpose to humiliate us. God, I hate her," she exclaimed again, clenching her fists.

"Joanna, this is no time for tantrums," Charles admonished.

"Charles is right. There's little use getting upset," Meredith countered in the vain hope that the meeting would not deteriorate further. She glanced at the other relations, who had remained silent. Ward was picking at a thread on the sleeve of his old tweed jacket. He had no real understanding of what was going on around him, but from time to time he pretended to listen. "I see no reason why Gallagher or I should refuse any reasonable requests."

"You don't understand," Joanna threw back bitterly. "She's humiliating us before this bastard, making us, her legitimate heirs, beg. It's disgraceful."

"I think you're becoming unnecessarily dramatic," Meredith answered quietly. "Soon we'll have more information on Gallagher and get a better idea of where matters stand. But for now, I'm afraid you'll just have to be patient."

It took Meredith another twenty minutes to calm Joanna down and bring the meeting to a close, but finally she was seated in her Jeep heading home, returning the calls she'd been unable to take during the afternoon and looking forward to another lonely evening.

That night, after the kids were in bed, Meredith sipped a mug of hot chocolate and tucked her slippered feet under the old cashmere throw, thankful the day was behind her. It was always hard to be the bearer of bad tidings. In a way she sympathized with the Carstairs relatives. After all, Rowena had always implied they'd share her estate once she was gone. But what surprised her most, what she couldn't fathom, was why Dallas had been so summarily cut out of the will. She and her grandmother hadn't seen eye to eye, but surely that didn't merit abandoning her?

Meredith leaned into the cushions and cupped the mug thoughtfully. She'd arranged for a phone conference with Dallas for the following morning, and was dreading telling her the news. Dallas had gotten a rotten deal all round. The property in Beaufort where Doug Thornton had raised thoroughbreds and where Dallas had spent the better part of her youth was mortgaged to the hilt. Presumably the only reason the bank hadn't foreclosed was because they knew of Dallas's expectations. Now that those were dashed, what would the girl's options be?

Taking a sip of piping hot chocolate, Meredith pondered whether Dallas could contest.

Analyzing the case from a legal standpoint, she realized probably not. The will was tight as a drum. Although it was her duty to see that the wishes expressed in the will were carried out, her sense of justice revolted. Somebody, she realized, pulling the file toward her, had to help Dallas. The girl couldn't be allowed to flounder out there on her own.

Should she appeal to Gallagher? No, a man with his track record would hardly have an ounce of compassion. And he certainly wouldn't feel any sense of loyalty to a family he hadn't even known existed. To him, Rowena's estate would be nothing but another windfall that some crazy old lady had seen fit to bequeath him.

And all at once she wondered if Rowena had known Gallagher, if they'd met. Somehow she didn't think so. Surely if Rowena had been aware of who Gallagher really was, she wouldn't have structured things as she had. On the other hand, Rowena was too smart to have made such a decision without a great deal of thought.

After flipping through several paragraphs of the long, detailed document, Meredith decided to go to bed. Tomorrow she would take steps to contact Grant Gallagher, and she would find some way to help Dallas.

Her determination to go to bat for Dallas increased as she remembered all the times over the past few years that she'd tried to ease the strained relationship between grandmother and granddaughter, and how Dallas had come to confide in her. She felt she couldn't betray that trust, couldn't let Dallas down, even though the girl refused to admit that she needed help.

By the time she turned out the lights, she'd sketched out the beginnings of a game plan. The first step was getting through to Gallagher.

Dabbing another lotion-bathed cotton pad over her cheeks, Joanna peered at her reflection and sighed. She must calm her frenzied mind. She must think straight.

Act. But how? Of course she would be in touch with Ross Rollins to see what could be done from a legal standpoint, but surely there must be something else she could do to sway things her way?

Rising from the dressing table and heading toward her lace-canopied bed, Joanna took off her peach-colored silk dressing gown and feathered mules, then climbed wearily into bed.

What a day. She'd woken up so happy, so certain that finally she'd hit the jackpot.

And now this.

She slumped against the pillows and wondered if she should visit her fortune-teller to see what she had to say. Oh, what the hell. That was just another expense. And God knows she had enough of those with a drawer full of bills sitting in her desk waiting to be taken care of.

But remembering the fortune-teller made her sit up straighter, brow creased as another thought crossed her mind. What was the name of that famous voodoo priestess Rowena had frequented? Miss Mabella. That was it. But now she also recalled that Miss Mabella was not easily available. There were times when she disappeared to the bayou, wouldn't speak English, would only communicate in Gullah with her close entourage.

She shivered, pulled the coverlet up to her chin, both encouraged yet scared that she'd remembered the woman's name. She knew it was dangerous to dabble. But still, Joanna wondered whether she was worth investing in. After several moments' reflection, she decided in favor. After all, things couldn't get much worse. She must use some kind of intervention if she wasn't going to be screwed. And from all she'd heard, Miss Mabella had a trick or two up her sleeve.

The question was how to contact her? Perhaps she would ask Josie, her cleaning lady, tomorrow. Josie had an aunt who lived in what she believed was the same neighborhood as Miss Mabella. Maybe she could make contact for her.

With a sigh Joanna turned off the light. Grant Gallagher, indeed. Fuck him. She was damned if she'd allow anybody, much less some illegitimate son of Isabel's—whom she'd never liked, anyway—to take what should be hers.

No siree!

Despite her laudable resolve of having a quiet morning, Meredith found it impossible to relax. Tweaking her hair back and donning her glasses, she rummaged for the Carstairs file. Sitting at her highly polished mahogany desk, an heirloom from her great-grandmother Rowland, Meredith admitted ruefully that relaxing was not her forte. Plus the task ahead of her was no light challenge. Setting the thick manila folder next to her laptop, she got online, determined to find as much information as she could about the man she already considered her adversary. All her legal training taught her never to get emotional about a case. Ross would have told her it was none of her business, that technically the man was her client now, and that her only agenda should be to defend his interests.

But how could she when so much was at stake for Dallas?

Typing his name into Google, Meredith learned it was distressingly easy to acquire information on Grant Gallagher—the man was probably a publicity hound. There were newspaper headings, articles and pictures of him at nightclubs with beautiful blondes hanging on to his arm. The fact that he appeared to be outrageously handsome only made her glare more coldly at his wolfish smile. No doubt his behavior in the bedroom matched his ruthless actions in the boardroom.

Logging off, she pulled out a thick sheaf of papers, realizing that even if the man willingly lived his life in the public eye, there were details in this folder that were intensely private. Details that he wouldn't want to share; information about himself that even *he* didn't know. Despite her contempt for him, she felt as if she were committing a violation. Rowena's detectives had been nothing if not thorough, she reflected, her lips curling cynically.

She skimmed once more over his case history. He didn't have much of a childhood, she admitted grudgingly, her brow knit. Grant had been adopted at birth by a wealthy couple unable to have children, who then divorced when he was four. Both parents had subsequently remarried several times. Judging by the frequent changes in address and the different schools he'd attended throughout Europe, it was obvious the man had lived an erratic youth in which his adoptive parents had figured little. They probably cared even less.

She studied a glamorous photo of Raymond and Gina Gallagher, clipped from some sixties-era society page. Although a handsome couple, they looked more impressed with themselves than with each other. Grant had probably been adopted to serve as a plug in a leaking tub. When the plug failed, the tub had drained and the child was left to fend for himself. Well, not entirely. There seemed to be some serious financial security. But that kind of life couldn't have been easy.

His experiences hadn't impeded his getting ahead

at the expense of others, she recognized, reaching for the bottle of Evian that she'd carried in from the kitchen. She would have imagined that someone who'd had an emotionally deprived childhood, albeit a financially secure one, would be sensitive to the needs of others. But apparently *empathy* wasn't a word in Gallagher's lexicon.

Meredith sighed, remembering her own happy childhood, her loving parents and sibling. Even when she'd been at her most rebellious—like the time she'd led a third-grade boycott of the Webelos for not admitting girls into their organization—her family had been there for her, offering their love and support. She'd been one of the lucky ones.

Slipping the documents back into the envelope, Meredith rose from the desk and headed upstairs for a shower, trying not to think about her upcoming phone appointment with Dallas. She had all of fifteen minutes to get herself cleaned up and dressed before she had to head to the office. Time to get the show on the road, she realized with a grimace, yanking off her tracksuit and heading for the shower.

"It doesn't matter, I wouldn't have taken a penny of her money, anyway."

Dallas's voice sounded harsh and determined, and Meredith sighed. She'd just pointed out a minor loophole in the will that she thought might give Dallas grounds to contest, but the girl wouldn't listen, despite the dire situation she was facing. Rarely had Meredith met anyone more stubborn and unyielding.

"Dallas, please, you need to think this over carefully. Let me give you the name of an estate attorney I admire. She can at least help you figure out where you stand."

"Nope. I don't care. I'll just let it go."

"But that's ridiculous. I know the mortgage company is breathing down your neck. At least let me talk to them, explain how things are, tell them there's still a chance you'll recover something, or at least enough to pay off a large chunk of the debt. That should keep them at bay for a while."

"Meredith, why won't you understand? I hated Grandma Rowena. She fucked up all our lives. I don't want any of her money. It's tainted. This guy Gallagher's welcome to it."

"You know, technically he's your half brother," Meredith said thoughtfully. She didn't know why it hadn't occurred to her before, but of course these two shared the same mother. They were siblings. Surely that had to count for something?

A short silence ensued. "So? What if he is my half brother? I don't know him, he doesn't know me. Just because we were born of the same mother doesn't mean we signify anything to each other. Why should I care about him? Or he about my problems, for that matter?"

"You're right, I guess," Meredith responded sadly. "Look, I've already sent him a letter to advise him of the inheritance, and I presume I'll be hearing from him shortly. I'll keep you informed."

"Fine. In the meantime I'll take that modeling job I was offered for that Australian magazine. At least that'll keep food on the table."

"Good. Go ahead."

Meredith was glad that Dallas was busy finding solutions to her plight. Although most people would assume she was a spoiled brat, given the way she spoke and reacted, she possessed the tough, determined streak of a survivor.

From all accounts, the girl had lived a solitary childhood. Apparently Isabel had shown little interest in her daughter, preferring her social life to motherhood. After Isabel's suicide, Dallas had lived alone with a father whose obsession with raising horses probably left little time or inclination to nurture the needs of a teenager. Lord only knew what kind of emotional baggage the poor kid carried.

Dallas wasn't precisely a child anymore, of course, but she was only nineteen. Such an age seemed a long way off from Meredith's own thirty-three. She thought of what that twelve-year difference amounted to in her own life. She had already experienced a wonderful marriage, two great kids and now widowhood.

Brushing the thoughts aside, Meredith turned to her computer screen and decided she'd better draft a follow-up letter to Grant Gallagher. She was surprised she hadn't heard anything from him yet, but she decided that he probably was having his lawyers look over everything before he took the next step.

3

Glancing at his watch, Grant Gallagher pushed himself into the last stretch leading up to the lawn and the castle. He'd been running for an hour on the wet Scottish moor and he was now ready for breakfast. But this final effort justified the rest of a day often spent seated in boardrooms or behind his desk. Today, he reflected, wiping his rain-swept black hair from his face, would be spent with his laptop, tracing the outline of a deal that was shaping into a winner.

Moving round to the east side of the ancient stone castle walls, Grant stepped inside the cloakroom.

At last. The reward. He shook himself like a St. Bernard, his large, well-formed shoulders soaked, and made his way down the corridor to the main part of the castle.

"Good morning. Yer breakfast's ready, sir," Mrs. Duffy, the housekeeper, said as she crossed him in the hall just as he was about to climb the vast oak staircase.

"Thank you, Mrs. Duffy. I'll take a quick shower and be down in a moment." He smiled.

The housekeeper later described his smile to Mrs. Cullum, the baker's wife, as a wicked yet wonderful one that lit up his fine features. Not that anyone, seeing her, would have guessed such a fanciful romantic lurked behind her severe expression. Two days later, Mrs. Cullum passed on the description to Mrs. Beatty at the butcher's. They both agreed, shaking their permed gray heads, that Mrs. Duffy read far too many romance novels for her own good. In their opinion, any woman who raved about bright blue eyes that sparkled in a way that left a female, even one of Mrs. Duffy's advanced years and station, with her heart fluttering definitely needed her head examined.

Unaware of the flattering descriptions being exchanged in the castle kitchen and elsewhere, Grant swung open the heavy glass door of the shower—the one area of the castle he'd agreed to modernize—and, after discarding his soaked attire on the marble floor, stood under the powerful hot-water jet. It felt like heaven after the rigors of the run he imposed on himself daily, rain or shine, wherever he was in the world.

Several minutes later he emerged, dried himself and, slicking his hair back, entered his dressing room where he donned a pair of navy sweats and the first high-necked cashmere sweater in the pile, which happened to be white. Next he slipped on his socks and sneakers and headed downstairs, humming a tune that for several days had been playing relentlessly in his head. That and the scent that Fernanda, his latest conquest, had worn on their last evening together in Paris. She was lovely, but far too young, of course. And she was beginning to cling.

He sighed. Time to bring that little interlude to an end before it became complicated and she turned on the waterworks.

Stepping into the breakfast room, he gazed satisfied at the round table covered with the usual white linen cloth, fine china and silverware. He lifted the cover of one of the Georgian silver dishes and sniffed. Mrs. Duffy's breakfast made every drop of rain of his run worth it, he reflected, serving himself a large portion of scrambled eggs, bacon and ham onto a plate, and spreading a thick lashing of homemade butter onto a piece of local granary bread.

This was the life. For a few days a month, at any rate, he reckoned, glancing at his watch, calculating the time difference with Sydney.

After breakfast, he headed straight for the study, intent on making his calls. He was deeply entrenched in understanding the legal implications of the deal he was handling, a meat packer in Australia that, if everything went right, would be his for the picking before the end of the week. He sat down and dialed the number of his lawyer in Sydney, sifting through his mail as he waited for someone to pick up. Just invitations and bank statements. They could wait. Then he looked at the last letter in the pile and frowned. It bore an American stamp and was postmarked Savannah Georgia. He turned it over, curious. He didn't know anyone in Savannah. Maybe it was another of those letters he received quantities of, people offering him deals right, left and center. Rita, his efficient secretary in London, must have forwarded it by mistake. The phone continued ringing just as he realized the letter was addressed to Strathcairn Castle, not to his office in Abemarle Street.

Odd, he reflected, hanging up when no one answered, noting the letterhead. Who the hell were Hunter & Maxwell, Attorneys at Law? Certainly he'd never dealt with them in the past.

Leaning across the desk piled high with scribbled notes, Grant reached for a letter opener. He pulled out a cover letter attached to a long white envelope with his name scrawled in large, spidery black ink.

He frowned, ignoring the uncanny frisson that gripped him. This must be a mistake, he reflected, ignoring a quickening of his pulse and a sudden need to swallow. Yet the letter was addressed to him, and now, as he quickly flipped through the rest of his mail a second time, he noted another missive from the same law firm. For a moment he hesitated, gripped by a sudden urge to bin the lot. For a moment he stared at them, then at the trash can, then back at the distinctive handwriting on the heavy white vellum envelope. But curiosity won, and with a shrug he slit the second envelope and pulled forth a single sheet of paper.

What he read made him sit up straighter. This had to be a joke, some crazy prankster playing tricks on him. But for some inexplicable reason, he couldn't drag his eyes off the spindly scrawl, words leaping off the page in quick succession, their significance hitting him like an inside curve ball.

Then, grabbing the cover letter, he skimmed through it rapidly, his pulse racing. This couldn't be real. It had to be a case of mistaken identity. There must be another James G. Gallagher somewhere, maybe even several, and they'd mixed them up.

But deep down, something told him it wasn't a mistake. He'd always known he was adopted. His parents had certainly never bothered to hide that fact from him. But they'd never told him anything about his birth mother, and he sure as hell hadn't wanted to ask. Surely it would be too much of a coincidence if…

Grant rose, still holding the letter, and gazed out of

the window. Rain poured, causing rivulets to trickle down the old panes before disappearing into the flower beds. What should he do? He had no desire to be connected with his past. A memory flashed—that of himself as a turbulent teenager ravaged with doubt. It had taken him long enough to force the hot, turbulent rage to subside and now that it was way behind him, he had no desire to revisit his past.

Turning his back on the window, Grant crushed the letter in his fist and pitched the crumpled ball into the trash can. He had no intention of replying. Would simply pretend it never happened.

But minutes later, and against his better judgment, he stooped and retrieved the two scrunched-up sheets from the trash, smoothed them reluctantly and read the letter over.

"Shit," he exclaimed, slamming his palms down on the desk. "Fuck Rowena Carstairs, whoever she is. And her damned attorneys."

But despite his desire to forget, he could think of nothing but what the old lady had told him in her letter.

"Damn," he muttered under his breath, glancing once more at the scrawled words. Why in hell's name would this woman who claimed to be his grandmother want to leave him some estate he didn't need? He could read some remorse between the lines, some desire to make up for a past mistake. But still, it made no sense.

He pushed the chair back abruptly, wishing he had time to take a trip, go scuba diving in Thailand or hiking in the Rockies. But he couldn't leave right now. He had to be available to jump on a plane at a moment's notice.

"Damn," he muttered again.

Leaving the correspondence on his desk, he shoved his hands in his pockets and left, slamming the study door abruptly behind him.

"I don't see what options are left," Charles pointed out to a recalcitrant Joanna. He disapproved of his cousin's house—wet bars did not belong in the home. Joanna was presently perched on a crimson leather bar stool, sipping a neon-colored cocktail at three o'clock in the afternoon. No wonder Rowena had entertained doubts about the woman's capacity to manage a few million dollars. Still, she needed to be humored.

"There really is no way we can contest the damn will?" Joanna asked for the hundredth time.

"I've told you. It's impossible. If we fail, we lose the trust income."

"But there must be a way," she said, twiddling the cocktail stick thoughtfully. "I mean, let's think. For instance, what would happen if, say, this Grant guy weren't in the picture?"

"What do you mean?" Charles looked at her and frowned.

"Let's say, hypothetically, that something happened to him. Who would inherit his share?"

"I guess that would depend on whether he has a will," Charles replied slowly. "In the event of his leaving no stipulated wishes, I guess the funds would revert to the next of kin."

"Thank you. From all I've gathered over the past few days, that's us." She pointed a red-lacquered finger at her voluptuous breast.

"Actually, it's Dallas. Joanna, you're not suggesting—"

"I'm not suggesting anything," she replied airily, waving the strawberry-blond mane from her face. "I'm merely trying to get a grasp on the situation."

"I see." Charles sat for a moment, elbows placed thoughtfully on his thighs. Joanna was a bloodthirsty sort, but at least she was being honest. Not like himself, he thought angrily, forced to pretend Rowena's will hadn't been a devastating blow. For three and a half years he'd been secretly nurturing a dream that would finally allow him to control his life and no longer depend on his marriage to Marcia for his status in society. He'd hoped to be able to afford an expensive yet discreet divorce, then marry his beloved Charlotte. Now, a few words from Meredith Hunter and all his hopes and expectations had flown summarily out the window.

It was a hard pill to swallow.

"Joanna, let's stick with what's real and not conjecture," he said, letting out a tight sigh. "The fact is both Gallagher and Dallas are very much alive. We might as well get used to it."

He felt suddenly old. The spring had gone out of his step. He'd told Charlotte the news yesterday. She'd taken it badly. The future struck him as incredibly gloomy.

"Don't be such a party pooper, Charles," Joanna countered with a moue. "Life is full of surprises. Tell me, have you seen Patricia? She looked as if she didn't care a damn about Ward and Mary Chris being cut out of the will. But I wonder…" She took a speculative sip of her cocktail and frowned.

"Oh, she's acting like a persecuted Christian, the usual pious dictums. God's will and all that jazz. Ward doesn't care. Rowena's money wouldn't make any difference to him. He has all the fishing rods he can use. As for Mary Chris, she probably would have given her share to the church, anyway. I wouldn't be surprised if one of Rowena's reasons for taking these measures was because of them," he added bitterly.

"Bullshit." Joanna set her cocktail down on the bar counter and came to sit next to her cousin on the sofa. "She did it to hurt us, to prove she could manipulate us from beyond the grave. The bitch. But don't get down, Charlie boy. Things may still take a turn."

"It's hardly likely. I doubt Gallagher's the kind of man to refuse a windfall."

"Well, I don't know. Sometimes the unexpected can occur." Joanna patted his hand with a cryptic smile and thought about the appointment she'd finally managed to arrange with Miss Mabella. "Remember that voodoo priestess Rowena was as thick as thieves with?"

Charles shrugged. "Don't tell me you're messing about with that lot?"

"Why not? Rowena seemed to think the world of her."

"I dare say." Charles shrugged, unconvinced. "Truth is there's nothing that can be done. And the sooner we get used to it, the better."

"Perhaps. Perhaps not," she replied with a Mona Lisa smile gracing her lips. "Only time will tell. I'll bet once Miss Mabella gets her spells moving along we may see some serious action. I'm going to visit her," she added, her voice laced with expectation.

Charles rolled his eyes and let out a sigh.

"I prefer to deal in the real world," he muttered caustically.

"I daresay you do," she answered smugly, "but a little nudge from the other side can't hurt. Not when you're in it up to your neck like we are."

After another week passed without a reply from Grant Gallagher, Meredith wasn't inclined to make any more excuses for the man. Surely someone who'd just been informed he'd inherited a sizable estate would at least respond to the news. This wasn't something to be ignored, she fumed.

"'Morning, Trace. How was the date?" she asked, grinning.

"It sucked. He turned out to be a total male chauvinist who thinks career women should be abolished from our society, period."

"I didn't know guys like that still existed," Meredith said with an expressive grimace, "but I'm beginning to think Gallagher may just be one of them. I've sent two letters via courier to his address at—" she squinted at her legal pad "—Strathcairn Castle. According to the detective, that's a place Gallagher bought up in Scotland a few years back. It's supposed to be a weekend home, but he spends a fair amount of time there. We know he received our correspondence because the housekeeper signed for it, but Gallagher hasn't shown any sign of life."

"Maybe he's away," Tracy murmured, scribbling.

"I guess." Meredith glanced at her notes. "The detective mentioned that Gallagher moves around a lot. Comes and goes from London and Paris and New York. He's not going to be easy to pin down."

And pinning Gallagher down was becoming more important with each passing day. Time was of the essence if Dallas was going to rescue her property. And Lord only knew what sort of plans Joanna and the other relatives were fomenting during this frustrating delay.

"Maybe he's left on a trip," Tracy pointed out reasonably. "I have Mrs. Fairbairn coming in at ten so we'd better be quick," she added. "I need Ali to print out those memos," she added absently, glancing at the run forming in her panty hose. "Shit, I knew that would happen."

"What?" Meredith glanced absently at the offending nylon, still absorbed in the report. "You know, according to the detective agency's latest report, he was seen in Strathcairn village last week. Surely they'd know if he'd gone somewhere. Oh, Lord." She eyed Tracy woefully, a new and horrifying possibility looming. "I'm sure he's received the information. Any normal person would have contacted us right away, knowing it's in his best interests to bring closure to everything. So is he *trying* to screw things up?"

"Maybe he thinks it's a hoax. There's no evidence to suggest he's ever heard of Rowena Carstairs. Men like him probably get all sorts of weird mail, fan mail, hate mail, you name it. He's somewhat of a swashbuckling figure in the corporate world." She tucked her tongue in her cheek and waited for Meredith's inevitable reaction.

"Swashbuck—are you nuts, Trace? The man's a heartless piece of—"

"Hey, don't go off at the deep end, girl. I was just reading some articles covering the Bronstern case. You know, if you analyze it from the shareholders' standpoint, he was probably right to do what he did." She twiddled her pen in her long, manicured fingers, a picture of sleek legal savvy.

"That doesn't justify the fact that he left a number

of hardworking American families unemployed,"
Meredith dismissed her. "Now," she said, sitting down
at her desk and removing her gray tweed jacket, "we
have to get the ball rolling on this."

"We?" Tracy shook her head firmly.

"Okay, me." Meredith rolled her eyes reluctantly
and let out a huff.

"Good. At least we've established that correctly.
Now, why do you think he hasn't answered? Maybe he
thinks we're not legit."

"But surely he could tell we're a legitimate law firm?
I wrote on our letterhead, I forwarded one of several
personal letters from Rowena, which I imagine told
him at least part of the story. She must have given him
some explanation for the inheritance. And although I
didn't get into specifics, I made it clear I needed to communicate with him ASAP."

"But the fact remains he's chosen to ignore your
correspondence." Tracy looked across the desk at her
thoughtfully, then hummed. "I think someone is going
to have to take a trip."

"Oh, no." Meredith raised her palms protectively.
"No way."

"I'm afraid there's only one way to deal with this,
Mer, and that's to contact him personally."

"Darn it, Trace. I knew you were going to say that,"
she muttered, shoulders drooping.

"Damn right. Start packing, partner."

"You don't think I could send someone from the
detective agency to speak to him?" she asked, clinging
to a last shred of hope that she wouldn't have to handle
this personally.

"Mer, get real."

"But surely they could handle it."

"It's hardly a detective's job to deliver important legal documents," Tracy answered witheringly. "And might I remind you that this man is now your client?"

"Oh, God, stop sounding like old Saunders. Two years of him at Yale was bad enough without you coming down on me like a ton of bricks." Her eyes closed as the truth and all its implications sank in. "Trace, I can't go. I simply can't."

"Why on earth not? You're the coexecutor. Now, stop whining and go find the guy."

Meredith swung in her chair, agitated. "But I have two kids and responsibilities. I can't just go to Europe at the drop of a hat because some moron doesn't have the courtesy to answer my letters," she wailed, knowing that Tracy was right and that it was useless to pretend otherwise.

"Should've thought of that before opening your own law firm," Tracy remarked unsympathetically. She did not add that Gallagher's silence had created the perfect opportunity to get Meredith out of the office and out of town for a much-needed break. She and Elm, Meredith's oldest and dearest friend, had discussed it on the phone only the other day. It was high time Meredith stopped hiding behind her job and those kids, wallowing in the past and afraid to face the future. She needed a trip, some time away. Finding Grant Gallagher might be the perfect excuse.

Tracy watched her carefully. She and Meredith had been close friends since law school, and if anyone knew what she'd been through over the past year, it was Tracy. Not that she ever complained, poor kid. Meredith was made of sterner stuff than that. But she knew what went on behind the facade, the lonely nights, the impossibly packed days. After all, she'd been through it herself when her own boyfriend, Jim, had died of galloping leukemia at age twenty-five.

"Look, Meredith," she said sternly, "get used to the idea and get out the luggage."

"But what'll I do with Mick and Zack?" Meredith murmured. She never let her personal problems interfere with work, but this was overwhelming.

"I'm sure Clarice and John will be only too glad to take 'em for you. If Carrie and Ralph Hunter hadn't moved to Charleston I'm sure they'd have pitched in. And I can help out if you need me."

"I know, all the grandparents love having them and spoiling them rotten," she muttered darkly, a tiny smile quivering, for she knew how her and Tom's parents doted on their two grandsons. "God only knows what I'd have to deal with once I got back."

"Oh, for Pete's sake, Mer, John and Clarice adore those kids. You couldn't leave them in better hands. Now, stop fussing and get on with it. It's bad enough having to deal with Rowena's relatives darkening our doorstep like a pack of vultures. And until you've definitely identified Grant Gallagher as Rowena's heir, you can't admit the will to probate."

Just then the phone buzzed.

"Yes?"

"Mr. Gallagher on line one."

"Oh, my God!" Meredith sat on the edge of her chair. "Pass him on through. It's him," she whispered, covering the mouthpiece. "Hello?"

"Good morning. Is that Ms. Hunter?"

"Speaking. I'm glad you finally called, Mr. Gallagher. I was getting worried you hadn't received my correspondence."

"Not only did I receive it, but I consider it a great

piece of impertinence," his deep, suave British voice replied.

"Excuse me?" Meredith swallowed, aghast. "I'm afraid I don't understand."

"Then let me explain. I have no interest in Mrs. Carstairs's inheritance. I suggest you find yourself another heir as I will not be accepting the bequest."

"But—"

"I also wish to make it abundantly clear that I do not want to be bothered with this matter now or at any time in the future. I expect you to take care of any details. Am I making myself perfectly clear?" His voice grated cold and unbending down the line.

"Mr. Gallagher, it isn't quite as simple as that," she said, bristling.

"I suggest you make it simple. I have no intention of cooperating, if that's what you're about to suggest. Good day, Ms. Hunter, I'm sure you will deal efficiently with any necessary details."

"Wait," she exclaimed, "you can't just avoid the issue as if it didn't exist. There are papers to sign, documents to be dealt with."

"Then deal with them. It's none of my damn business. Goodbye."

The phone went dead in Meredith's hand. "I don't believe this," she muttered, outraged. "The guy just brushed me off like a fly. I knew I was right about the kind of person he is. Jesus."

"What did he say?" Tracy prodded. She'd followed the conversation closely, had seen Meredith change color, the embryonic glint in her eye.

"You know what? That's it." Meredith slapped her palms down on the desk, eyes blazing. "I'm going after the bastard. Thinks he can just walk, does he? Well, he'll soon find out that ain't happening. Not on my watch."

"Go, girl, that's the spirit," Tracy encouraged, smothering a smile. There was nothing like a challenge to get Meredith off her butt.

"Fine," Meredith muttered, slamming the Carstairs file down before her. "If I have to go, I'll go. Even if it does mean sussing him out of his den. The nerve of it," she added, smoldering, "the sheer rudeness of the man. I knew this was what he'd be like. Didn't I tell you?" She whirled around in the chair, pointing her pen.

"Absolutely. The sooner you get going, the better. Well, since that takes care of that, I'll be off," Tracy answered, rising and straightening her skirt while hiding a smile. "It'll be fine. You'll see."

"Damn right it will," Meredith answered, throwing her pen onto her desk.

She already detested Grant Gallagher.

4

After realizing that her kids weren't in the least bit upset over her departure—indeed, they were clearly relishing the chance of being thoroughly indulged by their grandparents—Meredith spent the better part of the nine-hour flight from Newark to Glasgow figuring out her approach. She was still steaming at how rude Gallagher had been on the phone. The man was totally irrational! She'd tried to call him back and make him see reason, but all she'd reached was the robotic voice of his answering machine. Now she was obliged to land on the man's doorstep and be civil, when what she really wanted to do was tell him in no uncertain terms what she thought of his manners and attitude. She sent up a silent prayer that the detective's reports reflecting he'd been sighted only two days earlier in the village were correct and that she wasn't off on a wild-goose chase.

Adjusting the airline pillow, Meredith pondered the best way to handle the situation. Perhaps she should suggest a meeting at her hotel. She didn't suppose the

Strathcairn Arms would have anything as grand as a conference room, but as it boasted to be the only hotel in the Highland village of Strathcairn she had little choice in the matter. Since she was planning on a one-, maybe two-night stay at most, the hotel's lack of facilities were not a priority as long as it had a half-decent bed and hot water.

Abandoning the morsel of cold chicken that she'd been shoving aimlessly around her plate, Meredith reclined farther into her seat and stared out the window. Stars dotted the horizon like Christmas lights. A full moon hovered illusively among the clouds. Without warning her eyes filled and she closed them tight. How ironic it was that after all the times she and Tom had talked about visiting Scotland she should be going there alone, and under such inauspicious circumstances.

She swallowed hard. Tom's family's roots were in Scotland, and traveling to the land of his forefathers had always been one of his dreams. Working in a side trip to St. Andrews or Troon—Tom had been an avid golfer—had held its own allure. They'd planned to make their way up the west coast and then travel to the Isle of Skye. *Just wait until the kids are old enough to appreciate it,* she'd always said.

Now she wished she'd shut up.

With a muffled sigh, she shifted the pillow farther into the crook of her neck and attempted to sleep. Regret wasn't going to change a thing, she reminded herself sternly. The reality was that she was traveling to Scotland on her own, in mid-November, and the bleak weather forecast predicted rain, snow and subzero temperatures. A freak cold spell, they'd called it. Meredith shuddered, opened her eyes once more, grimaced at the chicken and the files in the neighboring seat and hoped the well-advertised central heating at the Strathcairn Arms really worked.

But after ten minutes it became obvious sleep was not on the agenda. Fiddling in her pocket for her Palm Pilot, Meredith turned on the overhead light and checked the weather report again, praying it wouldn't interfere with the tight schedule she'd set herself. With any luck she'd be back home in time to make Mick's baseball game on Saturday.

Closing her eyes once more, she tried to stop her thoughts from drifting to Tom and then back to Rowena, wondering what her client's letter to her grandson contained. Had it been a sentimental soul cleansing, an expiation of her sins or merely a history of past events? Perhaps it was a justification of her actions.

But somehow, knowing Rowena, Meredith didn't think the latter was the case. Accepting a bottle of water from the flight attendant hovering in the darkened aisle, she turned her thoughts to Dallas, who was still being thoroughly obtuse. The girl was obviously angry and confused by Rowena's rejection, even though she'd had every intention of refusing the money she'd expected Ro would leave her. The real question, though, was why the relationship between grandmother and grandchild had deteriorated so badly in the first place.

From comments Dallas had made, it had become clear that Rowena and Isabel had been forever at odds. Was that why Dallas professed so little love for her grandmother? It would be natural that she'd side with Isabel, however inadequate a mother she might have been. Or maybe Rowena had created a barrier between them—perhaps when she lost Isabel, she simply turned her back on Dallas, unable to accept her daughter's death.

Recalling the numerous conversations she'd had with Rowena, Meredith knew she'd loved Dallas deeply and that she'd spent many hours trying to breach the rift between them. It was therefore shocking that the granddaughter she clearly cared about was so summarily cut out of the will.

When Meredith last spoke with Dallas before boarding, she'd noticed something in the girl's voice—a note of near-hysterical despair—that made her determined to try to secure some kind of financial benefit for her. Perhaps she should hint to Gallagher that he might be sued if he didn't make a settlement with Dallas, although that was hardly ethical. Besides, something as trivial as a lawsuit would hardly faze a man used to taking on unions. He probably got sued so often he had a bevy of lawyers at his disposal to swat down anyone impertinent enough to assert he'd done anything wrong.

As dawn broke, Meredith watched the misty, translucent glimmer on the distant horizon turn into soft gray. It was only another couple hours before they landed. Changing positions, she rolled her shoulders and decided this whole situation had an air of the absurd. What must it be like to be left a large fortune? What would she do if Great-Aunt Agatha left her one hundred million dollars? The thought lightened her mood considerably. Aunt Agatha was the meanest old scrooge. She'd probably leave whatever she had to the cat-and-dog home. Yet she liked Mick. Imagine if her aunt died and suddenly left her son a fortune?

Meredith would not want that kind of responsibility for herself nor her kids. They were doing okay as they were. Of course, since she'd taken on the new responsibility of her own law practice, she exercised caution where spending was concerned. But she'd received a comfortable sum from Tom's life insurance, her client list was growing and she had a paid roof over her head. What more could she ask for?

Tom.

She would give it all up in a heartbeat if only she could have him back, at her side, laughing that rich, deep laugh, teasing her. Oh, for the warmth and security of his strong arms enveloping her. What wouldn't she do, Meredith asked herself, for just one more night curled up against him in their big, soft bed, cuddled under the goose-down duvet?

She must have dozed awhile for she jolted from a strange dream as the flight attendant's voice came on the loudspeaker, announcing they were about to land.

Fastening her seat belt, Meredith dragged her fingers through her hair, then gathered her thoughts and her papers. She must stop feeling sorry for herself and concentrate on her client. For even though she despised everything Grant Gallagher represented, like it or not, he was now her responsibility.

He woke up stiff and bad-tempered.

It did not take long for him to remember why.

Now, as he walked along the bluff, doing battle with a sharp east wind and driving rain, Grant muttered a string of oaths. He'd been doing a lot of that over the past couple days, he realized, as anger coursed through him as furiously as the bleak waves pounding the jagged rocks below.

"Damn Rowena Carstairs," he muttered, half to

himself, half to the two pointers, Monarch and Emperor, scampering at his heels. Stopping at the edge of the cliff, his black hair whipping across his face, Grant gazed out at the water. Somehow she'd managed to resurrect the niggling demons he'd believed long put to rest. Questions about who his real parents were had haunted his childhood. His endless wishful thinking had always entailed the secret hope that someday, by some miraculous act of God, he'd wake up to discover that the handsome jet-setting pair of Raymond and Gina Gallagher, who, for some incomprehensible reason, had adopted him, would return him to two mythical figures he envisioned as his birth parents.

Of course, at this point in his life, he couldn't give a damn about the past. He'd emerged unscathed and had built a life that suited him fine—no long-term attachments, no personal commitments except to himself. That some unknown woman should claim to be his grandmother and unearth his past was nothing more than a practical joke—and a poor one at that.

Except that he wasn't laughing. Because, he admitted as he breathed in the salty, damp November air, he'd never doubted the letter told the truth. Had it been sentimental or soppy he might have been suspicious. But Rowena Carstairs offered no mushy regrets, no pleas for forgiveness. Just the bare facts. And to his annoyance, he couldn't get it out of his mind.

Moving forward in long strides, Grant wished now that he'd followed his first instinct and thrown the bloody thing into the fire. He wanted to distance himself from all its implications. But even as he resolutely ignored the couriered packages from the lawyer's office in Savannah, he found himself hypnotically drawn to all that they represented. For in Rowena

Carstairs's letter lay the embryos of answers to the mystery of his past.

Now, if he wanted, those answers could be his.

Grant threw a stick idly across the weather-beaten grass and watched the dogs hurl themselves at it.

"Hell," he exclaimed, turning quickly about, his Wellington boots squelching in the mud as he marched back toward Strathcairn Castle, hands stuffed in the deep pockets of his Barbour jacket, each word of Rowena's spidery black writing stamped in his psyche forever. It was an undeniable reminder that the world he'd created was an illusion.

With the wind to his back, Grant climbed the last few hundred yards to the castle. The black mood that had settled over him for the past few days was affecting his work. The deal in Sydney was full of loopholes. There was a possibility the principals might pull out. He couldn't stand failure, yet here he was obsessing about ancient history. He better damn well get his act together, he reminded himself grimly, or the Sydney deal would evaporate.

He recognized, too, that his refusal to talk to the Savannah lawyer was his way of avoiding reality. By the time Grant discarded his Barbour and rubber boots in the cloakroom and reached the warmth of the library, he'd decided he had to tackle the Carstairs problem head-on, defuse its mystery and then put it back in the past where it belonged. Only then could he return all his attention to his present obligations.

Flopping onto the sofa, he analyzed the facts coldly. His birth family obviously had some degree of stature. After all, the tone of Rowena's letter resonated power and wealth. Wouldn't it be ironic if it was from her that he'd inherited his domineering nature? His mother had presumably been a more malleable sort—likely a society teenager who got pregnant, regretted her mistake and wanted her little problem to just go away.

Then why an adoption? Why not arrange for a quick abortion? Surely that would have simplified matters?

He sucked in his cheeks and viewed the facts through a distant lens: the pregnant young girl, the boyfriend who perhaps refused to marry her and a dictatorial mother accustomed to being obeyed. He wondered if his mother had wanted to keep— He stopped that thought in its tracks, brushed it off with a nonchalant shrug. What did he care?

The dogs, who'd followed him inside, now lay stretched out before the fire, the scent of their damp coats blending with fresh baking. Grant sniffed and glanced down at the tea tray set on the ottoman before him, realizing he hadn't eaten all day.

Absently he picked up a flaky scone and spread it with a thick layer of creamy yellow butter and homemade strawberry jam. It was only late afternoon, but already the lamps were lit, their gentle glow illuminating the mellow hue of the ancient oak-paneled walls. For no specific reason, he recalled the feeling of pride and possession that had swept over him when he'd acquired Strathcairn Castle. It had been more than just an acquisition, more important, somehow, than his London flat or his New York pied-à-terre. It had solidity, a sense of history—something he'd never had. Maybe that's why he'd refused to take out a mortgage and had paid the full five million gladly. By owning the castle outright, he immediately became a part of its legacy. Its history became his own.

Except now, thanks to Rowena Carstairs, he was reminded that the history he'd created for himself was a lie.

He pictured again his mother, a petrified young woman, betrayed by a man whom she'd once fancied but now abhorred, and bit into the scone, feeling almost sorry for the woman he'd created in his own mind. He was good at imagining deals. Now he imagined Rowena, the willful mother rushing to her flailing daughter's rescue, like a battleship headed to war, determined to protect her child regardless of the consequences.

In the distance the phone rang, but he ignored it and poured himself anther cup of tea. He had no desire to talk to anyone.

The phone persisted.

Defying it afforded him a degree of satisfaction. He supposed it was that lawyer from Savannah again—the self-righteous one. Well, it suited his mood not to answer it, even though he realized that at some point he'd have to deal with her. Letting out a low laugh, Grant flung his feet up on the ottoman and crossed his ankles. Rowena Carstairs obviously hadn't the first inkling as to what kind of a man he'd become. If she had, she wouldn't have wasted her time trying to dump her estate on him.

Staring at the crackling logs, Grant listened to the continuous drone of the phone. "Bloody nuisance," he muttered as it rang on persistently.

Then, rubbing the sticky jam from his fingers on one of Mrs. Duffy's carefully ironed linen napkins, he hauled himself out of the armchair. The Australians and his assistant all communicated on his mobile. Whoever was calling the castle could stay on the line until the cows came home.

No one—and that included Rowena Carstairs—was going to make him do anything he didn't want to do.

* * *

What on earth was Joanna doing coming out of Old Miss Mabella's place looking anything but delighted? he wondered. Following her a few blocks, he watched her hurry down the street and cross into the park. He must definitely arrange another one of their little "get-togethers" and learn more. Why did the woman look ready to murder when he'd supposed she would be crowing? It was well known that the Carstairs family had lived for a while in the expectation of all Rowena would leave them. Had things taken a different turn? He doffed his hat to Miss Biggles, who was taking her pooch for its afternoon stroll. Perhaps he'd drop in on Ross Rollins. If anyone had the scoop, it was usually him.

The thought that the Carstairs estate might hold surprises left him strangely uneasy. Not that there was anything to worry about. After all, as he reminded himself several times a day, Rowena was dead and buried. She could harm no one now.

Or could she?

5

Meredith landed at Glasgow Airport remarkably refreshed, even hopeful, assuring herself that although she didn't approve of Grant Gallagher, he was, after all, a highly efficient businessman. No doubt he'd come to his senses and realize it was in his best interests to address the questions pertaining to the will and settle matters quickly.

But four hours later, as she drove deep into the Scottish Highlands through torrential rain, Meredith's enthusiasm had waned considerably. The rental vehicle didn't have a global positioning system. There was a map in the glove box, but half the roads weren't even marked. There were no signs indicating Strathcairn, though she supposed she must be somewhere close. And there was no one to ask on this dreary, gray, foggy afternoon except a few motley sheep, huddled near a barbed wire fence, that looked about as happy to be there as she was.

Tired and hungry, Meredith pulled onto the side of the bumpy road and, switching on the overhead light, studied the map. With any luck, Strathcairn should be only a few miles away. Refolding the map, she let out a huff, started the engine and drove back onto the road. At last, she caught sight of the sea, a churning gray mass in the distance. Her hopes soared. Switching on the bright headlights, Meredith peered through the veil of mist, relieved when at last she noticed some cottages up ahead and a dilapidated, weather-beaten sign that read Strathcairn, Sister Town to Mondreux, Belgium.

Crawling at a snail's pace down the main street, she searched wearily for the Strathcairn Arms. What wouldn't she do for a hot bath and a hot meal.

Just as she was sure she'd taken a wrong turn, she saw it, a stark white edifice lit up by a blue neon sign. Relieved, Meredith parked, grabbed her luggage and hastened to the front door.

She was met by a dizzying vision of bright red-and-gold carpet and blue velvet sofas dotted around what must be the lobby. Meredith blinked. But despite the garish decor, the place seemed warm and bright, and she could smell something cooking in the distance, a reminder of how hungry she was.

Moving toward the front desk, she put down her bags and pressed her palm on the bell. Hearing sounds from behind a glass door, she looked up hopefully. The door burst open and a large woman with vivid red hair, dressed in fuchsia leggings and a heavy Shetland sweater, appeared.

"Hello," she said, a smile reaching from ear to ear on her freckled face. "You must be the American lady."

"That's right." Meredith smiled back, thankful that she was expected.

"We'd begun to think you'd got stuck on the

moors," the woman said with a kind laugh and outstretched hand. "I'm Moira MacPhee, the owner. Now,
if you'll just fill in this wee form, I'll take ye up to yer
room. Och, ye must be freezing to death. Drove all the
way from Glasgow, did ye? My, my. That's a long trip,
is it not? Now, let me take yer bags for ye, dearie. What
ye'll need is a hot bath and a bit of tea, nae doubt."

Meredith filled in the short registration card and
followed her talkative hostess up the brightly carpeted
stairs and down the corridor.

"It's our best room," Moira announced proudly. "We
had it redecorated last year," she added, unlocking the
door and showing Meredith inside.

"Lovely," Meredith said weakly, staring at the
boldly patterned purple curtains and matching bed-
cover, the plush orange armchair and Formica closet.

"Yes, well, Jim and I decided to go the whole hog
and do it right," Moira replied complacently. "Now, if
you get yersel' sorted out, dearie, I'll be getting yer
high tea ready for ye."

"Thank you. Uh, what's high tea?" she asked, curious.

"Oh, that would be somewhere between tea and sup-
per."

"Ah. That would be wonderful," Meredith responded, laying her briefcase down on the table, trying not
to blink at the color scheme. As the landlady closed the
door, she sank into the orange chair and let out a sigh.
At least the central heating worked. It was almost too
hot. Well, she reasoned, if all went according to plan,
she wouldn't be here long.

After phoning her parents to tell them she'd arrived
safely and a quick word with the kids, Meredith slipped
into the bathroom, glad to see that Moira and Jim's im-

provements had included functional plumbing. The shower worked fine and she relaxed under the hot-water jet.

She must, Meredith reflected as she dried herself, try to reach her quarry before nightfall. Who knows, with a bit of luck he might even receive her this evening. Not that she held much hope of that, Meredith conceded, brushing her hair back. After all, if the man hadn't had the courtesy to answer her mail, it was doubtful he'd be willing to see her outside of business hours. Still, it was worth giving him a call before going down to what Moira had described as "high tea."

She checked her notes for the number, then dialed and waited, listening impatiently to the double-burr ring and drumming her foot on the colorful carpet. After several rings a female voice answered.

"No, I'm afraid Mr. Gallagher isn't available," the woman responded to her inquiry.

"Could you leave him a message?" Meredith asked.

"Aye, I could," the dour voice on the other end replied.

"Tell him that Meredith Hunter called. I'm in Strath-cairn. I need to see him as soon as possible."

Silence followed.

"Did you hear me?"

"Aye, a heard ye. But a doubt it'll do much good. He's been in a terrible mood the past few days."

"Oh. Well, could you try, anyway?" Meredith insisted, hope plummeting as she tried to shake the nasty feeling that her trip might well prove to be a waste of time. Surely he would have to see her now that she'd made the flight from so far away?

With a shrug Meredith donned a warm sweater and made her way downstairs, hungrily following the scent of freshly baked scones that led her directly from the lobby through an adjoining door into the pub. Right now she was ready for anything they were prepared to offer. And as she followed Moira's waving arm to a table in the corner, the noisy, welcoming atmosphere of the pub made her forget that tomorrow morning she must hunt the lion in his lair.

For now, she'd content herself by indulging in what was certainly the best meal she'd had in a while.

"A lady called, sir." Mrs. Duffy stood in the doorway wrapped in her heavy blue coat.

"What lady?" Grant dragged his eyes away from the computer screen, annoyed at the interruption. The deal was still in jeopardy. He did not need a disturbance.

"An American lady, sir. A Miss Meredith Hunter. She's at the Strathcairn Arms," Mrs. Duffy added, pursing her lips, as though staying at the hotel implied bad news. "And," she added, "she wants to see you as soon as possible."

"Damn her," Grant muttered, swiveling his office chair and facing Mrs. Duffy. She looked almost triumphant standing there in her old head scarf, coat and gum boots, rather like the prophet Jeremiah on a bad day, he reflected gloomily. Mrs. Duffy had little sense of humor and fewer words. He'd noted that her general outlook on life was negative. On the rare days when the sun had dared peek from beyond the heavy expanse of cloud hovering overhead, she'd assured him it would undoubtedly rain later in the day.

"Thanks, Mrs. Duffy, that's fine. I'll deal with it." He smiled with an effort.

"Very well. Good night, sir. I left a pot of Scotch broth on the stove for ye."

"Thanks. Great. Good night." Grant nodded automatically, then swiveled back toward the computer screen. What the hell did this American lawyer think she was doing pursuing him when he'd already made it abundantly clear that he wanted nothing to do with Rowena Carstairs or her goddamn estate? When he talked to her it would be in his own good time and on his terms. Not at her behest.

For a few seconds Grant tried to recapture the possible solution to the standoff he'd been working on before he was interrupted, but it was no good. He rose crossly and, glancing at his watch, decided it was time to pour himself a whisky.

Meredith Hunter.

She was like a dog after a bone, refusing to let go. Well, he was damned if he was going to make her task any easier. Why should he? Didn't she represent the people who'd cast him out of their lives?

He'd thought quite a bit about his life during the past few days, and not by choice. An irritating series of memories flashed when he least expected them, taking him down distant paths he'd no intention of traveling again. Now as he poured the amber liquid into the crystal tumbler, the questions he'd ignored for years resurfaced. Why had the Gallaghers bothered to adopt him? That had been puzzling him for as long as he was old enough to analyze.

Telling himself for the umpteenth time that it didn't matter, Grant took a long sip. Cold logic told him there were probably a million valid reasons for what had taken place in his life. He of all people should know that. Weren't there a million valid reasons why he'd closed down the factory in Illinois last year? It simply wasn't productive. The fact that fifty or so families had ended up jobless was irrelevant. What mattered was the outcome. Life moved on. Results had to be achieved.

Maybe Rowena and her daughter had thought the same way about him. He was an inconvenience that needed to be eliminated for the show to go on. Despite this logical reasoning, he found it surprisingly hurtful.

All at once he wondered what those Illinois families were doing today. They were probably fine, he justified, draining his glass. After all, they'd received appropriate compensation and the job market was improving. The latest economical statistics for the third quarter had shown that the recession was on the mend.

After pouring himself another whisky, Grant threw himself into the armchair by the fire—his favorite spot in the castle—hating himself for allowing any sentimentality to surface. It was all this Meredith Hunter's fault, he reflected bitterly.

If she hadn't stirred up the dust like this, his life would have continued on the even keel he'd set, rather like a tightrope walker who's finally found his balance but must look straight ahead in order to reach the end of the rope. Now, thanks to her interference, he'd realized just how brittle his well-constructed world was. Why, he'd even called his adoptive mother Gina Gallagher at her luxurious old people's home in Surrey, thinking he'd finally ask her the question that had been on his lips for as long as he could remember.

But when it came to the crunch he hadn't asked, merely murmured the same old platitudes, then hung up none the wiser.

He passed a hand through his thick black hair, always a tad too long at the collar, and took another gulp of whisky. Of course, he hadn't asked his mother why she had adopted him. Gina probably didn't even know. Just as she didn't really know why she'd married the other two husbands that had followed his adoptive father. And he couldn't ask Raymond Gallagher, as he was long since dead.

It was just as well, he decided, thinking of how little he recalled of his father—of both parents, actually. There wasn't much to remember but occasional visits from boarding school where he'd been shipped off at five, the sporadic perfumed kiss, the new husbands and wives to whom he was expected to be polite and charming and whom he didn't give a shit about except that they were the momentary cause for his parents' absence and therefore deserved blame. The only remarkable incident had been with Emily, the luscious blonde his father had married when Grant was sixteen. They'd gone on a trip on his father's yacht in the south of France. Raymond Gallagher had been called away on urgent business, and Emily had wasted no time in expertly seducing her stepson.

Grant smiled at the memory. At least he'd lost his virginity in style.

But all that was history. At least the Gallaghers had never rejected him outright. Quite the opposite. On those rare visits home during his school years, they'd always been pleasant and generous. Too generous, he realized now, remembering the never-ending flow of checks that substituted for affection.

And now Meredith Hunter had pursued him to Strathcairn.

Grant got up and moved impatiently across the room to the window and stared out through the dusk across the lawn to the tossing sea beyond. Ignoring Meredith Hunter was probably childish, obtuse and unbusinesslike. But he really didn't care. She could stake out at the Strathcairn Arms for as long as she liked. He was damned if he was meeting any lawyer until he felt ready; he didn't care how far she'd traveled. After a while she'd get the message and leave.

Ignoring his earlier reasoning—that the issue needed to be faced—he ran his fingers through his hair. He was prone to willing problems away. It was a strategy that worked nine times out of ten. After all, it was much easier to forget the whole thing, decline the inheritance and the hassles it surely entailed. He'd let them give it to the next in line. That was fine by him.

Turning his back on the fading Scottish scenery, he marched into the study and without more ado sat down at the computer. If there was one guaranteed way to avoid reality, it was wheeling deals, and as luck would have it a new one had come onto his radar screen this very morning: an old-world resort hotel sitting on a huge chunk of valuable land in the Adirondacks. Definitely a good time to tap into his creative juices and work the magic he was renowned for, Grant decided, skimming through his latest e-mails. Of course, if he carried out the plan at present burgeoning in his mind, he would close down the resort, he realized, eyes focusing on the potential offer. But hey, that was par for the course. Win a few, lose a few. That was his life philosophy.

And he planned for it to stay that way.

6

The next day dawned cold and dreary as the previous one. Meredith peeked out the window and sighed. A native Savannahian, she was used to sweltering summers and mild winters, not this persistent bleak chill. How on earth did people keep their spirits up around here?

Slipping on a smart gray gabardine business suit and high-heeled shoes, she made her way downstairs for breakfast, her briefcase tucked under her arm. She was not going to be put off by last night's reception. She had every intention of pursuing Grant Gallagher as soon as she'd had a large cup of coffee. She'd ask Moira how to get to the castle and be on her way. In fact, she'd be willing to bet that Moira might prove to be a good source of information. No doubt Grant Gallagher's presence in Strathcairn had set tongues wagging.

Meredith settled at the same table she had the night before, and gave Jim, the landlord, who was busily polishing glasses behind the bar, a cheery good-morning.

"Morning to ye." Moira came bustling in with a bright smile and a pot of steaming tea, which she placed on the table in front of Meredith. "What'll ye have for breakfast, dearie, porridge? Black pudding? Scrambled eggs and sausage?"

"Oh, no, thanks, I really couldn't. I'm still digesting last night's meal. Just a piece of toast would be great." So much for coffee. She hardly dared refuse the tea when it was so graciously offered.

Moira looked disappointed but soon produced the toast.

"Tell me, do you know the owner of the castle?"

"You mean Mr. Gallagher?" Moira cocked a sandy brow.

"Yes. That's right. I wondered if you knew anything about him?"

"Not much." Moira shook her head and wiped her hands on her apron. "He comes in here once in a while for a dram, and although he's pleasant enough, he keeps himsel' to himsel', if ye know what I mean. Not one for conversation by the looks of it. Mrs. Duffy—she's the lady who manages things up at the castle—says he's always polite and nice to her, but never gets into a chat. Just closets himself up in the study and talks on the phone when he's not working on his wee machine, she says." Moira pursed her lips and leaned forward confidingly, her red curls bobbing. "It takes all sorts to make a world, but can ye imagine staying cooped up there in that pile o' stone all day? It's not healthy if ye ask me." She shook her head once more.

Meredith nodded in compliant agreement and sighed. "I have some business to conduct with him. I have to go up there this morning. I hope I'll get a decent reception."

"Well, I wouldna count on it if I were you." Moira sniffed and placed the marmalade on the table. "The last person that went to visit left with a flea in his ear, according to Mrs. Duffy. Still, I wish ye luck." She smiled and returned to the kitchen.

The pub was empty except for Meredith and the big sheep dog lying before the open fire. Although the establishment could hardly be five-star rated, it was warm, welcoming and cheery. Her host's extravagant taste in color schemes hadn't extended to the pub, which boasted traditional paneled walls, muted green and tartan cushions on the chairs and benches and a mellowed oak bar counter. And her host and hostess couldn't have been kinder, she reflected with a smile. The pub was the gathering place for the locals, and last night a man in a tartan tam had played Scottish tunes on an ancient squeeze box. Very picturesque. A pity she didn't have more time to appreciate it.

As she sat and sipped her tea, Meredith weighed her options. She'd wait until ten o'clock and then make her way up the hill to the ancient Highland keep just visible through the rising mist. She peeked gloomily at the stark, forbidding structure through the net curtains. It looked about as welcoming as its tenant. When she bit into a piece of warm raisin toast spread with butter and delicious homemade marmalade, she wished she could sit here all day and soak in the atmosphere, but she had a job to do.

Taking another sip of strong black tea, grateful for its reassuring warmth and smothering an inner hankering for espresso, Meredith thought about her boys, asleep now at Ranelagh, their grandparents' home, the family plantation that they loved dearly. She glanced at her watch and calculated the time difference between Scotland and Savannah with a sigh. Not a good time to call. In a few hours her father, John Rowland, would drive them to school in the new four-wheel drive he'd acquired last week and the kids would love it. Would her mother remember to tell Nan, the maid who'd been with her family forever, to send Mick's soccer shoes along for his afternoon practice? Perhaps she'd better leave a text message on her mom's mobile just in case.

Searching her purse for her cell phone, Meredith suddenly stopped herself. She was being ridiculous. She would only risk waking the household, and there was little use worrying about matters over which she had no control. She'd do better to apply her thoughts and energy to the upcoming meeting.

At ten o'clock precisely, Meredith left the Strathcairn Arms, and after a deep breath of damp, misty morning air got into her rental car and drove through the tiny village of Strathcairn. Now that she could see it properly, she realized it was quaint. Little whitewashed cottages bordered each side of the street, lending the impression of a Grimm's fairy tale. She saw the butcher, the baker. She grinned. All that was missing was the candlestick maker.

What, she wondered, could have induced a man like Grant Gallagher, a man who moved in pretty sophisticated circles, to come to an out-of-the-way spot like this?

Not that it was any of her business, she reminded herself as the car wound up the bumpy narrow road toward the castle. Her only interest was the execution of Rowena's will and perhaps to persuade him to do something for Dallas. In fact, all she really needed to extract from Gallagher was a commitment to come to the U.S. sometime in the next three months so they could have the meeting Rowena had insisted on and go ahead with probate. She also would require some material for an extra DNA test that would shut up the Carstairs relatives if they made a nuisance of themselves, an increasingly likely contingency. She sighed heavily, wondering why her gut was telling her it wasn't going to be that easy.

The mist had lifted as she reached the top of the steep hill where the castle loomed, severe and uninviting. Slowing the car, Meredith glanced at the huge wrought-iron gates, surprised to see them open. Raising her brows, she drove on through, past a couple ancient oak trees, tended grass and onto the gravel drive, wheels crunching loudly as she came to a smooth stop in front of the massive front door.

Picking up her briefcase, she checked her lipstick in the rearview mirror, then stepped out of the car, almost tripping on a large jutting root. Recovering her balance, she straightened her skirt and, securing the briefcase firmly under her arm, walked up the wide, well-trodden shallow stone steps that led to the front door. There she tugged a rusty iron wire to her right, presuming it must be the doorbell. Sure enough, a distant clanging somewhere in the castle's nether regions confirmed she was right. Taking a deep breath, Meredith stood straighter and braced herself. Then she heard a cough and a shuffle of feet and slowly the ancient door creaked open.

"Good morning," she said brightly, smiling professionally at the stooped elderly woman in a flowered, pale blue, mid-calf overall. She presumed this must be Mrs. Duffy. Her hair was scooped up in a tight bun secured by a net. A pair of clear blue eyes stared inquiringly at her. "I've come to see Mr. Gallagher. Is he in?"

"And who might ye be?" the woman asked warily, looking her up and down.

Undeterred, Meredith kept the smile in place. "I'm Meredith Hunter. I'm an attorney from the United States. I believe we may have spoken yesterday. I've come to see Mr. Gallagher on important business." She shifted her weight to the other foot while the woman continued to eye her with misgiving. "Well," she asked, trying not to sound rude or impatient, "is he in?"

"A couldna say."

"Look, either he's here or he isn't," Meredith responded, her patience withering, wondering if Gallagher had instructed his housekeeper to be unwelcoming only to her, or if the frosty reception applied to all visitors. "I've come all the way from Georgia to see him," she pleaded. "At least you might let me in."

The woman's expression unbent slightly and her blue eyes softened a tad. "Well, he won't be pleased, but I suppose there's nae use ye standing out there in the drizzle. Come in. You can wait in the living room," she offered, then shaking her head and muttering under her breath, she turned and led the way. Meredith followed her inside.

The hall was vast and drafty. A gaping medieval stone fireplace large enough to roast an ox stood against the far wall. It looked as if it hadn't been lit in a while. A threadbare Oriental rug covered the floor and a wide oak staircase led up to a Gothic-arched gallery above. The owner of Strathcairn Castle hadn't done much to modernize the place, she noted. It also felt distinctly chilly, and she shivered as Mrs. Duffy showed her grudgingly into the parlor. She wished she'd brought her coat.

"I'll go and tell Mr. Gallagher you're here," she said as they entered the oak-paneled living room.

"Thanks," Meredith murmured, stepping closer to the fireplace, glad of the warmth of the crackling logs. Placing her briefcase on a tapestry chair, she took a look about. There were portraits—under the circumstances, they could hardly be Grant Gallagher's ancestors—hanging on the walls, as well as miscellaneous ornaments, some ugly, large, empty porcelain vases and an expanse of draughty French windows framed with faded chintz drapes that looked out over a lawn. Meredith stepped over and looked out at the view. The lawn was pristine and stretched toward the edge of the cliff. Beyond that she spied a fishing boat bobbing back and forth, tossed by the strong wind as it ploughed the leaden waves. She could hear the squawk of gulls in the distance and the windows shook in their casements when a strong gust of wind hit.

She crossed her arms tightly over her chest, wondering whether to sit or remain standing. Gallagher had certainly chosen an eerie spot to work. She wondered if it was here he planned his Machiavellian takeovers. The venue certainly lent itself.

After a ten-minute wait, Meredith's mood had deteriorated significantly. Surely the man must realize that she wasn't here by choice but that she was merely doing her job. She wondered again if Gallagher had read Rowena's letter and whether she had revealed the truth. What if he hadn't known he was adopted? It was a definite possibility. Some adoptive parents never disclosed the truth to their child. How, she wondered uneasily, was she going to tell him the tangled story if that proved to be the case? Meredith shifted nervously before the fire, tweaked her chestnut hair behind her ear and wished it were all over.

Then, just as she was about to go and seek out Mrs. Duffy, the noise of a squeaking door handle from an adjoining room had her spinning on her heel and a tall, remarkably handsome, dark-haired man in old jeans, a baggy gray sweater and a day's growth of beard appeared. In the pictures she'd seen of him, he'd always been immaculately dressed. She didn't know what she'd expected, but it certainly wasn't this George Clooney look-alike who was taller than she'd imagined. For a second Meredith caught her breath as his eyes bored angrily into hers.

"What the hell do you want? I made it clear, didn't I, that you and I have nothing to say to each other?" he growled, shoving his hands into the pockets of his pants and eyeing her malevolently. "My advice to you is to get out. I hate being disturbed."

Meredith gasped and squared her shoulders. "You know perfectly well why I'm here."

"Oh?" A thick dark brow shot up.

"I'm here because I have important business to discuss with you. You cannot simply ignore my correspondence, Mr. Gallagher," she added in a clipped tone. "Presumably you have questions about what the letters contained."

"I'm not interested in the damn letters," he muttered, casting her another blazing glare from under thick, dark brows. That and the day's growth of beard gave him a rugged, devilish look. As he approached her, Meredith felt as though the large reception room had suddenly shrunk. She drew in her breath, then pulled herself together.

"There are matters to discuss that will significantly impact your future," she insisted, determined to stay the course.

"Ha!" He let out a harsh laugh. "My life is just fine as it is, thank you very much."

"Fine. Once we've gone over things, I promise you'll be left in peace and your life can go on," she said, standing her ground.

Gallagher gave her a thoughtful look. "I suppose I'm not going to be rid of you until you've had your say," he muttered. "You'd better sit down."

"Thank you," Meredith retorted sweetly, pleased her veneer of professional patience had at least got her through stage one. "As you rightly pointed out, I'm not leaving here until I've dealt with business. But neither am I here by choice."

His brows shot up. "Well, as I've already made it plain to you I'm not interested in what you have on offer, unless…?" He eyed her up and down, then met her eyes with a speculative look.

Meredith gasped, wondering briefly if he was mad and whether it was against the Georgia bar's code of conduct to kick a client in the balls. Clearly he was trying to needle her into losing her composure. Well, she wouldn't give him that satisfaction.

Seeing that he'd dropped into a wing chair opposite, she sat down on the couch and carefully removed the file from her briefcase. She should have expected a man of his ilk to lack gentlemanly courtesy, she reminded herself as she put on her reading glasses. Still, despite her growing anger, Meredith couldn't help noticing how sharp the contrast of his blue eyes was to his dark hair and tanned skin.

"As you know, I'm here at the behest of your American grandmother," she began in a crisp, nonemotional tone.

"Ah, yes. The prodigal grandmother," he murmured ironically in a pronounced British accent, "the famous Rowena Carstairs." He let out another cynical laugh.

Meredith eyed him over the rim of her glasses, glad that at least he seemed to be *au fait* with the facts. "So you're aware of the circumstances of your adoption?" she said, relieved.

"Aware? I'm not bloody aware of anything," he scoffed, eyes piercing hers. "Until the momentous revelation in your client's letter, I only knew that Raymond and Gina Gallagher had adopted me in a moment of misguided altruism that I'm sure they afterward came to regret."

"I realize this must all have come as something of a shock to you—"

"What? That some crazy old bat wanted to salvage her conscience before she moved on to a better world?"

"Something like that. I guess—"

"Ms. Hunter," he said, "nothing surprises me. In my line of business I've seen it all. Now, do me a favor, cut the formalities and let's get to the point, shall we?" He glanced at his watch. "I have work to do."

"Fine," Meredith snapped, pushing her glasses farther up her nose. She'd rarely come across anyone quite so uncivil. "You were adopted at birth, as you know. Your birth mother, Rowena's daughter, was Isabel Carstairs."

"Ah, the delightful Isabel," he drawled, crossing his ankles and clasping his hands behind his neck. "Go on. It makes a good story. Perhaps I should pitch it to Hollywood and pick up a few bucks along the way."

Paying no attention, Meredith continued as though he hadn't spoken. "As you know, Rowena, your grandmother, has named you in her will as her sole beneficiary."

His eyes shifted and settled on her. "Odd, isn't it? I can't think why she'd do a thing like that."

"Whatever her reasons, it's a huge bequest."

"I'm not interested in her money. You can give it all to charity as far as I'm concerned."

Meredith tipped her glasses and stared at him over the rims. "Perhaps you'd like to know what kind of inheritance we're talking about before making that decision."

"I couldn't give a damn." He shrugged and rotated his neck, his expression challenging.

Meredith stifled a desire to snap closed the file and tell him to go to hell. Instead, she gripped it and controlled her temper, knowing she had Dallas to think of. Maybe if he really didn't want the money, he could be persuaded to give his half sister a portion of the estate.

Pushing her glasses back up her nose, she focused. "Most people wouldn't be quite so cavalier about inheriting a hundred million dollars," she observed casually.

"A hundred million dollars? That's what the old bat was worth?" he asked, sitting up straighter and letting out a long, low whistle. "Well, well. Grandma must have been one smart cookie, as you Americans would say. I hadn't realized the estate was so huge."

"Something worth thinking about," Meredith pointed out, eyeing him closely.

"Certainly. If one was interested or needed the money," he replied, a scathing note entering his voice. "It so happens I'm not in either of those positions."

"I see. I must say, I hadn't anticipated this."

"No? Well, I made it plain to you over the phone. You should listen more carefully."

"Excuse me for asking," Meredith said, genuinely

curious, "but why *aren't* you interested? You have to admit this is rather an extraordinary circumstance. Surely you must be curious to find out more."

"Why should I be? I make a very good living doing what I do, and I've already got more money than I could ever spend," he said conversationally, studying her from his wing chair, enjoying her discomfort. "As for the so-called *family* connection—" he shrugged "—why should I want to know anything about Rowena Carstairs?"

"I thought perhaps you might be eager to learn more about your past."

"Ha! Not in the least. I don't need any more skeletons in my closet."

"Look, I'm aware that you find all this very amusing. But there are some serious issues to be dealt with. Whether you accept the money is your call, but you need to be aware of all the facts before you make a final decision. Surely you can see that? I need you to attend a meeting in the United States so that we can process the appropriate paperwork."

Grant snorted. "You have to be joking? First you have the gall to come wasting my time when I've already told you I want nothing to do with your client's estate, then you expect me to cross the pond because of this nonsense? Look, Ms. Hunter, I haven't got time for any meetings except those of my choosing. And for the record, I don't consider this amusing. Quite the opposite," he bit back icily. "She can stuff her money where the sergeant stuffed the pudding."

"Excuse me?"

"An old British expression, which I believe speaks for itself."

Meredith remained silent, looking at him as she

might a recalcitrant teenager who sat sulking and scowling into the flames.

"Well, Rowena had a great sense of humor," she remarked finally, "and she probably would have found that funny. As for me—" she sat up straighter "—I just keep wondering how a savvy businessman like you could be so foolish." Gallagher sent her a sharp look, but she plowed on. "Surely you didn't get where you are today by making final decisions without deliberating. That's a recipe for disaster, as you well know. I can inform you of all the facts, then leave you to make up your mind."

Letting out a huff, Grant turned and looked at her with a new, arrested expression. His chin went up and his eyes pierced hers, as though seeing her for the first time. "You really aren't going to leave me alone until you've hashed this damn thing out, are you?" he challenged.

"No, I'm not," she agreed, a smile twitching her lips.

He rolled his eyes. "Well, get on with it, give me the scoop. Then you can legitimately go home and tell your boss that you did all you could to get me to accept the inheritance and that I refused. There, satisfied?" He quirked a cynical brow at her, his eyes never leaving her face.

"As I'm the boss, that won't be necessary," she retorted, eyeing the documents before her. "Now, as things stand at present, you have been declared undisputed heir to the Carstairs holdings. One of the provisos of the bequest is that you attend a meeting at Rowena's house in Miami."

"Which, since I'm refusing the lot, won't be necessary," he responded smoothly, leaning farther back in the armchair.

"Would you mind not interrupting until I've finished?" she shot back.

"Excuse me," he said with exaggerated politeness.

"As I was saying, there are documents that must be signed and lodged in court. Then there's the question of your sibling."

"Sibling?" His hooded eyes shot up and he straightened. "What sibling?"

"You have a half sister."

"Where in hell's name did she come from?"

"Her name is Dallas Thornton. She's nineteen years old and is the issue of your mother's marriage to a man named Doug Thornton."

"I see. Why didn't the money go to her?"

"That, I'm afraid, is a mystery that has been bothering me ever since Rowena's death. There seems to be no specific reason why Dallas should have been cut out of her will, but she was," Meredith said, lifting the file. "Here, it might be easier if you took a look for yourself."

Grant stayed quiet for a moment, then he leaned forward and reached for the file, taking it from her outstretched hand. His eyes skimmed rapidly over the contents.

"How can you be certain that I'm the rightful heir?" he asked finally. "There must be a number of Grant Gallaghers running about the world."

"Because I've had it thoroughly checked out. About ten years ago, Rowena hired a private detective agency that traced all your adoption records. It's all in there. There is no doubt. Of course, another DNA test would determine undisputable proof."

"*Another* DNA test?" His eyes narrowed and Meredith felt her cheeks warming, cursing herself for the blunder. She'd found the detective's idea of taking a hair off the shoulder of his jacket invasive, and had said so at the time.

"Do you mean to tell me that, unbeknownst to me, someone has tampered with my private effects and taken material with which to do a DNA test?" he asked in a menacing tone.

"Well, not exactly."

"What do you mean, not exactly?" He rose and paced the room, body tense and taut. "Ms. Hunter, how dare anybody invade my privacy and mess with my stuff? Or didn't you think I knew how a DNA test works?" He stopped next to the couch and loomed over her. "Next you'll be saying you know what my damn blood type is. Or when I lost my virginity."

"According to your birth records, it's AB negative— just like your mother's. Quite rare," she observed mildly.

"My moth—God, that beats the lot. I suppose I'm meant to be grateful that I have that in common with her," he added bitterly before glaring down at her. "You know you've got some nerve coming here, disrupting my life. As for Rowena, I don't want her damn money and neither do I wish to acquire a herd of bloody relations."

"But Dallas is your sister."

"Good for her. I'll bet she has as much desire to meet me as I do her. That is, if you've told her about me?" he asked shrewdly.

"I have. Dallas is expected to be present at the Miami meeting."

"I thought I'd already made it clear that I've no intention of attending any meeting," he said harshly. "Who does that woman think she is—was, rather, manipulating people like pawns on a chessboard? She must have been raving mad to want to leave her money to me. She had no idea who I was or what I'd turned into. And she obviously cared even less."

"She clearly had some notion of who you were, since she compiled a file with ten years of data about you," Meredith reminded him bluntly, thinking privately that had Rowena actually met this boor, she might very well have made other provisions.

Scowling, he handed her back the file. "This is like a bad B movie." He sat down again. Then, mercurial as ever, his expression changed and he proceeded in a conversational manner, "By the way, just out of interest, why was I put up for adoption? Did my mother get knocked up by some worthless boyfriend?" The tone was blasé but Meredith caught the edge in his voice. Although he put on a good show, it was just possible that beneath his harsh front, Grant Gallagher was coping with deeper emotions he was determined to conceal.

"I don't know, I'm afraid."

"Well, neither do I, and, frankly, I don't care. I had parents—for what they were worth. And now I'm my own man. So let's forget the whole thing. You pack your papers up, go back to Savannah, and I'll get on with my life. If you need a release, send me the documents and I'll return them to you duly signed and sealed."

"It's not quite as simple as that," she demurred, standing her ground.

"Why not? I don't want her money. Give it to somebody who does, for Christ's sake. I'll bet there are dozens of relatives lining up for that kind of dough."

Meredith hesitated. She sensed it was too soon to place the chips on the table.

"Mr. Gallagher, any decision you make will directly impact a number of people. Should you continue to not wish to accept the inheritance and instead choose to hand it over to another party, it will still require going through the legal formalities."

"Well, you're the lawyer, you find solutions. What 'other party' were you thinking of?" His eyes met hers head-on, his hypnotic gaze impossible to ignore.

Meredith took a deep breath and hoped she wasn't jumping the gun. "If you don't want it, your sister, Dallas, could use it," she said at last.

"Great. Tell her she can have the lot."

"Unfortunately, the will has certain stipulations."

His eyes narrowed. "What stipulations?"

"I guess Rowena may have anticipated that you might refuse the inheritance, and established a provision that will take effect if you fail to undertake certain actions. For you to alter this provision, you have thirty days, as of now, to take the necessary legal steps. Included in those steps, as specified in the will, is your attendance at a meeting with Dallas in Miami. If you don't come to the meeting and sign the proper paperwork, then the money goes to a foundation set up by Rowena, the, um—" she paused "—the Society for the Advancement and Protection of Poodles."

He laughed now, a rich, deep laugh, and his eyes rested on her with the first glimpse of real feeling she'd recognized in him yet. "Very savvy," he exclaimed. "You sure this is for real? You're not making it up to try to persuade me to go to this famous meeting you seem so determined about?"

"Jesus! You have nerve," Meredith burst out, finally

losing her cool and jumping out of the chair. "If you'd bothered to read all the letters I sent, you'd know all about this already—"

"I rarely read my correspondence."

"Well, that's just too goddamn bad," she flung, throwing down the file. "Maybe when you've come to your senses, you'll read that through properly. I'm going back to the Strathcairn Arms."

"What for?" he goaded, crossing his arms, arrogantly looking her up and down. "I have no intention of changing my mind. I plan on ignoring the whole thing."

"Mr. Gallagher," Meredith said through gritted teeth, "I am not to blame for the manner in which your grandmother chose to bequeath her fortune. I'm merely an emissary. I have no pleasure in being here, I assure you. But I have a fiduciary responsibility to act on behalf of the beneficiary, and a legal duty to act in managing and administering the estate," she continued bitingly. "The law requires a high standard of ethical and moral conduct of fiduciaries. There are many specific duties. Some are imposed by statute, some by case law and some by the will itself. But none of them can be ignored."

"Bravo. An impressive speech." He clapped his hands and looked her over, amused. "I guess law school is good for something after all."

Mastering the urge to knock his well-aligned teeth down his throat, Meredith took a deep breath. "In case I used too many big words," she said sweetly, "it means that, like it or not, I now represent your best interests. I need you to cooperate. Do you understand?"

"Perfectly. Now, if you'll excuse me, I'm very busy this morning. Goodbye, Ms. Hunter." With a sharp nod he rose, turned on his heel and marched out of the room the same way he'd entered. The door snapped shut behind him, leaving Meredith openmouthed in the middle of the room.

"Well, that does it," she muttered, angrily clamping down the lid of her briefcase and leaving the file where he'd abandoned it on the side table. She crossed the room, then marched into the great hall. The man's obtuseness—not to mention his incredibly rude behavior—was intolerable. How could she be expected to deal with such a creature? There was no sign of Mrs. Duffy. In fact, the place seemed deserted. Reaching the huge front door, Meredith dragged it open and headed down the steps.

So much for wrapping this up in forty-eight hours, she reflected bitterly. She had to get back to the Strathcairn Arms and think out a new strategy, one that did not involve her personally, she vowed. As soon as the office opened in Savannah, she would phone Tracy and brainstorm with her. Surely she couldn't be expected to stick around while Grant Gallagher decided whether he could be bothered to accept a hundred million bucks?

Or, like it or not, would she have to?

With a sinking heart, she drove down the hill. It was her case, her responsibility. There was no senior partner to run to with complaints any longer. *She* was the senior partner. It was her show.

Realizing she must cool down, Meredith made her way along the seafront. She'd come across difficult clients before, but none as handsome, arrogant, offensive and irritating as Grant Gallagher. He obviously had a very high opinion of himself.

"Aargh!" Meredith let out a low growl and, spying

a convenient parking spot, decided to take a walk.
Some fresh air would help clear her brain. She would
not allow this man to throw her out of kilter, which was
his obvious intention. She must remain cool, think of
how she should deal with him. After all, there was Dallas to consider. Heck, if he really didn't want the
money, then she had to find a way to get him to follow
the conditions of the will and still cede some to his sister.

Surely he had some shred of humanity under that
tough facade? However deeply hidden.

The wind whipped her hair as she pulled on the
beige cashmere coat she'd retrieved from the back seat.
Whatever happened, she was not about to give up.

As Grant Gallagher would learn shortly, she had
not yet begun to fight.

From behind the mullioned window, Grant watched
her cross the gravel in her high heels and climb into her
car. She had good legs, he reflected. Then, as the vehicle headed down the drive, he shrugged, shook his
head and, crossing the study, headed back into the living room.

The file lay where she'd discarded it. He stared at it
with mixed feelings. If Rowena Carstairs were still
alive he would have had the immense satisfaction of
shoving her damn money in her face. But now that
was denied him. The clever old witch had seen to that,
hadn't she?

He remembered each word of her letter and ground
his teeth. She'd guessed exactly how he'd react—and
then had pulled the rug from under his feet by calling
his bluff. Poodle society, indeed. She'd known the notion
of so much money going to something so ridiculous

would give him pause. A cunning smile hovered as he shoved his hands deep in his pockets and his creative mind went to work. He wasn't going to be bested. Rowena would not win this battle of wills. Of that he was increasingly determined.

Still, like it or not, he was intrigued. At what point, he wondered suddenly, had the question of Rowena's estate gone from being an annoying interruption to becoming a challenge? He glanced down at the file once more, a half smile hovering. So she thought she'd get to him with the poodle bit, did she? Well, she was wrong. He didn't give a damn who her money went to. The poodles were welcome to it. Though Meredith Hunter was unlikely to give him any peace until he'd taken an ultimate decision in writing, based on legal argument.

Flinging himself down once more in the chair, he gave the material his full attention, still torn between a desire to consign it to the flames and a growing need to get the better of Rowena Carstairs, dead or alive. As he studied the specifics of the bequest—the various estates, the museum-quality artwork, the extraordinary stock-and-bond portfolio—he let out a low whistle. By any standard, this was a hell of a lot of money to leave to one person, let alone an unknown illegitimate grandson. What, he wondered, stretching his long legs toward the fire, had she meant to achieve by it?

In all these years—at least not since adolescence—he'd never allowed himself to wonder about the man and woman who had sired him. That they hadn't wanted him was all he really knew. And so he'd simply expelled them from his mind, concentrating on himself and the present, discovering early in life that self-preservation was the safest route to avoiding pain.

Now, for some reason he could not explain, this whole thing got his back up. What, he wondered, would his reaction have been if he didn't own all he had today? Would he have accepted gladly? Been thankful to Rowena for remembering him?

He didn't think so.

Still, it was a tidy sum that, well invested, could be put to good use. The rational thing, of course, would be to forget any personal issues and take the money, assuming it didn't inconvenience him to do so. But the fact of the matter was that Rowena seemed to have set out to inconvenience him, to capture his curiosity and force him to reconnect with his birth family. Why? he asked himself again. Why bother? What could the woman have wanted from him? For all at once, he was certain the bequest was not an outright gift—Rowena definitely wanted something in return. But at this point he just couldn't figure out what.

Rising, he returned to the cluttered study and sat down at his desk, determined to forget. Work was an infallible antidote.

But after several minutes spent trying to concentrate on the zoning restrictions on undeveloped parkland, he gave up, threw his hands in the air and groaned.

"Damn the lot of them," he growled. Rowena, Meredith Hunter, this unknown half sister—they'd all slipped through his well-honed defenses.

Leaving the study, he headed into the hall and placed the file on top of his jacket on the chair where he'd left it lying earlier in the day. He'd never had any brothers or sisters. Hadn't wanted any. Could do without any now, thank you very much.

And that's exactly what he planned on telling the lovely Ms. Meredith Hunter, he decided as he headed upstairs to change.

7

Back at the Strathcairn Arms, Meredith lay down on the purple bedspread and closed her eyes. The brisk walk along the seafront had done little to calm her irritation. Here she was, stuck in the boondocks, thwarted by the selfish whims of an insufferable man she thoroughly despised. She could barely recall the last time she'd experienced such total frustration. Hadn't she come here for his benefit? Perhaps digging up his past wasn't the easiest thing to accept, even for a man like him. But still. He was an adult, a man of the world—supposedly—who could at least act with common courtesy. Glancing at her watch, Meredith let out an impatient huff and drummed her foot rhythmically against the side of the bed. It would still be several hours before she could reach Tracy and discuss this latest development. She had a feeling that although Gallagher was determined to be recalcitrant, his curiosity was whetted all the same. What, she wondered, dropping her chin on her palm, would it take to persuade him that coming to the States was a good idea?

Slipping on a pair of jeans and a thick sweater, she went downstairs for a drink in the pub, grateful for its cheery warmth after such a dreary morning.

"Hi, Jim," she called to the landlord, who was cheerfully chatting to several customers. Then she sat down at what she was fast coming to consider "her" table, the cozy nook in the corner under the beams, with the sagging bench heaped with tartan cushions.

Determined not to dwell on Gallagher's insufferable behavior, Meredith ordered a gin and tonic and began thinking of persuasive arguments to lure Grant Gallagher to the U.S. Unless he came to Miami, there was little that could legally be done for Dallas. And if he insisted on ignoring the bequest, well, she sighed, there were going to be some pretty pampered poodles in the state of Georgia. What an awful waste, she decided, watching Jim as he stood behind the bar carefully pouring a pint for an elderly white-haired man seated on a stool at the bar.

It was barely twelve o'clock, but as she took the first sip of her drink Meredith felt that after her morning's travails she deserved every last drop. Once she'd convinced Jim to load her drink with ice—an unknown concept, apparently—she listened as he and the two white-haired kilted customers exchanged views on the weather and local politics.

Meredith listened, amused, thinking how similar life was around the world: the same complaints, the same worries and exigencies. Then Moira came in and assured her that it was close to lunchtime and that today there was excellent steak-and-kidney pie on the menu.

Feeling more relaxed, Meredith pulled a road map from her purse, determined to make sure she got on the right road back to Glasgow. As soon as this matter with Gallagher was settled, she was heading straight back to Savannah. She was just seeking Jim's advice on the quickest route when the door to the street opened. Poring over the map, she didn't notice a shadow standing next to the table until it was on top of her.

"Ms. Hunter?"

"Oh!" Meredith jumped and looked up with a start, astonished to see Grant Gallagher's tall figure looming over the table.

"May I?" He didn't wait for an answer but pulled off his Barbour jacket and slid down opposite her onto the bench. Recovering from her amazement, she watched warily as he retrieved the file from his capacious pocket and placed it on the table. He looked different. He'd showered and shaved, and Meredith caught a whiff of cologne. He might have a number of defects, she admitted, but she'd have to be blind not to recognize what an extremely attractive man he was.

"You left this behind," he said, indicating the file.

"Right." Meredith regrouped and, adopting a professional attitude, smiled briefly. "I presume you've read it?"

"Yes."

"So you've seen the provisos?"

"Yes. I did." He leaned back against the cushions, his eyes hooded.

"Good," she replied briskly, "then you realize something needs to be done."

"No. I haven't changed my mind. I just came to give you your file back." He pushed the manila envelope across the table.

"I wish you—"

"She and her daughter had a choice," he interrupted, the trace of the bitterness she'd heard earlier entering his voice. "They made their decision. They probably had a number of perfectly good reasons for doing so. It doesn't matter anymore." He gave a shrug. "But I have my life, and I'm not going to let Rowena or anyone else foist their bad conscience on me. It's too easy."

Meredith watched an angry, cynical expression cover his handsome features, amazed when she experienced a flash of pity. She shoved it aside. Winning this battle had become a personal challenge. Never mind that she was embroiled up to the neck in Rowena's affairs or that she wanted to do right by Dallas. The truth was that this was starting to mean something to her personally. She wanted to sort this mess out properly. For a moment she recalled Professor Morecombe's advice when he'd told his students never, ever to become emotionally involved with their clients. They were a case. That was all.

She certainly hadn't succeeded this time.

"I don't need Granny's charity," he continued in the same ironical tone.

"Nobody thinks you do, Mr. Gallagher."

"Grant," he answered, looking straight at her, his inscrutable blue eyes gazing directly at her.

Meredith hesitated. "Okay, then, Grant," she answered, surprised.

"At least Rowena was right about one thing," he said, raising his brows. "I've made my own packet and don't need anyone else's. Perhaps I do have some of her in me after all." He let out a dry, low laugh. "I don't suppose my moth—Isabel—is pleased with all this, is she?" he asked, his voice dark and cynical. "I mean, she must have done something pretty terrible—besides getting pregnant with me, of course—to get on old Rowena's bad side, because she's been cut out of the will, too, right? You haven't mentioned much about her," he said, barely masking his hostility.

"I'm afraid she's dead."

He looked at her, completely expressionless, then rose quickly to his feet and moved toward the bar. After exchanging a few words with Jim, he returned with a pint of Guinness and a fresh gin and tonic. Placing them on the wooden surface, he sat down again. "Dead," he commented, as though the conversation had not been abruptly interrupted. "How old was she when she had me?" He tipped back his glass.

"About seventeen, I guess."

"Exactly what I thought." He sounded satisfied.

"Maybe your grandmother was trying to make it up to you in some way," she murmured, trying a new approach.

"With a payoff, you mean? Like they did the first time around? Paid to have her 'little mistake' taken care of?"

"Maybe." Meredith shifted uncomfortably. "Or maybe Isabel wasn't able to care for you herself and they wanted to find you a good home," she said, keeping her voice neutral.

He let out another bark of humorless laughter, took another sip and eyed her cynically. "Don't try to sugarcoat this, gorgeous. I'm a big boy. I can take it."

"My name is Meredith Hunter, not 'gorgeous,'" she bit back. "And I'd appreciate it if we could keep this conversation professional. I'm not interested in your dysfunctional psychological issues."

"Dysfunc—what the hell are you talking about?" He slammed the tankard down abruptly.

"Forget it. All I want to know is how we're going to proceed with the inheritance. You are aware that if you don't come to the U.S. and attend the meeting Rowena intended within thirty days, you lose any right to direct how the estate's funds are disbursed?"

"So?"

"So, I thought you might at least consider doing something worthwhile with the money."

"You don't consider the poodle home a worthy cause?" he inquired with a ghost of a smile.

Despite the tension, Meredith's lips twitched. "Actually, I love dogs, but there *are* better ways to spend a hundred million dollars."

"Why poodles?" he asked, watching her over the rim of the tankard.

"Oh, Rowena was crazy about them. She had a pair of neurotic toy poodles. Used to dye them to match the color of whatever headdress she was wearing."

"You have to be joking?"

"Not at all. Did it for years until the day I told her it was probably the dye that was making them totally hyper. That's how we became friends."

"You liked her?"

"Yes, I liked her. She was a difficult client, trying and eccentric, but also generous and highly intelligent. She didn't suffer fools kindly."

"Why didn't her generosity extend to what's-her-name? The girl you mentioned earlier."

Meredith's pulse skipped a beat. "You mean Dallas?"

"That's it. Odd name for a girl, but typically American, I suppose."

Meredith let it pass. "I have no idea why she cut Dallas out of her will. Dallas didn't get on with her grandmother, but that wasn't a reason to leave her nothing—particularly when she's in one hell of a fix."

"What do you mean?"

"Her father died a few months ago and left her a pile of debt. The family has a gorgeous old horse farm near Beaufort, but the mortgage company is about to foreclose on it."

"Ah. Life can be tough sometimes."

"And sometimes it can give you a break," she flashed back, eyes blazing.

"I suppose she's dying to get her greedy little hands on anything she can," he muttered, thinking of the last girlfriend he'd ditched and what it had cost him.

"Actually, Dallas has made it clear that had she been a beneficiary, like you, she would have refused the inheritance," she countered wearily, removing her glasses and laying them on the table next to her. "I think it's safe to say your stubbornness is a family trait."

There was a moment's silence. Then, when she least expected it, Grant looked at her across the table and sent her a dazzling smile. Meredith caught her breath, unable to draw her eyes from his face. The smile transformed him completely. Hastily, she reached for her glasses and forced her mind back to the issue at hand, while telling herself that he should smile more often as it improved him no end.

"You should get rid of those glasses and use contacts," he remarked. "You have beautiful eyes. Great shade of gray. Haven't seen that color too often."

"I—" Meredith fumbled, taken aback, still reeling from his change in attitude.

"It's true," he insisted, the devastating smile still in place. "They're a great contrast to that chestnut hair. I'll bet you look wonderful with it loose."

"I don't see what my hair or my eyes have to do with the will," she muttered defensively, suppressing the desire to straighten her ponytail.

"You don't like being paid a compliment?" Now he grinned at her complacently, a very different figure to the man she'd been addressing seconds earlier. "What's wrong with the men in your life—are they blind?"

"I don't have a man in my life," she bit back. "Now, can we stick to business, please?" She slipped the glasses back on and opened the file, her hands trembling slightly.

Grant continued to watch her, intrigued by the flash of pain he saw flicker in her eyes. "I'm sorry if I said something to offend you. I can be, uh…abrupt sometimes."

She nodded curtly, muttering, "Now, there's a news flash." Then she straightened, all business. "I really think you should at least consider availing yourself of the option to redirect the funds," she said briskly.

Taking her cue, Grant leaned his elbows on the table. Despite every urge to resist, he was nevertheless intrigued as much by Meredith as by the subject he'd been so determined to avoid. "So now I'm expected to toe the line for her sake. That's rich. But clever of the old witch. The poodle home is, I have to admit, tempting, but as you pointed out, not a very worthy cause. What do you think was in her head when she devised this whole scheme?" he mused.

"I have no idea," Meredith replied truthfully.

"No. I'll bet no one did."

"Probably not. The point is, Mr. Galla—I mean, Grant, you have to come to a conclusion about this."

"I thought I already had," he murmured, fixing her with an amused stare.

"Could you please be serious about this for a moment?" she replied, raising her eyes and staring right back. "Surely you can't be totally impervious to Dallas's plight?"

"Why not?"

"Because she's a human being." Meredith threw up her hands in despair. "She's your half sister. She's family. Surely that must mean something to you?"

"Not a damn thing, I'm afraid." He shook his head mournfully.

Meredith pulled off her glasses angrily. "Despite your determination to make it into one, this is not an amusing situation. Unlike you, Dallas desperately needs funds. It would be a shame if her life was ruined because you were unwilling to spare the time for one trip across the *pond*, as you like to call it," she said recklessly, trying to gauge his reaction.

"Your defense of the underdog does you credit, Ms. Hunter. Or may I call you Meredith?"

"Whatever. I really don't care. As long I can persuade you that you just can't ignore all this. Won't you at least consider coming to the meeting? I'll make sure the date suits your busy schedule," she said, suddenly changing tactics. "It would really help clarify matters. Make my job a heck of a lot easier."

Grant looked at her for a long moment. "Why should I want to do that?"

"Because we're both busy people with lives we need to get on with," she retorted, her pleasant tone belied by her blazing eyes. "I don't have time to spend twiddling my thumbs here while you consider your options. I must ask you to give me a definitive position by this evening. I have a plane to catch."

"Back to Savannah?"

"Yes."

"What's the hurry?"

"I have—" Meredith cut off and took a deep breath. The man was impossible. "My personal life is none of your business. All I need is your answer."

"Sorry, just healthy curiosity." He leaned back, still watching her closely.

Meredith took another sip of her drink, trying to control her frustration and regain the upper hand. "Look," she said calmly, "I'd appreciate it if you would think carefully about what we've talked about here, about the people and lives you could help if you at least made the effort of this one visit. And I'd like you to give me your position as soon as possible," she replied sincerely. "I've got an early-morning flight to catch." With that she closed the file, removed her glasses once more and waited for him to rise.

Grant toyed with the Guinness and surveyed her, strangely unwilling to let this remarkable interlude end. She was lovely when angry—probably delicious when aroused—and her orderly, intelligent, well-trained brain and her obvious passion for justice intrigued him. He hadn't felt this intrigued by anyone for a while. It might even be entertaining to see how long he could drag this out now that his Australian deal had fallen through. He'd been too preoccupied to give it the full concentration it deserved.

Following her example, he rose. "I'll give you a call later today."

"Make sure you do."

"And if I don't?" he taunted.

"This is not a game, Mr. Gallagher."

"Grant. How many times do I have to remind you?"

"One way or another this has to be settled," Meredith said, ignoring the interruption. "As a lawyer and businessman yourself, I'm sure you understand that." She glanced at him haughtily.

"Point taken." He pulled on his jacket, feeling a reluctant admiration for this petite woman's self-assurance and dignity. She really was very lovely, and although she was apparently oblivious to the fact, highly seductive. Her severe expression gave a first impression of icy impenetrability. But he'd watched her carefully for the past half hour, and he'd seen her eyes flash. He'd be willing to wager that she dealt the ice-princess act in her profession. But what, he wondered curiously, lay beneath the surface?

They stood for a moment, then Meredith extended her hand. "I'll look forward to hearing from you later today."

Grant took her hand in his. Liking the feel of her tapered fingers, he held them a second longer than necessary. Then, with an abrupt nod, he turned and walked out of the pub.

It was five o'clock and she still hadn't heard from him.

She'd called home, spoken to her mother and the boys, and even answered questions concerning Zack's science project. It was a relief to know all was well and to be able to tell them that she hoped to be leaving for Savannah the next day. But now she was frustrated and hoped Grant wouldn't keep her here twiddling her fingers for another day.

Her conversation with her partner had been less fulfilling.

"What's he like?" Tracy asked.

"Unbearable."

"No, I meant what's he like as a guy?"

Meredith rolled her eyes. "Trace, for Christ's sake, what does it matter?"

"A guy's a guy. Of course it matters."

"Trace, when will you ever grow up? You sound exactly the same as you did in college."

"And you still haven't given me an answer," her friend replied mischievously.

"Okay. I'll admit he's extremely handsome."

"Tall?"

"Yes."

"Dark?"

"Yes." Meredith let out an irritated huff and shook the phone.

"Good muscles?"

"I couldn't tell. He was wearing a loose sweater," she replied stonily.

"Rats. Sounds pretty good to me."

Meredith burst out laughing despite her irritation. "Yes, the guy's a hunk, okay? And he knows it, and he probably lays everything in the modeling world and a few movie stars on the side. Now, will you get serious?"

"Gee, and you want to come home? I'd be looking for an excuse to stay."

"That's you, sugar, not me," Meredith pointed out firmly. "All I'm interested in is getting him to cooperate, and right now it's not looking good."

"Well, sorry I can't help, hon. If I come up with answers, I'll call you, okay? Maybe I should've gone after all."

"I wish you had."

Their discussion had left her more irritated than she already was, and when the rain finally subsided she decided to go for another walk by the sea.

Following the coastline, her face to the wind, Meredith dwelt again on her recalcitrant client. He definitely had a strong, unbending, selfish nature. Quite like Rowena's. As she expected, he seemed to care little for anything except his own welfare. Then, as she was stepping back into the garish hotel lobby, she recalled the touch of his fingers on hers and the ensuing frisson.

Frowning, Meredith climbed the stairs, telling herself that she must better compartmentalize the emotional and practical aspects of the case. He was a difficult client, one who needed the kid-glove treatment but also a measure of firmness. It was obvious from their conversation in the pub that, although he'd never admit it, this sudden revelation of the circumstances of his birth was causing him considerable emotional upheaval. And why wouldn't it? But that, she reminded herself, was a job for his shrink, not his attorney. Now, as her phone tinkled and she read the castle number on her ID, her heart beat faster. *Please say you'll agree to come to Miami so I can go home,* she pleaded, waiting a moment before answering, aware that she still didn't have a contingency plan if he refused.

"Hello?"

"This is Grant Gallagher speaking."

"Hi. What can I do for you?" Meredith asked in a brisk, professional voice.

"Come to dinner tonight and I'll tell you."

"I'm afraid that's not possible."

"Oh? Do you have alternate plans? Soup at the pub, perhaps?"

"I didn't come here to socialize. This is business."

"Exactly. What I'm suggesting is a business dinner. Here, if you don't mind. We can discuss the will over a decent meal and a bottle of wine without exciting the curiosity of the entire village. I prefer to keep my affairs private."

It was a reasonable request that she could hardly refuse. "Okay. What time?"

"I'll expect you at seven for drinks." He didn't wait for an answer.

Meredith stared at the phone. God, the man was intolerable. Then she grinned. At least it looked as if she'd finalize things tonight and be able to leave tomorrow. Cheered, she opted for a relaxing hot bath in the big tub, turned on the taps, then added some scented floral bath oil to the steaming water before undressing. As she did so, she glanced at herself in the mirror. Unconsciously she loosened the ponytail and shook her hair about her shoulders. It had grown considerably this past year. Not because she'd intended it to, but simply because she hadn't bothered to have it cut.

Tom had never worried about her hair and had said he liked it any way she chose to wear it. That was typical Tom, she reflected, turning away from the mirror to test the temperature of the water, her mind filled with memories of her husband and the teasing way they used to treat each other. Slipping off her cotton underwear, she took another peek in the mirror. Lord, she was skinny. Always had been. But this past year had taken its toll. Suddenly, peering at herself in the full-length glass, Meredith realized she hadn't looked at herself properly since Tom's death. Her figure was still good, she observed, her skin smooth and soft, and she supposed that as always she still looked much younger than her age. There had been times not that long ago, she recalled nostalgically, when they'd gone for a drink and she'd been carded.

Meredith blinked back the unshed tears and dipped the tip of her toe into the hot water, testing it before sinking into the bath. Forcing her thoughts away from Tom and the past, she wondered if Grant Gallagher was right. Was Rowena's bequest motivated purely by guilt? A desire to make up for something she'd maybe come to regret? Knowing Rowena, there had to be a greater reason. For the first time Meredith realized that her own curiosity was whetted.

What, she wondered, lay in all those thick white envelopes back in Savannah? Rowena had left a pile of sealed correspondence, with strict instructions as to when each was to be opened. Grant had already received the first letter; there'd be another for him, and Dallas as well, in Miami, presuming she could get him there. Yet others would be distributed at additional, and supposedly critical, junctures in the probate process. It was all very mysterious, and she'd couldn't help but wonder what the old lady had up her sleeve.

As she rubbed herself with her natural sponge, she thought of Grant. It seemed obvious that both he and Dallas were carrying considerable emotional baggage—and considering their respective childhoods, she supposed that was to be expected. Meredith trailed her fingers through the water, aware of just how lucky she was to have such a close-knit family. She couldn't imagine what it must be like to grow up a lonely only child.

Instinctively, her heart went out to both Dallas and Grant. Grant the child, of course, she reminded herself quickly. She had little time for the man he'd become. But Dallas was different. She'd sounded so defensive and angry on the phone, as though she needed to inoculate herself from Rowena and anything to do with her. The result was almost childlike in its violence.

For a while she lay in the hot bath thinking of her own kin. Her parents and her brother Jeff were as dear to her as her kids, all part of the orderly, secure pattern that formed her existence.

Just as Tom had been.

God knows how she would have handled his death without the staunch support and love of her family. The mere thought made her shudder.

As she lay in the cooling water, Meredith recognized the need to go beyond the boundaries of her professional duty. Although it wasn't essentially her job, she knew she owed it to Rowena to try to bring Dallas and Grant together. After all, even though they didn't know it, they really had only each other—and a bevy of Carstairs relations they could well do without. It made her feel almost guilty for the privilege of having had such great relationships, not just with her own family, but with Tom's as well.

It had all been so simple and healthy and right. Tom's father was a well-respected doctor in the community, from one of the founding families of Savannah, just like hers, and from the time they'd first started dating in tenth grade, everybody had assumed, quite rightly, that they would graduate and marry.

And unlike Elm, her best friend, who'd had such a disastrous marriage to her college sweetheart, Harlan MacBride, she'd never experienced any regret. In fact, quite the opposite. There had been no discord, no unhappiness or dissatisfaction, and ten years into the marriage she'd been happier and more content than ever.

Until disaster struck. Leading a prosperous, well-balanced life hadn't made her immune to tragedy.

She sighed, then, realizing that she was shriveling

from staying too long in the water, Meredith pulled out
the stopper and got out of the bath. Drying herself with
one of the large mauve terry-cloth towels, she moved
back into the room and debated what to wear to dinner. She'd brought one dress. Should she wear that, or
go in pants and a sweater? She was damned if she was
going to get sick in that drafty old castle. Still, it would
be embarrassing to arrive improperly dressed.

Finally, she opted for the black Gucci cocktail dress,
glad now that Elm had insisted she buy it. It was sleek
and well cut and it made her look a bit older and more
professional. Returning to the bathroom, she dabbed
on a little makeup and a touch of lip gloss.

Then she brushed her hair. For a moment she hesitated
before deciding to leave it loose. After slipping on her
pearl-and-diamond studs, she picked up her purse and
the file and made her way downstairs with her coat over
her arm.

"Oh, my," Moira exclaimed from the bottom of the
stairs, her hands straddled on her wide hips. "You look
smashing, dearie."

"Thank you." Meredith exchanged a surprised
smile with the landlady.

"Off to dinner up at the castle, are ye?" Moira asked
in a conspiratorial voice.

"Uh, yes. I have business to discuss with Mr. Gallagher." Meredith grinned weakly, realizing that
Grant's instincts were correct and the entire village
was probably conjecturing her reason for being here.
No doubt a private dinner at the castle would be infinitely preferable to a public meeting in the pub.

Moira winked and helped her on with her coat.
"Dinna catch yer death up there, now, will ye? It's
a chilly night. Ye'll be needing a scarf." She tugged

a bright woolen scarf off a peg and handed it to Meredith.

"Thank you. I won't be late," she added hurriedly.

"Och, dearie, you come in whenever ye like," Moira said, a grin spreading across her broad freckled face. "I'll leave the door unlocked for ye."

"Thanks, but that won't be necessary."

"Well, ye never can tell how an evening'll turn out, can ye, now?" With another wink Moira waved an embarrassed Meredith on her way. It was mortifying to realize the natives obviously thought she was having an affair with their most prominent resident, she reflected, climbing into the car.

Gunning the engine, she drove through the dimly lit village and up the hill toward the illuminated castle. It seemed to rise eerily from the damp evening mist, mystical and mysterious, like a beacon. And although Meredith prided herself on being sensible and logical, she suddenly understood what had attracted Grant Gallagher to this remote spot. Strathcairn was a dramatic reminder of another world, a world of old values, of tradition. Of roots. Was that what he'd been seeking when he'd bought the place?

To her surprise, Grant himself opened the heavy front door. He'd changed into a wine-colored velvet smoking jacket over dark pants and looked quite the lord of the manor. Meredith congratulated herself for having gone for the chic Gucci dress.

"Good evening."

"Hi."

"Come in." He held the door for her to pass through. "May I take your coat?" He seemed distant, excruciatingly polite. And all at once she wondered which she preferred, the rude creature of this morning or tonight's painfully civil stranger. Her heart sank. Somehow she didn't think his cool, formal attitude boded well. Had he made a decision? she wondered.

She accompanied him through the echoing, dimly lit hall and into the drawing room. The fireplace glowed and several heavy wax candles flickered on wrought-iron holders, creating an enchantingly medieval effect. Had he done it on purpose to impress her? Intimidate her? Or was this the way he always lived? Like some personage out of an nineteenth-century novel. It didn't tally one little bit with the corporate image he portrayed.

She sat down on the wide bottle-green velvet couch.

"Champagne?"

"Please."

Grant Gallagher appeared to be very much in the driver's seat tonight, and she wondered warily what he had up his sleeve. Perhaps he'd had time to think things over and was prepared to concede some, she reflected hopefully, watching him pour the champagne and replace the bottle in the massive silver ice bucket, noting how very handsome he looked. She thought suddenly of Tracy and bit back a smile. What would her partner say if she saw this man, his long, nearly jet-black hair glinting in the candlelight, his near-military stance and the well-cut jacket emphasizing his powerfully built shoulders?

He turned to face her, holding the two frothing flutes. "I read Rowena's letter again," he remarked, his eyes scanning her as though seeking something that eluded him.

"Good. Did it clarify anything?" she asked, determined not to appear anxious.

"That depends on how you interpret it. I've tried to

give it a rational spin. I'm still trying to figure out her motives, uncover the plot, so to speak."

"I see."

He handed her a flute, raised his, and Meredith followed suit.

"Cheers."

"Cheers," she murmured, taking a sip, studying his expression, hoping it might be indicative of his decision.

"Basically," he continued, "I still think Rowena was a manipulating old harridan, and I have yet to figure out what her goal was in trying to lure me to the U.S. Any ideas on the subject?" He sent her a penetrating look from his position by the fireplace, where he stood erect, his back to the crackling logs.

"None, I'm afraid."

"Well, why don't you take a look at the letter yourself and give me your opinion. After all, as you pointed out earlier, you now represent my interests." She caught his ironic inflection. He reached into his breast pocket and handed her the letter, his face inscrutable.

Meredith scanned the missive. The letter was typical of Rowena, dry, with a touch of wry humor and some self-deprecation. But there was nothing here to indicate any specific motivation.

"Not very enlightening, is it?" he remarked, leaning an arm on the mantelpiece.

"No," she conceded, struck by the picture of him standing by the fireplace, for all the world like some 1920s aristocrat, the flute caught lazily between his long fingers, an autocratic air on his striking face. "I found that last sentence intriguing, the manner in which she recorded your date of birth, that she considered it her lucky number," she finished, hoping to strike a chord. Sure enough, she saw his eyes flicker.

"That could simply be a ploy, emotional blackmail, bait to get me to go to the next level."

"It could," she admitted, "but knowing Rowena, I doubt it. She was a straight shooter. Not that she wouldn't have been capable of inventing some gambit to try to influence you."

"Then what?" He peered at her, eyes narrowed.

"Rowena was a superstitious woman," she said slowly. "All her codes, be it to her safe—even her phone number, which she went to great trouble to acquire—held a special significance for her."

"Interesting." He quirked a brow, sipped champagne and stared across the room. In a way he reminded her of Rowena, Meredith realized. Perhaps it was that air of confident nonchalance they shared. As though they both knew they could reset the chessboard to their advantage at any time. Except this time, Grant couldn't forecast all the moves. And for a man who crafted intriguing, even devious deals with consummate flair, that must be frustrating.

"Tell me," he asked suddenly, "did you really like Rowena?"

"Yes. I already told you I did. We got on well, I think because I was one of the few people who refused to take any nonsense from her."

"But she was a manipulative old biddy."

"In many ways, yes. But she had a good heart. I could name a number of folks who benefited from her generosity. But she never let on."

"Please—" he raised his palm protectively "—don't try to paint me a paragon."

"I wasn't. Just giving you a better idea of who she was."

"Then tell me the truth," he said dryly. "Don't try to

make her in to some benevolent, grandmotherly figure. Maybe she did do a lot of charity—obviously she could easily afford it. I want to know who she *really* was."

Realizing her mistake, Meredith took a deep breath and returned to the drawing board. No clever legal cover-ups for Gallagher. He wanted the truth. Grudgingly she respected him for it. "Very well. Maybe I should tell you more about my first encounter with Rowena, which might help clarify how our relationship developed. I already gave you the bit about the poodles."

"Go on." He was all attention now, and by the end of the anecdote he threw his head back and laughed engagingly. Again Meredith experienced the same frisson of awareness she'd felt this morning. It certainly wouldn't do him any harm to laugh some more.

"She obviously held a very high opinion of you."

"I hope so. I always tried to do my best for her. I'd like to continue doing that now," she added, posing her glass on the coffee table and meeting his eyes straight on. "Look, perhaps if you came to the Miami meeting, it might shed some light on matters. There are more envelopes addressed to you that can only be opened at different stages of the procedure. The next one is at the meeting itself."

"Casting bait, counselor? I have no intention of going anywhere near Florida, now or anytime in the near future, however intriguing Rowena intended to make this," he answered, his expression closing again.

"Well, it's heartening to know you can so easily deny your half sister a helping hand," she remarked tartly, leaning back against the cushions and crossing her arms. "She's a lot like you, you know. Stubborn, full of hurt pride, carrying baggage about from her childhood," she added airily. "I wonder how Dallas will feel when she's evicted. It's one thing to say you'd refuse a fortune had it come your way, another to actually realize you're going to be out on the street in less than sixty days," she murmured dryly, hoping she might hit home.

"Too bad. Maybe she'll have to hock some of her Prada handbags."

"Not much for worrying about other people's wellbeing, are you?"

"No," he replied, facing her now, body tense, eyes gleaming, "I'm not. This girl is no concern of mine. I don't wish to meet her or have anything to do with her."

"No doubt she feels the same way about you." Meredith shrugged, noting how riled he'd become. She ploughed ahead. "Still, I think you owe it to each other to at least meet."

"You make it sound so easy, so—" he waved his long fingers in a cynical gesture "—so simple. As though life was ever simple," he muttered bitterly, draining his flute.

"Give me some credit," she flashed back, sitting up straighter. "I never said it would be easy. Merely that I believe it's the right thing to do."

"Ha! The right bloody thing to do. You sound like a Sunday school teacher." He shook his head, his bitter laugh echoing among the solemn portraits of someone else's ancestors gracing the walls. "I wonder how she'll feel, suddenly having me flung on her out of the blue. Don't you think it will be a bit daunting to discover a half brother out there that nobody bothered to mention?"

"No more daunting than suddenly discovering you

have a half sister," she responded, the tense he'd used sparking hope in her breast.

"Touché. It is strange. But not enough to lose any sleep over. More champagne?" He lifted the bottle from the chilled ice bucket, eyes impenetrable as he reached for her glass.

Meredith winced inwardly. She was losing ground again. "Maybe you're right," she agreed, accepting the flute. "After all, you're a full-fledged adult, financially stable and a success. As for Dallas, she's only nineteen and has her whole life ahead of her. I guess she'll land on her feet somehow. Actually, your refusal to help her out may make things easier for her to accept in the future."

"Why is that?"

"Well—" Meredith gave a short laugh "—at least she'll have someone other than her father to blame for her misfortune."

"Oh?" He quirked a brow.

"I doubt the knowledge that you considered the poodles more worthy of assistance will be easily forgotten." He glanced at her appreciatively, eyes laughing. "Very smooth, Ms. Hunter. Did they teach you that at law school, too?" His lips curled and he tapped his glass on the mantel.

"Yale taught me the basics of legal reasoning," she said tartly. "It's life that's taught me about having a heart."

"Well, I suppose I must have been absent that day. I don't recall the subject being on the Oxford syllabus."

"Either that, or there's something missing in your chest," she said witheringly. "It's clear I came all this way for nothing. If you'd simply acted like an adult and responded to my letters, I wouldn't have had to waste my time or yours," she flung, wishing she could think of something, anything, that would persuade him not to reject the inheritance outright. It seemed so unfair, so callous, and went against her sense of justice that he could be so utterly selfish. Surely the man couldn't be as egotistical as he'd like her to believe? Then she recalled the families he'd so coldly put out of work and berated herself.

Of course he could.

Meredith wanted to get up and leave. But she restrained herself, knew she owed it to Rowena to give it her best last shot. "Would it really be so hard for you to meet Dallas in Miami?" she pleaded, raising her eyes to his. "I know you don't believe you owe it to her, but what about yourself? Don't you think you deserve the chance to at least take a look at what you're walking away from?"

Leaning against the mantelpiece, Grant watched Meredith's eyes darken. He was fascinated by the depth of her feelings. Here was a well-trained lawyer prepared to deal with tricky clients and situations, actually fighting for what she believed to be right. This, he realized with a jolt, went way beyond the boundary of her fiduciary duty.

It had been a while since he'd seen anyone exhibit such sincerity, such a display of steadfast dedication. She reminded him of the woman who'd represented the families who'd lost their jobs in the Bronstern takeover, a battle-ax filled with righteous fervor who had called him every name in the book. It all had slid off him like water off a duck's back. But Meredith's sincerity and passion touched him as few arguments could. Pulling himself up, he looked down at her, intrigued, too, by the fleeting sadness in her eyes.

"I'm sorry I put you out," he said in a softer tone, surprising himself. "I probably should have answered your letters and made it easier on all of us. I just didn't want to have anything to do with the past. What I'm trying to make clear to you is that what I am, I created. Nobody owes me and I don't owe anyone. And I want it to stay that way," he finished bluntly, holding her gaze.

She sighed. "Then there's nothing left to say." She lifted her hands in a gesture of defeat.

He could sense her disappointment. Damn, why should he care if she was disappointed? Why did he feel as if he'd just slapped her?

"Perhaps I should leave now," she said finally, glancing at her gold Cartier watch.

"Leave? But we haven't had dinner."

"I don't feel that hungry."

"Don't be ridiculous. You have to eat. I can assure you the food here is infinitely better than at the Strathcairn Arms." His smile turned persuasive.

She hesitated, then shrugged. "I must admit, the prospect of another steak-and-kidney pie isn't especially appealing." She looked up at him and smiled despite an obvious desire to refuse his invitation. "I suppose as your dinner guest, I should take my cue and politely change the subject, hmm? So," she said, rising and smoothing her skirt, "have you lived here long?"

"No." He laughed. "Only a couple years. I was looking for peace and quiet. I wrongly assumed this was a spot where I wouldn't be interrupted or bothered," he drawled.

"Yes, well, I shouldn't think you're bothered as a rule," she said, sucking in her cheeks. "I imagine Strathcairn is sufficiently removed from civilization to put most people off."

"But not you."

"No, not me. But then I didn't come by choice."

Grant's lips twitched. "No. I don't suppose you did," he conceded. "Shall we?" He offered her his arm in a surprisingly courtly gesture. "And now that business is behind us, perhaps we can enjoy the evening."

Business over, my foot! Meredith reflected as they entered the high cathedral-ceilinged baronial dining room and she surveyed her surroundings. The place certainly had character. A huge table that could easily sit fourteen guests was laid at one end. More candles flickered in a large eight-piece silver candelabra. The sideboard stood stacked with Renaissance pewter, some of which appeared to be quite distinctive. As she took her seat, she wondered if, like the portraits, it had come as part of the package.

"Not the coziest spot," he remarked apologetically, "but it seemed appropriate."

"Thanks. But do I look as though I expect the royal treatment?" she asked, twisting her head, unable to resist the mischief in his eyes as he pushed in the high-backed brocade chair for her.

"That remains to be seen," he answered cryptically. "I just thought you might enjoy the historical ambience. Americans always like things like that."

Meredith rolled her eyes, then shook her head, amazed to feel at ease with him. She quickly reminded herself that however charming he might appear, he was still the guy who had no qualms at leaving entire towns unemployed.

"Isn't that a rather broad generalization?" she queried.

"Far be it from me to ignore the power of a good cliché now and then. Besides, you must admit that the room's very picturesque." He made a grand gesture with his hand as he sat down. "Just think of all the murders that might have taken place right here in this room. It has quite an aura."

"Ugh." She shuddered, sitting down. "I thought it was just the Campbells and the MacDonalds that murdered one another over dinner."

"Oh, no, murdering one's neighbors was rife among the clans. Invite 'em over and whack 'em." He brought his hand slashing across his throat.

"Do we have to talk about this right before dinner?" she murmured, trying not to conjure up images.

"Don't tell me I've managed to scare the tough lady litigator." He poured from the crystal decanter. "I'd have thought you were made of sterner stuff."

"I'm as brave as I need to be. But the prospect of ax-wielding Scottish ghosts can be a bit off-putting," she murmured, unfolding the white linen napkin. "Seriously, isn't it creepy being here all by yourself?"

"No. Why should it be? I'm not frightened of ghosts—and that includes Rowena," he said, pointedly catching her eye before ringing a small bell placed next to him on the polished oak table.

"I doubt Rowena would try to haunt you—not that she wouldn't know how. That woman had standing accounts with every voodoo priestess and shaman in Georgia—anything to give her an edge, she told me. One in particular that she favored was with her when she died. Rowena was a tough old bird who stopped at little to get what she wanted. She's become quite a legend in Savannah."

"I see. What did she get up to?"

"Oh, all sorts of things. The parties she'd give, the stunts she pulled."

"Such as?" He leaned forward to pour her some water.

"Let's see," she mused, pausing a moment. "There was the time she was so furious with the mayor that she told him a dog could do a better job of running the city than he did. When he basically told her she didn't understand politics, she bankrolled a get-out-the-vote drive to put Uga—that's the bulldog who is Georgia University's mascot—on the ballot for the next election." She reached for her glass of wine, a smile playing over her face as she recalled the countless posters and flyers and rallies for Uga all over town. The press had had a field day. "Anyway," she continued, "the mayor did manage to hold on to his seat, but even he was forced to concede the margin of victory had been uncomfortably slim."

"Ha! That's rich. I'll bet he didn't mess with Rowena Carstairs again," Grant observed, sounding almost proud.

"Nope—even offered her a seat on some citizen's council he'd pledged to create. Of course, she turned him down—said she'd be bored to tears. Besides, the proposed meeting time conflicted with her morning yoga."

Grant reached for his wine and took a thoughtful sip. "Sounds as if she prided herself on being an eccentric," he said, tone laced with new curiosity.

She considered the statement, staring at the fire that had been set in the grate. "You make it sound like it was all an act—and I suppose part of her behavior must have been. But she was a genuine free spirit. People always talked about her extravagance—she had a small army of servants at her various properties. There was even one sweet old man whose sole job was to talk to the flowers and plants in her garden. Five days a week, he'd be there, coaxing them to grow, singing gospel songs, reading poetry to the petunias."

Grant snorted. "I'm amazed there's any money left in her estate if she spent it so frivolously."

Meredith leaned forward, her expression earnest. "It sounds frivolous, yes, until you realize that old Elijah was in a wheelchair and had to support not only his wife, but also three of his grandchildren. Talking was just about all he could do, so Rowena found him a job—an odd one, yes, but something where he could feel useful and take home a respectable paycheck."

"So now you're telling me she was Mother Teresa?" He snorted, eyebrows raised.

"Oh, no." Meredith laughed. "She was no saint—she knew more swearwords than the entire U.S. navy. But there's no disputing she found unique ways to help others while making sure her own needs and desires were met. She gave Elijah a job, and in exchange she got the most spectacular gardens in Savannah." She tilted her head, bemused. "It defies logic, but something about all that talking really worked."

"Okay, so maybe she wasn't exactly what I envisioned, but nothing you've said changes my impression that she used her money as a tool to get what she wanted."

"You should know. Isn't that what you do?" she challenged.

Grant stared at her, taken aback. "No, it is not what I damn well do."

"It certainly looks that way," Meredith murmured, buttering her roll and avoiding his cold gaze.

"We were talking about Rowena," he snapped. "Obviously, she wants to use me—for what, I have no idea—and the huge bequest is some sort of bribe. This meeting she orchestrated in Miami—I'm sure that's just the first step in whatever scheme she cooked up. Well, you can count me out," he muttered darkly as the door opened and Mrs. Duffy appeared with a large soup tureen.

Meredith smothered her impatience and smiled at Mrs. Duffy, accepting the ladle even as she racked her brain for a truly persuasive argument to entice him to Miami. He simply had to meet Dallas. She watched as Grant served himself a large helping of pea soup, sensing this was a man who never wavered once he'd made up his mind. But surely there must be a way? After all, she'd had difficult clients before and had never failed to sway them. Plus now it wasn't just her professional pride at stake. It had become a personal challenge. She could not, would not leave here without convincing Grant Gallagher to come to the States.

After a rich and satisfying meal—the food had indeed been as good as he'd promised—Grant suggested they retire to the drawing room for an after-dinner drink. Meredith knew she should refuse—at this rate, she'd never drag herself out of bed to catch her flight—but the dinner had been such a welcome surprise, with Grant displaying a subtle wit and rare intelligence, that to her surprise she was reluctant for the evening to end. He'd regaled her with hilarious tales of his first, disastrous deal and, with prodding, had shared stories of the more intricate aspects of some of the better-known ventures he'd been linked to.

It had been a while, she realized, since she'd exchanged ideas over dinner with anyone but her kids. Little had she imagined dining in a Scottish castle with one of the world's more notorious corporate raiders and actually liking it. As Grant crossed the room and turned on a CD of baroque music, she questioned her sanity. Was she really relaxing and forgetting her own responsibilities in the company of a man whose checkered history she knew by heart?

Yet he had turned out to be a charming host—so very different from the self-centered egotistical man of this morning. Maybe he practiced his own brand of voodoo, she reflected, accepting a snifter of brandy and gazing into the flames as the soft seventeenth-century music filled the silence. The scent of the logs and the atmosphere eased the tension and jet lag.

For a while they sat in congenial silence. Then the clock chimed in the hall.

"Oh, my, it's already midnight. I'd better be off," she said, laying her glass down and preparing to rise. Good Lord, had she really let herself be lulled into forgetting why she was here? After her initial effort to get him to Miami, she'd completely let him off the hook.

She looked into his eyes and smiled dolefully, using the one weapon she hadn't tried yet. "Won't you please just make this one effort toward resolving the issues of the will? It wouldn't take that much time out of your working schedule and it would help me so much."

"You're not easily put off, are you," he remarked, a touch of humor twitching his lips.

"When I take on a case I like to win."

"But this isn't a case. There is no win or lose," he answered softly.

"But I need to see this through to a satisfactory conclusion," she said firmly, trying to pretend she hadn't completely forgotten about the will until two minutes ago.

"How about we cut a deal?"

"A deal?" Meredith frowned. He was standing close to her now and her eyes flew to his. "What kind of a deal?"

"This kind."

Before she could react he stepped forward, slipped his arms firmly around her small waist and, lowering his mouth to hers, drew her close.

Meredith froze in shock. Then, to her horror, searing heat shot through her. She stood in his arms, allowing his tongue to taunt hers, too surprised to do more than give in to the unexpectedly devastating sensation. Then, just as quickly, she pulled away abruptly, her face flushed and her eyes blazing.

"How dare you," she whispered, eyes bright. Her hands shook and her eyes filled as she grabbed her purse and, turning, ran through the hall toward the front door.

Grant saw the tears and frowned. Damn. Why on earth had he done that? And, equally disturbing, why was she so unduly upset? He hadn't wanted to hurt her, had merely given in to the tempting vision she'd offered. When she ran out the door, he didn't follow or try to stop her, he merely watched as the oak door shut with a heavy thud and listened to the sound of the car engine disappearing down the drive.

Then he returned to the drawing room and sipped the rest of the brandy. *Well, Gallagher, that's one way of making sure you won't hear about that damned inheritance again*, he reflected grimly.

But despite a desire to feel pleased with himself, Grant couldn't suppress the niggling shame of knowing he'd acted like a cad. Perhaps he'd done it on purpose, he decided moodily, downing the last of his brandy, determined to justify the act. Perhaps now she'd leave him be and life would go back to normal. But as he refilled his glass from the crystal decanter, he was truthful enough to admit that his reason for kissing this woman had little to do with Rowena and her impossible will, but rather an excruciating need to taste her lips, feel the curve of her slim, taut body against his.

"Damn it!" he exclaimed, angry at himself for his weakness, for being unable to deny himself. Denial was usually one of his strong points. He'd spent a lifetime training himself to accept it.

But, hell, he'd made it clear he wanted to be alone, hadn't he? With an oath, he brought his fist down on the mantelpiece and stared angrily into the flames.

It was her fault, not his.

Or was it?

He'd been forced to face a part of himself that he'd believed dead and buried, but deep down he knew that Meredith was right. He owed it to himself to learn more. While he could not turn back the clock, he was going to have to meet the truth head-on however inconvenient and disturbing it might be.

Glancing at the ormolu clock adorning the mantelpiece, Grant hesitated. Meredith should be back at the Strathcairn Arms by now. He twiddled the snifter thoughtfully. He owed her an apology. He was not in the habit of acting on impulse. Plus he never treated women in the disrespectful fashion he'd displayed tonight.

Reluctantly he moved toward the phone and, heaving a sigh, dialed the Strathcairn Arms.

If he was going to humble himself, then the sooner he got it over with, the better.

Shaken, Meredith cradled the phone and tried to assimilate the evening's goings-on. He had kissed her and now he'd stiffly apologized. Even more shocking, he'd agreed to attend the meeting in Miami. She didn't know whether to be furious or thrilled.

"To hell with him," she muttered, slamming the receiver down and reaching for a tissue in her purse. She was too tired and stressed, that was what was wrong with her. First the journey, then the nerve-racking task of dealing with Gallagher and now this unexpected conclusion.

Sitting on the edge of the bed, Meredith kicked off her shoes, wishing she could erase the feel of Grant's lips on hers. His kiss had been insulting, something to be expected from a man like him. But she was finding it hard to sustain her wrath. Instead, she was unable to shake off the searing heat rushing through her body when his lips touched hers.

Just a hormonal reaction, she justified, rising and carefully slipping the dress off. It didn't mean anything other than that she was a healthy, red-blooded woman; of course she'd react to being in such close contact with a man. But why, then, had she slapped Ron Ferguson's face when he'd attempted to do the same thing after a concert three months ago? She'd felt nothing then but disgust.

Turning her thoughts down more positive paths, Meredith did what she did best: compartmentalized. What mattered was that her objective had been reached.

Grant had agreed to come to Miami. The rest was just par for the course, and the best way to deal with it was to forget it.

8

The Chatham Club buzzed with the usual Tuesday lunch crowd. Ross Rollins sat down at his favorite corner table, ordered a Scotch and water and awaited his guests. He knew that drinking alcohol at lunch was frowned upon these days in places like L.A. and New York, but thank God Southerners didn't fret about such things. After the phone call he'd just had with Joanna Carstairs, he needed something strong to bring down his blood pressure. That woman was a trial, no two ways about it.

The waiter brought his cocktail, and he took a long, satisfying sip as he waited for the rest of his party to arrive. He soon spotted Judge Coburn's impressive girth across the room, shadowing but not quite concealing Drew Chandler's tall, immaculately clad figure approaching the table. They were old friends who'd been getting together once a month in this same spot for more than fifteen years.

"I hear you've been hired to represent the family's interests in the Rowena Carstairs estate," the judge commented after they'd finished their dinner and the better part of a bottle of fine California merlot. "Bet that's giving you a headache. Old Rowena was never one to do things by halves, was she?" He looked shrewdly at Ross.

"Nope, she sure wasn't," Ross agreed, twiddling his glass, reflecting that it was most unethical of his old friend to ask him such a question. The temptation to reveal the secret was tremendous. "And with this crazy will of hers, she's making damn sure she goes out with a bang."

"Really?" Drew raised a silver brow, his tanned features breaking into an enigmatic smile. "Always full of surprises, wasn't she? Remember that Halloween party she hosted out at Montalba, the one with the ghosts coming out of the water? Never seen anything so damn spooky in all my life."

"I recall that party," Ross said thoughtfully.

The three men remembered Rowena and laughed while Judge Cockburn ordered dessert. "I shouldn't, of course," he said with a rueful glance at his paunch, "but I sure love apple fritters. Can't resist 'em. All right for the likes of you," he added to Drew, "you're one of the lucky ones who doesn't have to worry about cholesterol."

"Just get out on the golf course more often and you won't, either," Drew answered, winking at Ross. "So tell us, what's the old lady sprung on you this time around?"

Ross took another sip of his drink. The news was going to get out eventually. He knew that in Savannah, even the streets seemed to have ears. The question was how to massage the news, tweak things so that the right impression was left and not too much revealed.

After all, he had his reputation to consider. "Well," he said confidingly, laying down his glass and leaning forward, "it's quite a shocker." Seeing that he had their attention, he continued. "It seems Rowena's daughter, Isabel, had a child."

"Sure, Dallas Thornton. We all know that," Drew murmured.

"I wasn't referring to Dallas. There's another child. A child born out of wedlock." He paused for effect.

"Jesus!" Judge Coburn's small eyes sparkled behind the thick lenses of his bifocals.

"A child?" Drew's brows met over the ridge of his nose. "When did that happen?"

"Oh, years ago. I figure Isabel must have been about sixteen or so at the time. You remember when she disappeared that year to some Swiss finishing school, Drew?"

"I remember." He nodded, frowning, and finished off the last of his wine in one gulp.

"Yes, well, I figure that's when she had the baby. I know there was talk at the time. Seems like the rumors weren't so far-fetched after all."

"Well, this is quite a surprise," the judge said with an air of disapproval.

"So what happened to the kid?" Drew asked.

"Arrangements were made to have the child adopted abroad. Pretty clever of Rowena to have kept it quiet all these years," Ross added.

The judge shifted his considerable weight and tried to lean forward across the table. "So the child's still alive?" he said incredulously.

"Alive and well. Needless to say, the Carstairs relatives are on the warpath," Ross added, looking up.

"This part, of course, is confidential—Rowena cut them out of the will. Everything goes to this mystery grandson."

"You're kidding!" Drew exclaimed. "What do you know about this child? And what does *he* know?"

"More particularly, what do the Carstairs know? Did they have any idea?" Judge Coburn asked. "I'll bet Joanna was counting on the old girl's money to feather her nest between husbands. So then they've hired you to contest, of course."

"It won't be easy, I'm afraid." Ross shook his head. "Rowena's will is tighter than a drum. I've been looking for loopholes, but she's got a no-contest clause. Unless the beneficiary generously decides to share the bequest, the Carstairs relatives are screwed."

"Well, I'll be damned," Drew murmured. "How old did you say the boy was?"

"Hardly a boy," Ross said slowly, taking a long sip of his wine. "He's thirty-eight."

"I see. And there's no doubt whatsoever that he's Isabel's son?"

"Nope. There's been a DNA test. No question about his parentage," Ross assured them.

"Well, I'll be danged," the judge murmured. "I wonder why she went to all this trouble. Knowing Rowena, I'll bet she had her motives."

"I'll know more in a week. Meredith Hunter is the executor of Rowena's will," he admitted, grimacing, "and she's set up a meeting in Miami between Dallas and the heir. Of course, I insisted on being there to represent the Carstairs family interests."

"And she agreed?"

"Meredith is a good girl," he said condescendingly, "she knows it will save her trouble down the road if she makes it clear she's not concealing any special arrangements from the family."

"What intrigues me," the judge interjected, reaching for the cream to pour in his coffee, "is who the boy's father might have been. Obviously, Isabel was involved with someone here in Savannah before her mother packed her off to Switzerland."

"Yeah." Ross nodded. "Do your remember anyone, Drew? You used to hang around that set."

"That's right. Was there someone in particular you recall?" Judge Coburn asked, grinning, as a large platter of apple fritters was placed before him.

"Not that I can think of." Drew shook his handsome gray head and shrugged. "She was quite a little flirt, our Isabel. Got around a bit. Might have been any number of guys, I should think."

"Might have." Ross sipped his espresso thoughtfully. "Although she never struck me as a girl who slept around. A flirt, yes, but pretty conservative just the same."

"Obviously, not conservative enough," Drew noted dryly.

"Right on the mark," the judge agreed, drawing a chuckle from Drew.

"Still," Drew continued, "it would be interesting to know who the father was. Did Rowena leave any clues?"

"No," Ross admitted. "So I guess we'll never know. The secret, whatever it was, went with Isabel and Rowena to their graves. And this, of course, remains strictly between us," he added with a meaningful look.

"Of course. Maybe it's better that way," the judge remarked. "What's done is done and there ain't no changin' it. Let sleeping dogs lie, I say." He exchanged a quick, piercing look with Ross, then continued. "Say, Drew, what's this I hear about you being nominated for an ambassadorship?"

"Well, nothing's final yet, but it's in the works. George Hathaway has his eye on it in D.C. for me. Should be coming up before the Senate Committee pretty soon."

"Finally looks as if the wind's blowing your way," Ross said.

"I'm mighty pleased for you," the judge added.

"Well, I've waited long enough," Drew murmured, a tinge of bitterness in his tone.

"Everything comes to he who waits, or so they tell us," Ross pointed out, a laconic smile hovering around his lips. "And as you say, all that's lacking now is the Senate's approval."

"Do you know where you might be sent?" the judge inquired.

"Not sure yet. Probably one of the Latin American countries, I would think."

"That's right. You speak Spanish."

"It would make sense. I hope it's Buenos Aires and not Bolivia," he added, laughing and laying down his napkin. "Now, if you gentlemen will excuse me, I have an appointment." He glanced at the flat gold watch on his bronzed left wrist and rose. "Thanks for lunch, Ross. Nice seeing you, Judge."

The three men shook hands, and Ross watched as Drew crossed the dining room, a fine figure of a man in blazer and flannels, saying casual hellos to friends and acquaintances.

"You know, it's odd that it's taken so long for Drew to get a break," he remarked thoughtfully. "He's a bright guy, but he's never really made it."

"Either in business or politics," Ross agreed.

"Luck of the draw, I guess." Judge Coburn wiped the last of an apple fritter regretfully from his lips and laid down his napkin. "Helluva good lunch, Ross. And now that the two of us are on our own, why don't you tell me exactly what's going on with Rowena's estate? I believe that file's headed to my courtroom for probate, isn't it?"

"Not yet. But it will be."

"Then the more I know about the case, the better." He winked at his friend, finishing his last sip of coffee.

"Sure, how about a brandy?" Ross answered with a noncommittal shrug. The two men exchanged an understanding look.

"Why not?"

The seven-bedroom mansion on Granada Boulevard facing Miami's Biltmore Golf Course remained staffed and in readiness, as though Rowena were about to arrive at any moment. This seemed an unnecessary maintenance expense, given that the only way Rowena could return to the estate was as a ghost, but since there was a clause stipulating that the house remain open until the will passed probate, Meredith had agreed. Even the poodles—the descendants of the original ones that had consolidated her relationship with Rowena—were in residence, cared for by Rodrigo, Rowena's longtime manservant.

Upon arrival, Meredith greeted the yapping dogs and, after being shown her room and unpacking for her stay, she took a walk, admiring the fine furnishings, the eclectic cocktail of contemporary art and handpicked antiques. Very Rowena, she reflected. An appreciative smile hovered as she recalled her client's winter stays here.

When she reached the bedroom Rodrigo had identified as Rowena's, Meredith hesitated, then carefully turned the doorknob and stepped inside. The room was intact, Rowena's sterling brushes still lay on the dresser as though awaiting her return. The lavish four-poster bed trimmed with antique lace and heaped with extravagant pillows had the sheets turned down, and an old-fashioned hat stand with her client's numerous eccentric headdresses stood in the corner next to a vintage Vuitton trunk. It was just as she'd imagined Rowena's bedroom would be: grandiose, eloquent and unconventional. A statement.

Stepping out onto the wide Mexican-tiled balcony overlooking the translucent pool, Meredith rolled her shoulders and savored the light breeze. She'd spent the past few days dealing with the minor domestic disasters that occurred every day at home. God, she needed a break, she reflected, staring longingly at the pool. But now that she'd finally convinced Grant and Dallas to meet face-to-face relaxation seemed highly unlikely. If anything, Dallas had been even harder to persuade than her half brother. The first meeting between them was bound to be tense.

Added to all this was the knowledge that Ross Rollins would be in attendance, too. She wished she could have ignored his request to be present, but now that he represented the Carstairs relatives—and, presumably, by extension, Dallas herself—she'd had no choice but to agree.

Breathing deeply, Meredith raised her face to the sun, enjoying the lull before what might very well turn into a storm. Temperatures were in the upper seventies. The sky was cloudless and blue, the greens of the Biltmore Golf Course immaculate. Perhaps things would turn out okay, she assured herself as she absently watched three brightly clad golfers tee off.

Then she remembered Grant and the unfortunate manner in which they'd taken leave of each other, and groaned. They hadn't spoken since he'd called to apologize, although his secretary had phoned to confirm his date and time of arrival for this Miami meeting. Despite her determination to banish it from her mind, she'd thought a lot about that evening at the castle, trying to understand why it had affected her so. It was only a stupid kiss, the kind of thing that had happened to her in high school all the time. The only problem was she wasn't in high school any longer, and since Tom had come into her life, there had never been another man.

She drew herself up and rolled her shoulders again, a habit she indulged in several times a day. It helped soothe the tension in her upper back. The best thing was to pretend the incident never occurred. But somehow it wasn't working out that way, and the memory of his prying lips, his tongue tantalizingly flicking hers, was disturbing. The guy was a jerk, she reminded herself. But he was also her client, which meant that like it or not she must be civil to him and concentrate on doing her best to serve his interests.

"Pull yourself together and stop being ridiculous," she muttered, glancing nervously at her watch and straightening the skirt of her business suit. Grant should be arriving shortly, and Dallas's plane would land soon after. She had separate limos waiting for them at Miami International.

What would the first meeting between half brother and sister be like? she wondered, reentering the room before making her way along the corridor and down the wide flight of marble stairs to the hall, anxious to make sure everything was in place as she'd requested. Although she was supposed to be the neutral party here, she couldn't help hoping the two would take a liking to each other, would realize they were bound by family ties that should be cherished, not despised. She crossed the hall to the living room, glad to see Rodrigo had already prepared a tray with champagne flutes and nibbles.

"Oh, shit," she exclaimed, suddenly remembering the call she'd promised to Mick's French tutor. Scrambling in her pocket for her phone, she punched in the number and pinned it to her ear before moving outside to the pool area for a better connection.

Just as the phone began to ring, so did the doorbell.

Oh, God, could that be Grant already? She glanced over her shoulder, ignored her racing pulse and took a deep breath.

Then Mademoiselle Delvaux's lilting French voice came on the line and she geared into the complexities of French grammar and Mick's apparent lack of understanding thereof.

Dallas slouched in the air-conditioned limo, staring belligerently at her pierced belly button hovering above the waistband of her low-slung Gucci jeans, arms crossed protectively over the breast of her skinny white Dolce tank top. She didn't want to be here. She'd decided long ago not to have anything to do with Grandma Rowena, as though by ignoring the connection she'd eliminate the shadow that for years had loomed over her life.

Then the letter from the mortgage company had arrived.

Dallas swallowed, remembering her horror as the

print swam before her terrified eyes: if she didn't come up with the mortgage payment in thirty days, they'd foreclose.

Grabbing a chilled soda from the small ice box set in the console, she popped it and leaned back, letting the cold liquid pour down her throat and her glorious long blond mane fan out over the black leather seat, paying no attention to the chauffeur's wandering eyes in the rearview mirror.

How had everything suddenly gone so incredibly wrong? First there'd been her father's untimely death, and then the shock of learning that financial matters were very different from what he'd led her to believe. She'd loved her father dearly, had looked up to him as she might a demigod. But before he'd even been laid to rest, her illusions had been summarily shattered. She'd thought he was indestructible—that nothing could take him down, just as nothing could come between them, father and daughter together against the world. Only by relying on each other had they survived the horrible betrayal of her mother's suicide, and in the ensuing years, they'd only grown closer, the connection so intense that it made other relationships unnecessary.

And now it was all over. Not only was she entirely alone, but Providence, the two-hundred-acre stud farm where she'd grown up, was about to be repossessed. There was no money to pay the bank; to her utter dismay, she'd discovered that her father's personal debts were astronomical.

Then Grandma Rowena had died. She swallowed. It was hard to admit, even to herself, but in the darkest moments after her father's death, she'd nourished the secret fantasy that her estranged grandmother would swoop down to Providence and bail her out of the awful mess she'd inherited. That's what grandmothers were for, right? Even ones you couldn't stand. But she'd never been able to bring herself to ask for help—had even turned her back on the old woman when she attended Daddy's funeral, because the prospect of speaking with her had proved too overwhelming. She didn't want anything to do with her. Not after what she'd done. Not after what she knew. Rowena Carstairs had killed her mother—not literally, perhaps, but in every other way, and that Dallas would neither forgive nor forget.

When Dallas learned she was cut out of her grandmother's will, she understood the loathing had been mutual. She wouldn't have thought that realization could hurt so much. Even though she'd vowed never to take anything from Grandma Rowena, the knowledge that her own flesh and blood couldn't be bothered to help save Providence from going under the hammer made her strangely miserable. Dallas squirmed uncomfortably in the back of the car, disgusted at herself for thinking of accepting anything from the woman who had destroyed her mother's life. Even from the grave, Grandma was asserting her control, doing what she'd so excelled at in life—forcing the world to play by *her* rules.

Meredith had said that if she attended the meeting in Miami, she might be able to do something for her. That meant there must be a manipulating clause in her grandmother's will that would tie her up in knots. But what choice did she have? Dallas wanted to scream. In three weeks she would be kicked out of the only home she'd ever known, the plantation where she was sure her father's spirit still roamed.

Oh, God. Dallas let out a frustrated sigh and stared

stonily out at the flowing traffic on I-95. She thought about the *other* surprise waiting for her at the Granada Boulevard mansion. The news *still* had her reeling.

Her mother had given birth to another child, a boy whom she'd given up for adoption. The information had hit Dallas hard. Her mother had never taken much interest in her, but knowing she'd had another baby that she'd abandoned left her horrified. And she'd immediately wondered if that was what her mother had been referring to in her suicide note. The words on the crisp sheet of vellum that she'd discovered next to Isabel's inert body that awful day ten years ago were as fresh in her mind as ever.

I should have kept it. You shouldn't have made me give it up. You never believed me when I told you the truth about him.

Up until a few days ago they'd been just meaningless words, part of some secret Grandma Rowena was determined to keep from her. She'd tried to question her grandmother several times, but the old lady had reprimanded her sharply, saying it was none of her concern. Sullenly Dallas had obeyed, swallowing her mounting resentment, creating far-fetched hypotheses of what her mother's message could signify. Strangely, she'd never confronted her father with it. He'd never had a chance to see the note because Grandma had carefully removed it from the scene immediately. And whenever she'd thought about raising the subject with him, Dallas had hesitated, sensing that the note had nothing to do with her father. Now it became clear that she'd been right. Whatever happened had occurred before her parents' marriage. Could the man she was about to meet be "it"? And who was her mother referring to as *him?*

She had so many questions and so few answers. But somehow she sensed it was all intertwined.

And that Rowena was to blame.

No, Dallas thought bitterly, swiping a strand of hair back, she was glad the old witch hadn't left her any money. Rowena was responsible for all the ills in their lives, and probably those in the life of this poor bastard as well.

Her brother, she reminded herself, the word still shocking and strange. It was one thing to know this Grant Gallagher existed, but it was quite another to actually meet him. She didn't want to face the implications of his existence. Neither did she believe Joanna's claim that the guy was a fake, an imposter trying to horn in on Rowena's fortune. Meredith was too smart for that.

As the limo swerved right onto Red Road, Dallas's pulse rate increased. What on earth was she doing here, heading to a meeting she'd so adamantly wanted to avoid? In a few minutes she'd be meeting the man whom Meredith had identified as her half brother. She grimaced, folded her arms tighter over her rib cage and stared blindly at the Coke can she'd let drop, watching it roll over the car floor, its contents seeping into the rug.

Providence, she reminded herself grimly. That's why she'd agreed to this insanity; because Meredith had said she might know a way to save it. She simply had to look after the folks who lived there, like old Dan, the stable hand who'd been there since before she was born, and Mercy and Jim, who'd taken care of the house for as long as she could remember. And the list went on.

Dallas let out a distressed sigh and peered out the

shaded window once more as the limo made a wide
curve, past Granada Presbyterian Church and onto
Granada Boulevard. It would be mere seconds now
until she arrived. As the limo rolled past the elegant vil-
las, she remembered those visits long ago with Mom.

A memory flashed.

Her parents had quarreled because her father had insisted they visit Rowena, and Mother hadn't wanted to
come. There'd been angry tears, urgent whispers, a bro-
ken sob as Mother finally agreed to go. Then Dad had
gone off to play golf while Mom and Grandma Rowena
had sat on the terrace drinking champagne, and she'd
played in the pool. The poodles had yapped at her in-
cessantly. She recalled her mother's unhappy expression and her own unexplained discomfort. It was *that*
day, she realized, sitting up straighter, that she'd understood Grandma Rowena was to blame for making her
parents fight.

From that day forward, whenever her parents argued, whenever her mother packed her bags in a huff
and went off on another shopping trip to New York,
whenever her father raised his voice and her mother
stared through her as if she didn't exist, Dallas had
known who was responsible: Rowena Carstairs.

So why the hell was she doing the old witch's bid-
ding now?

The limo pulled up to Rowena's mansion and
parked in the drive. Stepping out of the vehicle, she
stared at the front door, caught between an urge to
dive back into the limo and flee while there was still
time, and the knowledge that this was, without question, her only way out of financial chaos.

For a despairing moment Dallas stared at the
house's gracious pink stucco, Spanish-Mediterranean

facade. She was still undecided, felt suddenly vulnerable and so much younger than her nineteen years, as though she'd gone back to being the same little girl splashing in the pool.

Then, with an angry shrug, she hauled her Dolce backpack over her shoulder. "Fuck it," she muttered, climbing the wide, shallow steps and pressing the doorbell. She was here, but she'd be damned if she let Grandma Rowena get the better of her.

9

Grant had always viewed regret as an appalling waste of energy. But right now, as he stood in the elegant living room of Rowena Carstairs's sprawling Miami mansion, he had the uneasy feeling that he'd let himself in for more than he'd bargained for. Why the hell had he risen to the bait Meredith Hunter had so cleverly set? He hadn't believed he would experience anything much, because the past was the past and he prided himself on caring only about the present and the future. Yet he'd allowed the whole affair to capture his curiosity—and now here he was in Rowena Carstairs's home.

He hadn't given much thought to how it would feel to be suddenly flung into an environment to which he was indirectly—or rather all too directly—related. It disconcerted him more than he liked to admit, and conflicting emotions warred as he glanced about the drawing room. His eyes skimmed the silver-framed photographs, the portrait above the fireplace, the treasures collected during a lifetime of which he had not been a part. It was damn stupid to have placed himself in this situation, he realized, angry at himself. He knew it made him vulnerable.

Moving toward the French windows, he looked out across the pool area, determined to recapture his usual detachment. He concentrated on the advantages of the property, viewing Rowena's pink-and-white-stucco extravaganza from a real estate angle, trying not to let the enormous home's eccentric beauty, the mark of an impressive personality, touch him in any way. But just as he was evaluating price per square footage, he caught the echo of voices in the hall, and for the first time in memory he wished for all the world that he could run. Despite his cool exterior, his pulse picked up at the sound of the front door opening, followed by the high-heeled staccato of approaching footsteps. He listened more carefully, dissecting each sound, catching the deep Southern drawl of the lawyer representing the Carstairs family, and Meredith's melodious voice. There was another female's voice as well—youthful, a little belligerent.

That would be Dallas, he guessed with a tinge of amazement, quickly reminding himself that sharing flesh and blood was inconsequential. Hell, 99.9 percent of every creature on earth shared the same primordial genes. But even as he tried to convince himself that this young woman meant nothing to him, the knowledge that they'd had the same mother left him both disturbed and irritated. He turned and cast a dark, reluctant look at the flamboyant portrait above the fireplace—no one had said so specifically, but he assumed it to be Rowena. Damn the old bat's interference.

Then the living room door opened and a blonde

bombshell who looked about eighteen entered, followed by Meredith and Ross Rollins. Grant stood by the window and observed the girl, masking any emotion. She had an amazing figure and must be at least five-ten. Her belly button was pierced. Good God, she looked more like a pinup than a horse breeder.

So this was his half sister.

A moment's awkward silence followed as the siblings sized each other up. Then Meredith stepped in.

"Dallas, this is Grant Gallagher, Grant, this is Dallas Thornton. Why don't we all sit down and have a glass of champagne?" she said in that quiet, firm, professional voice of hers.

"I'd like a Coke," Dallas muttered. She'd made no attempt to take Grant's outstretched hand and he stuffed it quickly into the pocket of his pants, regretting the spontaneous gesture. His color heightened. Damn it, he didn't want to be here, didn't need to be here, yet he'd come. And now this sulky, beautiful, spoiled blond brat—for that was exactly what she looked like—had the nerve to ignore him outright. Was this what he could expect from his "legitimate" relations—humiliation? He watched haughtily as she flopped into one of the big chintz armchairs, lips pouting. Well, fuck her. Fuck them all. He didn't need this, didn't need to be reminded that his misbegotten past was something he could no longer ignore.

He glanced at Meredith, calmly asking the butler to bring a selection of beverages to the far table. This was all her fault. If she hadn't pursued him to Scotland, hadn't looked so damned attractive that night in the library, hadn't—

He caught himself, realized that wasn't entirely fair and resolved to get his raging emotions under control.

Instead he would seek the humorous aspects of the situation. A cynical smile hovered about his lips as he focused. Ross Rollins was standing by the mantelpiece, his chest puffed out. He obviously considered himself important. Dallas pouted in the armchair, looking for all the world like some inconvenienced rock star; he himself was brooding darkly by the window, like some clichéd romance character; while Meredith quietly eyed them like a patient nanny assessing what to do with her recalcitrant charges. Then, as if reaching a decision, she grabbed the champagne bottle and began struggling with the cork.

"Allow me," Grant said, stepping forward and removing the bottle from her grasp. Seconds later he expertly popped the cork, then poured three flutes. Handing one to Meredith and ignoring Dallas, he raised his glass. "Cheers," he said, clinking crystal to crystal, meeting her gaze. How was she going to manage? he wondered, catching Dallas's sulking gaze as she eyed them askance from her slouched position in the armchair. She certainly didn't inspire compassion.

"This is a very pleasant house," he remarked to Meredith, paying the girl no attention. "I suppose it must be worth a fortune."

"The most recent property appraisal valued it at about five million," Ross said with a satisfied nod. Grant caught the quick glance Meredith flashed him. Apparently this was not how she wanted the little meeting to go. Well, tough. This was all her fault so she would have to deal with it.

"Five million. Hmm. Not bad. Looks like a decent golf course, too. You play?"

"Occasionally," Meredith replied. "Ross has a single-digit handicap. Dallas, are you sure you wouldn't like some champagne? After all, this is an important occasion in both your lives. One that should be celebrated."

Grant turned and observed this half sister of his. And Meredith. Under that calm front he'd be willing to bet she was a pile of nerves. Raising his glass he nodded to her, still ignoring Dallas, and took a sip.

Meredith watched as the brother and sister resolutely ignored each other. She hadn't expected this meeting to be a picnic, but this threatened to become out-and-out war. And yet how very alike they were—particularly when they scowled—despite one being so dark and the other so fair. All at once her heart went out to both of them, and she wondered absently what it must feel like to suddenly be confronted with a family member you'd never known existed. She wondered, too, if the obvious likeness between them was leaving them uncomfortable.

Neither spoke. Caught between exasperation and pity, Meredith cautiously sipped the chilled Cristal. Typical of Rowena to stock only the best, she reflected dolefully. At what point, she wondered, should she intervene? Dallas looked so unhappy and so young huddled there in her armchair, her perfect body encased in her designer garb, chugging Coke out of a can like a rebellious teenager. Grant, on the other hand, looked as if he were trying out for the part of Heathcliff with his windswept hair and impeccably cut suit, an air of brooding mystery masking studied nonchalance. Ross looked pompous, as usual. This was a *very* rocky start indeed, and Dallas was doing nothing to aid her cause.

"You've been here before, haven't you, Dallas?" she asked, sitting down in the chair next to her, trying to strike up a conversation.

"Yeah." Dallas carelessly plunked the Coke can down on the small antique table next to her chair. Meredith cringed, repressing the urge to reach for a coaster.

"Did you come here often?" she asked, hoping to break the ice.

"Nope. Mom hated it here. We rarely visited."

"I see." This was not getting her very far. "But you must have enjoyed the pool when you were little, didn't you?"

Dallas shrugged, chugged more Coke and peered at Grant out of the corner of her eye. "Not really. Those damn dogs were always yapping away whenever I got in the water. I hated them. They're still here, aren't they?"

"Yes. Your grandmother made provisions for their care."

"Who in hell's going to want them?" Dallas gave a disparaging laugh.

"Well, that's one of the things we need to discuss," Meredith said carefully. Then, glancing from one to the other, she made up her mind. "Perhaps we should leave you two alone for a little while to get acquainted?" She glanced at Ross.

"No!" brother and sister responded emphatically.

"Meredith," Grant said coldly, "I came here to learn about the will, not to socialize. Perhaps we should get on with it." Setting his glass on the Spanish rojo marble mantelpiece, he folded his arms across his chest and stood next to Ross.

"Yeah," Dallas corroborated, "I didn't come here to party. In fact, I'm not too sure why I am here at all," she added in an undertone.

"Very well." Businesslike once more, Meredith rose,

picked up her briefcase and slipped on her glasses. "It might be better if we did this in the dining room. There are a number of papers to sift through."

She headed through the double doors into the large, airy room and laid her briefcase on the surface of the Georgian dining table. Dallas, Ross and Grant joined her.

Sitting at the head of the table, Meredith smiled and gestured first to her right, then her left, letting Ross take the bottom. She was actually glad of his presence. She had a sinking feeling she'd need reinforcements.

Removing the will from her briefcase, Meredith handed Grant a copy. "Do you mind if Dallas and Ross get copies, too?" she asked of the stony-faced Grant.

"By all means."

"Very well." Meredith passed a copy on down the table to Ross and slipped one to Dallas, who left it closed in front of her on the mahogany dining table.

"Right," Meredith began, pushing her glasses back up her small nose and focusing on the will. "As I've explained, Rowena made Grant the sole beneficiary of her last will and testament. While there are, of course, several trust provisions that determine the dispersal of the assets, you, Grant, stand to inherit somewhere in the region of one hundred million dollars in liquid assets—" she ignored Dallas's small gasp "—as well as hard assets such as gold and gems, real estate and assorted stocks. Here is a complete list of the contents of the estate," she added, handing another copy to each. "If you like, we can go through it."

Dallas, seemingly over her initial shock, cast the document a cursory glance. "This means nothing to me. I wouldn't touch that old witch's money with a ten-foot pole even if she had left me a share." She flung the papers on the table and bit her lip.

"I understand your relations with your grand-mother were strained," Meredith conceded coolly, "but I'd prefer that we not speak ill of the dead. Also," she added, sending a significant look in Dallas's direction, "we're here to try to find solutions. You told me that your father died leaving a large amount of debt. I'm hoping we may be able to come to some kind of set-tlement."

"It wasn't his fault," Dallas flashed, blue eyes blaz-ing. "He got into problems and—" She cut off, biting back the unshed tears.

"Dallas, I'm sure there were all sorts of reasons why your father got into debt—it can happen to anyone," Meredith said quietly, "but that's not what we're here to discuss."

"Yes, it is," she tossed back, eyes narrowed, her hands clenched nervously. "I know that Dad asked Grandma to help him and she refused. I know because Joanna Carstairs told me when she came up to Beau-fort last week. She told me she did everything possi-ble to persuade Rowena to give Dad the money to save the property and Grandma refused."

"Joanna?" Meredith's antennae were immediately on alert. So the Carstairs had been working on the girl, had they? Very clever. She wondered what other doubts they'd seen fit to plant. Judging by Dallas's chilly reception of her half brother, quite a few.

"Yes. And as for you," the young girl continued, glaring at Grant seated calmly opposite, his face an unreadable mask, "Joanna said you were a fake."

"It would appear that 'Joanna,' whoever she is, is misinformed," he drawled, raising his brow.

"Dallas, that's ridiculous. You know very well I never would have asked you to come here on a fool's errand. Grant is Rowena's legitimate heir," Meredith exclaimed, annoyed.

Dallas looked away, as though suddenly aware of the resemblance between them. Then she faced him again and crossed her arms defiantly. "Joanna said you ought to be ashamed of yourself, coming here after our money. She said your existence is bad enough without rubbing our noses in it and trying to get hold of what's rightfully the family's."

"Dallas, that's ludicrous and you know it," Ross interrupted in a deep stentorian tone. "It has been legally established that Mr. Gallagher here is the heir. Naturally the Carstairs relatives are disappointed," he said, turning to Grant, "understandably so. They were led to believe that they would inherit a sizable chunk of Rowena's fortune. One can hardly blame them for feeling ill-served by this surprising turn of events."

Grant's expression remained inscrutable.

"One thing must be made clear," Meredith said, picking up the ball. "Rowena had every right to leave her money to whomever she chose. Personally, I think she should have included Dallas in her will. That notwithstanding, she elected to leave her fortune to Grant." Meredith looked from one to the other, wondering if either had even bothered to listen to her. It was evident that war had just been declared. Grant's next words left her in no doubt of just how matters were shaping up.

"It's amazing how wishful thinking can distort one's view of reality," he drawled, eyes never leaving Dallas's tempestuous face. "Still, this Joanna has a valid point. Unexpected and unwanted relations can be a terrible nuisance. In fact, thinking it over, I agree with her entirely. I have absolutely no claim to Rowena's fortune whatsoever. Joanna and her cohorts, whomsoever they may be, are welcome to Rowena's money. There," he said, bringing his palms down on the table and turning to Meredith. "That solves the problem nicely for all of us. And if it's too complicated to turn it over to them, then may the poodles make good use of it. Perhaps they're the ones who really deserve it. After all, Rowena must have given some thought to the matter before she cut out her relations." He checked his watch. "Now, if you'll excuse me, I see little point in carrying on this conversation. If I'm quick I might just make the next flight to New York." He rose, nodded coolly at Meredith and Ross, then at Dallas. "Nice meeting you. Have a good life." Then he spun on his heel and walked toward the door.

"But, Grant, no, please. This is absurd." Meredith shot a panicked glance at Ross before jolting to her feet, her glasses slithering down her nose as she hastened after him, catching up with him halfway across the hall. "Please," she begged in a low murmur, laying a hand on his arm. "I know Dallas is being difficult, but Joanna's been at her."

"Successfully, it would appear." He accepted his raincoat from the uniformed manservant and turned toward the front door while Meredith made an anguished effort to retain him.

"Grant, please, take a look at her. She's just a lonely, frightened kid. Give her a chance."

"Why should I?" he queried. "She's a spoiled brat. I don't owe her shit."

"No. But I'll bet Joanna's been making all kinds of trouble. Trust me, if you knew her, you'd understand. Ross told me as much before you arrived. I don't approve of a lot of my old boss's doings, but he's a top-flight attorney and I know that he must have made it very clear to Joanna and the others how the land lies. You can't blame them for feeling angry that they've got to kowtow to you if they hope to get anything."

"Sounds like I'm well rid of the lot of 'em," he muttered. Then he frowned. "Just who exactly is this Joanna?"

"One of Rowena's more unpleasant nieces. She thought she was going to inherit a substantial portion of the fortune and is livid that you've popped onto the scene. I doubt she'll accept this without a fight."

"Well, I guess the poodles better watch their backs, hmm?"

"Will you please stop acting in this childish manner?" Meredith exclaimed, irritated. "Of course you can't let the money go to the poodles. It would be utterly wrong. At least give it to charity. Surely even a man like you can't be that coldhearted and obtuse." She met his stare boldly, her eyes blazing with the injustice of it all.

"What do you mean, a man like me?" he murmured, arrested.

"I mean a man who has no thought for anyone but himself," she replied bitterly. "But since you don't care about all the hardworking employees you fire when you mount your little takeovers, why should I expect you to care for anyone else?" she cried, clenching her fists.

"Are you referring to the Bronstern case?" he said smoothly.

"You know perfectly well I am."

"I see. Perhaps you should check your facts before making statements like that."

"It was all over the newspapers, common knowledge."

"Yes, as usual the press reported matters as they saw fit. Now, I'm afraid I really must leave." He looked pointedly at his watch.

"Look," Meredith snapped, her gray eyes flashing, "you're the adult here, okay? So start acting like one."

"Me? Why me? I never asked to be thrust into the middle of a damn family feud. You're the one that created all this," he goaded, brow raised.

"You know that's not true," Meredith sputtered angrily.

"It's your mess, darling, you sort it." He shrugged and turned for the door.

Moving quickly in front of him, Meredith blocked his path, planting her hands on her hips. "Why are you determined to make my life so fucking difficult?"

"Me?" he exclaimed, astonished. "I've never made anyone's life difficult. I'm a very easygoing sort of chap."

"Yeah, you and Genghis Khan," Meredith muttered, eyes narrowed as she peered up into his face. "Grant," she growled, voice low, "if you leave this house right now, I swear I'll never forgive you."

A slow smile spread across his face as he stared back at her, gripped by the sudden challenge she offered.

"Well, put that way, I suppose I might be persuaded to stay under certain conditions," he murmured in a low, seductive voice that left her in no doubt of his meaning.

"Don't even think about it," she retorted, shaking with anger. "You're an impossible, presumptuous son of a bitch who cares for nothing and nobody but himself. If you don't know why you should stay, then I wash my hands of you."

"Good. That's exactly what I've recommended from the start. You just don't listen properly."

"How dare—"

"Don't." Grant caught her hand inches from his cheek. Their eyes held, will pitted against will, and time stood still.

Back in the dining room, Ross stayed seated at the table while Dallas got up and walked nervously to the French windows, the heels of her Manolos clicking on the parquet floor. She was at a loss now that the wind had been taken so summarily out of her sails. She hadn't meant to sound mean, but guessed she had. It was just that when Meredith had mentioned her father, she'd felt so mad. Dad wasn't perfect, she knew that. She knew all about the racing and the women and the drinking. But he'd been hers. The only person who'd truly loved her. Not like Mom, whom she'd adored but who'd never given a shit about her. Or Grandma Rowena, with her stupid dyed dogs and her crazy turbans, always so managing and imperious.

Closing her eyes tight, Dallas bit her lip and pressed her hand on the glass, realizing that she'd blown it. Meredith had explained that if Grant refused to help her she would lose Providence. Taking the damn money went against every instinct, but what else could she do? One hundred million dollars! Why had Grandma Rowena done something so unfair? Even if she didn't want the money, refusing it would have been difficult. But the old harridan hadn't afforded her that satisfaction. And if Grant could only be persuaded to concede her some funds, then maybe she would be able to save Providence. She'd gone half-crazy trying to find an answer that would allow her to avoid Rowena's tentacles.

Suddenly she wished she could take back the bitter words she'd uttered so arrogantly only minutes earlier.

Actually, Grant seemed, well, solid and serious and smart. She supposed she could have liked him under different circumstances. Hands shaking, she turned and looked through the doorway at the two figures conversing in the hall. He wasn't at all what she'd expected. Joanna had made him out to be a greedy, vulgar, smarmy business type whose sole aim was to steal from them. But she didn't think he was.

Hesitantly Dallas moved toward the hall. When she reached the double doors she closed her eyes and took a long, deep breath, leaned against the doorjamb and crossed her arms protectively against her body.

"Look, I'm sorry, okay?" Her voice rang loud and clear across the hall. It hadn't come out quite as she'd wanted, but it was the best she could do. Buffing the toe of her shoe rhythmically against the door, Dallas stared stonily at the floor, then, with a shrug of her slim shoulders, she spun back into the dining room and walked back to the window.

At the sound of Dallas's voice, Grant and Meredith turned simultaneously in surprise.

"So, we've changed our mind, have we?" Grant watched Dallas's slim figure walk through the dining room doors and sucked in his cheeks thoughtfully. "Let me guess. She just realized I'm her ticket for maintaining her present lifestyle? That would make her like most women."

"No, it's not," Meredith retorted. "Dallas is terrified of losing her home, of the consequences not just to herself but to all those who've worked there for years, good people who'd have to leave their home and find a new living. But I suppose that means nothing to you," she said, taking a deep breath, determined to compose herself. It was absurd how riled up this man could make her.

"You have a wonderful opinion of me, don't you," he said, staring down at her, his eyes narrowing.

"Come on," she said at last in a quieter voice, "give the kid a chance. I know you don't give a damn about the money, but she stands to lose so much. If the bank forecloses, I don't know what she'll do."

Dismissing a quick flashback to his own feelings when he'd bought Strathcairn Castle, Grant looked down into Meredith's stormy eyes and experienced a jolt.

"You really want this to work out, don't you," he said suddenly.

"Yes," she nodded, back to her normal composure, "I do."

"Why?" He sent her another curious glance.

"Because—because Rowena was my client, my friend, and I feel that she made a mistake in cutting Dallas out of her will. I don't understand why. Unless—" She paused, as a possibility dawned, something she hadn't considered.

"What?"

"Unless she wanted you to protect Dallas."

"Protect Dallas?" He raised a quizzical brow. "Looks to me as if she's pretty capable of protecting herself."

"Not really. Not when there's so much money at stake, and the relatives all believe they're entitled to some of it. Imagine if Rowena had left everything to Dallas instead—Joanna and the others would still be fighting tooth and nail to get their share. Dallas would be in the same boat as you, but without your resources to fight back.

"Just look at Ross in there. He has something up his sleeve. I know it. I've seen him look all Cheshire catlike all too often. The Carstairs are livid." She shook her head and dragged her fingers through her hair. "Look, this is all conjecture, okay? I just know there is more to Rowena's decision than meets the eye."

"But it's not just that, is it?" he continued, pressing.

"No. You're right. It's, well—you two don't know what you're throwing away," she implored. "This may seem stupid and sentimental and corny to you, but family *matters* to me. I can't think how I would have survived without their support," she said, raising her eyes once more.

Grant smiled. A cursory, cynical twist of his lips. "You would have," he murmured, glancing toward the dining room. "We all do. Now, come on. I suppose we'd better get on with it." Laying his raincoat back down on the nearest chair, he raised his dark brows. "Shall we?" He indicated the dining room and Dallas's stiff back facing them through the gathering evening shadows.

"Thanks," Meredith murmured, stunned by his sudden change of heart. Maybe there was hope after all. She regrouped and led the way back, grateful for whatever had inspired Dallas to back down, and for the fact that Grant Gallagher apparently had some decency after all. She sat down in the stiff-backed chair and quickly glanced at Ross, who sat unperturbed and silent, an unmistakable gleam in his eye. Meredith knew that look. It erased the elation she felt at bringing all parties back to the table.

"Okay. So that takes care of the bulk of the assets," Meredith explained, after reading them the text, "and now for the provisos."

Both Dallas and Grant looked at her with renewed intensity. Dallas tweaked the corner of her copy of the will and glanced nervously at Ross, who already knew the contents. He merely leaned farther back in his chair, looking smug.

Meredith cleared her throat, hoping the roof wouldn't blow off when she began. "You, Grant, as of this moment, are responsible for the well-being of Ruby and Emerald, the poodles. Their present level of comfort and care is to be maintained for the duration of their lives. Rodrigo, who is to be kept on for the purpose of maintaining the house and the dogs, must also be cared for in the manner to which he is accustomed. Once a year, the dogs are to be dyed purple—Rowena's favorite color," she added as an aside, "and a big party is to be hosted here in their honor."

"Oh, Jesus, that's ridiculous," Dallas exclaimed.

Meredith ignored her and peeked at Grant out of the corner of her eye. His face betrayed nothing beyond the casual interest of an observer.

"By accepting the inheritance, you will automatically become a trustee of an existing trust whose beneficiaries are the Carstairs relations. Rowena suggests—not stipulates—that you establish another trust in favor of Dallas."

"What?" Dallas's mouth dropped open. "First she leaves me nothing—not that I wanted her to—and now she wants him to make a trust? She must've been crazy."

"Or very, very clever," Ross murmured, twiddling his pen thoughtfully before scribbling a note on his pad.

"If, as I said, you establish the trust in favor of Dallas—Rowena's recommendation, by the way, is that it be in the order of twenty million dollars, but she leaves it to your discretion—Rowena wants you both to spend at least one month a year here, together, for a duration of five years."

"But that's absurd," Dallas burst out.

"Perhaps, but the establishment of the trust is subject to this condition."

"But—"

"Grant will automatically act as Dallas's guardian," Meredith continued doggedly. "Should she wish to marry anytime before turning thirty she will have to seek your approval of the match."

"Married? I've no intention of getting married," Dallas exclaimed, crossing her arms belligerently.

"Never?" Meredith quirked a brow.

"Never. Marriage sucks."

"Hear, hear," Grant murmured approvingly, eyes gleaming. If nothing else, Meredith realized, she'd thoroughly captured his interest.

"Besides, what would my eventual marriage have to do with Grant?" Dallas frowned. For a moment, Meredith thought things might deteriorate, but knowing that a glimmer of hope still flickered at the end of what for the past month had constituted a very dark tunnel restrained her from saying more.

"Apparently quite a lot. Rowena must've felt that your choice in boyfriends wasn't, er, very felicitous."

"Oh." Dallas stared down at her fingernails and bit her lip. "I guess she must have heard about Proctor Brady. He was a piece of shit. He dropped me like a hot biscuit when he found out Dad had left me with a pile of debt." She shuffled her feet and looked down, flushed. "That sucked."

"I should think it did," Meredith agreed sympathetically. "Sounds as if you're well rid of him."

Dallas nodded. "Yeah. But what about Grandma, what did she say?"

"That any husband you choose has to meet with

Grant's approval or you'll not get any money from the trust."

"What did she care?"

"I think maybe she cared a lot more than you think and that this was her way of seeing you didn't fall into the hands of another Proctor Brady," Meredith said quietly. Ross nodded silently.

"She tied things up very nicely. Meredith, I think we're both aware that she's protected Dallas from any possible counterclaims from my clients."

"Precisely," Meredith said, nodding. "I'm beginning to think this is what it's all about."

"Very likely."

"But I'm an adult," Dallas interrupted, still stunned by the news that Grant was going to be allowed to veto her choice of men. "Anyway, what could happen? If I get the money now, then get married in a couple years, it'll be a moot point," she said smugly.

"Who says you're getting any money, young lady?" Ross's deep Southern drawl echoed through the room. "It's up to Mr. Gallagher here to decide whether you get anything at all. He's not obliged to comply. Did she mention the others at all in any other documents, Meredith?"

"Uh, sort of." She'd read the documents thoroughly on the plane trip down from Savannah, astounded when she'd read that Rowena was leaving it to Grant's discretion whether the relatives received anything. She certainly hadn't made Meredith's job any easier, she reflected, turning to Dallas. "Ross is right, Dallas," she said, stressing the point, "you're dependent on Grant's goodwill. It's up to him whether he establishes the trust."

Dallas's face dropped comically. "So we're back to

zero again? But if I can't pay the bank by the end of the month, Providence will… Oh, my God." She stopped, tears filling her eyes.

"Well?" Meredith queried, looking Grant straight in the eye and keeping her voice neutral, "Have you any thoughts on the matter?"

"Why don't you keep on reading. Let's see what else Rowena had to say."

"Very well." Meredith swallowed. She could read nothing in his bland expression. "Hmm, let me see—" She pushed her glasses back up her nose. "If you decide to go ahead, Grant, then a party is to be held at Montalba that will include all the Carstairs relations. Rowena suggests that after you meet them, you can decide whether you want to bequeath any part of the inheritance to them. You are entirely free to choose one and leave out another at your discretion. But," she added, sending Ross a fleeting look, "should any member of the family try to contest this will, then she asks you not to give them a penny. And that includes you, Dallas."

"I don't believe this," Dallas muttered, clenching her hands, outraged. "As though *I*, of all people, would try to get anything from her." She gestured angrily at Grant. "And why should she want us to spend time together? It's ridiculous."

"Absolutely," he agreed, observing her critically. "I mean, you don't want to spend time with me and I don't want to spend time with you. In fact, why should we sing to her tune?"

"Yeah." Dallas nodded in agreement while Meredith eyed him suspiciously. "Why the big deal? If she wanted to give me any of her money, why didn't she go ahead and do it straight out? Why all the hassle? It's not fair on either of us," she argued, looking at Grant for approval.

"I agree entirely," he murmured, shaking his head. "In fact, it's downright barbaric."

Meredith glanced at Dallas. "I've no idea why Rowena made these determinations, except that it appears she wanted to protect you. If she'd left the money to you outright, then the other relations might have contested the will and that could have gone on for years without you touching a penny. In any event, you'd still lose Providence. And so," she noted, eying Grant, "it appears you're the only one who can save Dallas's home."

"Hey, I can easily live somewhere else," Dallas chipped in, eyes filled with false bravado. "Grant, if you don't want to accept the inheritance because you feel badly about it, don't worry about me, I quite understand. Quite honestly, if I were you I'd refuse it. The last thing you want is Grandma Rowena ruling your life. You'll see," she added, nodding wisely, "even from beyond the grave she'll get her tentacles around you and—"

"Dallas, we can do without your input right now," Meredith interrupted hastily. "This is a question for Grant to decide on his own."

"Meredith, you're a honey. I know what you're trying to do," Dallas said, stretching her hand across the table and pressing Meredith's. "But it's only fair he should know what he's getting into. She's trying to get at him like she did my mother and everyone else whose path she's ever crossed. I don't want to owe her anything. I'd rather be homeless," she ended in a shaking voice.

* * *

Grant had remained silent during this exchange, summing up the scene and placing himself in Rowena's point of view. He now had a clearer idea of what the old lady was trying to do. A few minutes in Dallas's company was enough to tell him she was an emotional roller coaster. But why did Rowena choose him to save the girl from herself? he wondered. Had his grandmother somehow found out about the children's charities and other youth organizations he contributed to? Surely not. His donations were always anonymous. But whatever her reasons, Rowena had very cleverly enmeshed him. If he accepted her provisos, he'd be stuck with this kid on his hands. If he refused to establish the trust and left the damn fortune to the poodles, he'd look like the biggest schmuck in Christendom.

Not that he'd ever cared what others thought of him, but Jesus, look at the kid. The girl was as raw as an open wound. Why? he wondered. Why should this pampered princess be so aggressive, so adamant, yet so honest—even though it was evident that she was desperate to save her home.

Her honesty finally did him in. All the women he knew would fawn all over him at the mere mention of twenty million. All except perhaps the other lady seated at this very table. He had a fair notion that Meredith would not be swayed by numbers, either.

All at once, Grant recognized that old familiar tingle that gripped him once a deal was under way. And just as abruptly, just as it did in business, his role of observer altered to that of participant. Shoving aside any misgivings and ignoring the niggling voice telling him this was the moment to back off, Grant succumbed to temptation.

"Okay. I'll do it." Raising his eyes to Meredith's, he read immense relief and something more. Was it surprise? He was surprised himself, now he came to think of it.

Not allowing himself time to think, he addressed her. "I think you'd better draw up the papers right away. Oh, and call the mortgage company and tell them I'll arrange to have the full balance wired within the next two days. Just get me the figures."

Dallas opened her mouth to speak, but nothing came out. Meredith was finding it hard to speak, herself. When finally they did, it was together.

"Thank you," they uttered as one, and for the first time in many years, Grant blushed.

10

Still reeling, Meredith breathed deeply, wondering how to proceed, when Ross cleared his throat.

"Meredith, if you'll excuse me a moment, I'd like to know what Grant has decided in relation to my clients." Ross peered at Grant, his bright gray eyes piercing from under bushy white brows.

"I think Rowena makes it perfectly clear," she responded before Grant had a chance. "He's to meet all the relatives first, then make up his mind."

"You in agreement with that?" Ross turned pointedly in Grant's direction.

"I suppose there's not much choice," he responded dryly.

"So you'll come to Savannah for this shindig Rowena has proposed?"

"Wouldn't miss it for the world," he drawled. "Besides I have a deal cooking up in New York State. I'll have to be around for a few days, anyway."

"Very well." Ross gathered his papers. "Meredith, I presume the funds for throwing this party will come out of the estate?" Seeing Meredith's nod, he stood up. "In that case, Mr. Gallagher, I expect your new relatives will be more than happy to throw you a real nice homecoming celebration. Now, if you'll excuse me, I'll be movin' along. Nice meeting you. I look forward to seeing you in Savannah shortly. Dallas, Meredith." He straightened his bow tie and, with a slight bow, departed.

Meredith could hardly fathom that Grant had agreed to pay Dallas's mortgage and establish the trust. Swallowing, she glanced out the window, catching sight of the floodlit pool and the palm trees swaying lightly in the evening breeze. Oh, my God! She scraped back her chair, realizing it was dark already, past seven-thirty, a reminder that she must ring Mick and make sure he had his science project under way. Then there was Zack's visit to the dentist that she needed to coordinate with her mother and—

"Meredith?" Grant's questioning voice and Dallas's curious stare turned her attention back to them.

"I'm sorry," she muttered, blushing, "just something I remembered I have to do."

"Go ahead, we're in no hurry," Grant replied, leaning back in the elegant designer chair.

"Yeah, go ahead," Dallas agreed graciously, glad of the break. "We've taken up enough of your time as it is."

Meredith caught Grant raising a cynical brow in his half sister's direction and hoped he wouldn't make a tactless comment after he'd done so well and when the girl was making an effort to be gracious.

"No, no," she answered quickly, "it's nothing that can't wait a few more minutes. I just need to speak with my kids before they go to bed."

"Kids?" Grant straightened, quickly looking her way.

"Cool," Dallas exclaimed, picking up the Coke can that was never far from her reach. "How are the boys?"

"Fine." Meredith gave her best professional smile and focused. There were still a couple legal points to go over.

"I remember when you brought them over to Grandma's once."

"They're fine, but I don't think my children are really of any interest to you right now, or the subject at hand. Why don't we just get this done? Then we can all go home and—"

"Go home? We can't go home. We have to stay here, in her fucking house," Dallas mumbled crossly. "And, anyway, who says I'm not interested in your kids? I like you. Always have. You were the only one who ever tried to make things right between Grandma and me. I want to know more about you."

"Hear, hear," Grant murmured.

"Then I'll tell you about them later, over dinner, okay?"

"Dinner?" Dallas cheered up. "I'm starving. Let's head out now and deal with all this tomorrow. There's supposed to be a great new place on—"

"I think dinner has already been catered. Rodrigo mentioned something earlier," Meredith answered guardedly. "Who cares?" Dallas pouted. "Let's go down to South Beach. Hey," she said, wiggling in her chair, a broad smile lurking behind her bright blue eyes, "I say we go party."

"I say we go Latin," Grant interrupted. "After all, none of us gets the chance to eat proper Latin food that often, do we?"

"So?" Dallas scowled at him, fast forgetting his role

of benefactor. "I don't want to eat Latin food. I hate rice and beans."

"Who says we have to do what you want all the time? Why not let Meredith decide?" Grant added. They both turned and looked at her, chins jutted in exactly the same challenging manner.

"Look, guys, I really don't care what I eat," Meredith replied, exasperated, her shoulders slumping as the strain of the day weighed upon her. "Couldn't we just eat here and be done with it?"

"No," brother and sister answered in unison.

"See?" Dallas argued, leaning across the table toward Grant. "She said she didn't care where she went."

"I don't care what she said, I don't want to go to South Beach."

"And why not? What's wrong with South Beach? You're just being selfish and mean. I'll bet you've never even been there," she added witheringly, sweeping her golden mane off her shoulders. "You Brits are too stodgy to enjoy any place that's *really* fun." She pronounced Brits with utmost disdain.

"Really?" Grant drawled. "You mean you haven't been to London? Goodness, what a slipup in your education. I would have thought that a sophisticated— well, pseudo-sophisticated—creature like you would know every aspiring club in Europe."

"Ha!" Dallas stared stormily across the dining table. "For your 411, I've been to London, *and* Paris, *and* Rome *and* Amsterdam *and*—"

"Oh, my goodness," Meredith exclaimed, finally losing her patience, "will you two please stop bickering and be quiet?"

They broke off simultaneously. Grant straightened his tie and Dallas muttered under her breath.

"May I?" Meredith asked sweetly, eyeing them severely over the rim of her glasses. "Thank you," she murmured in the same tone, pushing her glasses back up her nose.

"Look, I vote we take a break and finish this in the morning," Grant said, noting how tired Meredith looked. Tired and worried.

He'd felt a stab of disappointment when she'd mentioned that she had kids. He'd not considered that she might be married. More fool him. Then he took a long look at Dallas picking at the corner of her copy of the will and biting her lip. He was sure she was a handful, but Meredith was right. There was something vulnerable hidden under her spoiled little rich-bitch exterior. Much to his horror, Grant actually experienced something akin to compassion, an emotion he hastily suppressed.

"Right," he said, rising, "I reckon we could all use a break before facing any more of Rowena's intrigues. More champagne, anyone?" He smiled at Meredith.

"Uh, no, thanks." She flashed him a tired smile.

"Hey, what about me?" Dallas got up, scraping the chair on the parquet floor. With a scowl, she moved across the room and grabbed a champagne flute. "I'll have some."

"Sure you're old enough? I'd hate to break the law," Grant murmured, tongue in cheek.

"Why, you—" Dallas was about to protest vehemently when she realized he was pulling her leg. And despite her determination to stay aloof, Grant saw her lips twitch.

"I'm old enough, all right. Can't help it if I'm too sexy for my age, too sexy for my…" She began humming, swinging her hips over to where Grant stood sucking in his cheeks, holding the champagne bottle.

"Good show. Do you always put on a performance?" he asked quizzically, tipping her flute and pouring the champagne.

"Oh, only when I have an audience," she countered. "Say, what was it like growing up in England, huh? Were your folks rich or poor?" she asked, leaning her curved butt against the dining table and crossing her ankles. "Did you know you were adopted?"

"You ask too many questions," he replied, in no mood for an inquisition.

"Why? You have a problem with questions? I don't, ask away." She shoved her chin out and gave him a sassy smile. "By the way, that's her over there in the living room," she added, moving swiftly and stepping through the double doors, stopping before the black-and-white photograph of a young woman he'd seen earlier.

Despite himself, Grant followed her. "What was she like?" he asked, staring down at the picture, admiring the beautiful face but unable to muster any other emotion.

"Mom?" Dallas shrugged a careless shoulder. "She was pretty, drank a lot, lived in spas and health farms, that kind of thing. She didn't like horses much. Scared of 'em. She spent most of her time in Houston and New York, shopping."

"How endearing," he murmured, watching Dallas as she spoke, seeing the emotions fleeting in her eyes, the flashes of pain and the bitterness disguised by humor and indifference. "Guess I didn't miss too much after all," he said finally.

Again Dallas shrugged. Grant glanced through to the dining room where Meredith was busily punching numbers on her phone. Calling her husband? he wondered angrily, then stopped himself, feeling slightly ashamed. "You know, I really don't think we should go to South Beach tonight," he remarked smoothly.

"Why not?" she exclaimed, about to protest.

"Because I think Meredith's tired. She's had a long day."

Dallas turned and watched Meredith standing by the window of the dining room, her back turned, intent on her conversation. "I guess maybe you're right," she muttered grudgingly.

"Good girl." He grinned at her and received a smoldering look in return.

"You win. And by the way," she murmured, her face turning pink, "thanks for helping me out with the mortgage. You didn't need to."

"Anytime."

"You're a pain in the butt, Grant Gallagher," she said, a slow smile hovering around her luscious lips. "Just like Grandma. Too bad you never met the old bat—you'd have had a lot in common. I hated her," she added conversationally, looking up at their grandmother's exuberant portrait above the fireplace. "She killed Mom, you know."

"Why do you say that? I thought—" he hesitated to say *our mother* "—I thought Isabel took her own life."

"Oh, she did. But it was Grandma who drove her to it. I found her, you know. I read a bit of the note before Grandma got rid of it.

"There was a suicide note? You found her?" Grant felt a rush of shock. "How old were you?"

"Eleven."

"Were you alone at the time?"

"Yeah. It sucked."

"I'll bet it did," he muttered, taking a long sip and casting a disparaging look at the woman in the photograph. She certainly hadn't bothered to spare either of them by the looks of it. Couldn't she at least have done away with herself in a manner calculated not to scar her only daughter for life?

"The weird thing is, she didn't really look dead at all," Dallas continued. "I went in the room and stood there talking to her awhile before I—" Her voice caught on a sob and she whirled around. "I don't know why I'm telling you all this, it's none of your goddamn business, anyway."

Then, before he could stop her, she rushed from the room. Grant watched her, wondering if he should go after her. Better not. They both needed time to adjust, he realized, listening to her high heels resonating on the marble stairs. He sighed. How selfish could one woman be with her kids? he wondered. Then, downing the last of the champagne, he glanced again at the dining room where Meredith was collecting her papers.

"Can I give you a hand?" he asked casually, walking over to where she stood.

"Thanks, I'm fine." She smiled briefly, slipped off her glasses and began sorting her papers. "Do we really have to go out to dinner?" she asked, dragging her fingers through her hair.

"Of course not. Dallas and I have both agreed that a quiet dinner here would be great."

"It's not that I don't want to, but—"

"Look, we probably all could use some time alone to digest everything. My advice is to go upstairs, take a nice hot bath and come down whenever you feel like it. We'll let Rodrigo know that we're going to play it by ear. Kids okay?" he asked casually.

"Fine, thanks. Mick—that's my eldest, he's ten—

has this really mean math teacher. She has it in for him and I'm worried about his self-esteem because she singles him out in front of the class and— Oh, I'm sorry to bore you," she exclaimed, blushing and picking up the file.

"You're not boring me. What's your other child's name?"

"Zack. He's eight and a half."

"And your husband?" Grant laid his hands on the back of the dining room chair and watched, frowning, as her face paled and she swallowed.

"My husband died last year in a boating accident off the Georgia coast," she parroted in a dull monotone, as though she'd learned the text by heart.

Grant straightened. His brows closed in a thick ridge above his bright blue eyes and he frowned. So that was the slashing pain he'd sensed in her. No wonder. "I'm sorry," he said, reaching out his hand and touching her arm, feeling doubly guilty for his behavior at Strathcairn, "I had no idea."

"That's okay," she said with a brave little smile, her chin up. "We survive these things. Now, I think I'll take your excellent advice and go have a soak."

"Of course." He moved toward the door, opened it for her to pass. But before she stepped through it, he touched her arm again. "I really am sorry," he said quietly.

"Sorry?" She looked at him nervously, dismissing the tingle coursing through her.

"For my behavior in Scotland. I had no right to treat you the way I did. No right at all. I hope you'll forgive me and that we can start again on a new footing?"

"Uh, yes, sure—I mean, that's fine, no problem." Then, before he could say more, she dashed across the hall and briskly mounted the stairs, leaving him alone, prey to a number of troubling thoughts as he watched her go. What was it about this woman that so disturbed him? In two short weeks his well-ordered existence had been shaken to the core. He should have heeded the inner voice that warned him Meredith Hunter was the kind of woman who could get under a man's skin. Already he felt a dangerous desire to learn what made her tick, to dissect what it was about her that made her so compelling. What, he wondered darkly as he headed toward the stairs, was he in for next?

"So, now that Rowena has unearthed this…*relative*," Joanna sneered, capturing her audience's attention, "she not only expects us to accept the situation lying down, but we're to throw a party for him at Montalba. Imagine expecting us to welcome the guy as though he was some sort of prodigal son! She had some nerve. Don't you agree, Charles?" She turned, hands clasped over the front of her pale pink Chanel suit, trying to look as if she actually cared about what he had to say. She'd dressed appropriately for the occasion, serious and chic, nothing too flamboyant that the others—in particular Charles's wife Marcia—might disapprove of. Normally, she enjoyed annoying her cousins, but when millions of dollars were at stake, it didn't pay to ruffle feathers.

There was silence in Charles Carstairs's distinguished antebellum living room. As the eldest son of Rowena's younger brother, he'd inherited the original Carstairs family home in Savannah when his father died. Joanna had agreed to have the meeting here rather than in her own house because she realized the setting had to be imposing and serious, and she needed every tool at her disposal to sway the other family members—like the pious Mary Chris—into doing what she wanted. She didn't anticipate that Charles would pose any problem—he had the most common sense and he was also the greediest. The trick with him was to massage his ego—he needed to believe he was in charge, and she was happy to promote that fiction as long as it suited her purposes.

"I agree it's very odd," Charles declared slowly, "but I think we'd all better get used to the fact that—according to Ross Rollins—the only hope we have of getting anything is if Gallagher gives it to us of his own free will." He rose from the tapestry armchair and moved toward the mantelpiece, adopting an authoritative pose, pausing to make sure all eyes were upon him. Then he cleared his throat. "I reckon we have two options. First, we either take the matter to court—and unfortunately, from what Ross tells me, we've virtually no chance of winning, and thus we will lose our chance of receiving anything from Gallagher, or do as Rowena says and invite this…this relation, for there's no denying that's what he is, to the party that she wanted."

"An olive branch," Patricia Lambert, Ward and Mary Chris's mother, murmured with a sweet, innocent smile.

"What you're saying is, we don't have a choice," Joanna rejoined bitterly.

"Quite so." Charles sent her a repressive glance. "At least we'd know exactly what kind of person we're dealing with," he added in an aside for her ears only.

"I'd like to meet him," Ward Lambert chipped in, brightening up considerably. A tall, genial man, he was Rowena's youngest nephew, and not, Joanna acknowledged, the brightest bulb of the bunch. "In fact, I've been thinking," he continued earnestly, thankfully not noticing Joanna's sarcastic look of surprise, "we may be all wrong about him. He may turn out to be a very nice guy."

"Quite." Charles exchanged a look with Joanna and continued. "The point is, unless we follow Rowena's instructions and hold the party at Montalba, we won't be able to assess the full extent of the, uh, situation. We need to see him ourselves, and this is the perfect opportunity."

"And I suppose we're expected to be nice," Joanna muttered under her breath. "I guess we should tell Ross we'll do it immediately, before Gallagher leaves again for the U.K. Perhaps with his mind already made up. Though I would think he'd want to take a look at his inheritance, wouldn't you?" she added significantly.

"And there's Dallas to think about, too," Charles mused, drumming his fingers rhythmically on the marble mantel. "The whole thing is quite extraordinary. I almost fell over backward when Ross told us the clause about the poodle home and that Gallagher's agreed to set up a trust for her. Quite extraordinary, the whole thing."

"Really weird. Still, if he's giving Dallas money, well, who knows?" Joanna cocked a hopeful brow at her cousin. "I can't think why Rowena didn't just leave her the money outright."

"Perhaps we should be thankful he hasn't washed his hands of us," Mary Chris piped up, hands clasped. "It shows a Christian attitude. Loving one's neighbor is—"

"Oh, shut up," Joanna muttered, casting her cousin a dark look.

"Perhaps with some small persuasion on our part he will realize that giving us a share of his wealth is not only reasonable, but also the Christian thing to do," Charles said placatingly.

"If the money's his, why should he give us any of it?" Ward asked, rubbing his brow ponderously.

"Ward, it's better you don't get involved in the workings of all this," Joanna purred, placing a soothing manicured hand on Ward's arm.

"Okay. I'll do whatever you all think is right," Ward agreed complacently. "I'd like to meet the guy, though. Maybe he likes fly-fishing," he added hopefully. "It might be nice to share the lodge in Jackson Hole with him."

"The lodge is his now, Ward," Charles said heavily.

"Hmm. I must say I'm most surprised Aunt Rowena didn't leave my Charles Montalba," Marcy murmured wistfully. "It's such an elegant plantation. I can't think what a corporate raider would want with it. So vulgar to have the place associated with someone like that. I wonder if he'd consider an offer," she mused thoughtfully in her waspish Bostonian voice that drove Joanna nuts. All she needed was Marcy buying Gallagher out and having her lording over them all at Montalba. That would just about crown everything. And Marcy just might. She was a Cabot and had inherited a sizable fortune of her own.

"Marcia, surely you wouldn't want Montalba after the way we've been treated?" she asked sweetly, batting her false lashes at her cousin's wife, glad to see that Marcy had aged considerably over the past year. It tipped the balance somewhat, made her detest Marcia a little less.

"Well, of course not, Joanna, dear. Far be it from me

to want anything but the best for *you* all. But if it were to come on the market, why of course we should consider keeping it in the family." She was careful to put emphasis on the *you*, as though the matter really didn't concern her. "Still, it might be good for Charles's standing in the community to have access to such a fine property."

"That's unimportant," Charles murmured.

Joanna looked up, surprised at the unease she sensed, the underlying irritation in his tone. So he didn't want Montalba. Well, well. That was something of a surprise, considering Charles loved promoting his personal image. Perhaps the rumors she'd heard around town were true after all, and he'd been expecting the money to buy his way out of his marriage. She frowned. Could the staid, ever-so-conventional Charles really be having an extramarital affair? He, who'd always judged her so critically? The idea sent an ecstatic shiver to her toes. Oh, to have leverage over Charles. She simply must do some sleuthing.

Then she reminded herself that what really mattered right now was Gallagher. She'd made it her business to go online and study everything she could get her hands on about the man. Single and undeniably good-looking, he made frequent appearances in the society pages. He was, she thought approvingly, exactly the kind of man she liked—though, frankly, even had he looked like a garden gnome, she'd do whatever it took to secure a share of his newly acquired assets.

At that moment the doorbell rang. "That must be Craig and Sally," Marcia said, rising and moving graciously toward the living room door to receive her brother-in-law and his wife. "Ah, Sally, dearest, you look gorgeous. That color truly suits you. And Craig, handsome as ever. Do come in."

Joanna plastered on a sweet smile and reminded herself that allowing Marcy the prominent role of hostess was part of her overall strategy.

"Hi, guys—" she waved "—so glad you could make it."

"Make it? We came as soon as we heard the news. We were in Monte Carlo. We got straight on a plane," Charles's good-looking, fortyish, somewhat beefy younger brother replied, thrusting out his hand to pump Charles's. "Have to put a stop to this nonsense immediately. I didn't gather all the details, but it sounds pretty bad. Amazing that Isabel's bastard should be Gallagher, though. Did you know that we met him at a cocktail party in London about a year ago?"

"No, did you?" Joanna looked at him, intrigued, her mind working fast.

"Yes," Sally chipped in, her voice excited, crossing her slim, sexy legs. Her breasts had to be silicone implants, Joanna figured. Nature could not be that generous. "We met him at this incredible house that belongs to a real sultan. You should have seen it, Joanna. The carpets were to die for."

"Hmm, I'm sure. So what was he like?"

"Gallagher? Divine. Simply divine. Very sexy. Has a great ass and a *je ne sais quoi*, a sort of aura of power. A real turn-on."

"I think what Joanna was referring to was his character," Charles admonished.

"Oh, that," Sally replied blithely, Charles's tone sliding off her like water off a duck's back, "I have no idea. He seemed like a nice guy, a bit aloof, but then I guess people suck up to him all the time. Prominent people are often distant, I find," she added, her look implying that of course she and Craig would know since these were the circles they moved in.

"I chatted with him briefly," Craig said. "He seemed pleasant enough."

"Did you talk to him at any length? I mean, did you exchange cards? Enough to renew the acquaintance?" Joanna asked, an idea forming in her fertile brain.

"Why, I don't know. I guess, maybe. But why would we want to make contact with him? Aren't we going to contest the will?" Craig looked doubtfully over at his wife and sat down on the nearest chintz sofa, accommodating his chinos, which had become tight of late.

"I'm afraid that's not an option," Charles said.

"Not an option? But the old lady was obviously crazy, surely—"

"Unfortunately she took good care to make sure there was no doubt regarding the state of her mental health."

"Are we sure Gallagher's legit? Maybe it's a mistake."

"Afraid not. Gallagher is definitely Isabel's child," he added somberly.

"I see. Well that certainly paints a different picture." Craig nodded. "You got a drink there, Marcia? It's been a long drive, I could use a Scotch on the rocks."

"Why, of course, Craig. What about you, Sally, double vodka tonic with a twist of lime, as usual?"

"Oh, yes. That would be lovely," Sally answered, smiling, failing to catch the honeyed irony in Marcia's voice. It was not lost on Joanna.

"Joanna, what about you?"

"Oh, a Perrier would be fine, thanks." Served the bitch right. She was just waiting for her to say she wanted vodka, too.

"So you see, Craig, there's not much we can do except agree to hold this party Rowena has insisted on. Really quite humiliating," Joanna said. "But since you have the advantage over us and have actually met Gallagher, you might be able to make an overture, make it seem less forced. After all, if we've got to meet him, the sooner we put him at ease, the sooner we'll know where he's coming from and what his intentions are."

"You mean ask to meet with him?"

"Well, not exactly. Of course, this is subject to Charles's approval, but I was thinking that since Rowena has stipulated we should all get together at a formal family gathering out at Montalba, you could be the one to pave the way. He's arriving on Wednesday. Perhaps you could meet him at the airport and all that. The more welcome we make him feel, the more likely he is to loosen his purse strings."

"You may have a point," Charles agreed, catching Joanna's eye. She took the Perrier offered to her and raised her glass. "To our success," she purred.

"To our success," they answered in unison.

Only Marcia remained silent, her lips set in a thinner line than usual. But Joanna didn't notice, her mind too taken up with plotting the next step in her scheme.

11

"Oh, no, Meredith, please," Dallas wailed from the yellow-and-white-striped cushioned lounger where she lay wearing a tiny bikini and a large straw hat, the colorful cocktail Rodrigo had prepared for her balanced elegantly in her left hand. "I refuse to go over all those papers again. Why don't you come and get the sun?"

"Dallas, I'm not here on vacation. We have to complete the proper paperwork," Meredith said, letting out a sigh. She felt worn down, overdressed and ridiculous, wandering out here by the pool in a navy business suit, nylons and sensible pumps, when Dallas looked for all the world like an ad for some tropical getaway.

"I'm with Dallas on this one. You look as if you need a break."

"Oh!" Meredith spun around at the sound of Grant's deep voice close behind her. "You startled me," she remarked, eyes darting away under his appraising gaze.

"You scare easily," he murmured. "I was merely going to suggest that a little time away might do us all good. There's not much more to talk about before we meet in Savannah, anyway. I suggest we go for a boat ride."

"Yeah, Grant, great idea," Dallas agreed wholeheartedly. "By the way, I'm reading that book you recommended, *Hell and High Water.* I really like it. Won't you tell me the end so I don't have to read it all the way through?"

"Nope," he answered smugly, pushing his hands into the pockets of his black jeans. Then he sent her an amused, appraising look. "The designer didn't spend much on fabric when he designed that bikini, did he?"

"So? What's wrong with my bikini? There's nothing in Rowena's will that says you can criticize my clothes, so leave me alone."

"Far be it from me to—"

"Oh, shut up, you two, for goodness' sake," Meredith exclaimed. "Neither of you seems to understand that I can't stay hanging around here forever." She wasn't aware that a desperate note had entered her voice. The children needed her, the dog had to go to the vet, another client was on the phone three times a day requesting her presence at a court hearing on Friday. "This isn't my only obligation, you know," she said, dragging her fingers through her hair and slumping onto the lounger opposite Dallas, feeling suddenly overwhelmed.

"Meredith?" Dallas pushed the pair of huge black sunglasses down her nose and sat up. "Why, you're crying," she exclaimed, astonished, sending Grant a panicked glance. "Oh, Mer, I'm sorry. We didn't mean to be selfish." She moved quickly to Meredith's side and slipped an arm around her as Meredith furiously brushed the embarrassing tears away with the back of her hand.

"I'm fine," she muttered hoarsely. "This is totally unprofessional, I—"

"And all the more reason why you need an afternoon off," Grant murmured smoothly. "Give yourself a break before you go home, Meredith. You'll do no one any good by getting stressed out and overtired."

Grant's calm British voice a few paces behind her made Meredith take a deep breath and recognize the truth of his words. Perhaps he was right. Maybe she needed time for herself. "Thanks, guys. Maybe I should get out on my own this afternoon. Then go home."

"On your own?" Grant interrupted, winking at Dallas. "No way. We're going out. We'll have lunch at the Cuban place that Rodrigo recommended, the one on Calle Ocho that Dallas wouldn't go to last night, then we'll take the yacht I've hired for the afternoon and sail around the bay."

"Yacht? Grant, that's a divine idea," Dallas exclaimed, jumping up and pulling Meredith with her. "Mer, we've got to lose this office look *now*. Go put some other clothes on and relax. Come on," she urged, giving Meredith a hug and grabbing her towel and her wrap. "I'm going to get ready before either of you changes your mind."

"Well, that's a switch," Grant murmured, watching her leave. "I thought I was supposed to be an ogre. Now, you, young lady," he said, eyeing her with mock severity, "are to follow Dallas's instructions and change out of that uniform. Like it or not, Meredith Hunter, you are going to chill out. Consider it part of the job. You can bill Rowena's estate by the hour if it makes you feel better."

"I'd never dream of—"

"Oh, shush," he said, slipping an affectionate arm around her shoulder, sending shudders running up

her spine, "where's your sense of humor?" He turned
her toward him, brow raised.

"I guess it got lost along the way," Meredith replied,
a rueful smile hovering about her lips. Grant had a
way of lightening the direst situations. How different
he was from the bad-tempered angry bear of their first
encounter. And he was infinitely more dangerous, she
realized, suspecting that, when he chose to, he could
be lethally charming. Still, she had to admit the thought
of an afternoon without work was incredibly appealing, even if she cringed at the idea of going out on the
water.

"Okay. I'll wait for you both in the hall in ten minutes," he said.

"Right," she said, banishing the conflicting thoughts
that surfaced whenever a pleasure boat was mentioned.
Still, there had to be a first time. It wasn't as if she could
avoid boats for the rest of her life. It wouldn't be fair to
the kids, particularly to Mick, who was dying to sail. She
swallowed a shudder. "I'll go and get ready." She moved
out of the shield of his arm and he did nothing to stop
her. She felt suddenly unsure of herself. What would she
wear? Had she brought anything suitable for a yachting
trip?

As she climbed the sweeping marble staircase, men-
tally reviewing her outfits, she wondered what had
happened to the self-assured Meredith who never gave
a hoot about how she looked. Hadn't she always had
more important concerns than her appearance?

Entering her room, Meredith chastised herself. Here
she was, a respectable widow, mother of two growing
boys, acting like a sixteen-year-old because a man had
asked her to spend an afternoon with him and his sister. It was ridiculous. Absurd. Where was her head at?

And to make matters worse, he was her client, and likely to remain so for a while.

Perhaps she should call on the intercom and say she'd changed her mind.

Perhaps she should check out her closet, another stronger voice admonished.

With a sigh, Meredith flipped through the few garments she'd brought and selected a pair of light jeans and a white button-down shirt. After a quick shower she donned the outfit, slipped on a pair of sneakers and grabbed her navy-blue gabardine blazer. At least she looked sporty but chic, she concluded, tilting her head so she could see herself in the mirror, pleased with the result. After giving her hair a thorough brush, she slipped on her diamond studs, added a dash of lip gloss and mascara and, without allowing herself to wonder why, sprayed on some Chanel No. 5. She glanced at the bottle sadly. The cologne was Tom's last gift to her, a little surprise he'd brought back after a trip to New York. She placed it tenderly back on the bathroom counter and swallowed the sudden pang of guilt. Was it right to wear perfume her husband had given her when she was trying to be attractive to another man? For there was no denying it; she was unequivocally attracted to Grant Gallagher. More so than she cared to admit.

"Shit," Meredith exclaimed under her breath. She clenched her fists. Why was life so damned complicated? Why did Grant have to hold this allure for her? It was so unexpected and out of character. Still, she could not suppress her excitement as she tripped down the stairs to join the others.

"We're going to take Rowena's old Cadillac," Dallas exclaimed, animated. "It's candy-pink. A 1950s classic, perfect for South Beach." She wore a very short flowered miniskirt that showed off her wonderful, tanned, never-ending legs and a short T-shirt that barely reached her midriff.

"Are you planning to go out on the street like that?" Grant asked, eyeing her disapprovingly.

"Why of course. Have a problem?" She swung her large Murakami Cherry Blossom Vuitton purse over her slim shoulder.

He shrugged. "I don't want to *have* problems because of you."

"Well," Dallas huffed, "you obviously don't follow fashion closely."

Lifting his brows and letting out a sigh, Grant turned to Meredith. "Shall we?" he said, glancing approvingly at her outfit.

Suddenly Meredith didn't feel outshined by Dallas, but amused at the young girl's obvious desire to garner attention.

Soon they were sailing down Red Road in the enormous Cadillac convertible. Dallas sat in the back with her arm draped carelessly over the roll-down canvas top, looking like a model and attracting exactly the kind of attention Grant had foreseen.

"We'll be lucky if we don't have an accident," he commented after two salivating young men in a delivery truck veered to the left just in time. "Now, if Rodrigo's directions are correct, we turn left here and head toward Calle Ocho."

"That would seem right." Meredith glanced at the piece of paper on which Rodrigo had drawn the directions. "Just keep going."

Several minutes later the landscape changed from the elegant old Spanish mansions and upmarket build-

ings of Coral Gables to the more modest dwellings of
Little Havana.

They made a right turn down Calle Ocho, abuzz
with street vendors, supermarkets, garish signs and
shop names written on walls. The cheerful chaos gave
Meredith the impression she was somewhere in Latin
America. She could smell the heady blend of fried
plantains and strong coffee.

Dallas was less enthused. "What is this place?" she
complained, disgusted. "If I'd wanted this kind of
atmosphere, I'd have hit the local Taco Bell."

"Wrong country, Einstein," Grant drawled as he
slowed the car and pulled up in front of Casablanca, a
typical Cuban diner where Rodrigo had assured him
they would eat the "real" thing. They found a parking
spot and then stepped inside the establishment. Dallas
trailed crossly behind.

"We could be at Alto del Mar on Ocean Drive right
now instead of this dump," she grumbled, sliding onto
the red plastic banquette. "And FYI, bro, I'm not the
idiot you seem to think I am. I graduated magna cum
laude from Vassar."

"Let me guess," Grant said, hiding the fact he was
impressed, "you majored in fashion?"

"Business administration," she retorted sweetly,
"with a minor in accounting. In fact—" she grinned
"—I did one of my senior papers on that M&A deal you
orchestrated in Bolivia."

"And what did you conclude?" Grant asked suspiciously.

"Not one of my better efforts, I'm afraid. While I
admitted that, technically, the deal was brilliant, I argued that the guy who thought it up must have had ice
water in his veins. No thought whatsoever given to

how it was going to impact the local economy—you remember, Grant. Anyway, my professor said I wasn't being, um, impartial. She thought you were a stud."

"Remind me to finance a chair in her name," Grant muttered.

"Good for you, Dallas." Meredith laughed as a pretty dark-eyed waitress slipped plastic menus in front of them. "I'm going to side with you on that one."

"Time to order, ladies," Grant said solemnly. "I'll have the *arroz con pollo*," Grant pronounced in what Meredith considered creditable Spanish. "That's chicken with rice."

"Just great." Dallas rolled her eyes.

"And *plátanos maduros*. Rodrigo told me that's fried plantains. A must."

"Good. I'll have that," Meredith answered cordially, determined to keep up the spirit of the expedition and ignoring her quickened pulse when Grant's fingers inadvertently touched hers. "Oh, and some rice and beans, of course," she added, tongue in cheek.

"Yuck!" Dallas threw the menu aside and sat sulking in the corner. "You guys order. I'm not going to eat, anyway. This peasant food sucks."

"Never mind, we can swing by McDonald's later if you're hungry," Grant said blithely, calling the waitress and placing an order for three Coronado beers to accompany their food. Dallas almost shrieked when they were served in the bottle with a slice of lime stuck in the top.

"So, after this is wrapped, are you going to stop in Savannah for the party, or head back to Providence?" Meredith asked, steering Dallas away form her pithy exchange with Grant regarding their present surroundings. "I've heard it's gorgeous, but a bit remote.

I imagine it must get a bit lonely now that your father's gone."

"Lonely?" Dallas looked at her, surprised. "It's not lonely. I have folks there, old Tom the trainer, and wacko Wally—he's the gardener. He's crazy, talks to himself all day, but does a great job with the flowers. No, I'm not going to be lonely. Plus there's Dad's breeding program." She bit her lip. "He never got it off the ground, but I plan to."

"That's pretty ambitious," Grant murmured.

"So? I've got the schooling *and* the background. Why shouldn't I raise horses?"

"No reason at all. I just thought it might be quite an arduous task for a young woman on her own."

"I'm gonna make Providence one of the best stud farms in the South," Dallas replied in a determined tone that neither Meredith nor Grant had heard her use before. "Providence is going to be a legend."

"Well, I admire your pluck," Meredith said as the waitress placed the delicious-smelling dishes before them and Dallas grimaced. As Grant and she quibbled over the beans, Meredith took stock of the diner. Chirpy salsa played on the radio, interspersed with fast-spoken Spanish commercials. At the bar three old men in *guayaberas*—the traditional cotton short-sleeved shirt worn back in Cuba—sat smoking fat cigars and sipping *colada*, thick, black, sugar-filled, syrupy coffee. They looked as though they intended to spend the rest of the afternoon there, chatting, laughing and playing dominoes. Meredith noted the men's mapped, tanned faces, the faces of men who'd suffered and lost yet had learned to move on.

Meredith did need to learn how to move on from loss, herself. Buried in her thoughts, she concentrated on the delicious meal. Even Dallas, after a few suspicious bites, ate the food with enthusiasm. By the time they'd finished, they were all groaning in satisfaction.

"That was great," Grant said as he beckoned the waitress for the check. "Now we'd better be off to the Key Biscayne Yacht Club. That's where the boat I hired is picking us up."

Half an hour later, they were strolling through the club to the dock when suddenly a voice called out. "Dallas Thornton. Well, well. What a surprise." A tall, well-built blond man in his late twenties swung off the gangplank of a large motor yacht and swaggered in their direction.

"Why, Proctor, what a lovely surprise," Dallas cooed, dipping her large shades and flapping her long lashes as the man approached.

"Never thought I'd see you in these parts, gorgeous. How you doin', Dallas?" Proctor swooped an arm about her and enveloped her in a bear hug.

"Who the devil is this guy?" Grant muttered, eyeing the scene suspiciously.

"I haven't the faintest idea," Meredith answered, amused at his hostile reaction. "An old friend, it would seem."

"Hmm. Better take a closer look."

"Here," Dallas was saying, "let me introduce you to my—" she hesitated, then continued "—my brother, Grant Gallagher, and our attorney, Meredith Hunter." The three shook hands. Grant's look of surprise when Dallas said *my brother* was not lost on Meredith.

"Say, Dallas, why don't you let me take you for a spin in the bay?"

"Thanks, but we're just about to take a spin ourselves," Grant cut in with a perfunctory smile, pointing to the large yacht docked alongside.

"Oh, I'd love that, Proctor," Dallas interrupted, ignoring Grant.

"Dallas, we had a plan, I think—"

"Meredith, you guys wouldn't mind if I spent the afternoon with Proctor, would you?"

"Of course not," Meredith replied spontaneously, then met Grant's fulminating look and wished she'd bitten her tongue. "Sorry," she murmured, smothering a smile.

"See?" Dallas asked smugly, and Grant sighed.

"So be it," he muttered. "Actually, it's not such a bad idea," he conceded, eyeing Meredith, a thoughtful, amused expression dawning as color rushed to her cheeks. "In fact, the more I think about it, the more I like it. Let her go with her beach boy. Dallas, we'll pick you up here around seven, okay?" he said, raising his voice for her to hear.

"Don't worry about me, Proctor'll see me home," she responded blithely, already removing her shoes to climb onto Proctor's fine-teak deck. "Have fun, see you later, guys." She waved jauntily, then hopped on board without a backward glance.

"Well. Not exactly homesick, is she?" Grant remarked, slipping a hand under Meredith's elbow and guiding her toward the shiny craft he'd leased for the occasion.

"It'll probably do her good to get away for an afternoon," Meredith countered. Containing her unease, she braced herself as they climbed on board and one of the crew greeted them. There had to be a first time back on the water, and it might as well be now.

Moments later they undocked and the boat glided

out into the bay, past the mangroves and the million-dollar homes that dotted the Key.

Meredith leaned back against the white cushions at the stern of the boat and closed her eyes, determined not to let fear overcome her. She took a deep breath and let the wind blow her hair off her face, trying to dismiss images of Tom flailing in the water that immediately assailed her. She sensed rather than saw when Grant sat down next to her.

"Feeling okay?" he asked casually.

"Fine," she lied. "This was a great idea." She let out a sigh and gazed at the sea, the deep blue water sending shudders down her spine. What if they had an accident and something happened to her? What would become of the boys?

"Good. I love getting out on a boat. It gives one the ability to cut off from reality for a bit." He leaned back on the cushions next to her and with an effort Meredith calmed her racing pulse. It was a very different craft to the sailboat Tom and his pals had been sailing. There was nothing to fear. She kept repeating this. But she sensed the rising panic. Why, oh why had she agreed to come? It was stupid and irresponsible. Probably, she admitted, trying to stifle a groan, the dumbest thing she'd ever done.

Like the sea breeze, Meredith was a breath of fresh air, Grant realized, contemplating her as they sat, relaxed at the back of the boat as the wind blew her hair off her face. A very lovely face behind which lay a fine-tuned brain. The past two days had proved to him just what a clever legal mind she had. But more than that, he'd learned just how sincere and dedicated she was.

Rowena had certainly chosen well when she'd hired Meredith as her lawyer.

For she cared.

At first it had shocked him to see just how much of herself she was prepared to give. He was used to professionals who disassociated themselves from the case, remained impersonal, did not allow their feelings to get embroiled. Some of them, like the chap he was obliged to deal with up in New York, he reflected wryly, were, frankly, distasteful.

But Meredith was different, a remarkable woman able to remain impartial yet stay concerned. She managed Dallas well, too, he reflected, a rueful smile hovering over his lips at the thought of his impetuous half sister. Strange that he'd felt an electric charge course through him when she'd introduced him as her brother. It was the first time he'd been recognized as anybody's anything, he realized, and it had felt strange. His parents had often said "our son," but he knew perfectly well that as soon as he was out of earshot they explained the circumstances of his adoption to the other party. He'd never once felt completely part of a group. Which was fine, since he'd never felt the need to be a part of any group. Much better to be footloose and fancy-free.

He turned slightly and watched Meredith out of the corner of his eye. Her eyes were closed, her silky chestnut hair blowing in the soft breeze, her cheeks gently flushed by fresh air. Without a second thought, Grant leaned over and dropped a soft kiss on her lips.

Her eyes flew open and she jerked upright.

"Shush, don't get upset," he said, drawing her into his arms. He'd already acted like a jerk once before, he realized, and must take care not to make another mistake.

Meredith felt his arms close about her, her breasts tightening against the hard expanse of Grant's chest.

"Grant, you're trying to seduce me. I'm your attorney, for Christ's sake. This is against the bar code."

"I know, deliciously unethical," he murmured, dropping more kisses on her throat and down toward her breast.

"But this is absurd, I can't—"

"Meredith, shut up," he muttered, covering her mouth again, his taunting tongue sending a delicious ache through every muscle in her taut body. Somewhere in the back of her mind she knew she shouldn't be doing this. It felt treacherous and wrong and, as she succumbed, incredibly satisfying. Meredith ached, caught between her anxiety at being out on the sea, that same sea that had taken Tom from her, and the need to be held, the need to feel Grant's mouth on hers, his hands gliding up and down her back, and her knowledge that this was crazy. After several seconds, she forced herself to pull away. He let her go.

"Grant, this is madness." Meredith dragged agitated fingers through her hair. "I don't know what's come over me, I—"

"Madness, because you're attracted to me?"

"Yes, no. You're my client, I'm a widow. This is totally unprofessional and unethical. I—"

"Meredith, why the hell did you think I bothered to come here?" he asked, taking her limp hand in his and stroking it gently.

"I guess because you finally thought the whole matter of Rowena's will over and realized that—" She raised her eyes to his, saw the flash of humor and blushed. "No," she said, pulling her hand away. "I should have guessed. You wouldn't care about what was right."

"Thanks for giving me so much credit," he said dryly, letting her move farther down the cushion. "Would it surprise you to know that I came because I very much wanted to see you again?"

"Me?" She looked at him, frowning. "But all I've done is cause you problems. I mean, that isn't a valid reason to come all the way across the Atlantic. It's totally illogical." She shook her head, uncomprehending.

"Who says everything in life has to be logical?"

"No one. It just is. People don't do things on impulse or because they feel like it. They do them for a purpose," she insisted as a gust of wind swept her hair off her face as they hit the open sea. "Are you sure we won't hit bad weather?" she asked, suddenly anxious.

"We're fine. And by the way, not everybody acts out of similar motivation. I do things on a whim. You were a whim," he added, eyeing her critically.

"Well, gee, thanks."

"I didn't mean to sound rude."

"Too late," she admonished, glancing at the sea uneasily now that they'd picked up speed. "Do we have to go so fast?"

"We're only doing about fifteen knots."

"Oh. It seems more. I—I think maybe we should go back." She clasped her hands and tried to quiet her churning stomach. Too much was happening, and too quickly. Her thoughts were jumbled. She was allowing this man whom she thoroughly disapproved of to kiss her. Where was her loyalty to the husband she loved, the man who'd died only a year earlier, a victim of this very sea?

"Meredith, what's the matter, you look pale. Is something wrong?"

"Yes!" she cried, suddenly gripping her knees and

letting her head drop in her lap. "I should never have come, never. I can't bear the sea. I don't want to stay here. I want to go back," she wailed, "now."

"But we just left."

"I don't care. Take me home. I don't want to die."

Suddenly realizing the truth, Grant slipped his arms around her and held her tight.

"My God, of course you're frightened," he exclaimed, angry at himself for his insensitivity. For not thinking of the association of the sea and her husband's death, which would naturally affect her. "I'm sorry," he whispered, holding her close, "I should have realized. I'm a thoughtless idiot," he muttered, stroking her hair and pulling her head onto his shoulder. "Why didn't you say something?"

"I thought I could master it, thought I should try to make myself get over it," Meredith replied shakily. "I can't go on being afraid forever. It's not fair to the kids, to anyone."

"You're right, but give it a little time. Fears go away in the end. We all have them." He sat her up firmly, holding her shoulders. "Good. That's better. Now, take a deep breath and look at me, not at the sea. Take a few deep breaths."

Meredith did as she was told, the breathing and the soothing motion of Grant's hand on her upper back helping to dissipate the anxiety she was experiencing.

"Feeling better?" he asked, eyes brimming with a gentleness she'd never seen there before.

"Yes, thanks." She swallowed and nodded, tweaked her hair behind her ears and released a long sigh. Grant's arm still stayed firmly locked about her shoulders and she made no attempt to remove it.

"Now, let me tell you something."

"What?" She looked at him inquiringly, glad of the distraction.

"I had a hard time getting over something myself once upon a time." He looked down into her questioning eyes, then reached out and touched her hair.

"You? You don't look as if you've ever been afraid of anything."

"It was a long time ago, and I'd forgotten it until now."

"Go on."

"I used to be afraid of getting into a limo."

"A limo?" She frowned. "Why?"

"Because my parents—that is, the Gallaghers—always left in limos. I suppose I associated limos with people leaving me behind. A psychiatrist would probably have a field day."

"I see. You felt abandoned." Meredith felt a deep rush of pity.

"Now, don't let's get soppy about it, I survived perfectly well. I take limos all the time," Grant said hastily.

"But it must have been so hard for you, being brought up by a callous couple like that."

"They weren't bad. They never mistreated me. Quite the opposite. It was a lot better than what some people go through, that's for sure," he dismissed. "Now, are you better?" He smiled at her, that same dazzling, mesmerizing smile that had left her transfixed that first day at Strathcairn. "What are you thinking?" he asked suddenly.

"Nothing. Nothing in particular," she fibbed.

"You're a bad liar, Meredith Hunter. Too bad a liar to make you a good attorney, and yet you are an excellent lawyer."

"Is that a compliment?"

"If you want to take it as such. But it's a fact."

"Thanks."

"You're welcome. Tell me, how do you juggle all your roles? I find it intriguing. Concerned mother one minute, fighting for your clients the next. Presumably you're a loving and conscientious daughter. Probably were a great wife as well," he commented, throwing this last in casually.

"I do my best to fulfill all the roles that are required of me," she answered carefully.

"Not always an easy task, I would imagine."

"No, but then who said life was easy?"

"It's not?" He gave a comical grimace. "You mean all these years I've been deluding myself?"

"Something like that," she said, smiling warily, the fear gradually dissipating. "Not that I believe a word of it. Of all people, you must have known some pretty hard times."

"Bah," he disclaimed, removing his arm and getting up to help to set up the table where the steward was laying a tray with champagne and two flutes. "Thanks. I'll pour."

"Very well, sir." The man smiled and returned below while Grant carefully unpeeled the wrapping off the cork.

"Grant, are you trying to tell me that being adopted by people like the Gallaghers was easy?"

"No, but as I said, they never abused or mistreated me. In fact," he added with an ironic smile, "they showered me with worldly goods." The cork popped abruptly and he concentrated on pouring the champagne into the glasses, then handed her a flute. "Cheers."

"Cheers. And thanks. I feel much better now."

"What you need," he remarked, sitting down next to her once more, "is a break."

"Oh, but that's impossible."

"Why?"

"Well, for one thing, I have too much work, then there are my kids to look after and—"

"Meredith, stop. What about you? Your life?" he asked, peering into her eyes, reading all the doubt there.

"What about it? That *is* my life."

"No. I mean you. Not Meredith the lawyer or the mother or daughter, but Meredith the woman?" He eyed her carefully, gauging her reaction.

"I—well, I don't know what you mean," she answered, flustered.

"What I mean is," he insisted, "that I'm very attracted to you, as I think you are to me. I want to spend a few days with you away, on our own."

"Oh." She swallowed, eyes arrested, wondering if she'd understood him correctly.

"Well?"

"I—no. That would be impossible. I have too many responsibilities—besides the fact it would be entirely disreputable. You're my client." She shook her head firmly. "It's out of the question, I'm afraid," she insisted, ignoring her pulse rate. "And, anyway, I hardly know you."

"But despite all these insurmountable impediments, you do admit that we're both extraordinarily attracted to each other?" His eyes bored keenly into hers, leaving little room for retreat.

Meredith shifted uncomfortably. "I—"

"It's silly to go on playing games, Meredith, we both know."

She spluttered as the champagne went down the wrong way. "I haven't thought about it. I—"

He laughed, a low, knowing laugh that sent shivers of repressed excitement coursing up her spine. What was it about him that affected her so? She disapproved of him, disliked so many aspects of his life. Yet, as he'd so blatantly pointed out, the attraction couldn't be denied.

"I'm not in the habit of slipping off for fun and games with my clients," she said stiffly, determined to retrieve some vestiges of dignity. "The mere thought is outrageous. Imagine, for instance, if Joanna Carstairs should find out, or Ross?"

"Is that what's worrying you?" he asked quizzically.

"That, and one hundred other things. Just because I let you kiss me doesn't mean—well, doesn't mean that—" She cut off, searching for words withering enough to crush his pretensions.

"Yes?" he said helpfully. "Go on, tell me all the reasons why the two of us spending a couple days together would be as absurd as you're implying."

Meredith took a deep breath, determined to keep a grip on her fast-fading arguments. Getting so worked up over Grant's proposal was ridiculous. "Grant, I shouldn't have to explain this to you. We both know it's impossible. I'm a mother, a breadwinner, I have obligations."

"Not good enough," he taunted.

"Then try this for size. I don't want to."

"Liar." His eyes brimmed with laughter and something more that left her swallowing. "We both want precisely the same thing, so stop being so damned prim and proper and admit it. You're just afraid of giving yourself a chance."

"That's not true," she blurted, staring up into his face in a vain attempt to recapture her dignity.

"Of course it is. And the sooner you recognize that you didn't die in the accident with your husband," he said, his voice soft yet determined, "the better it will be for you and everybody around you."

"How dare you?" she said, wrenching away.

"Because it's true," he said matter-of-factly, "and at some point you're going to have to face it, recognize that you're still alive. You can't bury yourself with him, Meredith."

"That's a horrible thing to say," she whispered, outraged.

"If Tom truly loved you, as I'm sure he did, I doubt he'd want you to live the way you're living now."

She gasped. How could he say such things? How could he callously utter such cruel statements? "Tom was worth a hundred of you," she responded angrily. "He was a wonderful, caring and kind individual who never hurt anyone. Not like you with your corporate raids and unfeeling behavior toward others," she spat. "I wouldn't go to the end of the street with you, Grant Gallagher, and that's the truth."

"Really?"

Before she could react, he pulled her roughly into his arms, his mouth clamped down on hers and he showed nothing but sheer, unadulterated desire. And to her horror Meredith melted in his arms all over again, unable to stop herself, caught on a wave of longing, her mouth as wild and hungry as his. The next thing she knew Grant had swooped her into his arms and was carrying her below.

"Leave me alone," she uttered hoarsely, legs flailing.

He laughed, a wolfish grin covering his handsome features.

"I'll scream," she threatened, struggling halfheartedly.

"You'd waste your breath. The noise of the engine is rather loud, no one will hear." He kicked open the door of the master cabin and laid her unceremoniously down on the king-size bed.

Pulling herself up on her elbows, Meredith tossed her hair back, her eyes blazing. "This is ridiculous. Now, stop it and leave me be, Grant. You're treating me as if I was a brainless bimbo."

"That's the last thing I'd call you," Grant said, lowering himself onto the bed next to her. "Meredith, relax, for Christ's sake. I'm not going to eat you. And you might just enjoy it."

Before she could say another word, he moved over her, his body pinning her to the bed, his lips seeking hers tenderly, playfully yet determinedly. She could feel the weight of him on her, the hardness of his desire, and she hated herself for the sudden rush of need seeping into every part of her body.

Relax, she commanded herself, you're a grown woman. You can have sex with a man you're attracted to—it's not a crime.

But it might be construed as such when the man was her client.

Pulling away, she shoved her hand against his chest, catching her breath. "Please, Grant, stop. You have to understand. If the Georgia bar were ever to learn of this, I'd be out on my rear end so fast—"

"Okay, I respect that," he said, dragging his fingers through his hair and staring down at her. "By God, you're lovely. Why did you have to come into my life,

Meredith Hunter? It was going so smoothly until you rang my doorbell. Oh, hell. I really would love to spend a couple days away with you." He sat up and sighed.

Meredith smiled despite herself, surprised at how feminine and sexy she suddenly felt. "I didn't say that I wouldn't *like* to spend a couple days away, I said I *couldn't.*"

He turned, eyeing her suspiciously, then a slow smile curved his lips. "I'll tell you what. I'll come to Savannah and do whatever it is I have to do with the relations. But on the condition that afterward we go away together."

"I'm not being blackmailed," she responded, pulling her shirt down and tidying herself. "Besides, you've already told Ross you were coming."

"Plans can change."

"You wouldn't!"

"Try me." He rose, still grinning at her, eyes gleaming. "Now, take a rest, my dear, and before you know it we'll be back on land."

He leaned over, straightened her on the bed and pulled the bedcovers over her. "There. I won't bother you any longer. I'll be up on deck if you need me."

Without another word, he turned and left.

Touched by his gesture, Meredith let out a deep sigh and looked about the elegant cabin. Inlaid wood, white cushions and clever mirrors gave the impression of size. She glimpsed herself, surprised to see how bright her eyes were. Oh, God. Did she really have the hots for Grant Gallagher? It was so inappropriate and embarrassing. But perhaps he was right, she concluded, dropping her head on the goose-down pillow, feeling suddenly drowsy. Perhaps it would be better to go away with him for a couple days and get him out of her system. No one would have to know. It was about time she faced the fact that she was a normal woman, with hormones and needs. It might be better to have a brief, purely physical relationship, one with no ties and a set end point. Grant would go back to Europe and it would all be over.

What would Tom say?

Nothing. He'd want her to move on. She knew that.

But not with a man like Gallagher.

She turned and let out another sigh, then yawned. As the boat rocked gently, Meredith's eyes closed and she fell asleep, assuring herself that this really was nothing but a physical attraction.

When she woke, she noted shadows and quickly headed up the narrow stairway. Leaning on the railing, Grant was gazing out at the glistening buildings of downtown, the sky a glorious turquoise bathed in soft pinks and slashing magentas as the sun set slowly behind Coconut Grove.

"It's beautiful," she murmured, settling beside him, strangely at ease in his company.

"I must say, the Miami skyline's quite a sight, isn't it?" He slipped an arm around her, making sure she stayed steady on her feet.

"Hmm-hmm." Unconsciously Meredith leaned back against his chest. For a moment she stood deathly still, knowing she must not encourage his advances. Or not until Rowena's will was wrapped up.

He began rubbing her arms gently. "Not cold, are you?" he asked.

"Uh, no, I'm fine, thank you." She didn't dare move lest he thought she was rubbing against him. This was most embarrassing and illicit. It was exciting, she recognized. Enticing. Different to anything she'd ever known. How could she, a respectable widow, the mother of two growing kids, feel such an intense surge of desire for a man she barely knew and didn't much like? Meredith closed her eyes and prayed. She simply must get herself under control. These absurd flights of fantasy must end at once.

Then Grant's hold eased, his hands moved to her shoulders and he flicked her hair back. "We're almost there," he commented as Meredith let out a long breath of relief. "We'll dock at Dinner Key and go for a drink at Monty's."

"Great idea," she said, turning and flashing a bright smile in his direction. "Guess I'd better get my blazer and my purse, then. It's been a great afternoon. Sorry I panicked earlier."

"I understand." His eyes lingered on hers a moment, then she turned.

He watched as she accepted her things from the first mate, then glanced out to sea, his expression thoughtful. Meredith was an intriguing woman, one he was fast coming to admire and desire. And maybe, just maybe, she wasn't quite as inaccessible as she'd have him believe. The only problem was that she had yet to recognize her own needs. She was caught up in a world of duty, loyalty and lingering pain. If anything transpired between them it might be quick and enjoyable, for them both, and it might even help her move on from her sadness. But that would be all. He glanced at the twinkling lights of the approaching marina and propped his hands on the rail.

Perhaps going to Savannah wouldn't be such a bad thing after all.

12

It was wonderful to be home, to take her boys in her arms, hug them tight and listen to their excited reports of all they'd done during her absence, pat old Mac and later collapse onto her own soft bed. Although she experienced a sense of achievement—Grant agreeing to come to Savannah was definitely a triumph—the tumultuous events of the past few days had proved exhausting. But now, thank God, she could take a few days' respite before Grant's arrival and the Carstairs party, which, according to latest reports, was getting well under way.

She happily threw off her traveling clothes and slipped on an old tracksuit as she settled in for an evening with the kids. She had determined to banish any troubling sensations that Grant's kisses had left.

"Yes, she's gotten back safely. I'll be home soon," Clarice Rowland was saying into the phone as Meredith came back downstairs and entered the den, where her mother had been sewing the badge on Zack's new baseball uniform. "There we go," Clarice said, hanging up the phone and dropping the scissors into the sewing basket. She was a good-looking, chic, dark-haired woman in her mid-fifties. "I think that looks okay, don't you?" She held up the shirt for Meredith to inspect while taking a good look at her daughter. "You know, the trip's done you good, honey, you look more rested." .

"Well, who would have guessed stress was so good for one's looks?" Meredith countered, dropping onto the sofa. "What a situation, Mom. Those two weren't easy to deal with."

"But you've solved the problem?"

"Yes and no. Grant's accepted the terms of Rowena's bequest and agreed to set up a trust for Dallas. In fact, he's been extremely generous and is advancing the money for her to pay off her mortgage," she added, fiddling absently with the fringe of a cushion.

"That's a surprise, isn't it? You gave me the impression he was a tough customer."

"He is, but I guess he has a softer side, too—one that he's not even really conscious of."

"You think so?" Clarice raised a brow but said nothing.

"We'll see. He certainly treated Dallas fairly. Next up now are the Carstairs relations. Rowena's left it up to him to decide whether he wants to give them anything, so they're running around like scalded cats preparing to throw him a party."

"Yes, I got an invitation in the mail the other day. It's going to be out at Montalba, right?"

"Yeah—another of Rowena's little schemes."

"I wonder what she had in mind," Clarice murmured thoughtfully, slipping her purse onto her shoulder. "And how the relations intend to react. I've known Charles Carstairs since we were children. He's the kind of guy who hasn't made a wrong move since kindergarten. As for Joanna, I dread to think what she must be concocting." She rolled her eyes. "Probably off consulting all her shamans and witch doctors. I'd keep a close tab on your Mr. Gallagher while she's around. You know what a man-eater she is. With all those millions in the offing, she's probably orchestrating some kind of voodoo love spell."

Meredith laughed. "I'm sure Gallagher's well able to take care of himself," she replied.

"Well, I must get going now or I'll be late and your father will worry that we won't get to the Maxwells' black-tie dinner on time. They're honoring old Grover Sanford, you know, fifty years of loyal service to the city and all that."

"Nice. Grover deserves it. I plan to stay right here at home with the boys and have a quiet evening for a change. Thanks for holding the fort, Mom," she said, throwing her mother an appreciative smile. "I don't know what I'd do without you and Dad and Jeff. It's wonderful to have a family you can count on."

"Of course it is." Clarice smiled at her affectionately. "That's what family's all about."

Meredith got up from the couch and led the way to the door. "Say, Mom, you don't really believe in soothsayers and all that, do you?" She shook her head, laughed and unlatched the door.

"Well—" Clarice tilted her head "—I do and I don't. I've been told some pretty tall tales in my time, but I've also heard some frighteningly accurate things over the years, too."

"That's all very well," Meredith answered matter-of-factly. "Probably pure coincidence." Then suddenly she thought of Tom and her heart sank. What if she'd been to see someone and they'd told her to stop her husband from going on a boating trip? Would she have listened? Could she have prevented it?

Telling herself to stop being ridiculous, she accompanied her mother out onto the porch. "Thanks again, Mom. I'll see you Thursday—I'm so excited that Jeff is bringing Melanie."

"Yes, I've got a feeling about those two. We'll be there around seven p.m. Your father can't resist an opportunity to be with those boys of yours. By the way, I think Mick's got a crush on a girl at school," Clarice said, lowering her voice and glancing up the stairs.

"Already?" Meredith dropped a kiss on her mother's cheek. "Time moves so fast, Mom. It seems like yesterday he was a baby." Her eyes melted at the thought, at the memories.

"I know, dear, but you just relax now and let life take its course." She touched her daughter's cheek briefly, stifling the sadness that always gripped her since Tom's premature death, and turned to walk down the garden path. At least Meredith looked healthier and more relaxed than she had in a while. Perhaps Rowena's will, with all its inconveniences, was forcing her to forget some of her more pressing problems and worry about someone else's for a change. Bless Rowena. Had the old lady somehow known it would help Meredith to move on? she wondered, igniting the engine of her Volvo. As Meredith's mother, she was grateful to anyone who directly or indirectly helped her child.

Arriving a couple days early struck Grant as a good idea. He'd finished his meetings in New York earlier than anticipated, and had been surprised to discover he truly missed Meredith's company. So here he was in Savannah, the city of his mother's birth. And perhaps his father's, too. More than likely it was also the spot where he'd been conceived.

It had seemed easy enough to agree to the meeting with the Carstairs family when he was seeking an excuse to follow up on Meredith and assuage the natural curiosity aroused by Rowena's eccentric demands. But now, as he sat in the back of the limo driving him into town from the airport, he realized that the world as he knew it would never be quite the same ever again. Up until now, he'd insulated himself from his unknown past.

But, he justified, he'd really come to see Meredith. He knew she couldn't stay in Miami, and since he was determined to learn more about her, the simple solution was to follow her back to Savannah. Why he was bothering to pursue a woman who wasn't his type was a mystery. But come he had, fascinated by her unfailingly honest streak. In a world where every trick justified the means to an end, Meredith's sincerity had touched something in him that he barely recognized.

Then, too—but this he barely admitted to himself— there was Dallas, who, under her worldly-wise veneer, was nothing but a wounded, fragile child let down by too many people, including and primarily her parents. Not that it was any of his business, he assured himself, peering out at the graceful city. In fact, it might have been easier simply to pay her mortgage, give her some cash and forget about the rest. But that, he realized with a sigh, would have been impossible. Neither she nor Meredith would have accepted such a proposal, simply because they were both examples of a breed he'd begun to believe didn't exist anymore in today's world.

Grant turned his attention back to Savannah, trying to recall what he'd read on the flight from New York. It was one of the few cities that had remained intact after the Civil War, Sherman having been dissuaded by a prominent local citizen and an abundance of Southern hospitality from burning it to the ground. Perhaps they were Meredith's ancestors, he reflected, lips curving. She'd been pretty persuasive in her arguments to lure him here. Perhaps they'd used those same tactics on the general. The thought appealed to him, and as the vehicle continued its ride into town, he admired the ordered, meticulously landscaped streets and avenues, the squares of varying dimensions, which obviously influenced the lifestyles of Savannah's citizens.

In one square he watched two old ladies feeding the doves, while other folks lolled on benches, chatting, passing the time of day, watching the strolling tourists and commenting upon life. The sounds of the carriages made him feel as if he'd traveled into the past, into a city brimming with life but whose residents still communicated in a gracious old-world manner. He saw one man doff his cap in a courtly gesture to an elderly lady in a feathered hat, and was amused by an elegantly suited woman in impossibly high heels walking three graceful Afghan hounds.

So this was where he belonged.

No, he reminded himself quickly, not belonged. Originated.

There was a huge difference.

As the car drew up in front of the Ballastone Inn, the elegant B and B that Meredith had recommended, Grant realized that he didn't belong anywhere, not even at Strathcairn Castle. It wasn't something he'd considered before, but thanks to Rowena's machinations, his rootlessness suddenly bothered him. He'd arrived here without much thought of what coming to Savannah would entail. Yet now, as the car came to a halt and he stepped out, he was convinced that whatever awaited him here would prove more than challenging.

Walking up the front steps of the inn, he wondered how far away Meredith's office was, overcome by a sudden urge to go there immediately. Maybe he could stroll there after he'd unpacked his bag. The thought of seeing her again helped him focus.

Taking a deep breath of fragrant southern air, Grant realized the prospect of strolling through the city was equally compelling, as if by doing so he could seek out the subtle undercurrents, discover its secrets, force it to reveal itself.

Grant registered at the front desk and was shown to his room. Would Savannah reveal its secrets to a stranger? Perhaps it was only true to its own, he reflected.

He pulled aside a lace drape determined to shake off his mood, but a rustle of wind swirling down the tree-lined street made him oddly pensive. Was his birth father still alive? he wondered. The man who had unwittingly fathered him, who might not even know of his existence, might still live here. Or had he been from out of town?

He turned his back on the window and, flexing his fingers, determined not to get caught in a trap of his own making. He was damned if he was going to go down endless paths in search of answers to questions that had absolutely no bearing on his present life. He was who he was. Learning a name or seeing a photo of the man who'd accidentally fathered him wasn't going to change that.

Was it?

Aware that this line of thought was getting him nowhere, he began unpacking his suitcase. With any luck
Meredith might be in. Thank God he'd avoided being
picked up by Craig Carstairs, whom he vaguely
remembered from a party in London. He'd made sure
nobody knew his date or time of arrival. He wanted
time on his own to absorb his surroundings, get a feel
for the place before he faced the family.

He glanced at his watch. Four o'clock. If he was
going to ring Meredith, he'd better get on with it. He
flipped open his cell phone and found her number,
smiling briefly as he recalled her anxiety to get home
to her kids' dental appointments and baseball games,
a world so alien to him. Had he been wrong to insinu-
ate himself in it? Was he intruding on her privacy?

With a shrug he placed the phone to his ear and
waited. He didn't plan to invade her world, but merely
ask her to dinner. Surely that couldn't turn out to be too
complicated?

Half an hour later, Grant left the Ballastone Inn and
walked across Forsythe Park. Meredith could give him
twenty minutes if he got over there right away. She'd
seemed surprised and not entirely pleased at his early
arrival.

Late-afternoon sun filtered gently through the fo-
liage as he entered the park. Doves hopped fearlessly
on the paths, seeking crumbs and absorbing the last
rays. Subtle scents, some reminding him of places he'd
visited, others enticingly new, filled his curious nostrils.
Had his mother walked these same paths? he wondered, stopping a moment as a sudden shiver tingled
down his spine.

Telling himself he was being foolish, Grant banished

the strange sensation. But as he began walking again he had the distinct impression that he was not alone. He glanced sideways to make sure he wasn't being followed. Christ, he thought, shaking his head. *Pull yourself together.* His clear thinking was one of his greatest assets, he reminded himself. He was not a fanciful man, and he planned to remain that way.

"He'll be here any minute." Meredith burst into Tracy's office, hair flying.

"What? Who?" Tracy sat back and watched her friend, frowning.

"Why, Gallagher, of course. He's arrived two days early. It's most inconvenient, what with the holiday coming up and all."

"Why the panic?" Tracy sent her friend a penetrating look.

"It's not panic, I'm just annoyed that he calls up and announces himself as though I had nothing better to do than change my schedule to accommodate him."

"Did you tell him that?"

"Not in so many words. After all, he's here. I'm going to have to make the best of it."

"Hmm." Tracy sniffed skeptically. She'd never seen Meredith fazed by a client before and was curious to meet Grant Gallagher personally. "So I finally get to meet Rowena's mysterious heir." She chuckled.

"There's nothing mysterious about him. If anything, he's a nuisance." Meredith flopped into the office chair and studied her nails.

"That wasn't how you described him when you got back from Miami," Tracy pointed out. "In fact, you were rather pleased with him. The mortgage on Providence was hardly chump change."

"It's the least he could do," Meredith muttered grudgingly. "Besides, it's probably just a drop in the bucket for him."

"Meredith," Tracy said, leaning forward in her chair, "why not simply admit that he's just a nicer guy than you first thought?"

"Okay, fine. He is. And?" Her eyes leveled with Tracy's, challenging.

"Nothing." Tracy raised her hands and shook her golden head. "Just an observation, that's all. So when's he coming?"

"As soon as he can walk here from the Ballastone. Oh, God. Do I look terrible?"

"No, you look frazzled."

"Oh, Lord. Lend me some lipstick, will you?"

Tracy reached in her purse and handed Meredith a tube of lip gloss. "Go sort yourself out, partner. I'll take care of him if he gets here before you're done primping."

Meredith glared at her friend, then accepted the tube and rose to go to the restroom. She must calm down. Just because the man had kissed her did not mean she could forget she was his attorney.

After dabbing on the lip gloss, she pulled a brush through her hair, then rushed back to her office and sat down, breathless, behind her desk. She must be calm, in control, in command of the situation.

Five minutes later when the doorbell rang, she was working at her computer, pretending to be absorbed in her work. When Ali knocked, then showed him in, she took a few seconds before raising her eyes and smiled politely.

"Oh, hi, come on in."

"Hi." Their eyes met and locked. Before she could react, Grant leaned over the desk and grasped her outstretched hand in his, holding it a fraction longer than necessary. His eyes roamed critically over her. "You look tired," he said bluntly.

She resisted the urge to smooth her hair. "I've had a lot to do. Please, sit down. How can I help you?" She tilted her head and smiled professionally.

"Begin by dining with me tonight?"

"I'm sorry, but that's impossible. I've got a school play to attend—last performance before the break."

"Well, then how about tomorrow?"

"Tomorrow? But it's Thanksgiving tomorrow. I've got a huge dinner to cook, family coming. I can't."

"I see." She caught the cool tone, the touch of disappointment. "Silly of me to forget, I know, but we don't do that holiday in Britain. Of course you'll be with your family. I understand completely." His face closed and she felt an odd twinge of regret.

And before she could stop herself, she blurted out, "Look, if you don't mind slumming it, you're welcome to come to my house for Thanksgiving. We'll have the usual stuff—turkey, trimmings, more pie than we can possibly eat—and there's always room for an extra guest."

Grant hesitated. Family dinners were a foreign concept to him; certainly, he couldn't remember any such occasions in his own youth.

"Really," she insisted, "it's a tradition you should experience. A stranger is never left out in the cold on Thanksgiving. It's what this holiday is all about."

It was hardly the quiet, intimate meal he'd been imagining. But to refuse her generous offer would sound churlish. "Are you sure I wouldn't be intruding?"

"Not at all. Why don't you take down the address. I'm not far from the Ballastone."

Meredith regretted her offer the moment Grant left her office, but she could hardly retract it now. What on earth had gotten into her? Hadn't she sworn to put as much distance between her and Grant Gallagher as she could? But then she could hardly leave him alone in a strange city on Thanksgiving. She didn't really have a choice, did she?

"Mom, phone for you," Mick called from the top of the stairs.

"Thanks. I'll take it in the kitchen."

Meredith finished basting the turkey and popped it back in the oven, then, wiping her hands, picked up.

"Hi."

"Hi. Just thought I'd check to see if you needed me to bring anything. I don't know the protocol at these things."

An odd tremor tickled her stomach at the sound of Grant's voice. She'd have sworn he sounded nervous, but the very notion of Grant Gallagher being anxious about anything was absurd.

"No, we're fine, but thanks for offering. We're getting together about seven. Oh, and we're not very formal around here—just wear whatever you're comfortable in."

"Well then, I'll just—"

"Mick, don't do that," she exclaimed as her son came careening down the banister.

"Excuse me?"

"Nothing. My son. You were saying?"

"Go upstairs and get ready for dinner," she mouthed at Mick, who was staring longingly at the banister he'd abandoned.

"Just that—"

"Just what? I'm sorry, I was distracted, could you repeat that?"

"Meredith," Grant said patiently, "I just wanted to say I'll see you at seven, then. That is, if you won't consider meeting me for a drink beforehand? Just the two of us?"

"Has anyone ever told you that you're brash?" she asked, realizing she'd forgotten to reset the oven timer. "I'm afraid it's out of the question. There's a turkey in the oven that, if I'm not careful, will be dry as leather unless I monitor it. We'll have to do it some other time—" She blushed, realizing that was hardly what an attorney should say to her client. "That is, I mean, not that I'm suggesting we have drinks, just…oh, never mind," she said, completely flustered. "I'll see you at seven. Bye."

She stared at the phone, then with an exasperated huff, went about setting the Georgian dining table. Thank goodness Beth had polished the silver and the butcher had given her an extra-large bird. She stopped, tilted her head and planned her seating arrangement, aware that it was a while since she'd bothered about anything so mundane. And what on earth should she wear?

And what about the kids? Oh, Lord, she reflected, throwing down the dishcloth and heading for the stairs, she'd better make sure they had showers and clean clothes.

"Zack, Mick, you guys need to take a shower before dinner," she called as she went up the wide wooden staircase and popped her head into their bedroom, where a huge electric train that had once belonged to her father took up most of the floor. "Guys, please don't leave pieces lying about," she pleaded, picking up a carriage and replacing it on the rails. "Beth almost fell over the stationmaster yesterday morning. And no more fishing flies, Zack. They get caught in the carpet. And I don't want to be sued for negligence," she exclaimed, heading to the boys' cupboard and taking out clean jeans and polo shirts.

"Aw, Mom, do we have to shower?" Zack turned up his freckled snub-nosed face, his big blue eyes pleading from under his thick blond mushroom cut.

"Yes, sir. And that includes ears. I noticed this morning that they were none too clean."

"Gee, Mom, it's only Grandpa and Grandma and Uncle Jeff. They won't care."

"And two extra guests," she slipped in casually, wrinkling her nose as she picked up a discarded pair of sneakers and popped them into the dirty wash. "Mick, those sneakers are disgusting," she exclaimed.

"Yes, Mom." Mick rolled his eyes. "Who're the other guests?"

"Oh, Jeff's girlfriend, Melanie, and a client of mine from out of town." Meredith busied herself folding the mess in the closet and pretended not to feel the heat in her cheeks.

"A client?" Mick looked up, curious. "But you never have clients over, you said—"

"I know. But this is different. This client's from England. It's Thanksgiving and he has nowhere to go. It would be most inhospitable if we didn't welcome him to Savannah," she burbled. "Now, come along, boys. And, Mick, wash your hair," she said, rubbing her hand over his chestnut mane and smiling down into his big gray eyes, so like her own.

"Okay, Mom." Mick sighed and gave her a hug. She held him close for a brief moment. Of the two of them,

Mick was feeling the loss of his father most. Zack had been much more upset at the time but was getting over it easier, able to relate to his grandfather and uncle. But for Mick it seemed worse. He was that bit older, more conscious of the finality of death.

Minutes later, Meredith sifted through her own closet. They were usually pretty casual, even on the holidays. Still, she felt an urge to dress up a little. Maybe she would wear the gray Armani pants and the silk shirt she'd bought on her stop-off in London.

An hour later she was buzzing nervously around the kitchen checking the turkey and the pecan pie, and making sure the ice machine, which was forever breaking down, now worked again. Did she have enough whisky in the house? What if he wanted gin and tonic? Brits often did. She didn't think she had any.

Her thoughts were interrupted by the doorbell.

"I'll get it." Mick was halfway to the door, skidding over the black-and-white marble hall and opening the door before Meredith had a chance to do more than hurry behind him. She heard voices and her heart rate quickened.

"Hi, you must be Mom's guest. I'm Mick. Come on in."

"Hello." Grant took Mick's proffered hand and they shook in a masculine manner. "I'm Grant Gallagher." Then he looked up and met Meredith's fine gray eyes over Mick's glistening, freshly washed hair, noted her hand slip protectively to the boy's shoulder, and he smiled. They were so alike, mother and son. "Good evening. Are you sure I'm not intruding?"

"Heavens, of course not. Come on in. Oh, you shouldn't have," she said, taking the bouquet of red roses he was handing her.

"Nothing much, I'm afraid," he murmured, glancing awkwardly at Mick gazing goggle-eyed at the flowers.

"That was very kind. Mick, put these on the kitchen counter, will you? And don't eat any of Grandpa's favorite chocolates before dinner," she added with a meaningful look.

"Not even one teensy-weensy-bitsy one?" Zack, who'd come down the stairs, asked, grinning up at Grant. "Sir, maybe if you ask, she'll let us," he said in a confidential tone. Both Grant and Meredith laughed and the comment helped break the ice.

"Sorry—" Grant shook his head and demurred "—but you'd better do as your mother says. I've barely walked in the door. I don't want to get into trouble right away." What the hell had he let himself in for? he wondered, following Meredith through the gracious hall into an attractive living room looking out onto the garden.

Zack followed on their trail, apparently delighted to see a man in the house. "Want to see our train?" he asked hopefully. "Mom doesn't like it too much 'cause it takes up all the floor, but you might."

"Now, Zack, Mr. Gallagher came here for dinner, not to see your train set," Meredith said quickly, not sure how he would react.

"Actually," he responded, seeing Zack's face slump, "I'm rather keen on trains. Would you mind?" He turned to Meredith and felt his sleeve being tugged.

"If you're sure you don't mind," she said, biting her lip. "What would you like to drink?"

"A whisky would be great. On the rocks."

"I'll bring it up. Don't let them bore you."

"Don't worry, I can take care of myself."

"Oh, sure," she said, rolling her eyes and turning to her elder son. "Honey, don't let Zack monopolize Mr. Gallagher."

"Grant," he corrected.

"Excuse me?" Meredith looked up. He was halfway up the stairs and Zack was babbling away, thrilled to have a new admirer to look at his beloved train.

"I said they could call me Grant."

"Well, that's very nice of you. Did you hear that, boys? Uncle Grant says you can call him—" Suddenly she realized she was all tied up. "I mean, you can call him by his name."

"Okay."

After having inadvertently dropped the ice, Meredith finally poured the whisky then jumped when the doorbell rang again. God, her nerves were shot.

"Hi, Mom. Hi, Dad. Jeff, keep an eye on the oven, will you? Mel, you look sensational, I love that dress," she said brightly, kissing them all and nervously tweaking back her hair. "Uh, I didn't have time to tell you, but we have another guest tonight."

"Oh, who would that be?" John Rowland asked, smiling at his daughter from under thick silver brows set in a good-looking, tanned, fine-featured face.

"A client."

"Oh?" Clarice's brow shot up.

"Yes," Meredith mumbled nervously. "Grant Gallagher. You know, Rowena's heir. He's in town and was on his own. I felt it was only right to do something about him on Thanksgiving," she finished lamely.

"Quite right. No one should be alone at Thanksgiving," Clarice said, giving her husband an imperceptible nudge. "Is that his drink, honey?"

"Yes. I was just taking it up to him," she said, blushing furiously. "You see, the kids have already dragged him off to see the train. Dad, maybe you could go and make sure they don't bore him to death?"

"Sure, give me that drink and I'll take it up to him. I'll pour one for myself, too."

Seated on the floor in the cheerful bedroom, examining the workings of the electric train that the boys were enthusiastically detailing for him, Grant experienced a strange jumble of unforeseen sensations. He'd never been in this kind of setting with children before. Usually he avoided them on principle. Yet tonight he was enjoying himself. The kids were spontaneous and fun, and as the carriages began to circulate, signals change and tracks converge, he found himself absorbed. Only for a moment did he recall his own lonely experiences playing by himself with the expensive, sophisticated toys that his parents were only too eager to offer, and which had piled up in the closet as he got bored of having no one to share them with.

It was only when Mick looked up and said, "Hi, Grandpa," that he realized someone had entered the room.

Rising, Grant turned to see a handsome man in his late fifties holding two glasses.

"Brought you some backup," John Rowland said with a grin, handing him the glass of whisky. "They can be a little overwhelming when it comes to trains. I'm John Rowland, Meredith's father. Pleased to meet you."

Grant experienced a moment's hesitation. But he liked what he saw. The two men shook hands, then the kids demanded their attention and soon all four were absorbed by the workings of the train.

Downstairs in the kitchen, Meredith kept determinedly busy checking on the turkey between sips of white wine while Clarice added cherries to the dessert plates. Through the half-open door they could see Jeff and Melanie seated on the couch in the den, holding hands and murmuring to each other.

"Those two look as though they'll end up engaged by the end of the year," her mother remarked, smiling. "But tell me about Grant Gallagher, honey. What a surprise to find him here. But I'm sure I'll like him," she remarked, taking out the petits fours and placing them on a silver dish.

"Consider yourself lucky he's in a good mood. If you'd first met him as I did, sporting a foul temper on a cold, wet day in a Scottish castle, you might think differently." Meredith concentrated on the vegetables she was about to steam.

"Hmm. But the past few days you spent with him and Dallas in Miami weren't too bad, were they?" Clarice watched her daughter thoughtfully, noting her air of tense excitement, and wondered if Grant Gallagher had anything to do with the subtle change she'd noted in her daughter. Too wise to put the cart before the horse, she changed the subject. "How long will he be in Savannah? Is he just here for the Carstairs bash?"

"I believe so, although there's also some more paperwork to be signed. Frankly, I'm a bit nervous about the party. Given what's at stake for them, I'm sure the relatives are going to be all over him. It's sure to swell the man's already super-size ego," Meredith muttered darkly, slipping the vegetables into the bamboo steamer.

"Well, the party sure sounds like it's going to be very grand," Clarice continued, sitting down on one of the counter stools and reaching for her glass. "Apparently Joanna's invited *le tout* Savannah. I heard she's taken charge of the arrangements. She's having a marquee put up on the lawn."

"Well, all I can say is that Saturday should be an interesting evening. Mom, do you think I should put out more appetizers?"

"No. We'll be sitting down soon, anyway. Ah, that sounds like your father and Mr. Gallagher coming down now."

Meredith looked up as her father and Grant entered the kitchen. "Come in the living room and have another drink," she said quickly, the intimacy of them all assembled in the kitchen strangely troubling. It reminded her of all the times they'd stood here with Tom. Somehow it didn't feel right seeing someone else standing next to the doorjamb.

"Hi, I'm Clarice, Meredith's mother," Clarice said, shaking hands with Grant.

"How about another drink?" John Rowland offered as the children burst on the scene, hugging their grandmother and talking ten to the dozen.

"Sorry about the racket," Meredith apologized. "Why don't you come into the living room and meet my brother and his girlfriend?"

Dinner was a lively affair, interspersed with amusing comments from Zack and Mick. To her surprise, once she'd gotten over not seeing Tom seated at the foot of the table, carving the turkey, Meredith found herself at ease, enjoying the conversation. This was the first time she'd had anyone outside the family to dinner since Tom's death, she realized as she took the plates into the kitchen. For a moment she stopped and let out a deep sigh.

"You okay?"

"Oh!" she exclaimed, spinning around to see Grant standing behind her, holding two dirty dishes ready to go into the dishwasher. "You shouldn't be doing that," she murmured, dropping the plates onto the counter and snatching the dishes from him, wishing her heart would stop pounding quite so hard. He was standing so close, his face inches from hers. Meredith swallowed, turned quickly away and busied herself with getting dessert.

"Shall I stack these dishes in the machine?" he asked casually.

"No, no, don't worry about them. Beth will deal with them tomorrow morning," she responded, trying not to sound nervous. Where was her sangfroid? The self-control she'd always prided herself on? "Anyway, the boys should be helping, not you."

"They are. They're bringing in the rest."

"Great." Meredith threw him a quick, nervous smile.

"Is everything all right?" he asked in a low, intimate voice, sending another shudder racing through her.

"Fine. I'll be right out with dessert."

"Are you sure I can't be any help?" His eyes bored into hers and she swallowed.

"No. That's fine. In fact, do me a favor and go back and sit down and I'll be with you in a second."

"Okay." He retreated just as Jeff entered the kitchen carrying some more dirty plates and Meredith let out a thankful sigh of relief. What was it about this man that left her quivering? It was absurd. She leaned a moment against the counter and caught her breath before the boys came hurtling in and she dashed to the rescue of her Grandmother Ponsonby's best Wedgwood china.

"Do be careful," she exclaimed, grabbing the plates from Zack's precarious hold.

"I am. Mom, Grant's really neat. Do you think we could invite him over on Sunday? That way we could show him the new tents that Grandpa bought us."

"I don't know, I don't think so," Meredith responded, feeling an absurd panic at the thought of Grant in her home again.

"Aw, Mom, why not?"

"I'm sure he has a lot to do. Plus he's not staying in Savannah that long."

"But it's only Thursday and he won't be leaving until Monday. He said so," Zack added helpfully.

"Look, guys—" Meredith whirled round "—I have no idea what Grant's schedule is for the next couple days, okay? He's here on business, not to play with you."

"Okay, Mom, don't get mad." Mick looked up at her, surprised.

"I'm sorry." Meredith dragged her shaky fingers through her hair and concentrated on getting the chocolate mousse out of the refrigerator.

After generous seconds of pecan pie and delicious chocolate mousse they sat in the living room drinking coffee and sipping the brandy John Rowland had poured. Grant was a good conversationalist and her parents were obviously enjoying his company. But Meredith couldn't suppress the thread of anxiety that buzzed just below the surface. Frankly, she was glad when at last he set down his snifter and said he felt it was time to go.

"We'll drop you off on our way home," Clarice said with a pleasant smile. "The Ballastone's on our way."

"If you're sure it'll be no trouble," Grant said, glancing at Meredith.

"None at all. A pleasure," John replied. "Great dinner, Merry, my girl. We'll be seeing you at the Carstairs bash on Saturday. Boys, we'll go on that hiking trip sometime next week."

Grant waved to Meredith and the boys standing on the porch, trying to analyze the uncomfortable sensation that had assailed him all evening.

Logically he could not explain it.

Meredith's family had been charming, intelligent and amusing. Her children were well brought up and delightful. What was there not to like about such an enjoyable evening? Except that it was a far cry from what he'd had in mind. He'd wanted to have Meredith all to himself.

Instead, he'd been introduced to a different type of intimacy, the kind that existed in a loving family. The kind that he himself had never known—and that he doubted he could ever fit into. He sighed and made polite conversation with Clarice and John Rowland, realizing that the sooner he forgot about their daughter, the better. Her life and his were too far apart. There were no common denominators.

All that existed between them was a red-hot attraction that would probably burn out the moment it was consummated. Which, he reminded himself as the car pulled up in front of the Ballastone, was exactly what he'd had in mind when he'd suggested they take a short trip together.

After thanking the Rowlands for the lift and saying good-night, Grant climbed the steps of the inn and went to his suite. "Damn," he exclaimed, throwing off his blazer and moving toward the window, realizing bitterly that his own loneliness seemed harder to accept now that he'd experienced the intimacy of Meredith's family.

Sitting down abruptly in the deep armchair and staring at the empty grate, Grant berated himself as a sentimental fool. He knew perfectly well that the last thing he wanted was to give up a lifestyle of fancy-free women who didn't tie him down and the freedom of moving from one spot to the next whenever he chose.

He went over to the high chest of drawers and pulled out a Cuban cigar. Snipping the end off with his cigar cutter, he lit it and remembered Meredith moving about her kitchen, elegant and at ease in that domestic environment. Tonight he'd been privy to all the facets of her personality that he'd tried not to think about. For it was easier to view her as an intelligent, challenging, attractive female than as a mother, an elegant hostess, a daughter, surrounded by an enchanting family.

Taking a long drag on his cigar, Grant stared into the starlit night. He was out of his comfort zone and beginning to feel vulnerable and in a position he didn't know well.

Damn the lot of them for bringing him here, he thought as he stubbed out the cigar. Grant turned back into the room, his mouth set in a stern line. He would see the weekend through now that he'd given his word. But that was it. The sooner he got back to New York and away from Savannah, the better off he'd be.

13

Everything was perfect, Joanna decided gleefully, gliding among tables covered with pale beige organza, sterling and fine crystal, on the lawn under huge *ombrellones*. The decorator, who'd flown in from Atlanta to set up the party, was worth every penny. It looked elegant, yet not over the top. Charles had quibbled at the expense, but, as Joanna had pointed out, the estate—or rather Grant—was paying for it and either they did it right or not at all.

The other argument had been over whom to invite. After much discussion they'd decided to keep the gathering select. Ross Rollins was invited, of course, as were Meredith and her family, Senator Hathaway and his daughter Elm, Lady Graney, at present home on a short stay. Several other of the city's notables, friends of Rowena's and members of the city's oldest families, were to be gathered here today for the return of the prodigal grandson.

It had required careful planning.

Everyone knew of the Carstairs' inherent expectations. It was important, as she had pointed out to Charles, Craig and that ridiculous wife of his, to make sure people saw them welcome Grant. It was bad enough to know the entire city would be agog with speculation and would be monitoring their every reaction. They mustn't give anyone food for gossip. It would be better to show the world a gracious united front. Such public acceptance of the bastard grandchild would pull the rug nicely out from under any spiteful speculative feet, she reflected, as she corrected the position of an orchid centerpiece.

But the party was not the only thing Joanna was feeling pleased about. She had, she noted triumphantly, discovered Charles's Achilles' heel. Once she'd set her mind to it, it hadn't taken her long to discover why he'd been so ashen-faced when Meredith had revealed the terms of the will. For her cousin, she'd discovered gleefully, had a skeleton in his closet: the irreproachably respectable Charles had a mistress.

How stupid men could be, she reflected, glancing at her watch, wondering why the bartenders weren't in place yet. How could he imagine he would be able to keep this a secret, especially from Marcia, who held the purse strings. Charles was entirely too accustomed to the lifestyle Marcia's money afforded him; she wouldn't have thought he'd be willing to give that up for another woman. But then Joanna had seen the other woman. Charlotte Parnell was not only beautiful but elegant, intelligent and charming. She was not the kind of woman who'd stick around for too long unless Charles took some serious action—which, of course, he couldn't do without Rowena's money.

It hadn't taken long for Joanna to put together a strategy. She'd dismissed her first thought of blackmailing her cousin. It was too crude and could always be brought on board as a last resort. No. It was much better to let him believe that she sympathized with his plight. Was on his side. Better still, that she was disposed to help him solve his problem.

All she would expect in return—at least initially— was that he help her look good in front of Grant Gallagher. According to her investigations, this Gallagher had neither a wife nor a steady girlfriend. He was incredibly handsome, and even wealthier than Rowena. Surely such a man would appreciate the effort being made on his behalf and realize that she was the author of the extravaganza? From there on, it might not be too difficult to persuade him to part with a portion of his riches. Perhaps he was even on the lookout for a suitable wife. And who better than his long-lost cousin?

With a sigh Joanna glanced once more at her watch. In an hour or so they'd all be here and the show would begin. She'd been to the hairdresser early this morning and had brought her outfit out to Montalba, where she planned to stay the night. Today she'd made sure to arrange matters so that she, and not Marcy, would act as hostess. Patricia Lambert and Mary Chris were no threat. But they needed to be prepped, told how to act. She wouldn't bother to worry about Ward—he was too dumb to pose any problems. Craig and Sally would gush and do their usual dog-and-pony show, she supposed, dismissing them as unimportant. What mattered was for Grant to realize that she was the one member of the family who could smooth his entry into society, the only one who really had *his* interests at heart.

Taking one last look at her handiwork, Joanna patted herself on the back. It was perfect, all in excellent taste. A man of the world like Gallagher would recognize that immediately. The perfect arrangements—orchids, camellias and trailing ivy, the sparkling Bohemian chandeliers hanging in the marquee, the carefully studied seating arrangements, the fine Baccarat crystal and English china. It all spelled elegant taste and refinement and she would make darn sure he knew exactly who was responsible for the arrangements.

Waiters in period costume were beginning to appear from inside the house. She'd had a moment's doubt about the costumes but was relieved to see they didn't look kitsch, but rather gave the right tone of old Southern elegance to the affair. Clasping her hands Joanna let loose a sigh as she envisioned champagne and whisky flowing, delicate finger food circulating, guests moving about the torch-lit lawn, and the white-gloved waiters roaming, their silver trays glistening in the shimmer of the crystals overhead.

If only she could become the mistress of this place. Grant Gallagher would just have to see that of all the women present, *she* was the only one who could truly do justice to his millions.

Another ecstatic sigh escaped her as she toyed with her dreams, so real now that she practically thought of Grant as her future husband. Rowena's injustice was about to be put right. Of course, she would need Charles's help to ensure that her plans came to fruition, but it would be worth every penny she spent on him. Plus there would be the extra delight of seeing Marcia bought down to size.

Making sure her elaborate chignon was still in place, Joanna hurried into the house. She exchanged a few words with the head caterer on the way, quickly checked that the florist had brought the sophisticated interior floral arrangements that she'd personally created. After all, this was to be her masterpiece. If all went according to plan, in a few weeks she might be in a very different position than she was now. But she mustn't gloat, mustn't count her chickens. A lot depended on luck, a commodity that she knew only too well could often run scarce.

As she climbed the sweeping marble staircase, Joanna gazed down, satisfied at the hall. It had to work out. *Would* work out. Tonight would be an event to be commented upon in years to come. Grant would be touched at his reception and grateful to the one responsible for such a welcome.

A satisfied smile curled her lips. All she needed to do was don the glamorous dress she'd chosen with such care for the occasion and keep her fingers crossed.

Grant had spent all Friday and most of Saturday morning roaming the city, walking the streets, the squares, admiring Savannah's brick houses hidden behind mysterious gardens filled with sweet-scented jasmine, camellias and oleander. Everywhere he went he recalled those perfect symmetrical features from the photograph in Rowena's Granada Boulevard mansion, as though Isabel's shadow was determined to haunt him.

It annoyed him, this sudden undesired connection with a mother whom he'd never known, one whose only claim to the title was that of giving birth to him.

But he couldn't shake it off.

Everywhere he walked, he wondered. Had she trod these same paths or sat on the same bench? Had she breathed this same soft breeze, lingered in this very spot? He tried to ignore the sensation. But for some inexplicable reason it stuck. A woman walking in front of him would make him think of her, a gesture or the look of a passerby would remind him in some uncanny way of the picture in the silver-framed photograph. It was as though Isabel was imposing her presence, demanding something of him, telling him to look deeper, search further, find out more about himself and the past.

It was ridiculous, of course. There were no such things as ghosts or spirits. Yet he wondered all the same.

He'd called Meredith Friday morning to thank her for dinner. He had thought about asking her to have lunch with him. Then he'd reminded himself that he wanted distance rather than proximity, and had said merely that he'd see her at the party.

He groaned, wondering what was in store for him tonight. According to Meredith, it was going to be quite a do. The prospect filled him with dread. The last thing he wanted to do was spend an uncomfortable evening with a passel of unknown relatives—especially since they'd likely stab him in the back the first chance they got.

Dallas arrived at Montalba in a vintage white Ford Mustang that had belonged to Doug Thornton.

She hadn't wanted to come tonight, but after Grant's generous gesture—the money had come through in forty-eight hours and the mortgage had been paid off in full—the least she could do was give him moral support.

The valet held the door of the vehicle as she stepped out, her white Versace sheath slit up to the thigh, mold-ing her exquisite body. The place looked spectacular. Footmen stood at the bottom of the steps, illuminated fountains gushed and candles and shimmering crystal chandeliers lent a magical touch. Even Dallas, who was generally scornful of anything any of her cousins did, was impressed.

"I have to give it to Joanna," she said, meeting Meredith at the top of the steps. "If this was done to impress Grant, she's done a bang-up job."

"Yes. The place looks splendid," Meredith agreed, wondering uneasily what lay behind Joanna's lavish display. "But it must have cost a fortune."

"Nothing like getting Grant to pay for his own party," Dallas giggled, moving into the receiving line hosted only by Joanna and Charles. "Where do you think she's stuck the others?" Dallas whispered. "How come they're not receiving, too? Aunt Patricia must be pissed as hell."

"Shush, Dallas, someone will hear you," Meredith admonished.

"Oh, who cares," Dallas muttered, looking Meredith over critically. "You look really good, Mer. That pale blue suits you. Oh, look, there's Elm Graney. Boy, that husband of hers is some hunk, huh?"

"Johnny's not only handsome, he's also a great guy," Meredith said, waving to her friend, who was chatting with her parents, already sipping champagne.

"And a great horse breeder," Dallas murmured.

"I wonder where Grant is. Wasn't he supposed to be a part of the receiving line?" Meredith frowned. It wasn't like him not to call back. Yet she'd phoned the Ballastone earlier and left several messages to which he hadn't replied. All at once a shiver ran though her. Surely he couldn't have backed out at the last minute?

Then she saw his broad shoulders behind Joanna, chatting with a guest. Thank God, she breathed, even as her stomach knotted with tension at the prospect of seeing him again.

Yet another piece of Rowena's elaborate puzzle had settled into place.

Meredith, however, hadn't the slightest idea of just how complex a puzzle it was.

14

*"S*ome party," Senator Hathaway commented as he and Drew Chandler handed the car keys over to the valet. "Right up Rowena's alley. She would be happy to see such a good turnout, that's for sure."

"Yeah. She sure loved a party. Was this initiative a disinterested gesture on the part of Joanna and her co-horts, or was Rowena behind it?"

"Dunno," the senator replied, picking up a glass of champagne from a roving waiter.

"Certainly no expense has been spared," Drew murmured as they headed outside where the company was assembled, sipping champagne and chatting to the backdrop of smooth jazz played by a quartet. "I wonder why they're putting on such a show. Ross isn't talking."

"Of course not. He's bound by client-attorney confidentiality," the senator harrumphed.

"Hmm." Drew glanced around skeptically. "Better go and say hello," he murmured, smiling and exchanging a quick greeting with two women in sequined dresses. "I see Joanna and Charles over there." He pointed to a small group standing slightly apart. He wished he knew more. But that would come, he hoped. Soon.

Very soon if he had anything to do with it.

Senator Hathaway nodded and the two men made their way across the grass under the moonlit sky.

The evening was proving strangely anticlimactic, Grant decided as he sipped his champagne, pretending to listen to something Joanna was saying. He'd expected fireworks, but instead he was being killed with kindness, he reflected cynically. Joanna—whose heavy, cloying perfume was fast giving him a headache—hadn't let him out of her sight. A shimmering figure in silvery silk and chiffon, diamonds glinting in her ears under her coiffed strawberry-blond hair, she was undeniably an attractive woman. In her early forties, he guessed, although she'd obviously already had one too many facelifts. It was quite evident she considered herself queen bee of the whole affair, he reflected, amused, remembering how she'd introduced him to the other cousins. Charles, a gray-haired man in his mid-fifties, was formal and discreet. His wife, Marcia, looked upper-class East Coast. Unlike Joanna, who was swathed in a long, tightly wrapped designer bombshell, Marcia was elegantly clad in fuchsia silk. She looked about fifty-something. No face-lift, he noted.

Mary Chris had struck him as a pious spinsterly battle-ax, but she'd been unfailingly polite. Craig and Sally Parnell, a sophisticated, chatty couple whom he wrote off as social butterflies, had accosted him as an old friend, obviously determined to be one up on the others for having met him once before. He'd met Ward last. A tall, thin man in his late forties, he stood shyly in a corner wearing a shabby tux that had seen better days. Joanna had introduced him briefly, barely giving him time to shake the man's hand. He'd been glad to see that when Dallas arrived, she'd gone straight up to Ward and given him a hug. He suspected the rest of the family treated their cousin like the village idiot.

As Joanna waved to someone in the distance, insistently beckoning them over, presumably to meet him, Grant considered Montalba. The place was undeniably lovely. As he'd driven the rented Jaguar up the long alley leading to the sprawling antebellum mansion lit with torches and floodlights, he was moved by how magical it all looked. That feeling had only been reinforced as Joanna dragged him on a guided tour of the place, then out into the meticulously maintained garden which stretched toward the river.

"Senator, how wonderful to see you," Joanna trilled as an elderly gentleman approached. "Come over here and meet our new cousin," she said, a fixed smile on her perfectly made-up face. "Grant, do meet Senator Hathaway. He's an old friend of Aunt Rowena's."

Grant turned, a ready smile on his face. "How do you do?"

"This is our cousin, Grant Gallagher, the *famous* businessman," Joanna purred, slipping her arm through Grant's in a possessive manner. "Imagine that!" He tried not to wince; her voice was beginning to grate on his nerves. Now, as he shook hands with the senator, he wondered if he could use him as an excuse to shed Joanna.

"So tell me, what do you think of this place?"

"Amazing. Exactly how one imagines a Southern plantation should be," he murmured. The senator

was very much what he imagined a Southern senator to be like on his home turf, exuding elegance and
natural power. Quite a collection of individuals, he
reflected. It seemed the Carstairs had gone out of
their way to invite Savannah's notables to meet him
en masse.

And suddenly he wondered why. He knew Rowena
had insisted on a party. But surely they could have
organized something more discreet? As he was pon-
dering this conundrum, Meredith sidled up to him.
Thank God she was here.

"So, how's it going?" she asked. She looked lovely
tonight, her hair pulled up on the side with a 1930s diamond hair clip. All at once he forgot his earlier plan
to avoid her. Meredith, he reminded himself as he studied her well-cut pale blue silk sheath, was just too
much woman to pass up. She seemed completely unaware of how beautiful she was. After Joanna's endless
simpering and the other, more subtle offers that several
women had already cast his way, Meredith seemed
like a breath of fresh air.

"Are you holding up okay?" she whispered, taking
a quick sip of champagne and eyeing him closely. He
seemed surprisingly at ease for somebody who must
know that he was under close scrutiny from everybody
present. The place was buzzing with curiosity about
him, his background and, of course, the identity of his
natural father.

"I'm fine. How about you?" He looked her over approvingly. "Nice dress. You look lovely tonight."

Meredith suppressed the immediate rush of heat
his words provoked. They made her recall the moment
in Scotland when his lips had come down on hers, and
she vowed not to think about that again.

"Thanks," she replied coolly. "I think dinner is about to be served. I should warn you, though."

"What do you mean?"

"You'll be seated to Joanna's right," she murmured, trying to suppress her grin.

"Good Lord," he muttered. "Can't we rearrange the seating?"

"Too late," she whispered, seeing Joanna bearing down on them. "Good luck." She moved away and Joanna moved in.

And as Meredith had accurately predicted, he was seated to Joanna's right at a round, beautifully laid table in the center of the marquee, surrounded by other smaller tables. As he held her chair for her, Marcia took the seat to his left. He surveyed his other table companions. Ross Rollins was on Joanna's left, he noted with relief, glad he was not stranded alone among the Carstairs clan. Rounding out the table were Dallas, who'd winked at him as she sat down, Charles, who was enduring some good-hearted ribbing from Dallas, and then Ward, who sat squeezed between Sally and Craig. They were nine in all, an odd number, but the relations were all at one table. The ones that mattered, anyhow. He'd been introduced to several distant cousins by Charles and Joanna earlier in the evening, but since they were of no direct interest to him he'd paid scant attention.

Now, with them all seated about the table he could observe them at ease. Although Charles and Craig were brothers, they looked nothing alike. Neither did Joanna resemble any of her cousins. In fact, the two that most resembled each other were he and Dallas, as Sally innocently pointed out.

"I think that is so cute," she said, folding her hands

in her lap with a girlish giggle. "You two really do look
like brother and sister. Who would have imagined such
a thing? Poor Isabel. She must have had a rough time."

"I suppose there's a likeness," Marcia murmured,
sending Sally a reproving look meant to put her in her
place, "but, Grant, tell us about your business interests.
I hear they're quite extensive."

"I never talk about my projects, I'm afraid. Super-
stition, I suppose. I don't want to jinx them." He
laughed easily, as did the others.

"He even sounds like Rowena," Sally continued,
undeterred by Marcy's disapproval. "That's the sort of
thing she would have said."

"Yeah, she was always doing things for luck. She
even made them change the street number from thir-
teen to fourteen. Caused the post office and the neighbors one hell of a problem."

"That's right," Ross agreed as the chilled vichys-
soise was served, placed simultaneously before each
guest by the liveried waiters. "It fell on me to handle
their complaints. Two wanted to sue her. Mercifully, I
was able to come to an agreement with their council."

"Sounds like an interesting woman," Grant replied,
determined now that he had them all in one spot to
gather as much information as he could. "What do you
think her idea was by leaving me her fortune?" He let
his gaze travel round the table, observing how each of
them received the question.

"Difficult to tell," Charles said, clearing his throat.
They obviously hadn't expected the direct approach.
Grant chuckled inwardly. They'd set the stage to take
control of him and the situation. By asking uncomfortable questions he was reversing the roles.

"Perhaps she wanted to prove something. Had

something she wanted us to find out," Grant mused, dipping his spoon into the creamy soup. "Something none of you knew about."

"Well, we certainly didn't know about you," Joanna said, her mask dropping for a split second.

"No. I can see my existence must have come as something of a shock," he murmured, withholding a smile.

"No kidding," Ward said cheerfully, unaware of the sudden tension surrounding him. "Everyone was very upset. In fact, Joanna wanted us to—"

"That's enough, Ward, eat your soup. Grant isn't interested in boring details," Joanna interrupted. "Of course, we were very surprised," she continued smoothly.

"After all," Charles added, coming to her rescue, "in all truthfulness, it was a bit unnerving to be told we had a cousin whom none of us had ever heard of."

"Who stood to inherit Grandma's fortune," Dallas said sweetly before popping a piece of bread into her mouth and chewing it smugly. "You guys must've shit in your pants."

There was an awkward silence. Then Craig raised his glass. "I say we drink a toast. To our new cousin, Grant. However we came to all meet, it's good we have."

"Hear, hear." Ross raised his glass and the others followed suit. "And to Rowena," he added.

There was a less-enthusiastic murmur before they drank, giving Grant the impression that none of them had liked their unconventional matriarch. They had tolerated her, put up with her eccentricities, all in the expectation of the day she died. And he was the result. It can't have been easy.

What, he wondered, was Charles's agenda? The man seemed well-off, but he suspected the funds were Marcia's. There was something about the patronizing way she smiled at him that smacked of control. Craig and Sally were easy enough to deduce. They were highfliers who needed all they could lay their hands on to keep up their expensive lifestyle. And Joanna, what about her motives? He'd heard she'd been married and divorced several times. Was she just greedy or did she really need the funds? The only one who didn't appear to have an ax to grind was Ward, who happily ate his soup. This suspicion was confirmed seconds later.

"Say, Grant, Rowena left you the fishing lodge in Jackson Hole. I was thinking maybe we could go up there and take a look at it if you'd like. I know the place real well. You do like fly-fishing, don't you?" he asked, an anxious crease forming on his brow.

"I do."

"Good. Then let's make a plan."

"I look forward to it."

"Really, Ward, stop bothering Grant with idiotic notions," Joanna cut in impatiently.

"On the contrary," Grant reassured him, ignoring the interruption, "it would be a nice break."

Ward turned to the rest of them. "See? I told you he'd be nice and that he'd like fishing. Perhaps we could go there next week."

"Actually, I have to be in New York next week, but we can arrange a visit."

"Ward's a great fisherman," Dallas chipped in, patting her cousin's hand and smiling at him. "He's won trophies, haven't you, Ward?" Ward flushed and murmured incoherently. "You must show them to Grant.

Maybe I'll come along to Jackson Hole with you guys. I like to fish."

"Would you?" Ward looked thrilled. "You're so nice, Dallas. I always liked you, better than Charles or Joanna, or Sally or—"

"Yes, Ward, I know," she murmured, squeezing his hand again.

"You never bitch at me."

"Really, Ward," Joanna tittered, "what an extraordinary thing to say. Grant will think we're mean to you."

"Well, you *are* mean to him," Dallas replied, tossing her blond mane and sending Joanna a challenging glare. "You never miss a chance to put him down. Nor does Charles, except he does it in that supercilious, condescending way he has, trying to make everyone think he's brighter than the rest of us, while you're just plain mean to everyone. Guess you were born that way and can't help it," she added smugly, sending Grant a mischievous look from under her long lashes.

"Well, really!" Joanna exclaimed, her face suffused with suppressed anger.

"Your mother should've taught you better manners," Ross drawled, taking a sip of white wine. "You've run wild, Dallas. Time someone took you in hand."

"My mother didn't have time to teach me manners," she retorted, "she was too busy shopping and having her hair done. Then she took the quick way out. I'm surprised you and Mother didn't get along better," she added, addressing Joanna. "After all, you like all the same things, primping yourselves, spending lots of money on clothes and jewelry."

"I think the fishing trip's a good idea," Grant intervened, feeling it was time he put an end to Dallas's diatribe before the atmosphere at the table deteriorated. Charles looked outraged, Marcia sat stiffly disapproving at his side, Joanna was nearly purple and Craig and Sally were shifting uncomfortably, trying to pretend that nothing was going on. "We'll talk about it later on, you, Ward and I," Grant said firmly, sending his sister a look that said "enough."

To everyone's surprise, Dallas nodded and went quiet.

The lengthy dinner progressed without further disruption, Grant guiding the conversation into safer avenues, ably assisted by Marcy, Charles and Ross. As the waiters served steaming cups of after-dinner coffee, Joanna sent Grant a bright smile. "Grant, would you like to visit the summerhouse? It's one of Montalba's most notable features."

"What's so great about it?" Dallas interjected.

"Well, you know," Joanna urged as though talking to a small child, "it rotates. The summerhouse was brought from England in the late nineteenth century," she added for Grant's benefit. "It's considered one of the most interesting specimens in the country. Quite unique, in fact. I'd be thrilled to show it to you."

"No, let me," Dallas insisted, practically leaping up from her chair. She moved quickly to Grant's side. "Anything to escape this lot," she murmured quietly. Then, in a louder voice, she called, "Joanna, do tell them to send over a bottle of champagne, won't you?" Joanna sent a look of loathing as Dallas blithely took Grant's arm. "Ward, you can come with us, too, if you like."

"I love the summerhouse," Ward said cheerfully, linking his arm with Dallas's spare one. "You'll like it, too. Joanna's right," he said to Grant, who couldn't help smiling at the man's open manner.

"We'll see you back here before the dancing begins," Charles commented in a genial tone.

"Let's get the hell out of here," Dallas whispered as they slipped through the wide marquee curtains. She caught Meredith's eye at a nearby table and gestured for her to join them. Meredith excused herself from her dinner companions, then walked gracefully to their side.

"I hate these people. Joanna's the biggest pain in the ass, and as for Charles and the rest of them, they're all a bunch of hypocrites."

"I didn't think they were putting up too bad a show," Grant murmured. "It can't have been easy learning they weren't going to inherit."

"It wasn't," Ward confirmed blithely. "I've never seen Joanna look so upset in her life. Boy, was she angry. She wanted us all to sue you, but Ross told her she'd be wasting her money."

"And did the others want to sue me?" he asked casually.

"Oh, yes. Well, not Craig and Sally, I don't think, but then they weren't there for the meeting, so I don't know," Ward answered as the summerhouse came in sight. "Maybe they would, too. Shall we ask them?" He stopped, frowned and turned to the others with a questioning gaze.

"No, Ward. It doesn't matter," Dallas said, taking his arm once more. "Look, there's the summerhouse. Remember when Grandma used to put us inside and spin it?"

"I remember. You were sick all over me once. Who's going to spin it this time?"

"You could. Grant, you and Mer can go in it and Ward and I will spin you," she said, hastily concocting a plan.

"All right." Ward nodded enthusiastically. He was good at anything involving physical effort.

Grant looked over the pretty summerhouse, so typical of nineteenth-century English gardens. Lit up with tiny lanterns, it was a small structure of painted white wood built close to the river. Tiny windows gave it a dollhouse appearance and he could see why children would find it enchanting.

"Excuse me, sir," a voice behind them called, and one of the liveried waiters appeared carrying a tray with an ice bucket, champagne and four flutes. "They said to bring this out here. Shall I put it up into the summerhouse?"

"Yes, go ahead," Dallas said, laughing. "I wonder why Joanna wanted you to see the summerhouse. To make you feel bad about your childhood?"

"You really don't like her one little bit, do you?" Grant said as the waiter entered the illuminated structure and set up the champagne.

"And neither would you if you knew her as I do. The woman's a first-class bitch."

"She's not that bad," Meredith countered.

"'Fraid she is," Ward replied, nodding glumly. "Always been that way. Mother said that's why her husbands didn't stick around. She was too mean to them," he confided.

"It's all set up," the waiter said, stooping as he exited the low wooden door. "Is there anything else I can get you?"

"No, that's fine, thanks." Grant smiled. "Dallas, you lead the way."

"No. You guys go inside." She pushed Meredith toward the summerhouse, which stood slightly elevated from the ground on the apparatus that allowed it to spin.

"Come on, Dallas, join us," Meredith insisted, not wanting to find herself alone in Grant's company once more.

"Just go," Dallas said, shoving her inside. With a sigh, Meredith entered.

"It's quite ingenious," Grant remarked.

"It's certainly quaint," Meredith said, perching on the edge of one of the faded chintz armchairs while Grant poured the champagne. Ward stood in the doorway, a happy grin on his freckled face.

"Shall I spin you around?" he asked like a hopeful child waiting for a treat.

"Not yet or we'll spill our drinks," Grant exclaimed, reaching for the champagne. "I'll say one thing for Joanna, whatever you all may think of her, she does know how to throw a good party."

"No one can deny that," Meredith agreed, a smile hovering round her lips as she watched Grant, a sigh escaping her. He looked as at ease here as he did back in his castle in Scotland. What was it about the man that left her breathless? she wondered, recalling images of his mouth lingering on hers.

Pulling herself together, Meredith sat straighter. It must be the champagne putting thoughts like that into her head, she reasoned, accepting the flute with a smile.

"Cheers." Grant raised his glass and Ward and Dallas followed suit.

"Please, let me spin you," Ward begged, his eyes bright and excited as he laid the glass on a small mahogany table and jumped up. "I'll close the door. It doesn't go fast. Don't worry."

"Okay." Grant caught Dallas's eye.

She nodded discreetly. "I'll give you a hand, Ward."

"Okay."

"Spin away," Grant murmured as the door closed. He hesitated, looked down at Meredith, then sat next to her. Ward hurried out, closing the door behind him.

"Ready?" he called.

"Yes," they responded.

Meredith shook her head. "Poor Ward, he's a sweetie. If only his mother would get off his back, maybe he'd have half a chance. But between her and Mary Chris..." She rolled her eyes as slowly the summerhouse began to rotate.

Outside under the moonlight, Ward held on to the side of the structure, tongue between his teeth, and concentrated on heaving his weight against the wooden wall. Finally, the house began to move and he pushed harder, thrilled at his achievement.

Dallas made a token effort to assist, grimacing down at the heels of her Manolos slowly sinking into the grass. "Okay, that's enough," she instructed, falling back once the summerhouse was rotating nicely.

"Why? It's fun." Ward gave the structure another heave.

"I know, but we have to go. I have something to show you." Dallas slipped a persuasive arm through Ward's.

Ward shrugged forlornly and did as he was told.

"Now, listen, Ward," Dallas whispered in a conspiratorial tone. "I saw a heron down on the river. If you like, we could look for its nest."

"But it's dark," Ward pointed out.

"I know." Dallas rolled her eyes, irritated and determined to find an excuse to leave Meredith and Grant alone. "But we can still think about where it might be."

"I guess." Ward seemed doubtful. But by this time they were nearing the marquee and were already distracted by the noise and bustle of the party. He was about to mention to Dallas that they'd left Meredith and Grant by themselves and that wasn't nice, when Joanna accosted them.

"Have you seen Grant?" she asked, peering over his shoulder. "I thought they were with you at the summerhouse."

"They are."

"What do you mean?" Joanna inquired imperiously, eyes narrowing.

"They're just coming," Dallas interrupted quickly, digging Ward in the ribs. "They'll be right back. Joanna, this is a great party," she said generously, determined to sidetrack her cousin. "You really have done a terrific job." She smiled encouragingly.

Joanna blinked. "Coming from you, that's quite something," she replied, surprised. "If you see Grant, tell him I'm looking for him." She turned to talk to an elegant couple getting ready to depart.

Dallas let out a long breath. The last thing Grant and Meredith needed was Joanna knowing they were by themselves in the summerhouse. A mischievous gleam entered her eye. She'd be willing to bet there was more to those two than they cared to make out.

Straightening her attractive shoulders, Dallas moved across the room and set about charming some of the older guests with vivacious small talk. Perhaps she had hidden talents after all, she reflected, surprising herself. Perhaps life wasn't just about photo shoots and raising horses. Perhaps having some friends—like Elm and the kind of people Meredith knew—was kind of nice after all.

"It's stopping," Meredith remarked as the summer-house slowed.

"I think they've given up on us," Grant remarked as he watched Meredith who looked so attractive and relaxed, curled up in the old chintz armchair. He leaned across and took her hand in his. "You look lovely." He drew her toward him.

It was impossible to resist, impossible to fob him off with excuses, when all she'd been thinking about for the better part of the evening was the taste of him, the feel of his arms around her. Now, as she gazed into his eyes, Meredith yearned for more. It was silly to deny it. She wanted to make love with this man, even though by taking such a step she would digress from all she'd held sacred for so long.

Her head spun and her body shifted gears, and all she could think of was the warmth of him, the strength of him, the deep-rooted need she felt to be held in this man's arms. As if in a slow-motion movie, she waited, anticipating his mouth warm and tantalizing on hers. And when their lips touched she gave way, kissing him back, unleashing myriad sensations she'd believed dead forever.

"We have to spend time together," he whispered into her hair, drawing it back from her face and caressing her cheek. "There's no use either of us pretending we don't want the other. It would be denying the obvious," he whispered, a smile curving his mouth.

Meredith drew away, trying to compose herself. It

was true. The attraction was impossible to just shove under the carpet.

"What if they find out?" she said finally. How could she be contemplating leaving on a trip with a client, abandoning her children for the sake of indulging in sex? For like it or not, that was what this was all about. She felt her cheeks burn.

"No one will find out. And if they do, we've the perfect alibi—sorting out Rowena's estate. You might even tell them you're in the process of persuading me to part with some of my newly acquired millions. That should keep the likes of Joanna quiet," he added, a wicked grin spreading over his face.

But she didn't resist when Grant pulled her firmly into his arms. Meredith quivered with anticipation. When the kiss came, when his lips feathered hers and his hands roamed over her rib cage, she sighed and gave herself up to the delicious sensations. Her pulse beat faster and a rush of molten heat soared from her head to down between her thighs. Unconsciously she arched, a tiny moan escaping her when his fingers fondled her breast through the delicate fabric. Her hand snaked around his neck and she responded fully to his demands, her mind hazy as his fingers caressed her inner thigh.

"Perhaps this isn't exactly the place to take this further," he murmured, raising his head.

"No, you're right," Meredith muttered hazily, sitting up. She was having a hard time staying lucid. The languid lazy trance that he'd cast over her was hard to dispel.

"We'll take our leave and get the hell out of here," Grant said, taking charge. As he did so, he stood her up and helped straighten her dress. "There," he said, studying her critically.

"Do I look okay?" Meredith searched around in vain for a mirror.

"Just a little mussed," Grant replied, tongue in cheek, seeing her face flush.

"Oh, Lord." She rummaged in her evening purse for her lipstick. "Is that better?" she queried, casting him a dark look and straightening her hair.

"Perfect. No one would dream what you've been up to," he said, a mischievous gleam hovering.

"Grant, you know this is ridiculous," she began, trying to remember all the justifiable reasons that made her present behavior deplorable.

Grant rolled his eyes. "Meredith, don't start, I beg you. We'll discuss it in the car."

She sighed. There was no resisting the tidal wave in which she was swept. Perhaps the best thing was to make a suitable arrangement, leave with Grant for a few days and get her yen for him out of her system.

"We'd better go and say goodbye," she said, stepping back onto the grass.

"I suggest we arrive back in the marquee separately. You go ahead and I'll take a couple minutes." He gave her a friendly nudge and dropped a kiss on the back of her neck.

Taking a deep breath, Meredith composed herself. As she reentered the house, she caught sight of Elm crossing the room. In a few quick steps, she reached her.

"I need to talk to you," she said in a rushed whisper, "and not in the ladies'."

"Okay." Elm glanced at the hall. "How about one of the bedrooms?"

"Yes. Rowena's upstairs sitting room. There shouldn't be anyone there."

Together the two women climbed the stairs and headed down the corridor to Rowena's apartments. Meredith slipped open the door and switched on the lamps. "At least here we can be private," she said, sinking onto the daybed with a sigh. "Elm, my life is a mess."

"Why?" Elm perched on a gilded tapestry stool opposite and looked at her friend inquiringly. "What's the matter, Mer?"

"It's Grant."

"What about him? Isn't he cooperating? Things seem to be pretty well on track. After all, if he bothered to come here I should think it wouldn't be too hard to get him to come to a suitable agreement with the family. Particularly after his generosity to Dallas."

"Yeah, I know. It's not that." Meredith let out an irritated huff and looked her friend in the eye. "Elm, I have a yen for the guy. I don't know how it happened, or why I feel this, but I have this—this…" She brought her hand down on the arm of the chair, unable to define her feelings. "This need, that's the only way I can describe it."

"You mean you would seriously like to go to bed with him?" Elm queried with a ghost of a smile. "Mer, that's the best news I've heard in a while."

"You can't be serious," she burst out. "It's all wrong. He's my client," she wailed. "It's totally, completely unethical."

"Now, don't make a drama out of it," Elm soothed, sweeping her long blond hair from her face and leaning forward to squeeze Meredith's agitated knee. "This is not the end of the world."

"Yes, it is," Meredith sniffed.

"But you're going to do it, anyway," Elm murmured

knowingly. "Meredith, stop denying yourself. Give yourself a break."

"But how can I feel something like this for a man I don't even like?" she exclaimed, jumping up and pacing the room. "It makes no sense whatsoever." She shook her head fiercely.

"Not everything needs to make perfect sense in life. Sometimes things just happen." Elm shrugged, raised her palms and smiled. "That's what makes life so wonderful, so unexpected."

"Maybe that's so for you," Meredith said witheringly. "I like order in my court. All this spontaneous stuff just isn't for me." She smoothed her dress and fidgeted nervously. "Elm, what am I going to do?"

"What does he suggest?"

"That we go away for a few days together somewhere. Can you imagine? It's totally unfeasible."

"Why?"

"Because it just is. I'm not that kind of person. I'm a mother, a lawyer. I don't disappear with strange men to get laid, for Christ's sake."

"Oh, Mer, are you serious? Grant is not just any man. Frankly, I liked him a lot. So did Johnny. And he has excellent judgment."

"You think so?" A sliver of doubt made her hesitate. Maybe Elm was right. Maybe she should just face the situation and deal with it head-on.

"I not only think so, I insist." Elm rose. "Come on or we'll be missed downstairs. We don't want Joanna looking for us. Take a leap, Mer. Don't be afraid. I know all the reasons that are holding you back. But remember," she said softly, "Tom would hate it if he saw you living the way you are now. You need to move on, however painful it may seem."

"I don't consider having gratuitous sex with a client moving on," she responded pithily.

Elm rolled her eyes and opened the door. "Just promise to give a full detailed report the minute you return, okay?"

Casting her a dark look, Meredith accompanied her friend down the stairs. As she reached the bottom step, she caught sight of Grant taking leave of Joanna and Charles. "Oh, Lordy," she muttered as he raised his eyes.

There was nothing she could do but to move across the room and say farewell.

"I can give you a lift back to town," Grant said casually for Joanna's benefit.

"Are you sure it wouldn't be too much trouble?" she answered sweetly.

"Not at all." He sounded bored enough to deceive even the sharpest sleuth.

Minutes later, they were descending the front steps and the Jaguar drew up.

As she got in the car, Meredith glanced up at the top of the steps. An uneasy sensation gripped her at the sight of Joanna watching their departure, a speculative look on her face.

"So when are you leaving?" She glanced at him sideways. Better get it over with if she was going to go for it.

"As soon as you agree to come with me." His hand reached out, touched her thigh, and she swallowed. "Sooner rather than later—we're going to make love," he said matter-of-factly, his hand stroking her leg now, sending shivers through her. "After all, we're both unattached, mature adults."

"I'm not unattached," she replied. It was probably

crazy, but she still thought of herself as married to Tom. Now Grant's words brought home the truth: she was unattached. Available.

"I didn't mean it quite like that. I realize you must have suffered a tremendous loss," he said, his voice serious, "but the fact still remains."

"I guess," she muttered as the car took off down the driveway. Meredith admitted that his practical approach was hard to resist. "Where were you thinking of going?" she asked. "I don't think we can afford to be too public."

"I have a house in Cancún. I believe it's very private."

"You believe?"

"I've never actually been there, just seen pictures. But it looks okay. There's a couple who takes care of everything."

"You mean you bought a house without actually seeing it?" Her brows shot up.

"Actually, it was thrown in as part of a deal. It seemed a good piece of prime real estate, so I accepted."

"I see." It all seemed painfully dry and unromantic. Not that she was seeking romance, Meredith assured herself, far from it. This was about dealing with needs that lately had become only too apparent. For an instant Tom flashed before her, but she banished the image. This had nothing to with Tom or what they'd experienced over the years. This was nothing but a passing fling that would in no way interfere with her life, she justified.

"Well?" Grant slipped his hand over hers and a shudder zipped up her arm, reminding her of just how deeply attracted to this man she was.

"I guess I could swing it," she said at last, hardly believing she was uttering the words. It went against all her principles, professional and private, but she knew she was going, regardless.

"Fine. We can meet in Miami. Better not fly out of here together."

"No, better not," she agreed with a shudder, imagining the embarrassment of meeting the senator or Judge Coburn at the airport. It was bad enough wondering what she would tell her mother. And Tracy— God, she'd have to tell her the truth in case there was an emergency. For a moment she thought of her children and closed her eyes. What kind of mother went running off with a lover, leaving her kids to their own devices? Not that that was quite the case, since she knew her parents would take the boys gladly.

"And now that you've made up your mind, stop thinking about it," he ordered, squeezing her thigh. "What's the earliest you can leave?" he asked as they drew up in front of her home.

"The day after tomorrow, I guess."

"Fine." He smiled at her, that rare smile that illuminated his face and lit up his eyes. "We'll meet in Miami on Thursday, then, and fly down to Cancún for the weekend. I'll make all the flight arrangements."

"Okay." She nodded, swallowing, getting used to the idea that she'd acquiesced.

"Then, good night, my dear." He leaned over, caressed her cheek gently. The tender gesture left her breathless and ill at ease. Somehow the sullen, difficult Grant was almost easier to deal with.

"Good night. No need to get out," she said hastily as he started to come and open her door. "I'll be fine."

Grant watched as she walked quickly up the path

and unlocked her front door. Was he crazy pursuing this woman? Perhaps, he reflected with a shrug. But he had her under his skin. The only way to make sure the fire burned out was by consuming it.

Fast.

15

It was one thing to decide to take a daring and unprecedented step, but quite another to actually implement her plan.

"I can't believe I'm really doing this," she said to Elm as they had lunch the next day.

"I'm glad you are," Elm responded quietly. "It's time you had a life, Mer. You can't go on living only for your kids and work."

"Look, this is nothing more than a fling, okay? Embarrassing, I know, but there it is."

"I don't see what's embarrassing about it. After all, that's what I had with Johnny before we realized things were more serious between us," she said fondly, a smile on her lips as she thought of her husband and their baby son.

"That's you, Elm, not me. I'm different. I'm practical. I do things because they make sense, not out of some metaphysical inspiration. The truth is," she said brutally, piercing the mozzarella of her caprese salad with her fork, "I'm going off to get laid. Sounds terrible, but that's the reality. And I'm not proud of it."

"Stop beating up on yourself."

"Elm, did you just hear what you said? I'm not looking for a long-term relationship. In fact, I thoroughly disapprove of everything about Grant Gallagher, his lifestyle, his values. He's the last man on earth I should be going anywhere with." She took a sip of white wine and let out a sigh. "I'm going because for some inexplicable reason I have this guy under my skin, and the only way I'm going to get him out from under there is by letting this thing burn itself out."

"Fair enough." Elm nodded, keeping her thoughts to herself. "But if you're going, at least enjoy it. I forbid you to spend the whole weekend berating yourself. You're a grown woman, Mer, unattached and attracted to a man who's attracted to you. Two consenting adults."

"Ouch," she grimaced. "That's basically what he said."

"Well, face it, he's right. Just go and enjoy it, for Christ's sake. Stop worrying. I'll take care of the kids, as will your mom and dad and at least ten other people I can think of. Mick promised to babysit for me, by the way."

"He's so proud of little George," Meredith said, momentarily forgetting her plight as she thought of her godson, presently at the senator's house under the vigilant gaze of the nanny Elm had brought with her from Ireland.

"How are you for clothes?" Elm asked as the waitress removed their plates and handed them the dessert menu.

"Oh, God, I don't know. The last time I wore a bikini

was on that trip to the Bahamas Tom and I took three years ago." Her expression fell.

"Don't." Elm pressed her hand on Meredith's. "No looking back. I say we go to the mall and buy you some new outfits for the trip—including a new bikini. Though hopefully you'll be undressed most of the time."

"Elm!" Meredith squeaked, then laughed and shook her head. "When would I ever have believed I'd be hearing you utter those words?"

After sharing a disgustingly fattening piece of chocolate cheesecake, they headed for the mall. Despite her reluctance, Meredith experienced a wave of excitement. She hadn't prepared for a trip or bought new clothes in ages. Maybe, just maybe, she was right to go after all.

Two days in New York had done much to exacerbate Grant's anticipation. His deal was shaping up nicely. He already had several prospective buyers lining up for the land, and pending a few final details he was pretty sure the deal was in the bag. Needless to say, the present owners, the Carringtons, weren't too happy with his plans, but business was business.

Now, glancing at Meredith sitting tensely across from him in the wide white leather seat of the nifty G6 he'd chartered to take them to Cancún, he cursed himself. All during the meetings her face had popped up. She represented integrity. For Meredith matters were black or white. The gray areas that in the past he'd glossed over seemed incredibly uncomfortable all of a sudden. Why had he let her get under his skin? he wondered. It was damned inconvenient. Why should he suddenly care that the Carringtons—particularly the elder—were unhappy?

Somehow he got the impression that if she knew about the deal, Meredith wouldn't be thrilled with his prospective strategy. In fact, he had little doubt that any attraction they felt for each other would be eradicated immediately. There would be little use explaining to her that his route would actually *enhance* the local job market. She'd just hold him accountable for destroying what was already there.

A smile curved his lips. Right now she looked tired. But the dark circles under her eyes just made her more vulnerable and appealing, exposed some of the fragility masked by an outer strength that she didn't recognize in herself but that he found intriguing. He wondered now about her marriage. It was safe to say the couple had been happy. You just had to step into her house and see her kids and her family to realize that.

Reminding himself that he was here to have fun, not to get emotionally involved, Grant got up and stretched.

"We should land soon," he commented, watching as she shifted her long, slim legs. He liked the dress she was wearing, the color—soft muted pink—suited her. He wondered if he should open a bottle of champagne to break the ice, then decided it was too clichéd.

"Kids doing okay?" he asked, regretting the question the minute he'd phrased it. What was the use of reminding her of what she'd left behind?

"Fine. Zack's staying with Elm this weekend."

"Ah. Nice people, Elm and Johnny."

"They are. Elm's my best friend."

"She seems an exceptionally pleasant woman," he said truthfully, for he'd enjoyed the short chat he'd had with Elm Graney.

"She is. I miss her now that she's living in Ireland."

"That must have been quite a romance," he said idly.

"It was—is. Elm had a rough time before Johnny came into her life. Her first husband, Harlan MacBride, was a worthless bastard." Her eyes gleamed with righteous anger.

"You obviously didn't like him one little bit."

"I don't like cheats. And Harlan was all of that and more."

"I see. Elm didn't have your luck."

Meredith's eyes flew to his. "What do you mean?" she queried, her defenses immediately on alert.

"Merely that you seem to have had an exceptionally happy marriage," he murmured carelessly. "A rarity these days. You were lucky, that's all. No need to poker up as though I'd punched you," he added, an edge to his voice. "I know you consider me a coldhearted son of a bitch, but believe it or not I can empathize with your feelings."

"I never said you were anything of the sort," Meredith countered, embarrassed.

"No, you're too polite for that. But you thought it."

"Well, your initial behavior didn't exactly put you in a favorable light," she said, sending him a rueful smile.

"I guess not," he admitted, a grin hovering as he looked down at her and leaned on the back of the opposite seat. "But you were invading my privacy."

"Not through any intent of my own," she answered primly, but he caught the twinkle in her eye and realized, relieved, that she was loosening up. A sudden desire to pass his mouth over those well-shaped lips, taste their subtle secrets, made him clear his throat and glance through the window.

"Hope this weather lasts. They say it should be sunny over the weekend."

"Good. I bought a new bikini."

"You'll have every opportunity to wear it. The house is right on the beach and has a pool on the deck."

"It sounds beautiful," she replied.

"If the photographs are accurate, it is," he responded, glad to see that she was more relaxed now. Perhaps some champagne might be in order after all.

Moving toward the galley, he extracted a bottle of Cristal from the refrigerator and two flutes.

Meredith sighed. The fact that he was about to pop open an extraordinarily expensive bottle of champagne made an already surreal situation seem even more so. Was she really on a private jet flying over the Caribbean with this unnervingly attractive man? The scene was such a far cry from her daily routine.

"Thanks," she murmured when, after deftly popping the cork, Grant handed her the flute and sat down opposite, his presence dominating the space between them.

"Salute!" he said, raising his glass with a smile that sent tingling shudders down Meredith's spine. His smile was full of sensual promise, she reflected, nearly spluttering on the champagne.

And the reality of those promises could well be just around the corner, she realized, swallowing hard, her gaze gliding from Grant's well-worked-out figure to the sparkling Caribbean below. She followed the white wake of a tanker and asked herself just how she planned to go about the next round. What if she got stage fright? What if this turned out very different from what she'd imagined? Now, there was a question. What exactly *had* she imagined?

Up until now, making love with Grant had remained a hazy area in the nether regions of her busy mind. Now, only hours away from it happening, her heart sank.

Shifting imperceptibly in her seat, Meredith masked her discomfort. She was a grown woman. She was single. She was allowed to have a life. All these things seemed perfectly reasonable. But when she balanced them against what it would mean to get into bed with any man other than Tom, she felt overwhelmed by shame.

She shouldn't have come.

All at once it was crystal clear to her that she'd committed a grave error. No way could she allow this to go further.

Meredith turned from the window short of breath, the flute trembling in her shaking fingers. She must do something immediately, get him to turn back the plane. Something.

As though sensing her anguish, Grant leaned forward and touched her hand.

"Something the matter?" he asked, his tone a caress.

"As a matter of fact, there is," she said, letting out a tight breath, eyes avoiding his keen gaze.

"Meredith, look at me." Grant reached for her other hand and peered straight into her wavering eyes. "I know very well this is hard for you. I realize that you've taken a huge step coming away with me on this trip. I want you to know that I appreciate it."

He felt her fingers flutter in his and squeezed them tighter. "You're here to relax and enjoy yourself. To take a break. Nothing more. You call the shots. Nothing will happen that you don't want to happen, understood?"

And the amazing part, he realized, looking into her worried gray eyes, was that he truly meant it. Somehow making love with Meredith seemed less important than making sure she felt at ease with him and with herself. He felt perplexed. When was the last time he'd thought of a woman in such a way? Certainly none that he could recall offhand.

"I—" She let out an expressive sigh. "I'm really sorry to be like this. I see I should never have led you to believe—"

"Shush." He placed a finger over her lips. "There are no conditions or expectations. No, I take that back," he said with a wicked grin. "One thing I do insist upon—having fun. We're here to have fun. Lots of it. Although you seem unaware of the fact, Meredith, there's more to life than simply doing one's duty."

"I'm very well aware of that," she replied stiffly. "But this year hasn't exactly been a party."

"I realize that. But tell me something," he continued, eyes unflinching, "do you really believe that Tom would want you to bury yourself for the rest of your life?"

"I don't see what that has to do with it." She shifted her gaze uncomfortably. Tom would hate her to be unhappy.

"Everything. You're caught up in a cobweb of guilt." He caught the quick intake of breath, read the refusal in her eyes. "I'm not asking you to rush anything," he said softly. "But at some point you must allow yourself to feel like a woman again. For his sake as well as yours. You need to move on. He would want you to. I'm the perfect sounding board for that."

"Oh—"

"Think about it." He raised his hands now, palms

up, and grinned. "No baggage, no commitments, here today and gone tomorrow. Whatever happens between us now or in the future, you'll be free as the air we're flying through." He leaned back, flung one loafer-clad foot across the knee of his faded jeans and ignored the voice inside telling him that his statement wasn't strictly true. No feelings. Just attraction. Wasn't that his policy?

"I don't know what to say," she muttered, shaking her head and pushing her hair back in a manner he was becoming used to.

"Because having a fling without a commitment is outside your normal code of ethics?"

"Something like that," she answered, trying to marshal her dignity.

"I can assure you that in your circumstances, you're doing by far the best thing," he said conversationally, reaching for his glass and taking a sip. "No rocking the boat. Just a simple clean-cut experiment that will help you loosen up—if that's what you decide you want," he added, tilting his head in an appraising manner. "Think of it as therapy."

"Therapy?" she exclaimed blankly, eyes meeting his hypnotic gaze. It was as if all at once her brain cells had gone dead and all she could take in was his presence.

"Yeah, therapy. People do it all the time. They go on singles cruises where nobody knows who they are, get their kicks and go safely home to the country club, no one the wiser." He sucked in his cheeks, his expression quizzical. "Just like us. On Monday we'll go back to our client-attorney relationship, no one the wiser. However much or however little happens, it really doesn't matter," he added with a shrug and a tantalizing smile.

Then, as though a window had burst open and a

strong gust of wind rushed in, she reacted. Sitting straighter, she plunked the glass down on the table and looked him straight in the eye.

"You're right," she said, nodding hard. "You're absolutely right."

"Good." He nodded back approvingly.

But as the word came out he couldn't help feeling disappointed that his argument had been so easily accepted.

Joanna fiddled around the outdated kitchen of her house on Oglethorpe, noisily spooning instant decaf into a mug. She cast the thirty-year-old Formica cupboards a look of disdain. She'd never bothered to renovate the kitchen, so certain was she that Rowena's mansion would one day be hers. Now that illusion was very definitely laid to rest.

Though maybe if she could get close to Grant it could still be wangled.

Letting out a frustrated sigh, Joanna poured the boiling water from the kettle into her mug, and dragged her robe-clad self into the dining room.

Sitting at the table, she cupped the mug in her hands and speculated, remembering the party. Undoubtedly it had been a huge success. But why had he left so abruptly? She'd been certain a meeting would be planned at Ross's office. But to her surprise and annoyance, he'd simply left town without a word.

Tramping crossly upstairs, Joanna decided to call his London office and try to track him down. Or maybe Meredith knew where he could be found. It might be worth giving her a call.

As she entered the bathroom, she frowned. They'd left together after the party. Could Meredith be competition? No, she reflected, peering at the packaging of the new face mask her beautician had recommended to ease some of the wrinkles she saw appearing. Meredith was as prim and proper as a nun. Grimacing in front of the bathroom mirror, doing her facial exercises, Joanna took a good look at her lips. Perhaps another collagen shot wouldn't go awry. But right now her financial situation wasn't too rosy.

All the more reason, she reflected, dabbing the face cream on sparingly, to get this business with Grant settled one way or another. Maybe she'd ask Drew, whom she was lunching with later at the club, for his opinion on the matter. He was a bright man, one that, had he been richer and more successful, she might seriously have considered as husband material.

But he wasn't.

Then, glancing at herself in the mirror, she heaved a heavy sigh. The truth was Grant was considerably younger than her, and although dreaming was a pastime she favored, Joanna had to admit that landing as big a fish as the thirty-eight-year-old Grant Gallagher was perhaps out of her reach now. Maybe she should consult Miss Mabella about it.

Feeling cheerier she stepped into the shower. You never knew what tricks the Miss Mabella's of the world had up their sleeves. And if Aunt Rowena had been satisfied with her services, there was no saying where this all might end up.

No saying, indeed.

16

Soft, balmy air, a stretch of white sandy beach and the sweeping expanse of turquoise sea viewed from the wide veranda of Grant's villa made it impossible not to be enchanted.

After being greeted by Chico, the smiling Mexican butler, and his wife, Lupe, they'd stepped out of the cool marble-floored living room strewn with local artisan rugs onto the large flagstone veranda, dotted with rattan furniture arrayed with plump earth-toned cushions, overlooking the beach and the sea.

Tilting her head up toward the cloudless sky, Meredith let out a sigh. "Acquiring this house blind wasn't such a bad idea after all," she said, sending him a mischievous grin.

"I'm glad that you approve," he murmured wryly, removing his blazer and rolling up his white shirtsleeves to reveal his well-toned forearms. "I'm favorably surprised myself. Though the pool could do with an extra few meters," he said, glancing at it critically.

"I think it's perfect just as it is."

"Then I shan't call in the builders right away. I suggest we get our things off and relax."

"Hmm."

Now that she had arrived, she could feel some of her anxiety dissipate. To her relief, Lupe, the maid, had placed them in separate adjoining bedrooms. That and Grant's sincere words on the plane had removed some of the pressure she had felt. Now all she had to do was forget Savannah, stop wondering if her world could go on functioning without her and let loose, she reflected, looking about her, admiring the attractive plants and the string hammock hanging lazily in the corner.

From a few feet away, Grant cast her a quick, appraising glance. The afternoon was fast ending, the sun shone as a hot ball of fire sinking on the shimmering blue horizon. She looked extraordinarily appealing perched there on the balustrade next to a cluster of potted palms, the highlights in her chestnut hair picked up by the setting sun as she looked out over the ocean. She was not his usual type, but as he studied her slim body, its curves subtly defined under the pink fabric, he realized he hadn't felt a similar desire in years. He swallowed, willing to place a bet that she had no inkling of just how sexy she looked.

Masking a sudden deep urge to kiss her, Grant spoke instead. "How about a swim before evening sets in?" he suggested.

"That would be lovely," she smiled. "I'll run upstairs and change."

"Me, too. See you back here in five." He grinned in anticipation. It would be intriguing to see Meredith—the sober classically dressed attorney—in a bikini.

Standing before the mirror, Meredith tugged at the snippets of pretty flowered Lycra that she and Elm had discovered at the mall. Damn. The bikini hadn't seemed this tiny in the changing room. She let out a long breath. Tough. It was too late to do anything about it. With a grimace, she scooped up her hair in a tortoiseshell clip, thankful that she'd had the good sense to buy the wrap that went with the bikini.

Taking a deep breath, she descended the stairs and walked across the gleaming marble living room—all white from the walls to the furnishings, the only splash of color a few large contemporary canvases and several clusters of tropical plants. The butler appeared, carrying a tray with margaritas and a dish of guacamole and miniature tacos, which he placed by the side of the pool before discreetly disappearing.

"This is the life," she murmured, very aware of Grant's muscled body close to hers. He looked great dressed, but undressed…well, she hadn't quite imagined him so lean and well built and his closeness left her both breathless and filled with undeniable desire.

She'd always equated sex with love and with Tom. Now, as she floated about in the warm water sipping the delicious drink, she knew that was not always the case. She had no love for Grant—in truth, the man represented everything she despised—yet it was futile to pretend she didn't desire him.

Meredith stood in the shallow end of the white stone-edged pool, the water lapping her well-defined breasts. Craning her neck skyward, she let her mind go blank.

"Relaxed?" Grant asked, sidling up to her and placing his hands on her shoulders. Meredith shuddered as he kneaded them cleverly, releasing the knots of tension that had been her constant companion for so long.

She let out a tiny groan. "Ah," she sighed, "that feels

wonderful." A bolt of white lightning hit her when she leaned back and encountered his firm, muscled chest. She shuddered when his arms slipped around her, but she did not resist. Closing her eyes, she let out a sigh. This was what she'd come for, wasn't it?

Slowly, Grant smoothed his hands up her rib cage, sending darts of pleasure threading through her. Then he expertly kissed the back of her neck while his hands moved upward, covering her breasts. A delicious light-headedness took hold and a soft moan escaped her as his thumb grazed her taut nipples.

All at once, need, vital and intense, spiraled. She longed to feel him, to touch him as he was touching her, to feel his weight upon her, his body plundering hers. She wanted to finally satisfy the longing haunting her like a silent ghost, ever since the trip to Scotland.

Grant let out a sigh of his own.

God, she was delicious.

He'd only intended to relax her, to break the ice. But how could he resist temptation when he knew so clearly that they both wanted the same thing? Slipping his hand under her top, he caressed her small, firm breasts, delighting in them and the need he sensed in her as she unconsciously arched against him, her small, firm bottom rubbing against him in the soft warmth of the water. He could barely contain his own sudden rush of desire. But he would take it slowly, he vowed, determined not to rush her, accepting that there was still a way to go before he finally bedded her, a thought that was fast becoming an obsession.

The water swished gently around them as Grant twirled her around and they faced one another. Reaching for one of the diminutive tacos, he slipped it into her mouth, while his other arm pulled her close, so close she could feel the hardness of him through their suits. He dropped a kiss on her lips, lingering awhile, drawing her lower lip between his teeth and savoring the taste of her, delighting in the feel of her body against his. Then, when he knew he couldn't stand it any longer, he backed off, leaving her strangely disconcerted.

"Better not stay in the water too long," he remarked brusquely, waiting for his body to quiet.

What had happened to make him desert her so abruptly? she wondered, paddling across the pool, unwilling to show how his action had left her feeling shunned and insecure. Which, she reminded herself severely as she did a few strokes, was ridiculous. There was no room for feelings here. This was about satisfying an urgent, untamed attack of desire so that she could get him out of her system and get on with her life.

Evening was fast approaching. Subtle spotlights came to life, lending the pool and the veranda a mysterious and magical aura.

Pulling herself out of the pool, Meredith glanced at Grant still lingering in the water, his hair sleeked back, and the broad expanse of his shoulders sending another uncontrollable shaft of longing through her. How could she be so attracted to a man merely because he looked good? Surely she didn't think of Grant as anything more than a potential weekend sexual partner?

Picking up one of the large terry towels, she wrapped herself in it and watched him ease, lithe and toned, out of the pool. Instinctively, Meredith picked up another towel from the pile and handed it to him.

"Thanks." He smiled down at her, gave his head a rub, then wrapped the towel around his hips. "So," he said, handing her the last of her margarita, "shall we dine in tonight, or would you prefer to go out and see the sights?"

"I don't mind," she replied truthfully. "It's lovely here, quiet and serene."

"Then let's stay put. Apparently Lupe is an excellent cook."

"I'm sure she is." Meredith's eyes brightened when Grant's hand slipped onto her shoulder. She wanted to speak, to say something coherent, something normal. But all she could do was stay caught in his powerful gaze.

"I want you, Meredith. I know I said on the plane that we'd take it slowly, and far be it from me to rush you."

A knot caught in her throat. "I—" It was so hard to admit it.

Grant's hand slipped down her goose-pimpled arm. "You're cold," he murmured, his voice low and seductive. "Let me warm you, Meredith." He brought her into his arms and held her so close she could hear the rapid beating of his heart.

It felt wonderful to be encircled by his strong arms, to experience that inner sensation of belonging that she'd missed so much. Not that this would ever be like what she and Tom had, she reminded herself quickly, her pulse racing as he raised her chin and searched her eyes.

"Just let this happen," he whispered.

Meredith trembled when his lips met hers. Until minutes ago, she'd known she could retreat at any moment. But now the die was cast. Even if she wanted to, there was no way she could pull away. As Grant's lips explored hers she felt her legs buckling, and her arms slid up his shoulders and around his neck. She was kissing him back now, every vestige of doubt scattering as their bodies cleaved to each other's, seeking, needing, begging for completion.

When Grant finally lifted his head, she swallowed in an attempt to stay the dizziness.

"I think we'd better go upstairs," he murmured, taking her by the hand and leading her through the living room and up the staircase to the bedrooms beyond. When he reached his door, he didn't hesitate. He pushed the door closed with his foot and pulled her roughly into his arms. Meredith gasped, not from fear but from excitement and anticipation as his hands roamed over her. The towel fell to the floor, followed by her bikini, and she stood naked before him. For a second she panicked. Then a new and hitherto unknown sensation took hold: the power of being a woman. Eyes locked with his, she reached out and pulled the towel away from his body. They reached for each other in a hungered frenzy, the overwhelming need to join near devastating in its powerfulness.

When Grant scooped her up and carried her to the huge California king, she caught her breath. No man had ever carried her. Not even Tom when they'd married. Had anyone suggested such a thing, she would have thought it ridiculous. Yet being carried in his arms felt wonderful, as though she was the only woman in the world.

As he laid her on the bed she reached out and pulled him down beside her. Together they explored each other, caressed, until they became familiar with each other's bodies. Then Grant pushed her back on the pillows and his lips followed a devastating path, taunting, tantalizing, his tongue flicking her taut breasts until she could bear it no longer. She let out a ragged moan when his fingers reached between her thighs, seeking her core, and something spiraling inside her seemed ready to explode. When she finally gave way, she found herself gasping in this new uncharted territory. Digging her nails into his shoulders, she threw her head back and let out a cry of delight as she reached completion.

Could this be the same woman? he wondered, letting his fingers trail over her exquisite body. He'd been certain in Scotland and Miami that under her cool and collected front, there lay a vibrant woman. But this went beyond the realm of expectation. He swallowed, watched her intensely as she opened her eyes, and a subtle, satisfied smile hovered on her lips. Then she reached up, unabashed, and he came on top of her, the need to bury himself inside her, feel her warmth and lose himself there too overwhelming to ignore or to restrain. In one swift thrust he entered her, felt her legs wrapping around him, knew the need to penetrate, to reach her core, to mate until they reached a point of no return.

There was no gentleness now, only undisguised desire, a stream of molten lava flowing unreservedly as together they peaked, touched the summit, then fell, spent in each other's arms, among the rumpled sheets.

Meredith could hardly believe that it was Sunday already and that later this afternoon they'd be leaving. It felt as though they'd been here forever, cocooned in a world of their own. She glanced down at her golden skin, surprised that she'd achieved a reasonable tan in such a short time. Closing her eyes, she rested on the lounger under the umbrella and let her mind drift.

"A penny for your thoughts." Grant's seductive voice reached her. She looked up to find him standing over her. She experienced a jolt. In three short days, they had become strangely but intensely intimate. But today that would all end. They would put this behind them, move back to their separate worlds.

"Hi." She shaded her eyes and watched as he sat down on the lounger next to her.

"I've ordered the plane for four. I'm dropping you off in Savannah, then flying straight on to New York. I have an important meeting tomorrow at noon." He poured a glass of water and handed it to her.

"Your new venture?" she inquired, taking a sip.

"Yes."

"Which unfortunate company are you buying this time?" she challenged, turning on her side.

"Not a company. A private property." He looked straight out to sea, his dark hair slicked back, and Meredith was able to appreciate the well-honed muscles in his back. The guy really was a hunk.

"Where?" she probed.

"Upstate New York. The Adirondacks."

"What do you plan to do with it?" she asked, curious. "Surely there are some restrictions on what you can do with land up there—so much of what's left of the Adirondacks is now protected."

"We've managed to work around any restrictions. I have several development opportunities, some mining, some retail. The owners are ready to cave in."

"Then why aren't they selling it to a developer themselves? Surely they'd make a bigger profit that way."

"Because the owners are against any development," he said bluntly. "They'd rather keep everything intact.

There's an old hotel called the Carrington House on the property, one of those places built in the nineteenth century with leaking plumbing and musty fabrics. They don't want to let it go."

"The Carrington House?" Meredith sat up, frowning. "I've heard of that. Massive old place, right? I think I remember Rowena telling me about it. Apparently she used to visit there in the forties and fifties. Said it was a gorgeous place, pristine land, one of its kind in America."

"Rowena? She was there?" He looked at her, surprised.

"Yes. I think she was friends with the owner."

"Old Carrington? Well, well." He shook his head and frowned. "There's a coincidence for you."

"The hotel must be lovely."

"I have no idea. Right now it's closed. They've no money to keep up the maintenance. It's useless. A white elephant. What I'm interested in are the thirty thousand acres surrounding it, bordering the lake. Once we've rid ourselves of the hotel, the land will be worth a fortune."

"You're going to tear it down?"

"No other answer, I'm afraid."

"But that's terrible. If I remember rightly, it's an architectural gem. I'm surprised it's not on the National Register. I can't think why you'd be allowed to tear it down—or why you'd even want to," she said, staring at him, eyes challenging.

"Because it's good business," he answered coldly.

"Is that all that matters to you? Making more money than you've already got?"

"It's a win-win situation. The land will be very valuable once it's properly zoned, there's a mining concern interested in ten thousand acres, the local economy will get a boost. What's wrong with that? Plus I'm going to make the owners very rich. Right now they're crippled by property taxes."

"Then why are they so loath to let it go? That should tell you something," she muttered.

"You can't be sentimental when it comes to business. I am a businessman," he said patiently. "I take companies or property and turn them around for a profit."

"Haven't you ever wanted to build something up instead of always tearing things apart?" she asked, shaking her head, uncomprehending.

"I've never thought about it. This is what I do for a living. It works. Why would I change? As you Yanks say, if it ain't broke don't fix it."

"Isn't that a pretty narrow-minded approach?"

He shrugged, swung around on the lounger and grinned at her. "Enough of business. The sea looks particularly nice today. We should take a walk on the beach and maybe have a swim later."

"I was just wondering," she murmured, raising herself on one elbow and tipping her designer shades to get a better look at him, "how did you get the permits sorted out? Rezoning is almost impossible in environmentally protected areas."

"I pulled a few strings. Now, can we talk about something else?" He slipped his hands behind his neck and rolled his head from shoulder to shoulder.

"You've bribed someone on the zoning committee!" she exclaimed, shocked, staring at him disdainfully.

"*Bribe* is the wrong word. Persuaded to see the benefits, is more like it. The local town council isn't above giving me a hand. They know the present situation can't last. The property is a dead loss for the area as it is. There was a bypass built ten miles away a few years ago. It's redirected most of the traffic away from the town, so people don't stop off there anymore. All the local businesses have suffered, and the little antique stores, the diners and so on, have closed. The place is languishing in the Dark Ages. My deals—the mine, the housing developments—will bring an economic boost to the area. There's a factory project in the offing, too. That means jobs, growth, a second chance for the town. People need to earn a living, Meredith. Surely you can't disagree with that?"

"No, but at what cost? Sounds like you're going to strip-mall the place out. Transform what's probably a charming, safe little community into another slice of overbuilt America."

"There's always a price to pay on any deal," he said curtly.

"But couldn't you consider keeping the hotel? After all, so many of the big luxury chains are going crazy trying to build simulations of the place you've described. But this is the real thing."

"Meredith, I still haven't fathomed how you can be such a good lawyer when at heart you're a softy." He reached down and skimmed his lips over her forehead while his hands gripped her arms to pull her up. "Come on, let's go take that walk and forget I ever told you about this deal, okay?" he murmured. Threading his fingers through her hair, he tilted her head up and planted a kiss lightly on her lips.

"I still don't understand why you consistently destroy what's taken people years to build up," she said, letting out a sigh and taking the hand he proffered.

"Life goes on, Meredith. Some companies or properties just aren't feasible any longer. They serve no useful purpose."

"It seems very cruel."

"Life is cruel," he answered shortly as they descended the stone steps leading down to the beach.

"Couldn't you try to find another way, look into the possibility of saving the hotel? Reestablish it as the focal point of the community?"

"I haven't thought about it. Frankly, the deal is ready to close."

"Maybe you should try."

"Fine, then *you* think about it. Personally, I don't want to spoil our last day here arguing."

It wasn't like her to drop the argument, but he was right. Plus it was none of her business, she reminded herself. When Grant laced his fingers with hers and their toes touched the soft, warm sand, she sighed, determined to enjoy the last few hours of the dream while it lasted.

17

Tension reigned in the boardroom of Grant's Upper East Side office. On the one side of the wide glass table sat the stately white-haired Aubrey Carrington. To his left were his lawyer and Carrington's nephew, Carl.

"I'm damned if I'll see you tear down what four generations of my family have been dedicated to protecting, Gallagher," Carrington muttered, barely controlling his rage.

"I'm afraid there's no choice. I own eighty percent of the property now. I can take a decision."

"You stole it."

"No, I bought the debt from the loan company."

"Which amounts to the same thing since your only intention was to use it to blackmail us into selling."

"Mr. Carrington, technically I could just take the property. You've defaulted on the loan. The property was the collateral. Instead, I'm offering you compensation for your twenty-percent stake—I'd say that's a very fair deal."

"The only reason we defaulted was because the

bank suddenly called in the loan, and then refused to give us another one," Carl declared. "I wonder why that happened. One day they were ready to talk business, the next it was out of the question. I don't suppose you had anything to with that, did you?" he asked belligerently.

"What are you implying?" Grant's eyes narrowed.

"Now, gentlemen, don't let's get heated here, this is business," Robert Schaeffer, Grant's lawyer, interjected. "Mr. Gallagher is offering you a generous deal here. Personally, I would have said too generous, but that's the way he is." Robert smirked at his client, whom he was only too pleased to suck up to.

"This is outrageous," Aubrey Carrington exclaimed, "and I'll fight you all the way. Even if I have to lose my shirt over it."

"I'm sorry you feel this way, Mr. Carrington. Business is business." Grant sat perfectly still, hands crossed on the table, watching as the two men grappled with their emotions.

"We have nothing more to talk about, then," Carrington said at last. He got up abruptly and pushed his chair back. "Come on, Carl, we have work to do."

Grant rose and watched thoughtfully as the two men left the room.

"We've got 'em by the balls," Robert responded gleefully after the door closed. He was a short, pasty man who'd spent too much time behind a desk.

"Yes," Grant murmured absently, "I believe we have. Still, I need to fine-tune some details. Call them up and set up a meeting tomorrow at the hotel."

"At the hotel? You're kidding? Why?" Robert demanded. "Much better to let 'em stew. When they realize they're beat—and that shouldn't take more than twenty-four hours—they'll cave in like the rest of them."

"Just do as I ask." Grant picked up his briefcase and walked out, leaving Robert shaking his head and muttering.

"Hi." Elm peeked round the door of Meredith's sparsely decorated office. "How was your weekend?" She entered, casually yet elegantly attired in a cream skirt and top and a beige sweater slung over her shoulders. Tweaking off her shades, she sat down expectantly.

"Well?"

"It was fine," Meredith muttered, pushing her glasses down her nose and shifting the papers on her desk. She was still dazed by events, confused by the intense connection with a man whom she otherwise disapproved of. It made no sense. And she hated lack of logic. Plus she was unwilling to admit just how much it had affected her.

"How fine?" Elm cocked her head. "You look good. The tan suits you."

"Thanks."

"Meredith, I don't want a blow by blow, I'm merely asking if it went well," Elm said mildly.

"Yes. Very well. Too well. Oh, shit, I don't know." She rose and paced the office. "How can I work like this? Why do I have to feel so attracted to the man? He's like a damn drug. I've never experienced anything like it before." She stopped and dragged her fingers through her hair. "With Tom it was different, warm and secure and wonderful, and I knew exactly where I stood all the time. We were a team. This isn't like that. I didn't expect or want it to be like that, but—"

"But?"

"It was disturbing," she said finally, stopping in the middle of the room and shaking her head. "It's ridiculous to be out of kilter because of a little fling, but I can't seem to set my mind to anything. Maybe I need more ginkgo biloba. I've never had a concentration problem but now I'm forgetting the simplest things."

"It happens."

"Not to me." Meredith gave a withering sniff. "This office is run in an efficient and professional manner. I don't have time for daydreaming—" She caught herself up short and let out a fair simulation of a wail. "I can't handle this, Elm, it's—it's complicated and uncomfortable." She threw up her hands and perched on the edge of the desk.

"And wonderful?" Elm murmured softly, studying her friend closely.

"Wonderful," Meredith scoffed. "There's nothing wonderful about having sex with a guy who's practically a stranger. And a client to boot. Do you realize that people lose their law license over things like this?" she cried, burying her head in her hands. "I feel so confused, so not me. Why, I almost forgot to drop Mick off at judo yesterday afternoon. I don't know what's the matter with me."

"Hmm." Not wanting to state the obvious, Elm remained quiet, knowing that Meredith needed to come to her own realization.

"And Grant, damn him. He was the one that suggested we have a fling. That's exactly what he called it. On Monday," she mimicked, folding her arms across her chest, "we'll go back to our client-attorney relationship."

"And?"

"Like hell we will." She leaned forward, frowning. "How can I possibly sit there with him across from me, cool as a cucumber, and pretend nothing happened, when all I can think about is when it might happen again?"

"You have a point," Elm conceded, muffling the gurgle in her throat. This was not the time to nag or pry, just listen.

"Oh, and hear the latest," she exclaimed, planting her hands on her hips, her face a picture of righteous anger. "He called here this morning, cool as you please—never even mentioned Cancún."

A knock on the door made her cut off. "Yes?" She looked up as Ali peeked in. "This just arrived for you FedEx."

"Thanks." Meredith took the package and frowned. It came from the Carlyle Hotel in New York. "Mind if I take a look at this?" she murmured, already reaching for the paper knife.

"Go ahead. Any chance I can get a cup of that herb tea Ali has stashed away in her desk?"

"Of course," Meredith said absently, retrieving the thick file from inside the cardboard wrapping, her eyes skimming the file. "I don't believe this," she muttered.

"Something the matter?"

"Yes, no. I mean this is crazy."

"I'm afraid you'll have to explain," Elm said patiently.

"Oh, right. Grant is doing a deal up in the Adirondacks. He's buying a property that he plans to cut up into little pieces and sell at a huge profit. There's a beautiful old hotel on the land, which he plans to bulldoze. Naturally I protested."

"Naturally."

"The Carrington House is a landmark set right on a pristine lake. I don't know how he got around the zoning laws, given that it's exactly the kind of place that should be protected from development, but he has. Bought someone off, I have no doubt. Anyway, I told him he should think of saving the property rather than destroy it."

"And?"

"He brushed me off. I'm ashamed to say that I didn't want to spoil our last day arguing."

"Quite right. After all, it's really not your business."

"That was my reasoning, too," Meredith agreed. "But now he's sent me the complete file, and look at this—" she waved a plane ticket "—he wants me to go up and join him there tomorrow. He says if I can propose a viable solution for the hotel he'll consider it before closing."

"Goodness." Elm's lips twitched.

"This is a damn challenge, he's throwing down the glove," Meredith muttered, dragging her fingers through her hair. "It's not my affair."

"You appear to have made it your affair," Elm pointed out. "He must think pretty highly of your business acumen to be willing to listen to your opinions."

"Yeah, right. As if I had the least intention of aiding and abetting him in destroying the lives of hardworking American families. I find his business practices despicable," she snapped.

"Exactly. And by the looks of it, he's offering you a chance to alter them," Elm's calm persuasive voice soothed.

"Oh, hell, I don't know." Meredith flung the file down on the desk. "Truth is, I never should have gotten mixed up with him in the first place."

"It's too late to regret that now. And besides, why

be sorry about something you appear to have thoroughly enjoyed?" Elm queried.

"Because it's messing up everything. Before I met Grant everything was going along just fine. My life was on track."

"Really? Are you sure of that?" Elm held her eyes a moment and waited. "Meredith, maybe it's time you recognized that since Tom died, you've had no life worth talking about."

"Of course I have. I have my kids, my work," she replied defensively.

"Your kids are wonderful. So are your parents and Jeff and everyone else. But, Mer, I'm talking about you," Elm appealed, "you as a woman. You have to think of your life, too. Even consider having someone in it on a more permanent basis," she added, hoping she hadn't overstepped the mark.

"Well, it certainly won't be Grant Gallagher," she replied hotly. "He's only in this for the sex."

"Isn't that what you wanted?" Elm cocked her head and refrained from pointing out that, if that were the case, he'd hardly be asking her friend to join him in the Adirondacks.

"Yes, yes it was," she responded, irritated.

"So you both got what you were after."

"I guess." Meredith's shoulders slumped and she doodled with a pencil on her legal pad. "I thought," she said slowly, "that once the weekend was over he would be out of my system and that life would go back to being the way it was."

"That's not always as easy as it seems."

"I just gathered that."

"After Johnny and I made love the first time it changed everything."

"But why?" Meredith brought the flat of her hand down on the desk, missing the stapler by half an inch. "Why can't it be simple?"

"Because relationships aren't simple," Elm replied quietly.

"But this isn't a relationship! Oh, Elm, what am I going to do?" Meredith dropped her chin on the palms of her open hands, her eyes one huge question mark.

"You want my advice?" Elm asked cautiously. She did not plan to have her head bitten off.

"Yes."

"Since you're the one that got yourself into this by vociferously expressing your disapproval—"

"I wasn't vociferous," she protested.

"Mer, I've known you all my life, of course you were vociferous. Now, will you listen?"

"Okay."

"My advice is to meet him up in the Adirondacks, see for yourself if the place is really worth saving. He's willing to listen to your suggestions, so obviously your opinion means something. Plus it'll give you an insight into how he conducts his business and a truer perspective of who he really is as a person. Right now, you've only your own preconceived notion to go on."

"Why did I open my stupid mouth? I should have never gotten involved." The chair jerked forward and Meredith leaned her elbows on the desk. "It's an inconvenience. I can't go away again," she mumbled, fingering the corner of the file, recalling the lazy days spent lounging around the pool laughing, discussing everything that came to mind from politics, to painting, to music. It came as no surprise that Grant was well traveled, but that he should have such a well-educated, intelligent and broad mind was. Somehow she'd imagined him a corporate raider who thought only of money and deals and who hung out in glitzy hotels and casinos. She was not ready for the refined man who liked to take long walks along the beach, mess around like a kid in the pool and dine on the delicious dishes that Lupe prepared so lovingly. Neither had she been ready for his expert lovemaking. Maybe Elm was right and she needed to see close up and personal what the man was truly made of.

"Hello?" Elm waved at her across the desk. "I'm still here."

"Sorry."

Elm smiled and laid her hand on Meredith's and squeezed. "Mer, accept his offer."

"But I have Rowena's estate to deal with, plus a hundred other things."

"You wouldn't be away long."

"You really think I should go, don't you?" Meredith hesitated as Elm rose and slung her designer purse over her shoulder.

"A definitive yes. As you pointed out, maybe you can influence the outcome. And, no, I don't want to hear about Mick and Zack being abandoned," she said, lifting her hand like a stern traffic cop, "because you know perfectly well I'll take good care of them."

Meredith's mouth opened, then closed. She sagged in her chair and let out a long-suffering sigh. "I suppose if you're determined I should go, then I will. Thanks for taking the boys. But I'm only going because I may be able to help those unfortunate people he's dealing with," she said dolefully, raising her eyes to Elm's.

"Sure," Elm nodded, managing not to smile. "Start packing."

18

A limo awaited her in Albany to drive her to the hotel. Thick snow covered the ground and the roads were icy. It was almost Christmas and she hadn't even begun shopping, she reflected, gazing out of the car window at the enchanting landscape, the shimmering white blanket dotted with trees, etched like an icy fairy kingdom under rays of elusive sunshine peeking from behind fast-moving clouds. *Magical* was the only word that came to mind. Few places like this existed anymore. When the vehicle finally turned into the massive gates of the Carrington House Hotel drive, Meredith caught her breath as a fox trotted calmly between the trees, leaving footprints in the virgin snow.

How could Grant even consider ruining such a spot? Why should Grant Gallagher, who was wealthy as Croesus, who'd already had Rowena drop a hundred mil into his lap, need to make yet another bundle on this land speculation? It seemed totally unfair. Then, peering up ahead, she saw the building and gasped, recalling Rowena's stories about the place.

"A beauty, ain't she?" The limo driver, a man in his mid-sixties, turned and smiled. "She's our grand dame, she is. Rumor has it that some jerk is going to buy the place and turn the property into an industrial park or something. I know things have suffered here since the bypass was built, but still. It's a darn shame."

"It is," Meredith murmured, recalling what she'd read in the file about the Carrington House's history. Back in 1870, Theodore Carrington, a wealthy businessman from New York, had traveled to this area with his wife, Clementine. Enchanted by what they found, they envisioned a peaceful retreat where people could enjoy the beauty of nature in a truly spectacular setting. Theodore purchased the property and the couple set about turning the ten-room inn and tavern into a magnificent Victorian castle bordering the shores of the small lake.

"Could you stop a moment?" she asked suddenly.

"Of course, ma'am. Step out and take a look. Those are local children out on the lake, skating." He pointed to the figures gamboling to the left of the massive, rambling stone hotel. "We've been very lucky until now. This is still an unspoiled part of the world," he said as he opened the door for her.

Meredith shivered. She hadn't thought of bringing snow boots. Pulling her cashmere coat close about her, she took a few steps down the drive, breathing the pure, invigorating mountain air. Then she paused and listened, to the sounds of nature, to the distant laughter of the children. She looked at the unblemished stretches of land and forest, the mountains rising to the north, and she knew that she must do something to save this place from destruction.

She glanced at her watch. Grant had mentioned he

would be arriving after her as he was held up in meetings in town. Rubbing her chilly nose, Meredith climbed back in the car.

"Have you worked here long?" she asked the driver.

"All my life, ma'am. I don't know what I'll do when they sell the place. The whole town used to depend on Mr. Carrington for employment. He keeps some of us on even now that the hotel is closed because we're too old to find other work," he said sadly. "He's a good man, and so's his nephew, Carl. Mr. Carrington's held on to this place as long as he could. He was hoping to pass it on to the next generation—that'd be his nephew, since his wife's gone and he has no children. God only knows what'll happen to him if he loses the House—that's what we call it in these parts."

Meredith felt tears in her eyes. Then, as the car drew up in front of the massive oak portals, she pulled herself together. Grant had challenged her to come up with a better solution for the place than he had. Well, she would do her best.

As she stepped inside the grand hall, Meredith's heart slumped. The remnants of its former majesty remained, but the hotel had lost its luster. Only one of the twelve chandeliers gracing the coffered ceiling offered minimum light. The dated, threadbare furnishings were dignified relics of another time. Only the marble floor glistened. She doubted the heating was working well.

"Ah, you must be Ms. Hunter," greeted a tall, elderly gentleman wearing a tweed jacket over his sweater and cords. "Welcome. Sam, you can leave the bag here. We'll take it up in due course."

"Very well, Mr. Carrington, have a good day. Oh,

and, sir, Mrs. Burton from the bakery says to tell you
she's making you a special pecan pie."

"Thank you, Sam. If you see her, tell her I'll be over
to pick it up."

Sam touched his cap and said goodbye.

"So, Ms. Hunter. I haven't gathered why you're here
or what this meeting Gallagher requested is about, but
if I can help you in any way, I will."

"Thank you," she smiled, liking this old-world gentleman already and wondering how to broach the subject.
"What a perfectly unique spot you have here, sir. It's
beautiful."

"I like to think so," he said, thawing slightly.

"Unfortunately it won't remain so for long." Meredith's head shot up to see a tall blond young man in his
late twenties wearing jeans and a thick gray sweater
standing in a nearby doorway. "Your friend Mr. Gallagher has bought up all the debt on the property. He
virtually owns it now." His voice sounded bitter.
Meredith watched as the older man's shoulders sagged.
"Don't, Carl. I've done everything I can for Carrington
House. I guess there comes a time when you have to accept reality and let go. This is my nephew Ms. Hunter."

"Hi. Nice to meet you," she said meeting his hostile
stare. "I—maybe there's a way to save it," she said,
grasping at straws. For anything to be done here would
cost a fortune.

"I've been telling myself that for the past ten years,
young lady. Unfortunately, we live in a tough world.
Nobody cares about the finer things in life anymore. Or
the peaceful ones."

"I read the history of Carrington House. I thought
your grandparents' philosophy was incredible. They
must have been very special people."

"They were. Very. But come on in and sit down in the living room. It's cold in the hall since we've stopped heating. Carl, you could show Ms. Hunter the place."

Meredith followed him up the wide marble steps and into a cozy oak-paneled room where a log fire burned. Carl stiffly brought up the rear. "This was the small parlor when the place was built. People would come up from New York and Philadelphia. Guests liked this particular room. They'd have cocktails here by the fire in winter, and out on the terrace overlooking the lake in summer."

"You can feel the history," Meredith murmured, taking the armchair offered to her by the fire. "I knew a lady who used to come here often in the forties and fifties. I think she was a friend of yours—Rowena Carstairs."

"Rowena, my goodness. That takes me back a while. What a woman. Is she well?"

"I'm afraid she died a month and a half ago."

"I'm sorry. She was a fine woman. I may even have some pictures of her in the old photograph albums."

She watched as he moved toward the wall and pulled out an album from among the many books gracing the shelves. "Did you know that Mr. Gallagher is her grandson?"

He turned, clasping the leather-bound book. "You don't say? A pity he doesn't have more of the old girl in him." He shook his head. "He's a tough cookie, that young man. A hard nut to crack."

"Doesn't seem to have any human feelings," Carl added, picking up the poker and stabbing the logs angrily.

"Well, in any event, he's certainly good at hiding

them," Meredith said quietly. "But I do think, with the right approach, we might get him to reconsider things."

Carrington sent her an arrested look and his eyes narrowed. Carl stopped poking the fire. "What exactly are you getting at, Ms. Hunter? Gallagher doesn't strike me as the type who ever changes his mind."

"Well, I certainly can't promise anything, but I'm here because Grant asked me to come. We had a bit of an argument about what he proposes to do here. He—he set me a challenge," she said, reddening.

"What do you mean?"

"He said that if I came up with a better or equally good solution for the property, he'd consider it."

"He did?" The old man's head jerked up and a glimmer of hope flickered.

"Ha," Carl muttered.

"So I'm asking you to help me find that solution," she said, clasping her hands together. "I want to help you save this place."

"Well, I never," Carrington muttered, staring at her, a slow smile curving his lips. "Perhaps my prayers are being answered after all."

"Please, I don't want to raise any false hopes. I can't guarantee anything. But at least he's willing to give it a one-time shot."

"Here, take a look at the photo albums."

"Why would she want to see what you're going to destroy? I don't believe Gallagher knows what the word *goodwill* means," Carl said, not budging. "Your client is scum, Ms. Hunter. If he hadn't personally put pressure on the bank, we would have gotten the loan. He's a filthy son of a bitch."

"Carl, that's no way to speak to a lady. And you

know very well it was that smart-ass attorney of his who swung that deal. Personally I'm not sure Gallagher was totally aware of exactly what was going on."

"Yeah, right. No one who associates themselves with the likes of that man can be up to any good. If that's the kind of legal representation Gallagher has, then good luck to him."

Meredith frowned. Grant hadn't mentioned his attorney. She laid her hand on the older man's arm. "Leave him be. He's sore, and he's right. Grant had no right to do that. And whoever this attorney is, he had much less right unless he had his client's consent."

"Well, I'm surprised to hear you say so. I thought you were a friend of his."

"I—I am, but—that doesn't mean I approve of certain things. It's hard to explain."

Carrington looked at her wisely, caught the flush in her cheeks and came to his own conclusions. Saying nothing he merely turned to his nephew. "Carl, ask Betty to make some coffee, will you?"

"Okay," Carl muttered grudgingly, casting Meredith a dark look before he stomped out of the room.

"I apologize for my nephew's rude behavior," he said with a weary smile, "but we've been under a lot of pressure lately. He's taking the whole thing very badly. You see, growing up, he was groomed to be the next caretaker of Carrington House. It's hard for him to see it go."

"I understand. Tell me, Mr. Carrington, before all this happened, did you have any ideas of what Carrington House could become?

"Ideas? Oh, yes. A ton of them. Carl had several projects plotted—we just couldn't get the backing." He eased into the armchair opposite and smiled sadly. "They've just remained on paper in a drawer somewhere."

"Could I see them? Are they feasible?"

He frowned, an arrested look in his eyes. "Carl's the one who really knows. He's got a degree in hotel management from Cornell. I think some of his ideas are great—and possibly extremely profitable."

"I'd love to hear them if he'd be willing to tell me—it would help me understand this place's potential," she murmured, ideas sprouting as she spoke. The hotel could be redeveloped as a resort, brought back to what it was in its heyday and serve a similar clientele. Why, people paid big money to go to places that were built from scratch to resemble gorgeous old hotels like this. Here was the real thing. All it needed was a good business plan and a serious injection of dollars.

"Besides being first in his class," the old gentleman continued, "Carl also has several years' experience working in top resorts around the world."

"So management issues are already taken care of. I love the concept of a family-owned hotel. I think there's a huge market for such places today. People are seeking personalized service."

"They'd certainly get that here if we were given the opportunity," Carrington replied. "I've lived here and run the place since I was a young man. Carl has the know-how, the modern management skills, knows what staff to hire and how to train a local workforce."

"Well, that's certainly a start, but let's not rush things. This is only an idea," Meredith said hurriedly, seeing the gleam in Carrington's eye. "Have you had any interested investors in the past?"

"Oh, yes. We've had a couple offers from the big

chains over the years. Maybe I should have accepted. But I didn't like what they planned to do with the place, though it sure as hell was better than what Gallagher has in mind."

"If you'll allow me, I'll study the files and talk to Carl."

"Of course. I'll go fetch them. Have some coffee, then we'll show you around. Take a look at the albums."

"Thanks, Mr. Carrington, I appreciate you sharing this with me."

"Very soon they'll just be a pile of old memories," he answered sadly. "Someone will stash them away in a box in the attic, and one day, a few years from now, they'll be thrown out in the trash. God knows what this place will look like by then." He paused, leaned his arm on the mantelpiece, looking suddenly weary. Meredith's heart bled for him.

And her anger toward Grant tripled.

How could he do this to people? Didn't he have a soul?

"Here's coffee," Carl said, coming back with a tray. He glanced over at Meredith reverently turning the pages of the ancient albums, raised his brow and looked at his uncle.

"You interested in old hotels?" he asked, laying the tray down on the large weathered ottoman before the fire.

"Yes. In this one, at any rate." She looked up smiled at him, hoping to break the ice. "Do you have any ideas of what this place could become?" she asked, looking him straight in the eye.

"Ideas! Don't talk to me about ideas," he muttered, sitting abruptly on the small couch opposite.

"Carl, you should share your ideas with Ms. Hunter.

She wants to help," he said simply. Meredith looked at him and their eyes met. "You really do, don't you?" he continued, his blue eyes holding hers. "The minute you walked in I could tell there was something honest and good in your nature."

"Look, I—" Meredith clasped her hands, worried at the pressure being laid on her. "I'll do all I can to try to help, but I can't guarantee anything. If I had something concrete to work with, if we could formulate something that looks worthwhile on paper, then I could try to reason with Grant."

"Are you serious?" Carl sat up and eyed her. "Why would you bother to try to help us? You're here with him. All he wants is to destroy this place and ruin the whole area."

"In principle, you're right. But he asked me to come and take a look. He's willing to listen to an alternative before closing the deal."

"You're kidding. Gallagher?" Carl looked at her, amazed.

"Yes. But we don't have much time. I suggest you find those files right away. We need to get to work."

"I'll go fetch them at once. You keep talking to Carl here," Carrington said, a new note of excitement entering his voice. "And whatever the outcome," he said as he reached the door, "we'll be grateful to you for trying. Now, Carl, instead of sitting there like an open-mouthed grizzly, you start telling Ms. Hunter here—"

"Please, call me Meredith," she interrupted.

"Okay, Meredith. Carl, I'm going to go get those business plans we put together a few years ago. They're somewhere in my desk," he muttered, leaving the room.

Carl watched his uncle retire from the room, then

turned to Meredith with a tentative smile. "I'm sorry I was abrupt. It just hurts to see him suffer. He's been like a father to me. This place means everything to him."

"And to you?"

"And to me," he agreed, handing her a cup of coffee. "But I'm young. Worst-case scenario, I can go work with one of the big chains. And after the deal goes through, it won't be money that's lacking," he added bitterly.

"It's motivation, right?"

"Yes. This place has been in the family right from the start. Before that there were Indians on this land and there still are. We've done everything to preserve nature. There're thirty thousand acres of wildlife out there that will be destroyed even if Gallagher only builds in the zoned areas." He dragged his fingers through his thick blond hair. "I guess this may sound dumb, but I still can't believe it's happening. Up until a few days ago I really thought the bank would bail us out one more time. But Gallagher got to them somehow. He has too much damn clout."

"You think he blocked the loan?"

"I'm certain he did. The reversal was too sudden. Somebody pulled the plug."

"I see." Meredith experienced a bitter taste in her mouth. And this was the man she'd slept with, made love with. "Why don't you share your ideas with me," she said, concentrating. If she was to do anything to save Carrington House she needed facts and figures, not just dreams.

Slowly Carl began to talk, about the hotel, its potential. His ideas were impressive and, Meredith acknowledged, her own excitement growing, eminently feasible with the proper backing. He painted a future where Carrington House was once again an exclusive and unique resort. He'd add the lures of a state-of-the-art business center for small high-level conferences, an exclusive spa run in conjunction with one of the big cosmetic brands, a range of outdoor activities, including shooting, fishing, hiking, rock climbing and water sports on the lake. He spoke of how the revived hotel would resurrect the dying town, bring back the antique stores and small boutiques and encourage an influx of new restaurants and bistros. As he talked, she could see it all happening. Carl, she realized with a grin, was a born salesman.

Then all at once the front doorbell clanged, resonating through the hall, and the conversation came to an abrupt end.

"These must be your buddies arriving," he said dryly. "I'll go see."

Seconds later, she heard voices in the hall. Her back tensed and she sat straighter. How could she face Grant, greet him civilly, knowing what his intentions were? Yet he had invited her here for a reason. Knowing that the Carrington House deal represented everything she abhorred, he'd offered her an opportunity to change his mind. Could she do it? she wondered, swallowing hard as the voices approached.

"Hello, Meredith. Have a good trip?"

Just seeing him sent her heart somersaulting. "Fine, thanks."

Grant came over and kissed her on both cheeks in a friendly manner. Her pulse raced and her warring feelings leaped.

"This is Robert Schaeffer, my lawyer."

Scaheffer gave Meredith a perfunctory smile that

didn't reach his eyes. She disliked him on sight, his fat, pudgy form poured into his Italian suit and Gucci loafers. How could Grant hire a guy who wore a tacky magenta tie, for Christ's sake? Because he was the best sleazeball in town, she told herself. She glanced at Carl and saw that he was having a hard time mustering enough grit to remain polite and offer them coffee.

"Isn't this place beautiful?" she asked Grant, who took a seat in the chair next to her, determined to begin her offensive.

"Yes, I suppose it has a certain charm," he replied blandly. "Have you come up with anything?" he murmured.

"I've barely had time," she replied sharply, "but, yes, Carl and I have been discussing some ideas. I'm waiting to see his business plan to make sure they're feasible."

"What business plan? I never saw a business plan." He turned and sent a questioning look in Robert's direction. "Have we seen a business plan?" he asked the lawyer.

"I didn't see any point in bothering you with non-viable options," he muttered, flushing.

"Really?" Grant's voice cut the air like a sharp knife and his eyes turned to flint.

"Grant, how about you and I take a walk in the park," Meredith chipped in. "I'd love to go down by the lake where the kids are skating. Do you mind?" She turned to Carl, standing poker stiff by the mantelpiece.

"Be my guest. I won't be able to say that in a few hours."

"A walk sounds good," Grant said, rising and setting the coffee cup back on the tray. "Robert, we'll see you back here in an hour or so."

"Don't be too long, I need to get back to town tonight to wind up the Philly agreement."

Grant sent him a cold, appraising look but didn't bother to answer.

"You'll need some gear if you're going to go out walking," Carl remarked, eyeing Meredith's tan cashmere coat with misgiving. "Come along to the cloakroom. I'll find you something so you don't freeze to death."

"Thank you, Carl." Meredith sent him a warm smile and she and Grant followed him out the door, leaving Robert glancing impatiently at his diamond-studded Rolex and fiddling with his Palm Pilot.

Minutes later, they were trudging through the snow wrapped in parkas, big snow boots, bright woolen beanies and Alaskan gloves.

"You look like a snowman." She laughed, reaching down and shaping a soft, pristine snowball in the palms of her mittens, then pitching it at Grant playfully. "You know, this snow is so clean and so pure, I find it hard to believe that a place like this still exists."

"That's precisely why it's on the block. It's not real in today's world."

Realizing that an argument would not further her cause, Meredith took a deep breath and recalled all Professor Hardwick's advice. "Today's world is the way it is because we allowed it to become that way," she said quietly. "It's up to us to make sure it doesn't get spoiled further."

"That will happen, anyway," he dismissed.

"Not if each of us helps to preserve the balance."

"What do you mean?" Grant stopped and eyed her closely, enjoying the flush the crisp air had brought to her cheeks.

"Well, take this place, for instance." Meredith took his arm and turned him around so they faced the back of the resort. "You're planning to bulldoze it. But just think what it could become if it was handled right."

"What did you have in mind?" he asked warily.

"How about the most exclusive, privately owned family-run five-star hotel in the country? With its kitchens run by a dynamic young chef using locally grown ingredients in creative ways? With a state-of-the-art business center for CEO get-togethers and a world-class spa, a Jack-designed golf course, eco-tourism opportunities, and you're talking big business."

"That would require a major investment."

"Money's not hard to find when you have the means to back up the loans. Grant, you could build this place into something spectacular."

"Build?" He frowned as though the concept were totally alien.

"Yes, build. Watch something grow because you've nurtured it, have something to show for all your hard work in a few years' time, build a future empire for your kids."

"What kids?" he asked, mystified.

"I don't know, the ones you'll maybe have one day."

"Oh, those," he replied, arching his brows dismissively.

"Tell me, why did you buy Strathcairn?" she asked suddenly, pressing her point, feeling she might just be reaching him.

"I liked it."

"Why?"

"I suppose because it had tradition, a sense of permanence and solidity."

"And you wanted that?"

He shrugged. "Something about it appealed, nothing more."

"This place has tradition, too. The hotel was founded by two people who had the sensitivity to capture the land's magic without disrupting its special sense of natural beauty and isolation. They created something unique, handed it on down to their children. Each generation has extended the gift they received, working to preserve this spot. You could be a part of that, of keeping it a wonderful place for people like yourself to come and enjoy."

"But my project would bring far more jobs to the area."

"Not necessarily. Talk to Carl. He has a master's degree from Cornell and several years' experience in running resorts, and he not only has plans for the hotel and the land, but for the town as well. The countryside would remain intact rather than filled with fast-food joints."

"Hey, wait a minute, I never said I'd put in place anything of the sort," he protested.

"No, because you're not thinking about what it'll be like in five years' time, when that gorgeous historic structure has been torn down and the beach and the lake are polluted by everybody's barbecue trash, beer cans and empty Coke bottles. Look," she said, pointing just beyond his shoulder, "where do you still see that?" she asked softly as two deer sauntered gracefully by the edge of the wood.

Grant gazed at the scene of the mother and fawn. There was something defenseless about them that made him swallow. He didn't know why the scene should remind him of Isabel, but it did. He shook his head, embarrassed by such fanciful thoughts.

"Let's go down to the lake," he said abruptly, turning his back on the deer and watching the kids who had returned to the ice. The boys were playing hockey while the girls practiced spins and figure eights at the other end.

"I used to play hockey," he remarked as they approached. "Helped get some of the anger out. It's a great game for venting your feelings."

"I'll bet you never played on a real pond," she murmured. "Isn't it a treat to see kids enjoying nature?"

"Hmm." All he recalled of his childhood were the well-tended gardens of the various five-star hotels his parents took him to. He'd particularly liked the one in Capri because it had a swing chair. He must've been five. Hawaii wasn't bad, either. He'd surfed there.

Together they watched the hockey match.

"A couple of those kids have potential," he remarked, shading his eyes from the rays of sunlight bursting out of the gray sky.

"You think so?" Meredith smothered the sliver of hope.

"Yes. See the one in the red parka?"

"Yes."

"He's good. So is the kid who has the puck right now." His face broke into a smile as the kid shot the puck into the makeshift goal. "Nice shot," he exclaimed as they reached the frozen lake's edge.

Minutes later the red-cheeked kids glided up, threw their sticks on the bank and reached for their thermoses.

"Great stick work," Grant said to the kid in the yellow jacket who'd scored the goal.

"Thank you, sir." The freckled, snub-nosed kid grinned. "We're playing New Paltz on Saturday, that's why we're practicing."

"I'd say you guys are in pretty good shape."

"Yeah, not bad—especially for a team without a coach. Our coach had to move away. He was great."

"Where did he go?"

"I dunno exactly, some place in Canada, I think. There wasn't any work for him here. Lots of folks leave 'cause there's no work. My folks are talking about it, too." He took a swig from the thermos. "They say this place is going to be sold to some real estate developer who's gonna build a bunch of ugly houses and strip malls here, and that the lake won't be the same anymore. That sucks."

"It sure does," Meredith agreed, calculating the child's age at around ten—he had that same puppy look as Mick. She peered at Grant out of the corner of her eye, wondering how he was reacting. Out of the mouths of babes, she reflected. If only he would show some sign, give her some indication that she was getting through to him.

After wishing the kids well in their upcoming match, they walked back toward Carrington House, the snow crunching under their feet.

"Grant, you asked me to come up with some alternatives for this place."

"Yes, I did."

"Well then, take a look at the existing business plan. I think there's a lot about this property that your two-faced, shifty-eyed lawyer in there hasn't let you in on."

"You don't approve of Robert?" he said, lips twitching.

"I most certainly do not," she exclaimed hotly.

"How you could have someone like that working for you is a mystery to me."

"It was an accident. I inherited him with the deal."

"Yeah, well, I think he's pushing you to do the deal because he's on the make and this is the quickest way to get his dough. He's not protecting your interests."

"Maybe I should hire you," he said with a quizzical smile.

"I wouldn't be any good, but I can certainly recommend a couple attorneys who would represent you a heck of a lot better than that piece of slime," she said.

"Okay, so what do you advise?" He watched her, intrigued, captivated by her passion.

"Let's take a look at their business plan before you make any final decisions. If you think there's a possibility it might work, then maybe you could commission one of your own."

They'd arrived back at the hotel now. "I don't know if Carl's plan is feasible, but I have the feeling he really knows what he's doing and—"

"Hi, there." Robert's strong Brooklyn twang interrupted what she was about to say. "Let's get on with the meeting and wrap this thing, Grant. Then we can get out of this hole and be back in town by dinner. Gee, the place is a goddamn freezer. Don't they heat it?"

"They don't have any money to heat it. Not surprising, since their loan was blocked," Meredith spat, tearing off the parka and stalking across the hall to the sitting room.

"What bug got up her ass?" Robert muttered, throwing up his hands. Then he turned to Grant, his beady eyes and ferret nose twitching. "We gotta close this deal now. Not tomorrow, buddy, but right now. Their ass is on the line and they know it. Shit, we've been at this for more than six weeks. Let's get the fucking thing wrapped and get our butts out of here."

"Did anyone ever tell you how vulgar your language is?" Grant remarked coldly, removing the snow gear and pulling on his shoes before sauntering back into the hall.

"What the hell does the way I speak have to do with anything?" Robert muttered. "You English are all the same, worried about niceties. Let's close, man."

They reached the door of the sitting room when Aubrey Carrington came out of his study, holding a file.

"Mr. Carrington, I wonder if I might have a word with you. In private," Grant said.

Carrington frowned, then nodded. "Sure, if you'd like. We can go into my study."

"Hey, why do you want to see him alone?" Robert whispered anxiously.

"All in good time," Grant said, cutting him off as he straightened the sleeve of his blazer.

"Look here," the lawyer protested, turning to Meredith, who'd stepped out of the living room, "you can't do this, every word can be important."

"It's my deal," Grant answered icily, "and I'll do whatever the hell I want with it. Mr. Carrington—" he turned and smiled at the older man "—I'm ready whenever you are."

"This way." Carrington opened the study door and the two men disappeared inside, leaving the furious Robert muttering to himself.

"Fucking crazy talking to the guy by himself when we're ready to cut his balls off. Jesus."

Meredith looked at him disdainfully, opened her mouth, then thought better of it. Would Grant give

Carrington House a chance? she wondered. Well, she'd done all she could in the short time available. It was up to the gods now. Impatiently, she returned to the sitting room where Carl was absently poking the fire. An Old English sheepdog wandered in and she crouched to stroke him between the ears.

"Ah, that's Mohawk. He's getting old now. Come here, boy. He likes snuggling up and snoozing in front of the fire."

"Your uncle and Grant Gallagher are in the study together," she said, crossing her arms and biting her lips as she stood nervously behind the couch.

"Yeah. Well, I guess this is it, then." He shrugged, placed the poker back on its stand and sighed. "How about a drink? Thanks for trying." He smiled at her, a sincere smile that left Meredith wishing she could burst into the office and ensure the outcome. It was her own fault for allowing feelings to interfere, she realized gloomily, accepting the offer of the drink. She could hear Robert talking on his cell phone in the hall. She glanced at the carriage clock on the mantel. They'd been in there for ten full minutes. What could they be saying to each other? Meredith tapped her foot impatiently. If only she'd had more time, even just a day more to get her ideas sorted out in a businesslike manner, they might have stood a chance.

Carl handed her a vodka and tonic.

"Thanks. I need this."

"Me, too. I wonder when we'll have to move out of here."

"I'm sure you'll have at least six months."

"Not from what he says." He jerked his head in the direction of Robert muttering on his cell phone in the hall.

"You have legal rights," she pointed out.

"Yeah. I know all about legal rights. They're subject to serious manipulation. We don't stand a chance. And, frankly, if we've got to leave, then I'd rather make a clean break and get it over with. I'm just worried about Uncle Aubrey. He hasn't been doing too great the past few weeks."

At that moment they were interrupted by the sound of voices. Meredith swallowed and her heart beat faster.

Then Aubrey Carrington walked in with Grant. Both men were smiling. Meredith caught her breath and glanced at Carl, who raised a haughty, surprised brow. Robert was fussing behind them, trying to get Grant's attention.

"Carl, Meredith, I have an announcement to make." Aubrey cleared his throat and Meredith read the emotion in his eyes. "Mr. Gallagher—or rather Grant, as he's asked me to call him—has decided not to buy our property."

"What?" Robert squeaked. "Are you fucking crazy?"

Carl stood straighter and swallowed. "What do you mean?"

"Instead of buying it, I'd like to become a partner and invest in it," Grant said quietly, ignoring Robert.

Meredith felt her legs go weak and her eyes water. She wanted to rush forward and throw her arms about him. Instead she blinked back the tears.

"Are you serious?" Carl murmured, trying to mask his emotions.

"Never more so."

"I don't believe this," Robert ranted. "This is fucking unbelievable. Are you nuts?"

"If I am it's no longer any of your business," Grant replied coolly, his eyes resting on Meredith. "As of this moment you no longer represent me, Robert." He looked at the man with disdain. "Take the limo, go back to town and send me your bill. I won't be requiring your services any longer."

"But—"

"You got the message, Robert. I don't work with anyone who withholds information from me. Just go."

Sending a frustrated look around the room, Robert turned on his heel. Soon the sound of the car engine fading in the distance sent a wave of relief through the company.

"What made you change your mind?" Carl asked once the champagne—vintage bottles laid down by the second-generation Carringtons—had been passed around.

"Your business plan, for one. I wasn't aware of its existence and it's very well put together, though it could use some updating. But mostly," he said, his eyes moving over Meredith, who'd joined him on the sofa, "it was what somebody said to me." He raised his glass and murmured for her ears only, "Something about building instead of demolishing."

Their eyes held and Meredith let out a sigh. Grant watched her carefully, enjoying a new and hitherto unknown sensation: that of looking toward the future. Usually he felt numb after he closed a deal and simply blocked it from his mind. Now he experienced the pleasure of anticipation. Reaching down, he kneaded the dog absently between the ears and listened to the Carringtons expand on their plans for the place. It was impossible not to get caught up in their enthusiasm. Glancing at Meredith sitting quietly next to him, he experienced a rush of unfamiliar warmth and satisfaction. Even if it cost him a few million, it was worth preserving this little bit of paradise. It was too special to let go. Just like Meredith herself.

The realization hit him hard and he choked on his champagne.

"You okay?" she murmured solicitously.

"Fine. Champagne went down the wrong way." He stole another look at Meredith, seeing her as if for the first time. Now that the thought was lodged, he knew he'd never be able to shake it. And maybe he didn't want to, he realized, shocking himself yet again. Gulping down the rest of his champagne he joined the discussion before any other errant thoughts could hit his well-ordered existence.

19

They'd left the party together, Joanna observed, and then Meredith and Grant had been out of town last weekend. Now they were in New York at the same time. Could there be more to this than met the eye? she wondered, tapping her fingers on the dashboard as the rain blurred the windshield. She recalled the familiarity with which Grant had slipped his hand around Meredith's shoulder as they moved down the stairway at Montalba. That certainly was *not* the impartial gesture of a client toward his attorney, she reflected, new excitement growing.

Lifting her umbrella off the passenger seat, Joanna toyed with this new vision of things. Could there be something going on between those two?

Her heart missed a beat. It certainly put a spoke in her wheel as far as her own plans for Grant were concerned. On the other hand, it opened up a plethora of possibilities. She'd have to ask Ross, of course, but surely it was highly unethical for an attorney to have any kind of intimacy with a client?

Determined not to get excited when there was probably no foundation for her imaginings, Joanna stepped out of the car and opened her umbrella. Why did these people always have to live in impossible parts of town? She winced, stepping carefully among the puddles and up the front steps. God, it was so wet and miserable, maybe she should have just stayed home. But when Miss Mabella granted you an appointment, it didn't matter what time of day or night it was, you accepted. Or she might never see you again.

After ringing the buzzer, Joanna waited. Soon the door creaked open and the same young mulatto girl dressed in a long white dress who'd let her in last time stood in the doorway.

Joanna stepped inside the dim hallway and was instantly assailed by the familiar aroma of incense, herbal potions and candle wax.

She slipped a bill into the girl's hand, then followed her into the mysterious inner sanctum of Miss Mabella's world. Joanna swallowed. The place didn't exactly give her the creeps, but it was hard to ignore the mysterious energy that pulsated in these rooms. It both excited and frightened her. Oh, to have Miss Mabella's powers, she thought, seeing the old woman seated as usual among a cluster of guttering candles. Today her amazing outfit was somewhat marred by a brightly striped sweater worn over her flowing garments.

"Bless you, girl, come on in," Miss Mabella said softly, her huge black eyes gleaming.

"Good evening, Miss Mabella. It was kind of you to give me an appointment."

Miss Mabella nodded regally. A tiny smile curved her lips. "I been lookin' into things since you visited last," she said.

"I'm all ears, Miss Mabella." Joanna sat down on the same uncomfortable chair, thinking that with all the money she charged, Miss Mabella could certainly afford better seating.

"You worried, girl, ain't you?"

"I sure am."

"You still afraid y'ain't gonna see any of that moola your aunt left behind."

"That's right. I told you she left it all to her bastard grandson," Joanna said bitterly. "I don't know why she did that to me. I was so fond of her."

Miss Mabella said nothing, merely looked at her silently. Joanna wished she would get a move on and talk.

"Why don't you tell me what's on your mind," Miss Mabella said finally.

"Well, a couple things. The first is Grant Gallagher, Rowena's grandson. Can you tell me any more about him? What he's thinking. Will he give us any money?"

Miss Mabella removed the shells from her pouch and Joanna waited while she murmured the incantations and threw the shells. "I told you before, girl, that man be badly hurt when he were a little thing."

"You said he had a dagger in his heart."

"That's right. But at last it's beginning to loosen."

"Why's that?" Joanna whispered, leaning forward and watching Miss Mabella's face intently.

"Because he found a woman who touched his heart."

"A woman?" Her head jerked up and her expression changed. "But he's not married, doesn't have a steady girlfriend. I checked."

"This be mighty recent. But it's hit him hard."

"How recent?" Joanna asked suspiciously.

"A little while, a few months. No," she decided, picking two of the shells up and throwing them like dice once more, "weeks is more like."

"Can you tell me anything about her?" The pulse in Joanna's throat throbbed, a sign that she was nervous.

"She be young but not too young," Miss Mabella said, once again throwing the shells. "She be very different to the other women he be used to beddin'. But she's got ache in her heart for another man. He be gone, but she still achin' for him for he was a good man. Let me see…" She took the shells and held them in her left palm, closed her eyes and chanted some words in a language Joanna couldn't distinguish. "She be afraid to love again. But he won't let go until she be his."

Meredith. It had to be Meredith. Aching for another man. Meredith was widowed. It had to be her. "Have they slept together?" she asked, flexing her fingers.

"Oh, yes, they been man and woman together." She gave a long, toothless cackle. "They be made for each other, those two. Ain't nothin' going to keep them apart. Seems like there's destiny involved." She paused, intent. "Someone on the other side wants it to happen."

"What do you mean?" Joanna's eyes narrowed.

"What I said. Someone who's passed over is watchin' over them. Strong spirit she is, too. She's still around, waitin' to make sure. Won't move on until all's settled."

"My God, it must be Rowena," Joanna whispered, seriously perturbed by Miss Mabella's words.

"Could be." Miss Mabella nodded wisely. "She were somethin' else, yo' aunt. She be quite a lady."

"Is there any way he'd look at me?" Joanna asked, smothering her pride, the need to know too intense to hide.

"You?" The old woman looked at her and shook her head. "You're too old for the likes of him. He needs babies, a future. You need to be lookin' for an older man, sister."

Joanna's shoulders slumped. "Tell me more about the woman. What does she do? Where is she from?"

Again the shells rolled. "She be an intelligent woman, a fighter. She protects her own and don't take no truck from nobody. She got a fine mind. She be a good mama to her babies, too."

"Babies?" It had to be Meredith.

"Why you so worried about her?" Miss Mabella sent her a piercing glance. "She don't mean you no harm."

"I'm not worried, I'm—"

"Don't you tell me no lies, girl."

"Where is she from?"

"She not be far away. She be on this side of the water. They two flew over water together recently," she added, nodding. "What else you want to know?"

"Will I get any money from Rowena's estate?"

The old woman rocked thoughtfully. "Maybe, maybe not. Early days yet."

"But he's met us. And he has so much himself. He doesn't need the money. What's he waiting for?"

"Things is too hazy to say right now. Come back and see me in a week or so and I'll be able to tell you more."

"Fine." Masking her irritation and dreading what the information would cost her, Joanna rose. "Goodbye, Miss Mabella."

"Bless you, child, may the gods be with you," she muttered as Joanna stepped back into the corridor and marched toward the front door, which the girl had already opened. It had to be Meredith, she reasoned, climbing into the vehicle, her Prada pumps soaked.

Everything Miss Mabella had said fit her own suspicions perfectly. But how could she prove it?

Time was of the essence. She sensed it, felt it. And if it was true, she realized, grinning suddenly, she'd just bought herself some serious leverage.

"Spend the night with me in New York," Grant insisted as they boarded the private jet that would fly them into La Guardia.

"I really have to get home," Meredith demurred, finding it hard not to resist the prospect of another night in his arms. Especially after what had happened at Carrington House.

She'd experienced such a rush of emotion when Grant had changed his mind and gone with her suggestion that it left her dizzy. This man had actually listened to her, gone ahead and looked at the business plan. And seeing it could work, he had agreed to do something he'd never done before. She was ready to burst with pride.

"It's only a night, Mer," he murmured, his blue eyes cajoling as he placed her hand in his and skimmed his lips over her pulse. "You can fly back in the morning. In fact," he added, eyes arrested, "I might come back to Savannah with you."

"I don't think that's a good idea," she said hastily. "This, us, our—" She cut off, embarrassed, then took a deep breath. "I think it would be preferable if we flew separately."

He eyed her carefully, then nodded. "Okay. I'll fly down in a couple days once I've wound up my business in New York. We have to make a decision regarding the Carstairs family. It might as well be sooner rather than later."

"Perhaps we could discuss it tonight over—"

"I have no intention of discussing anything tonight except the best way to get you naked," he murmured as they climbed on board and took their seats.

Meredith let out a stifled sigh, torn between her duties and the guilty knowledge that she was committing a grave breach of conduct that could put her reputation on the line. But she couldn't seem to help herself.

Grant pulled her close and she leaned her head on his shoulder. It felt strangely right to be here with him. She felt so close to him, so honored by the way he'd acted. She knew how hard it had been for him to change his plans for the property. Yet he had. That said a lot for who he was as a man. Knowing it was crazy, Meredith snuggled closer. She'd at least enjoy it for one more night, she argued. Tomorrow she would straighten herself out and get her life back on track.

"I checked with his office in London, Ross. The girl was a temp, a silly little thing, and she looked up his agenda for me. She said he was in Cancún last weekend and right now he's in New York staying at the Carlyle."

"Yes, and?" Ross leaned back in the wide leather chair and twiddled his Mont Blanc pen, his expression bland.

"And so's Meredith," she said, eyes gleaming as she leaned forward and placed her hands on the desk between them. "Meredith is *also* in New York, staying at the Carlyle. I checked."

"So?" Ross quirked a bushy white brow. "A lot of folks go to New York and stay at the Carlyle."

"That's not all," she said, her voice throbbing with repressed emotion. "I discovered from Carla Miles, who works at the airport, that last Friday Meredith got on the Miami flight. Carla saw her board."

"Joanna, what exactly are you getting at?"

"If you were flying to Cancún, where would leave from?" she asked.

"Miami." Ross sat up straighter, eyes narrowed, the connection suddenly clear to him. "Good Lord. You think that—" He cut off, drummed the pen against the desk. "Joanna, if this is true," he said, a slow grin creeping over his weather-beaten face, "Meredith could find herself in a serious predicament."

"That's what I thought," Joanna agreed smugly. "I think Little Miss Goody Pop is screwing her brains out with her client. Now, tell me, Ross, isn't that a serious breach of fiduciary duty?"

"It could be very serious indeed if it came to the ears of the Georgia Bar Association."

"Exactly." Joanna clapped her hands gleefully.

"But for this information to be of any use," he said cautiously, "we'll need proof, absolute proof that she's been sleeping with him. It's no good if they've just been seen eating together in a restaurant."

Joanna's shoulders slumped.

"Don't worry, I can get a private eye to look into it."

"Yes," Joanna cooed. "Oh, I can't wait." She clasped her hands, relishing the moment. "What'll you do, Ross, if it's true? How'll you get me my money?"

"Hold your horses, Joanna. Let's collect the facts first. Then, depending on what those facts are, I'll have to formulate a strategy."

"Okay, but don't take too long. We need to act fast."

"Don't worry, I will. You've done well, Joanna, very well indeed." He sent her a warm, admiring smile across the desk.

"I have to be going," she said, soaking in his praise, certain that now, by some magic means, her funds would be liberated. "Keep in touch, won't you?" She rose and Ross followed suit.

"I'll call you as soon as I have any news," he assured her, accompanying her to the door. He closed it thoughtfully. If Meredith really was having an affair with Gallagher, it could turn the tables radically. She would find herself in a most vulnerable position.

He let out a long, low whistle. What wouldn't he give to see her ass backed against a wall after all the moral wrangling she'd put him through when she'd left Rollins, Hunter & Mills.

But as he sat behind his desk, his mind was absorbed with practicalities, not revenge. Dealt with right, this could be the goose that laid the golden egg. After all, Meredith was not only executor of Rowena's will, but also cotrustee with Gallagher of the Carstairs family trust. That entailed legal work. No doubt a yearly retainer had been fixed, a percentage of the trust's income to be disbursed to her for her services. He would not be loath to take over those duties.

But first things first. He must have confirmation of the facts before engaging in any type of speculation. Where there was smoke there usually was fire, and he'd be willing to bet some serious money on Joanna's hunch being right.

The dinner reservations that Grant had made over the phone were forgotten once they'd reached the suite at the Carlyle. She'd called home, said she'd be there in the morning, and then blinded herself to any possible consequences. Tonight was hers for the taking. And take she would, Meredith decided, as Grant unhooked her dress and it fell about her in a heap on the carpet. For tonight went far beyond desire. Grant's actions had altered their relationship. By taking a leap of faith with the Carringtons, he'd unblocked a dam, and emotions long held in check now flowed freely.

Trying to loosen his tie, Meredith experienced the same impatience she read in Grant's eyes. There was no time for niceties, no time for seduction. Tonight they needed to feel their bodies melt, blend, fuse.

With their clothes discarded on the floor, they fell on the turned-down bed, silently seeking each other's secrets, driven by a new irresistible force that took no prisoners, left no terrain uncovered. Together they explored uncharted territory, as each experienced an unprecedented torrent of wondrous emotion. Never had sex been so entire, so whole. And as he buried himself deep within her that night, Grant knew he'd never known the need for more as he did now.

20

The first thing to catch Meredith's eye when she walked into the office the next afternoon was the pile of phone messages.

"Anybody need urgent answering?" she asked as she slipped off her jacket and sat down at her desk, ready to sign the documents Ali offered.

"Mick's drama teacher wanted to speak to you about the Christmas play. He needs a crook for his shepherd's costume. And Ross Rollins called twice asking when you'd be back." Ali rolled her eyes. "I think that's all. I sent out the Christmas cards to everyone on our list."

"We have a Christmas card list?" Meredith tipped her glasses, surprised.

"No. But when we left Rollins, Hunter & Mills, I thought it would be expedient to acquire theirs," Ali said primly.

"Al, you amaze me. I never thought of you as devious." Meredith laughed.

"I can't help it if my hidden talents aren't recognized," she murmured, grinning. "Call Ross. He sounded ready to blow a fuse."

"Okay." Meredith yawned, forcing herself to concentrate. The day was by no means over, and the lack of sleep last night was beginning to catch up with her. She smiled as she lifted the phone, and thought of Grant's ruffled hair as he took her in his arms this morning.

Pulling herself together, Meredith listened to the private line of Ross's office ring.

"Hello, Ross Rollins speaking."

"Hi, Ross, it's Meredith."

There was a split second's silence. "Hello, Meredith. Have a good trip?"

"Fine, thanks." She experienced a shudder of anxiety. How did Ross know she'd been away?

"I'd like the two of us to get together tomorrow sometime."

"Is it anything important?" she asked, flipping through her agenda. "I've got a pretty busy day."

"Yes, I would say it's important," he replied blandly.

"Can you brief me?"

"Actually, I'd prefer to talk to you in person, not over the phone."

Meredith frowned and raised her brows. Weird. "Okay. How about four p.m.?"

"Perfect. Can you stop by the office?"

"That'd be fine. Sure you don't want to give me a hint? If there's any paperwork needed, I could bring it along."

"That won't be necessary," he answered.

Perplexed, Meredith laid the receiver back in the cradle. It wasn't like Ross not to get straight to the point. Brows knit, she sifted through the mail, wondering what could be so mysterious that he shouldn't want to talk about it over the phone.

No use conjecturing, she decided. She'd find out soon enough. Banishing tomorrow's meeting and the lingering thoughts of Grant, she attacked the pile of paperwork on her desk, determined to get through it before she left the office that evening.

It was three-forty-five the next day when Meredith set out across the park, taking advantage of the fair weather to get a little exercise. There were few people about as she walked through the orderly paths. Soon she was ringing the buzzer at the wrought-iron portals of her old office.

"Hi, Patty," she said, waving to her old pal seated as always in the reception area. "Ross is expecting me."

"I'll tell him you're here." Patty picked up the phone and spoke into it while Meredith gazed around. Her time spent in this office felt like part of another life. And in a way it was, she realized, as Patty motioned for her to go ahead. So much had changed since then.

Meredith knocked on Ross's door and waited.

"Come on in."

Pushing the door, she entered.

Ross rose graciously to greet her. "Hi, Meredith, good to see you. Come on in and sit down over here on the couch."

Meredith sat down on the leather chesterfield, surprised. Ross rarely used this area of his office, preferring his leather swivel chair behind his desk.

"Coffee?" he asked solicitously.

"No, thanks, I'm fine. So what's up?" she asked, watching him carefully ease into the armchair opposite. Posing his elbows on the arms of the chair, he steepled his fingers thoughtfully.

"Meredith, as you know, I hold you in great affection and esteem, sort of like a surrogate daughter," he began benignly. "It was a great sorrow to me when you left this office for reasons which were not, if I may say so, totally justified." Meredith shifted, alert now, wondering where this was leading. "Still, I bear you no ill will. I was young myself once and full of idealism. I know what it's like. You got certain impressions and you acted upon them without too much reflection." He eyed her carefully, his bushy white brows meeting across the bridge of his nose. "The truth is, I'm very fond of you and your family." He stopped, let the words sink in. "And that's why it troubles me that certain disturbing facts have come to my attention," he said at last, looking her straight in the eye, "facts that have put me in a mighty difficult position, Meredith."

"What do you mean?" Meredith crossed her legs. Her hands clasped her purse tensely and her heart sank.

"I've been alerted to the fact that you have been seen socializing with one of your clients. Is that so?"

"Do you mean Grant Gallagher?" she said, feeling the flush pinkening her cheeks.

"Yes. Of course, I imagine it's all quite innocent. That, let's see, two trips together—one a weekend in Cancún—were strictly business. Still, you know what wagging tongues can be like, especially here in Savannah. It would be a terrible shame if something like this were to reach the wrong parties. Could be damaging to you. I would hate for that to happen...."

"Ross, I can explain." Meredith felt her world collapsing about her. Her stomach jittered, panic set in. Ross knew. She could tell by the look in his eyes.

"Meredith, it's not me you have to worry about," he

said in a solicitous tone. "But we both know that this could have disastrous consequences for you should it, by some mischance, reach the Bar Association," he continued quietly, eyes pinning her.

She was about to deny the truth of it, then flinched. Swallowed. Tried to find words but couldn't. She'd thrown herself into the lion's den because of her inability to control herself. It was horrendous. Her mouth went dry, the pulse in her throat beat hard. She knew perfectly well that Ross's feigned solicitude was nothing but a foil. He could destroy everything she'd built over the years. Panic gripped her. What would she do? How would she provide for her kids?

Some of her anguish must have shown on her face, for Ross said soothingly, "Now, there's no need to get upset, Meredith. We're all human, after all, we all make mistakes. I'm prepared to overlook your little lapse in judgment," he said, eyes settling on her, "provided we can come to an agreement on certain matters."

She stiffened. Blackmail. She should have known he was setting her up. "Why?" she asked, struggling to retain her dignity despite her humiliation.

"For old times' sakes, and because I'm sure that we can come to a good working arrangement," he said, leaning back and crossing his legs with the confidence of one who knows he has his victim cornered. "I'm sure I can count on your cooperation in the Gallagher-Carstairs matter. Now, don't come to any rash conclusions," he said, raising a hand when he saw she was about to respond hotly, "give the dust time to settle and we'll talk. No hurry. You just think things through."

Meredith squirmed, wishing she could get out of her chair and spit in his face. Instead she sat, hands clenched, desperately seeking an out, knowing she had no option but to comply or see her life shattered. He would have no compunction, she realized, perceiving the gleam in his eyes, no mercy, because he still hadn't forgiven her for leaving, for the moral high ground she'd assumed. Oh, how she regretted those priggish words. Why hadn't she found an unrelated excuse to leave this office instead of making a point of letting him know what she felt about his involvement in covering some of Harlan MacBride's dirt, even though it was impossible to prove. There would be little use in trying to discredit him. Once again the old-boy network would close ranks around him and she'd be the loser.

"You're right," she said finally. "I'll need a little time to think this over."

"But of course, my dear, far be it from me to put pressure on you."

Meredith nodded and rose. "I'll be in touch with you in the next few days."

"Perfect. I'm sure we'll come to a satisfactory arrangement."

Her legs felt like jelly as she walked toward the door, head high. Ross opened it and showed her out. "Always a pleasure to see you here, Meredith. Take care now, and say hello to your parents." He stood in the doorway watching her as, mustering all her strength, Meredith made a calm and dignified exit from the building.

Once she was safely outside she closed her eyes and reached for the railing. Oh, God, what was she to do? How could she have allowed herself to be so stupid? How on earth had he known? Someone must have seen them together and told him.

Slowly she moved down the street. She needed a drink. A coffee. Anything. She picked her mobile out of her purse and stared at it. Who could she call? Grant? That was out of the question. No way could she tell him the truth. She needed time to think, to reassess, to come up with a plan.

But what plan? There was no alternative but to agree to his terms.

Meredith stopped at a coffee shop, sat down on one of the metal chairs on the sidewalk and ordered a café latte. Never before had she felt so impotent, so vulnerable, so close to losing everything she'd fought for. And what about those who worked for her, who'd thrown their lot in with hers and courageously gone out on a limb? If her reputation were ripped to shreds, she'd have to leave the area she loved so well, move to someplace like California where nobody knew her, leave her family and…

When the coffee arrived, she took a sip of the steaming liquid and forced herself to settle down. Now, more than ever, she needed to think clearly. She mustn't despair. She must set her feet solidly on the ground, review her options—and try to ignore the fact she was standing in quicksand.

Her entire existence was at stake. And all she had to help her were her wits.

Grant was surprised at how much he missed Meredith. Most of his romantic interludes faded from memory as soon as he delved back into the intricacies of his business affairs. But Meredith was different. Now that she was gone, he felt bereft, unable to concentrate; he wondered if she was thinking of him, too. Perhaps it was because he hadn't set about finding a new takeover target, he justified, as he sat by himself in Bemelman's bar, listening to the pianist and drinking a whisky while waiting for Carl Carrington, who was coming to town to discuss more details regarding the project.

Carl's excitement and enthusiasm were contagious. Already over the phone they'd had an in-depth discussion regarding the craftsmen and designers who could bring Carrington House back to its former glory. And Grant found himself caught up in the details, putting pen to paper and jotting down ideas, even formulating a few sketches of his own as the thoughts sprouted. It was the first time he'd ever been a part of creating anything. He found the notion both intriguing and satisfying. And it was a step he never would have considered without Meredith's prodding.

God, how he missed her. Missed her scent, her sincere gray eyes looking at him so appealingly. He was sure that since they'd returned from the Adirondacks her eyes had shone with something more than mere attraction.

He took a long draft of whisky and listened for a moment to the chatter around him, the strains of the piano in the dimly lit bar. He wasn't entirely certain, but was it pride he felt when Meredith looked at him in such an admiring and gentle manner?

He was being ridiculous. But still, he knew he wanted it to continue. Which, of course, was also unrealistic since Meredith lived a predictable, well-regulated, family-oriented life. She was everything he was not. It was unthinkable to envisage any kind of future with her. It simply wasn't possible.

He let out a huff and popped a cashew. He didn't like to be faced with impossible dreams. Coveting any kind of illusion regarding Meredith was both foolish and self-destructive, two failings he'd tried all his life to avoid. Mick and Zack flashed before him. She couldn't just put everything on hold and spontaneously join him in Monte Carlo or Portofino, as his other girlfriends had. No, he reasoned, seeing Carl standing in the entrance looking for him and waving a hand in his direction, it just wasn't feasible. And the sooner they both resolved the Carstairs business and got on with their lives, the better it would be for both of them.

"Boy, it's hot in here today," Ross muttered, wiping the sweat from his face with the hand towel hanging around his neck. "You been playing any golf lately, Drew?"

"Just nine holes here and there," the other man responded through the veil of steam.

"And how's the State Department appointment progressing? Any news yet?"

"Still waiting. The Senate Foreign Affairs Committee has been stalling again. There are dozens of appointments—including mine—that are being held hostage to politics. It's amazing anything ever gets done up in D.C., hmm?"

"Amen to that."

"And you, still working on the Carstairs estate?"

"Yeah." Ross shifted on the tiled ledge and leaned forward. "I'm hoping to make some significant progress. By the way, I might just have a buyer for your shrimp farm." His voice was noncommittal.

"You know I've been wanting to get rid of it for a while. Is it Gallagher?" he asked, wiping some sweat from his eyes.

"How did you guess?"

"Just a hunch. He's quite an impressive guy, isn't he?"

"Sure is. Apparently, he's got his fingers in deals on

every continent. Sure would be nice to get a piece of that action, huh? Oh, jeez, I have to get out of here, it's too damned hot." Ross rose and, securing the towel around his waist, pushed open the door.

"I'll be out myself in a couple minutes," Drew answered as Ross hastened out of the steam room. He heard the splash as his old friend dipped into the cold pool. Interesting. Perhaps it was time he got to know Grant Gallagher better. A man with such possibilities shouldn't be ignored.

21

This couldn't be happening, Meredith told herself for the thousandth time. She was lying in bed, unable to sleep, haunted by Ross's words. She was screwed. Totally and utterly screwed. From now on she would be at his mercy whatever she did.

Realizing sleep was out of the question, she slipped on her dressing gown and padded downstairs to the kitchen to make herself a cup of tea. What on earth had possessed her to put so much on the line for the sake of an inconsequential sexual attraction?

But that was half the trouble. The attraction didn't seem inconsequential. And Grant felt like more than a client. How could she have imagined the relationship they'd developed would grow so unexpectedly?

Sitting on one of the counter stools, she let out a long, anguished sigh. Should she try to appeal to Ross? No. If she were still a part of his firm he would have protected her. Now she'd become the enemy, the competition. He'd never forgive her for the humiliating showdown they'd had right before her departure.

She'd considered confiding in her mother but had thought better of it. This was her fault, her responsibility. She could not involve others. She'd been round and round it now for two whole days, barely able to work because she was so worried. She had to come up with an answer by tomorrow.

Grant had called to say he was arriving tomorrow afternoon. A few days ago, she would have felt excited, happy at the thought of seeing him again. Now she felt only dread. She was going to bail out on him. She had to. To save her skin, her livelihood and her position in the community, she was going to have to fall in with Ross's wishes, resign as trustee and suggest to Grant that he make the settlement on the family. His note had made it abundantly clear that if she didn't comply with his terms, the information regarding her private life would be circulated.

Meredith heaved a sigh and stared at her hands. Grant was probably disposed to settle, anyway. They'd discussed it a little over the phone and she knew he wanted to be fair to the Carstairs.

She was ashamed at how wrongly she'd judged him. He had revealed a generous and sincerely different side of his personality during those twenty-four hours in New York. They'd grown closer and Meredith sensed that in breaking the mold of his old habits, he'd opened a new side of his being.

And just as she knew she was finally touching the real Grant, she was going to have to deceive him. That, she reflected bitterly, hurt more than all the rest. He didn't deserve that. Not one little bit.

Taking a tentative sip, Meredith held the mug in her cupped hands, glad of the warmth. She glanced over into the hall at the Christmas tree, already decked, its fairy lights flashing on and off in the darkness. Then she burst into tears.

Returning to the Ballastone Inn felt strangely like coming home, Grant realized as the concierge welcomed him back. He'd even kept him the same suite, which now felt comfortably familiar. All he needed to do was unpack and call Meredith. Maybe she could take the evening off and they'd dine together somewhere nice. He was anxious to see her, to talk to her, watch her tweak that rebellious lock of hair behind her ear, then look into his eyes with that sincere, half-questioning expression that he'd come to enjoy.

Despite the pretense of dealing with Rowena's estate, he knew he was in Savannah for one reason only: to see her. For the past few days, he'd found himself wishing he could build a future with her, however unrealistic that might be.

Still, seeing her would do him good. They needed to discuss the Carstairs relatives and what he planned to settle on them. He glanced at his watch and wondered if she was still at the office. Better try her right away.

He dialed the number and Ali put him through.

"Hello, Meredith. Still slogging away?"

"Not for much longer. It's been a long day." She sounded exhausted, he noted, growing worried. "How was your trip?" she asked.

"Fine. I was hoping we might be able to dine together tonight."

"I don't think that will be possible," she said hurriedly. "But perhaps I could meet you for a drink downstairs at the Ballastone."

"How about a drink and dinner?" he cajoled.

"I really can't. It's...look, I'll explain when I see you, okay?"

"Okay," he answered, determined to twist her arm once she arrived. However much she might pretend, the truth was he believed she, too, was aware of the changing nature of their relationship.

An hour later, after asking her mother to watch the boys, Meredith entered the Ballastone Inn, heart sinking. She'd purposely stuck her briefcase under her arm to make herself appear as professional as possible. But when Grant rose to greet her, when her eyes met his and his smile caressed her, she nearly caved in. But she mustn't, couldn't. Too much was at stake.

"You look tired," he murmured, reaching over to kiss her on the cheek.

Meredith drew back. "Not here," she said quickly, slipping off her raincoat. "We can't...it looks terrible."

"Sorry." He raised his hands, rolled his eyes and backed off. "When will I get to see you in private to catch up?"

"I—look, we need to talk," she said in a rush, falling silent while Grant ordered their drinks at the small, intricately carved mahogany bar.

"What do you wish to talk about?" he asked, taking in her nervous demeanor. "Is something wrong?"

She hesitated, longing to tell him the truth, knowing it was her problem to handle alone. "The thing is, I've been thinking," she said, tweaking her hair in a nervous gesture.

"That's always dangerous. What about?"

"About us," she said, swallowing. "I mean, not that

there is an 'us' of course, just a figure of speech," she added quickly, twisting her glass of white wine.

"Well, what about us?" He watched her now, a new wariness in his eyes.

"I can't see you anymore. I'm taking a huge risk that could seriously damage my career. It must stop." It hadn't come out quite as she wanted it to, but she felt relieved at having said it.

"Just like that?" He flopped back in the chair and eyed her askance. Her words felt like a slap.

She nodded, looked away and let out a heavy sigh. "I want you to understand my reasons for taking this decision," she continued, fiddling with the clasp on her purse. "It is totally inappropriate for me to be having any kind of—of intimate relationship with a client. It's unethical, plus I can't be impartial any longer. Frankly, Grant, I don't think I can serve your interests properly."

"You have up until now."

"That was different."

"In what way?"

"I—I don't know, exactly, but it was. It's not correct for me to place myself in this position."

"But, Meredith, that's absurd. Next thing I know you'll want to resign as trustee and executor," he said, shaking his head and letting out a low, mirthless laugh.

"You're exactly right," she answered quietly. "I do plan to resign."

"On what grounds?" he asked, seriously taken aback.

"The ones I just told you. I'm sorry, Grant, but I can't do it. I don't feel right. It's wrong and we both know it. And since my impartiality is...compromised, I can't serve as a trustee to an estate to which others believe they have a claim." She held up her hand as he started to protest. "I've given this a lot of thought, and believe you should contact a colleague of mine, an estate lawyer in Atlanta. I've brought her name," she added, seeking the card in her purse. "She's exceptionally well regarded, and will do a great—"

"Damn, Meredith, I'll not hire another attorney, I want you," he pronounced harshly, eyes boring into hers, leaving her weak and confused.

"I'm sorry, Grant, but it's just not to be."

"Why? If you were resigning because you wanted to continue our relationship, I could understand, but to resign *and* give up on us. That doesn't make sense."

"Grant, I just explained, there is no us."

"Are you so sure about that?" He leaned forward, forcing her to meet his gaze. "I didn't think there was, either. But in the past couple days I believe I've changed my mind."

"I'm sorry, but I can't handle this right now," she murmured, dropping the attorney's card on the small mahogany table between them. "You really should consider talking to Amy Margulies. She's top-notch."

"You're serious about this, aren't you?" he said suddenly, backing off, baffled, a strange niggling pain gripping his gut.

"Yes, I am. Thank you for respecting my decision." She glanced at him quickly, then looked away, eyes prickling. "I have some more of Rowena's correspondence for you," she said, swallowing, determined to stay businesslike. "I was meant to give it to you once you'd made your final decision regarding the family. But I don't feel I could hand these over to another attorney. It seems—well, rather personal. Rowena entrusted the letters to me and I'd rather give them directly to you."

"Fine," he said blankly, unable to process her distant, almost detached manner.

"Very well. I'd better get going." Meredith glanced at her watch. Her wrist was trembling. "If you call the office in the morning, we can set up a time for me to hand over the file."

"Fine," he repeated, rising automatically as she did. When she extended her hand, he took it, held it a moment longer than necessary and looked into her eyes. What he read there was a mass of confusion that left him frowning. For an instant he thought of forcing her to sit back down and tell him exactly what was going on. But she removed her hand and smiled a brittle smile that didn't reach her eyes. "Goodbye, Grant. I'll talk to you tomorrow."

"Goodbye," he muttered. Standing rooted to the spot, he watched as she disappeared down the steps and out of his life.

This is what happened when emotions got involved, he reminded himself bitterly, sitting back down and throwing back the rest of his whisky. It was his own damn fault. When had he started wanting something more than just the passion between them?

In New York, he realized. The Carrington House had changed everything. By accepting his challenge, by helping him rethink how he could manage his career, live his life, she'd shown him she cared.

Ordering a second whisky, he thought about Meredith and what she'd come to represent for him—the future, he acknowledged, swallowing hard. He'd never thought of building any kind of relationship with a woman. But neither had he thought of building a hotel. Any sort of deeper relationship would automatically entail commitment. But then so did the project he'd just gotten himself tied up in. And he felt good about that, didn't he? Could it be possible that he might feel good if he were to assume some of the responsibilities that only days earlier he'd argued would make any type of future relationship with Meredith impossible? Now, all at once, those same insurmountable hurdles seemed trivial.

For a moment he pictured the two kids he'd met and a slow smile curved his lips. He, of all people, knew what boys of that age needed. Particularly ones who, one way or another, had been deprived of their father. Perhaps, and this, of course, was a daring thought, he might just be able to contribute something to their lives.

He quickly reminded himself that the last thing he wanted was responsibility. But to his amazement, assuming some of the burdens in Meredith's life didn't seem a major issue any longer. The existence he'd fought so hard to protect seemed strangely unappealing. Now, as he looked back, he wondered if his celebrated ruthlessness had just been a kind of revenge, a way to mete out to others some of the pain and hurt he himself had felt. The thought sickened him.

And yet he was trying to change, wasn't he? Meredith had helped him see the value of building things up rather than tearing them to pieces. And that had brought a rare feeling of satisfaction and accomplishment into his life, recognition that he could be a positive force for change. Jesus, he was getting sappy, he reflected, but that didn't alter the truth that, for the first time in memory, he felt good about himself, about what he was doing, about what he could do.

And it was all because of Meredith. He wasn't prepared to give her up. She was an integral ingredient of this new future he envisioned, whether or not she admitted it. He knew a thing or two about fighting for what he wanted, he acknowledged with a half smile. And Meredith Hunter was in his crosshairs.

Still, he realized, sobering, he'd have his work cut out for him. After all, she'd just told him she didn't want him in her life any longer. That hurt, he admitted. That she should want to back out as his attorney made a certain amount of sense since she felt it was unethical to be romantically involved with a client. But she'd made it clear she wanted nothing more to do with him.

Grant frowned, going back over their conversation word by word, remembering the nervous way she'd twisted her glass, her anxious expression. It wasn't like Meredith at all, he concluded. There had to be something else at work here, a deeper link than she'd admitted between her desire to resign and her rejection of him. She definitely hadn't been herself tonight. There'd been dark rings under her eyes, as though she hadn't slept.

Later, as Grant climbed the polished oak stairs to his suite, he decided he'd visit her office in the morning and see if he could do some damage control. Something—or someone—had upset her, and he had every intention of finding out exactly *what* or *who* it was.

After that, they'd have him to reckon with.

Meredith lifted the phone and dialed Ross's number. He would be out of the office by now so she could leave a message. She didn't want to talk to him.

The phone rang several times, then went on to the voice mail. She waited for the beep. "Hi, Ross, it's Meredith Hunter. I'm calling to tell you that I spoke to

Gallagher and tendered my resignation. It is now up to him to decide how he wishes to proceed."

She laid down the receiver heavily, her only consolation a meager one: that whatever the consequences she had not caved in to Ross's unscrupulous demands. Maybe he would be angry and take his revenge if and when Grant appointed another attorney in her stead.

So be it. She glanced around the hall, through the living room door at the Christmas tree. Would this be the last Christmas she and the kids would spend in this home? God, she hoped not. But if it was, she would have only herself to blame. Her lack of control would haunt her for the rest of her life.

The weight of her sin hung over her like Damocles' sword. Everything about her felt heavy, from the feet she dragged up the stairs to her bedroom, to the heart that ached as she'd never believed it could again. Seeing Grant tonight had brought everything into focus. She'd lied to herself, pretended that her feelings were not involved when, in fact, they were. It hadn't been just a fling, at least not for her. She had feelings for him, impossible feelings that entailed a future together. She wanted everything she knew he didn't. She would never have imagined that she could conceive of it all with anyone except Tom.

Yet she did.

And now it was over.

Burying her head in her pillow, Meredith allowed the tears to flow, crying this time not for the past, but for a future she longed for and that could never be. Tomorrow she would hand over Rowena's file and the final letter to him and that would be that. There would be no reason for them to meet again. Which in the long run was for the best, she justified with a sniff, since it wouldn't have worked out, anyway.

Blowing her nose hard, she turned the light out and tried to sleep.

"You close them shutters, girl," Miss Mabella ordered her assistant. "It ain't hurricane season no more, but tonight we're in for a big one."

"I hate storms." The girl shuddered, heading toward the window.

"Ain't nothing to worry about. You be protected," Miss Mabella assured her. Then she moved her bulk back to her wide stool and sat down once more, the folds of her wide white-lace skirt falling about her. The wind picked up and she glanced at the ceiling. The stuffed blackbird swung on the string from the rafters and she eyed it warily. "Ain't no good when you starts movin'," she muttered, shaking her turbaned head and inspecting the glasses of water standing next to the statuettes she'd placed on the altar after that Carstairs gal's last visit. "Ain't no good, that one," she muttered, refilling the glasses with water from her special pewter jug. She needed to keep the two figures' cups full, otherwise things might go drastically wrong.

Slowly she rocked, back and forth, murmuring incantations. The spirits were about tonight, and as the wind whipped up, she sensed a powerful one right next to her.

"You still here, Miss Rowena?" she whispered. "Yep, you still hangin' around waitin'. Well, you's right. That boy of yours be needin' some help—he's a changin', jes like you hoped, but things ain't done yet. Those two got some workin' to do. They got the bad one fightin' them. I'm doin' all I can, but people be a meddlin' in what don't be no concern of theirs. That ole rooster, he be just as nasty as that Joanna. Got our girl frightened out of her wits, poor child. Just lucky your boy got a mighty lot of good sense in his head. And he be a strong man. Ain't no one gonna roll over him, no siree. Not after what Miss Mabella been gettin' up to." She let out a low cackle that ended in a hacking cough. "Gimme my pipe, girl," she called out.

"The doctor said you wasn't to smoke it no more, Miss Mabella," she ventured timidly.

"That damn doctor's a quack who don't know nothin'. I ain't got no time for him. He's an ole woman."

Taking the gnarled old pipe, she filled it with herbs and tobacco, a special mixture handed down to her from her African ancestors. It had proved helpful in the past, would be so again. As the smoke spiraled toward the ceiling, Miss Mabella studied the patterns forming. And didn't like what she saw. She could feel the spirit's agitation, knew Rowena was calling upon her to take stronger action.

"You know interferin' directly in people's personal bizness ain't my style," she argued back, "but you's right, they be unprotected, those two. But I got to get closer, can't do no more without seein' them personal. You tell your li'l girl that in the end it'll be okay."

The wind howled and the rafters shook as Miss Mabella rocked, pipe in hand, watching the pictures in her other world fall into place.

She rocked until the pipe burned out, then sighed. She'd have to wait until dawn to get a better reading. Too dang much negative energy floating about just now.

Leaning her elbows on her wide thighs, she closed her eyes and allowed the trance to take over. It was time, and she needed to be prepared.

22

"Giving this party was a brilliant notion," Joanna said to Craig as she lifted another champagne cocktail off the tray of a passing waiter. "You're sure he's coming, right?"

"Absolutely. He assured me he'd be here. I told him the small gathering was in his honor. He can hardly fail to show."

"Good." Joanna nodded and took a long sip that emptied half her flute. "Lovely stuff, this champagne cocktail," she murmured, glancing cheerfully at her glass.

Craig sent her a skeptical glance. Joanna was halfway soused already.

Seeing Grant appear in the entrance, he moved forward to greet him. "Come on in, nice to see you back in Savannah," he said cordially, "Sally, dear, our guest of honor has arrived."

"Oh, Grant, how great you could make it," she cooed, straightening the tight black cocktail dress that hugged her voluptuous figure, leaving little to the imagination.

"Nice to be here," he answered, his smile polite as he scanned the room. Dallas, who'd reached town yesterday, had told him that Meredith would be here tonight. He hadn't been able to see her at the office. She'd been conveniently "out" and had her secretary hand over the file, but he had every intention of pinning her down and having a talk.

"Hi, there, gorgeous."

He glanced over his shoulder. Joanna Carstairs, dressed in a slinky gray silk cocktail dress, sidled up to him, a champagne flute balanced precariously in her long, manicured fingers.

"Good evening," he responded, peering over the heads of the other guests to see if he could catch sight of his quarry.

"Don't forget about me, darling." She stood next to him and smiled archly. "You went away without saying goodbye," she pouted, pushing her index finger into the front of his blazer, "you naughty boy, you."

"I've been traveling." By the looks of it, Joanna had already consumed a fair amount of champagne.

"I *know* you've been traveling," she responded in a confidential tone, pulling his shoulder down and whispering in his ear. "I know where you've been and who you were with," she added triumphantly.

Grant experienced a shiver of unease. "I don't how my personal travel plans can be of interest to anyone," he responded blandly.

"They are to me," Joanna cooed, gulping more champagne and flapping her eyelashes. "You've been a very bad boy," she repeated, wagging her index finger. "It's not eth—" she hiccupped "—ethical to fuck your attorney, you know. It'll set people talking," she said, reaching out and grabbing his forearm. "There're all these rumors about."

"What kind of rumors?" he inquired, controlling his anger as all at once Meredith's sudden actions began to make sense.

"Oh, well, you know how it is," she said, smiling coyly up at him. "No rumors yet, but there *could* be. She's no good for you, Grant. Now, you and I, I'll bet that could be something," she cooed, letting her scarlet nail trail down his sleeve.

Grant took a step back, wondering how to escape Joanna's persistent attentions. Raising his eyes, he caught the eye of a man he'd met at the party at Montalba. They exchanged a glance and again he experienced a strange sense of familiarity. Then the man smiled and, as though understanding Grant's plight, approached.

"Hi, you may not remember me, I'm Drew Chandler. We met out at Montalba."

"Yes, I remember. Have we met anywhere else before? You strike me as familiar."

"I don't believe so," Drew said carefully. "But I was wondering if you'd like to join me for lunch one day?"

Grant hesitated, gripped by a strange sensation he couldn't define. "Why not?"

"Good. Then I'll call you. The Ballastone, isn't it? Maybe we could fit in some tennis, too."

"Fine. I'd enjoy that," Grant replied, smiling, surprised to realize that he would. The prospect of whacking out all his frustration on a tennis ball seemed instantly appealing.

"Oh, Drew, I was having such a nice chat with Grant, here. Why do you have to be a party pooper?"

"Excuse me. Sorry," he said in an aside for Grant's ears only, "I'm afraid I have to go. Just tell Craig to take her home if she gets difficult."

"Right."

"What'd he say?" Joanna lurched, nearly losing her balance.

"Nothing, just good night. Now, tell me more about those rumors," he insisted, securing her arm and replacing her empty champagne flute with a full one.

"Rumors?" She frowned. "Oh, yeah, Meredith. Yeah, well as I was saying, she'd better look out. She could get into some deep shit if she's not careful and that's the truth." Joanna nodded between sips. "She'll have to mind her step from now on."

"What do you mean?"

"Why should I tell you?" She sent him a languorous look from beneath her mascara.

"Because," Grant murmured seductively in her ear, "you want me to make you a very rich woman."

"That's true." She nodded, slurring her words. "You're darn right I do. Ross says it'll happen now that Meredith's screwed up. But I don't know."

"Ross?"

"Oops, sorry, didn't mean to say that." She hiccuped once more and brought her hand to her lips. "Sorry, this champagne's kind of getting to me. Will you take me home?"

"Why, it would be a pleasure," he responded, taking her arm and guiding her toward the door. "Why don't you give me your car keys and I'll drive you?"

"S'good idea." She gulped, nearly losing her balance on the step. "I'll just get my coat."

"Allow me." Grant beckoned to a waiter and Joanna described her coat to him.

"I like your style," she said, swaying on his arm in the hall under the chandelier, "you've got class. And money. That's a pretty lethal combination."

"Let's see if you can help divest me of some of it," he said dryly as the waiter returned with the coat and he helped her struggle into it. If Joanna had any pertinent information, he was willing to pay to extract it from her.

"Well." Meredith bristled as she and Dallas drove up and she watched Grant help Joanna into her car, then take the wheel. "He hasn't wasted any time, has he?"

"Oh, Joanna's probably drunk and he's taking her home," Dallas answered indifferently. "Hey, you're not jealous, are you?" She quirked her brow and grinned, her expression arrested.

"Of course I'm not jealous. What an absurd statement," Meredith said in a withering tone.

"You *are* jealous." Dallas nodded knowingly. "Now, don't deny it, Mer. I just *knew* there was something going on between you two!" She clapped her hands, delighted.

"Dallas, will you shut up? Of course there's nothing going on between Grant and me. I'm just surprised to see him with Joanna, that's all."

"Oh, sure. That's why you're bristling like a hedgehog. You can't fool me, Mer." Dallas rolled her eyes. "Do you really want to go to this party?" she asked. "After all, the one person we came to see just left." She peered at Meredith out of the corner of her eye and stifled a giggle.

"Dallas, you're impossible," Meredith exclaimed, exasperated.

"Well, it's true. I say we go get ourselves some ribs at the Pirate's House. I have a craving for some Carolina Honeys."

"I couldn't eat anything right now."

"Why not? It's dinnertime."

"Because I'm not hungry."

"That's 'cause you're in love."

"Rubbish, it's—what did you say?" Meredith squeaked. "Dallas, don't say things like that, you'll get me into a shitload of trouble, okay?"

"But it's true," Dallas insisted. "You're in love with my brother. I think that's cute. I mean, it's obvious to any discerning human," she said with a confident laugh.

"I am not in love with anyone, so shut up. Now, tell me where I should drop you off. Where are you staying?"

"At Rowena's."

"You are?" She looked at the girl, surprised. "Who gave you the key?"

"Nobody. I kept one."

"It's not strictly ethical for you to stay there while the will's in probate," Meredith said, frowning.

"Neither is it ethical for you to have the hots for your client," she countered, laughing, stopping short when she saw Meredith's eyes fill. "Hey, I'm sorry, Mer, I didn't mean to hurt your feelings or say something out of line. What's the matter?" She reached over and squeezed Meredith's arm.

"Nothing. I'm just tired, that's all. I'll drop you off and go home. I need an early night."

"Okay, if you're sure you don't want to come in for a while and talk," Dallas murmured as they turned into Rowena's street. "You seem really stressed out, Mer."

"I have a lot of work right now," she said, slowing in front of the house.

"You sure you don't want to join me for an hour or so?"

"Thanks, but I need to get home," she answered, kissing Dallas goodbye.

"Well, hang in there. And don't let things get you down, okay?"

"Okay." Meredith nodded and smiled gamely as Dallas got out of the car and moved toward the gate.

She must assume control, Meredith realized, shocked at her own reaction. She simply must sort her life out. Tomorrow she would call Ross.

She hated herself for thinking of giving in to him. But her whole future hung in limbo.

Her mind wandered back to Joanna and Grant driving off into the night. Well, regardless of what Dallas had said, it was obvious he hadn't spent much time mourning her loss, she reflected bitterly. If that was the kind of man he was, well then she was better off without him.

But as she drove up in front of her home, taking a deep breath so that she could pull herself together to face the kids, she knew that getting over Grant Gallagher would take her longer than she cared to think about.

A satisfied grin swept over Ross's tanned features as he checked his phone messages. Very good. Meredith had fallen in line just as he knew she would. He'd talk to her later in the day to smooth out any glitches, but what mattered was that she'd resigned and told Gallagher so. Now the road was free for him to act. The first step was to get in touch with the man and set up a meeting so that he could reach a final settlement for the Carstairs relations. This, of course, would demand a substantial fee. But they would be only too glad to pay whatever he asked— indeed, they should be thrilled to be receiving anything at all!

The phone rang and he picked up.

"Ross Rollins speaking. Who?" His brow creased, then lightened. "Ah, of course. Put him on." His face broke into a grin. Already the chain reaction was at work. "Good morning, Grant," he called jovially into the receiver, "glad to hear you're doing fine. You're in town, right?"

"That's right. I wondered if we could set up a meeting. I have a couple things I'd like to discuss with you."

"But of course." Ross flipped through his agenda. "How about four o'clock today?"

"Perfect."

"I'll see you then."

He set down the phone and let out a gusty sigh. Everything was going according to plan. Obviously, Meredith had pitched the ball his way. Good girl. He'd be willing to bet she was ruing the day she left the firm.

As he walked across the park to Ross Rollins's office, Grant's mind focused on the upcoming meeting. Something was definitely amiss, and he planned to find out exactly what. The picture of Meredith's white features and Joanna's drunken comment were clearly etched before him as he reached the fine wrought-iron gate of the imposing offices. Time to test the terrain, he reflected as it opened. And let Ross Rollins walk into the spiderweb he planned to set for him.

* * *

Ross saw Grant into his office, offered him a seat, then settled behind his desk. He peered at Grant over his glasses. "So, you've come to talk about the Carstairs family settlement. I understand it was too much for Meredith to cope with."

"So it would seem." Grant leaned back and observed the man before him. He looked at ease, comfortable. As though he knew exactly where he stood.

"Right." Ross cleared his throat and rummaged through some papers on his desk. "You know all the main issues so I won't bother going over them again. What I wanted to focus on are the investments and how we could manage them better. "Take this copper mine in Bolivia, for instance."

"We?" The word cut the air and Ross looked up, surprised.

"Yes. After all, I'll be handling the estate from now on, so I thought we should think of diversifying the portfolio."

"Not so fast, Mr. Rollins." Grant's gaze pierced and he saw the flash of doubt in the other man.

"Well, it all seems pretty straightforward," Ross countered, smiling once more in what Grant recognized as his reassuring manner.

"I'm afraid I don't think so. Perhaps I'd better make my position clear to you. I have absolutely no intention of leaving the estate in your hands."

"Wh-what?" Sweat broke on Ross Rollins's brow.

"Exactly what you heard. I don't know what you've said or done to intimidate Meredith, but I'd be willing to bet big money you persuaded her to hand over the file through foul means. Now, perhaps you'd like to see the file I have on you." He slipped a buff envelope across the desk.

Ross stared at it. "I don't know what you're talking about. This is ridiculous," he blustered. "Intimidating Meredith, indeed. That's slanderous."

"No more so than the information in that envelope. It could stop you practicing. In fact, the Georgia bar would be very interested in all it contains. Not to mention the fact that you would most probably end up behind bars."

"How dare you? This is outrageous," Ross spluttered.

"Really? I'll leave you to take a look at it. Maybe after you've read the contents you may not feel quite as outraged at my words," Grant said deliberately, rising from the chair. "Good day, Mr. Rollins. I'll be taking care of my own estate in the future, and as for Rowena's relations, tell them to get in touch with me personally. I'll keep them posted on any decisions in due course."

With that he left the room, leaving Ross dumbfounded behind the closed door. Grant smiled at the secretary as he passed in the hall, then stepped out into the street feeling a lot lighter than he had half an hour earlier.

It was hard to get motivated when her mind was filled with worry and her heart heavy with loss. Meredith sat staring blindly at the papers on her desk, aware of a deep sense of emptiness, eerily similar to what she'd felt when Tom had died.

That was coupled with an intense level of anxiety zapping every ounce of her usually buoyant energy. She'd taken a huge risk in flouting Ross's plans—he'd be furious when he realized she hadn't advised Grant to transfer Rowena's estate business to his firm. Even though she could hardly be blamed if Grant chose to hire outside council, she suspected Ross might well spill the beans on her, anyway, just out of spite.

She'd been up since three this morning, painting progressively grimmer scenarios of what her and her children's future would be once the sword came down. Now, at ten-thirty, her head jerked every time the phone rang in the reception area, certain it was the bar association, inviting her to appear before an ethics panel.

Unable to think straight and feeling increasingly queasy, Meredith decided she could not stay in the office. She'd better go home and try to get some sleep. She dragged on her coat with an effort, caught a glimpse of herself in the mirror in the hallway and grimaced at the wan creature reflected there. Her life was collapsing around her and there was nothing she could do to avoid the fall.

"I'm not feeling great," she said to Ali as she passed her desk. "I think I'll go on home and take a rest. Tell Trace, will you?"

"You, sick?" Ali looked surprised. In all the years they'd worked together, Meredith had never once been out on sick leave.

"Hold the fort and call me if anything major occurs." *Like my license getting revoked*, she thought bleakly as she walked out the door and got into the car.

At home everything was quiet. The boys still had several days of school left before the vacation. She dropped her coat and briefcase in the hall, went into the living room and stared at the Christmas tree. When the doorbell rang, her mouth went dry and she swallowed hard. Had they come to seek her out at home?

Moving heavily toward the door, Meredith opened it. She stopped short and her pulse jumped a beat when she saw Grant standing in the doorway.

"Wh—what are you doing here?" she murmured, her voice a thin semblance of its usual self. Automatically she pushed her hair back. She looked a mess. But then again, at this point, what did it matter?

"Ali told me at the office that you were ill. I came at once. What's the matter, Mer?" He stepped forward, strong and vibrant, his eyes brimming with concern.

"I wasn't feeling great," she managed to say. His sympathy and having him so near brought her close to tears. Without waiting for her to answer, he pulled her into the crook of his arm and, moving her inside, closed the door behind them.

"Start by telling me what Ross Rollins was threatening to do to you if you didn't resign," he said, tilting her chin up and searching her face.

"Ross? How do you know?" She gulped.

"I put two and two together. It wasn't difficult after Joanna told me about the little plan they'd cooked up."

"So that's why you were driving her home the other night."

"Yes. Did you think it was something else?" His eyes filled with tender mirth and her cheeks flushed. "Go on, I want to know exactly what he said to leave you in this state."

"He's threatening to tell the Georgia bar about us," she said, letting out a miserable sigh but relieved to finally be voicing her worry.

"Well, you can forget that," he said harshly, moving

back a step and taking her hands in his. "Ross Rollins will be lucky if the bar doesn't come after *him*."

Meredith looked at him in confusion. "But he's a very powerful man, Grant. The Georgia bar will believe every word he says. Plus I'm at fault, that's the truth of it."

"Trust me, Ross won't go anywhere near the bar association," he said deliberately, "for the simple reason that if he does, a package containing a fully documented file on his activities during the MacBride campaign will be anonymously placed on their doorstep."

"But that's never been investigated. Ross hushed it up. I knew some of it, but not enough to nail him." She dragged her fingers through her hair and looked at him, the dark rings under her eyes telling him just what sort of a night she'd had.

"Darling, my investigators unearthed enough dirt on Ross Rollins to send him to jail for quite a while. He's not going to harm you or anybody else. Not while I have anything to do with it," he pronounced grimly.

Meredith stared at him in wonder. The hard expression on his face gave her an inkling of what he could be like when he became angry. Little by little the reality of his words sank in. "You mean you've told Ross this?" She could feel a lightening of the weight in her chest, relief rushing through her.

"I have made it abundantly clear to Mr. Rollins that if he ever lifts a finger against you he'll have me to deal with." His fingers trailed down her cheek and skimmed her jaw. Then, cupping her neck, he drew her close. "You don't think I'd allow anyone to harm you, do you?" His lips touched her brow, the tip of her nose, her lips.

"I've been so frightened, Grant," she whispered between his kisses, "I can't begin to tell you." He guided her to the couch and pulled her gently on top of him until she was sitting in his lap.

"I know," he soothed, "I realized that as soon as Joanna spilled the beans. The bastard." He ground his teeth on the word and Meredith felt strangely comforted.

"I still think I'd better resign as your council, though," she said, sitting up, still dazed by the unexpected turn of events. "I'd feel happier. It's hard to explain, but I don't really want to be your legal representative anymore." She frowned, it was so unlike her to say a thing like that.

"Good. Because as it happens, I have other plans for us," he murmured, hand snaking up behind her neck and bringing her lips down on his.

Unable to resist the deliciously familiar taste of him, Meredith responded. Her arms slipped around his neck and she gloried in the security and strength she experienced as his arms surrounded her and she melted into them. It was as if no harm could ever come to her while he was here.

"I don't think I can live without you," Grant murmured into her hair.

"Neither do I," Meredith whispered, biting her lips. "But we both know it's impossible for us to be together," she added, pulling away.

"Why?" Grant asked, gently moving her hair behind her ear and cocking his head. "I don't see why it should be impossible. In fact, I can think of a number of perfectly reasonable options. It may take a little thinking out, but I'm sure we'll manage it."

"Maybe," she retorted, determined not to be caught

up in his enthusiasm and lose sight of reality. "But the truth is that we lead such different lives. Right now you don't think it matters," she continued, playing with his fingers absently, "but in a while you'll get bored and want to move on. I don't want a relationship of forty-eight-hour stopovers in fancy hotels. I don't think I could handle that."

"You mean you want more?" There was a gleam in his eye, which should have warned her.

"I guess you could say that," she admitted, a trembling smile hovering as she looked into his eyes. "Our lives are poles apart. We have nothing in common except...except...well the fact that we—" She cut off, looked away. "I can't expect something from you that you never promised and are not prepared to give," she finished in a rush. "It's not your fault I got myself into this. I don't want you to feel bad."

His hands gripped her shoulders. "You insult me," he said quietly, forcing her to look at him.

"I never meant to."

"But you did." His voice was quiet now and intense, and she cringed.

"Meredith, if you think that for one moment I want anything less than the whole enchilada, you're dreaming."

"The whole enchilada?" she repeated blankly.

"That's right, you and everything that comes with you. The house, the kids, the dog, even that damn hamster," he said, pointing to Ronnie's cage, which Mick had left in the kitchen doorway for its weekly clean. "The lot."

"You can't be serious." She let out something between a sigh of longing and a stifled laugh. "You may think that's what you want, but in a practical sense it's just impossible."

"Give me two good reasons why."

"Well, to begin with, either I'd have to move to London, which would upset the kids, and I don't think I could do it—"

"Or I could move to Savannah," he supplied.

"You'd consider moving here?" Her hands dropped in wonder.

"As I recall, I inherited a very nice house. There's no reason why we shouldn't move in there."

"Grant, you don't understand," she said, tears of tenderness welling. "This isn't London or New York. People don't just move in together."

"I meant after the wedding," he said, eyes filled with tender mirth.

"Wedding?" Meredith's eyes flew to his. "You want to marry me?"

"Yes, of course. And as I pointed out only a moment ago, I'm willing to do anything to get you—even live with that menagerie of yours." His lips twitched and he looked her over lovingly.

"What about the ferret?" she queried faintly, her heart racing as the realization of what he was saying sank in.

"I must admit the thought is daunting. Couldn't Zack be persuaded to find it another home, in favor, let's say, of a new bike?"

"I should think that might be negotiable. But, Grant, seriously, you can't want to take on my kids as well. This would change your entire life. And mine," she added, the realization finally sinking in. It was all so sudden.

"You don't think I'd make a good stepfather?" He quirked a brow at her. "You know I may not have much experience, but if anyone knows what a child desperately longs for and needs, I do."

"I don't doubt that," she answered sincerely. "I think you'd be a wonderful dad. I just worry for you. This might get old after a bit. And then everyone would be hurt."

"This is the first time I've asked a woman to marry me," he said, getting up and standing over her. "I never realized it could be so damn complicated. Meredith, why won't you give us a chance?"

"I want to," she conceded. "I guess I'm scared." She raised her hands palms up, then dropped them in her lap.

"I'm scared, too. Who wouldn't be? Change is always hard. But I'm willing to give it a hell of a lot more than just a try. At least give me some credit," he muttered, still gazing down at her, determined to get his way.

"I do."

"But not enough to take the plunge."

"It's not that." Meredith looked into his eyes and caught her breath, the pain and rejection she read there too much for her to bear.

"Then what is it?" he insisted.

"Grant, I—"

"Yes, say it, for Christ's sake," he insisted, frustrated. "Tell me what it is you find wrong with this and we'll try to find a solution."

"I really don't know. I need time, I—"

"You don't want to marry me," he said suddenly. His face paled and he nodded. Suddenly he realized he'd read her wrong. Of course. He should have known, should have realized. "I was a fool," he murmured, turning away. "A bloody fool. I should have realized this didn't mean the same for you as it has for me." He dragged his fingers through his hair and stared out the window. He'd just made an idiot of himself. He'd believed, wanted to believe so badly that Meredith had changed something in his life. But she obviously didn't love him. Well, he was used to rejection. He'd rebuild the barriers he'd so foolishly let drop.

"Grant, please, let me explain," Meredith pleaded.

"There's no need," he said, cutting her off, raising his hand. "I understand. I never should have put you in this position. I'm sorry. Now, you mentioned a letter of Rowena's you wanted to give to me. It wasn't in the file. I plan to leave late tomorrow morning."

Meredith swallowed, at a loss as what to do. It was as if in a few short seconds he'd withdrawn from her life, leaving her feeling empty and alone. She didn't know what to say.

"Look, Grant it isn't what you think, I—"

"Just get the letter please," he answered curtly.

"Grant, please, listen to me. I need to explain."

"Meredith, I'm not a dimwit. I got the message loud and clear. Now, would you please give me that letter so that I can leave?"

He sounded cold, almost rude.

"Okay," she muttered at last, not knowing how to proceed, how to reach him. How could she make him understand that she couldn't just decide her and her children's future in a few minutes? That she needed time to consider his offer?

Moving to the hall, she opened her briefcase, hands agitated as she retrieved the letter. "Here it is," she said, looking up to see him right behind her.

"Thanks." He slipped it automatically into his breast pocket. Looked at her long and hard. "I'll miss you, Mer," he said at last.

"Grant, I—please just give me a chance to think this over."

"Please." He raised a restraining hand, his expression cold. "Let's make this easier on both of us, shall we? Don't feel you have to soften the blow. You'll only prolong the agony." He smiled down at her ironically, a self-deprecating smile that left her wishing she could just throw herself in his arms and say yes.

She wanted to stop him, to tell him she'd made a mistake, that she wanted to be with him more than anything in the world. But she knew she couldn't truthfully decide without first taking the time to be sure. And that was not acceptable to Grant. He wanted her to commit to him here and now, for her to place her future and that of her children in his hands with no questions, no doubts.

But how could she?

They stood for a moment, the silence heavy between them, when all at once the doorbell rang.

Meredith jumped. "Oh, God, who can that be?"

Grant said nothing, just watched as she went to answer the door.

"Hi, darling, I called the office and Ali told me you were sick so I popped by. What's the matter? You look terrible," Clarice Rowland exclaimed, walking inside automatically. When she saw Grant, her eyes flew from one to the other; it was evident she'd just stepped into the middle of something. "Oh, hi, Grant, I didn't realize you were here. I'll just drop these cookies off in the kitchen," she said hastily, "and then I'll be on my way."

"Please, don't go on my account, I was just leaving myself," Grant said with practiced ease. "Nice seeing you again, Mrs. Rowland. I shall be leaving Savannah tomorrow so I probably won't see you again." He shook her hand, turned to Meredith. "Goodbye,

Meredith. I'll advise you once I've talked to Ms. Margulies and you can have the files shipped. Thanks for all your help." He dropped a chaste kiss on her cheek, then walked out the door.

Meredith's limbs simply wouldn't react. She murmured goodbye and watched, confused, as he headed down the path and out into the street. Then he was gone and the tears she'd been holding back poured down her cheeks.

"Meredith? What on earth's the matter, honey?" Clarice rushed forward as Meredith closed the door and, placing a comforting arm about her shoulders, led her into the kitchen.

"He's never coming back," Meredith sobbed, "and it's all my fault. I sent him away. Oh, Mother…" She buried her head in her mother's shoulder and wept as she hadn't wept since Tom's death. "I—I never thought I'd fall in love again. It was meant to be a fling, a—a way of getting him out of my system."

"And now?" Clarice asked softly, stroking her daughter's hair.

"Now I've screwed it all up," she wailed. Raising her head, she accepted the handkerchief her mother handed her and dropped onto the counter stool.

"Tell me about it." Clarice moved toward the kettle and turned it on, then popped two tea bags into mugs.

"There's nothing much to tell." *Nothing that's not incredibly embarrassing to admit to one's mother*, Meredith thought miserably. Then, gathering her courage, her face flaming, she spoke about Cancún, about the trip to New York and how proud she was that Grant had changed his mind about destroying the hotel. "And I guess I've finally realized," she finished, "that he's so much more than the man I thought he was."

"And now?"

Meredith sniffed and twisted the damp hankie methodically. "Now he wants to marry me," she muttered. "And of course I can't because it would be crazy."

"And why is that?" Clarice asked, her voice neutral as she poured the boiling water into the mugs.

"Well, for all sorts of obvious reasons," Meredith declared.

"Such as?"

"The children. It wouldn't work with the children. They're not over Tom's death yet."

"And never will be," Clarice said, placing the mugs on the counter and sitting on the stool. "But they're ready to move on, to have a happy, fulfilled mother rather than a nervous wreck, which is what you're fast becoming."

"I'm not a nervous wreck. It's just something that happened," she replied, not even wanting to go into the whole debacle with Ross, knowing he was one of her father's old friends.

"Meredith, I know this is not my affair," Clarice said carefully, understanding how risky a mother's intervention could be. "But Grant strikes me as a very special man. Are you sure you're not prejudging him when you say a life together would be impossible?"

"I don't now. That's what makes it so hard. I have no firm answer. There's nothing to assure me that it would work out. If I was certain, had a concrete answer…"

"Well, that's one thing you'll never have," her mother said firmly. "Nothing is sure in this life except death. But I do know life can be very sad and boring and empty if you don't take the opportunities that are put in your path. Life isn't an equation, Meredith.

There's no one right answer. You of all people know that life takes twists and turns when you least expect it."

"I guess," she murmured doubtfully.

"Think about Tom," her mother insisted, placing the cookie jar between them. "You had twelve wonderful years with him. Would you have given them up if you'd known they were going to end so abruptly and so tragically? Or was it worth it?"

"Of course it was worth it," she retorted defensively.

"So tell me, honey, what's so different? You have a wonderful man ready to turn his life upside down for you, to give you and your children love and a safe, secure home, maybe even kids of your own."

"Kids?" Meredith looked at her, shocked. "You think he'd want kids?"

"Why not? You're not too old. I think the boys would love having a baby brother or sister."

"Oh, my God." Meredith stared into her mug as a picture formed in her mind and her hands trembled. "Mother, I've been an idiot. I have to go after him." She pushed back the stool abruptly. "Will you pick up the kids later?"

"Don't worry about a thing. Just go after your man, Meredith, and make sure you make him happy. He deserves it."

Grabbing the car keys, Meredith rushed down the path and into the street. It was probably crazy, but she must catch Grant, must tell him she'd changed her mind before it was too late.

Hands trembling, she drove the Jeep down the street toward the Ballastone Inn. She had to find him before she lost her nerve. Oh, God, how could she ever have thought of living without him?

23

Walking usually helped clear his mind. But not today. Not after what he'd just experienced. How foolish of him to believe that Meredith felt the same way he did. She'd always said it was a fling. And she'd been telling the truth.

The truth hurt.

He walked past the attractive houses hidden behind luscious vegetation. It was only as he saw a familiar white Mustang slow down across the street that he realized it was Dallas and that she was pulling in front of Rowena's sprawling Savannah home.

Crossing the street, he came alongside the car and smiled down at her.

"Hi."

"Hey." Dallas tipped her black designer shades, a broad grin stretching her generous mouth. "Good to see you, bro. Come on in," she said, jumping out of the car, her pink Gucci jeans hugging her slender hips. As usual her midriff appeared below the tiny black T-shirt.

"I didn't realize you were still in town," he said absently, glancing up at the elegant redbrick home, peeping through the trees. "I suppose I could come in for a while. I don't have anything else to do," he added glumly. Being at Rowena's place reminded him of just how lacking in purpose, how senseless this whole adventure had turned out to be. Why had she bothered to make him her heir? he wondered morosely as he followed Dallas inside the large, white-stuccoed hall. He would have to get rid of this place, he reflected, banishing the earlier images of he and Meredith living there, having a family. They'd been nothing but stupid childish fantasies.

"Let's have a drink," Dallas said, entering the generously proportioned sitting room. "Sit down on the couch and I'll get you a—" She tilted her head and looked him over critically. "I'd say you look like you need a pick-me-up, so how about a Bloody Mary?"

"Sounds perfect," he replied, sitting down on one of the wide beige couches piled with tasseled cushions. He glanced at the art books adorning the huge ottoman. They were as diverse as their owner had been. Then his eyes moved to the fireplace and to the imposing portrait above it. She'd been a fine-looking woman, his grandmother. The artist had captured her strong features and her personality. It was easy to imagine her laughing, telling stories, to sense her quick change of mood.

Remembering the letter he carried, Grant slipped his hand into his pocket and withdrew it. What would this one reveal? he wondered, sending the portrait a skeptical glance. Should he open it now or wait till after he'd had the drink with Dallas?

Fingering it thoughtfully, he decided to go ahead

and give it a quick perusal. He slit the top of the envelope and withdrew a folded dog-eared sheet of writing paper. But as he opened the missive he became immediately aware that this was not Rowena's distinctive black scrawl, but rather a slight, almost childish script. The note wasn't addressed to any specific person, and he looked at it more closely, frowning. An unprecedented surge of anticipation gripped him as he glanced at the printed address in the right-hand corner, his pulse leaping when he realized that it was Dallas's address in Beaufort. As his eyes closed in on the words his heart missed a beat, his breath caught and his pulse changed gear.

"Here you go." Dallas reappeared with a tray and hastily he stashed the letter back in his pocket, barely able to disguise his agitation. She set the tray down on top of the piled books on the ottoman, handed him a tall glass with a celery stick protruding, then sat down opposite.

"How long are you planning to stay in Savannah?" she asked, raising her glass, then taking a long sip. "You should come and stay here instead of the inn. Ah, this stuff is good." She closed her eyes as the first sip lingered.

"I don't know yet," he muttered absently, too taken up with the few powerful words he'd just read to pay real attention.

"What about Christmas?" she asked.

"What about it?"

"Well, it's only a week or so away."

"What do you plan to do?" he asked her, trying to quiet his thoughts.

"Don't know." She shrugged. "Dad and I always spent Christmas together."

"Maybe we should fly somewhere," he murmured vaguely. "Better than sticking around here."

"What about Meredith?" Dallas asked, eyeing him thoughtfully.

"What about her?"

"Well, I thought you might be planning on spending Christmas with her and her family."

"What gave you that idea?" He eyed her askance and sipped his Bloody Mary.

"Oh, nothing, just a thought." She shrugged her attractive shoulders and sank farther into the cushions. "Why don't you stay and we can eat lunch? But first I need to go check my e-mail."

"Good idea. Take your time, I'm quite happy here browsing around Rowena's stuff."

"Fine," she said, rising. "Give me twenty minutes and I'll fix us some quiche and a salad. Then maybe we can make Christmas plans."

"Great," he encouraged, anxious for her to leave the room. The missive was burning a hole in his pocket.

As soon as he heard her high heels mounting the stairs, he withdrew the note carefully, almost reverently, fingers trembling. It was, he had realized, his mother's suicide note. The shock of seeing her writing combined with the words swimming before his eyes was indescribable. Forcing himself to stay calm, he began at the beginning.

I saw *him* yesterday. Dallas and I were in Savannah shopping. And he actually came up to me! Brushed himself against me as he tousled Dallas's hair, as if nothing had ever happened between us. I should have bitten his hand off, but I couldn't. I just stared at him, and he looked back at me, smirking. Then he whispered, "Pretty daughter," and I wanted to scream.

All these years, and it's still as vivid and painful as if it were yesterday. I can't bear it anymore. I can't pretend I've forgotten what happened because the shame lives with me each and every day. But I won't let him hold this over me any longer. Today I'm going to put an end to it, Mother, something you never bothered to do, even when I needed you most.

Why didn't you believe me? Why was protecting one of your friends more important than protecting me? You saw him that night at the Murphys' fund-raiser, saw him lead me out into the garden. And yet you refused to accept that he was the one. Even when I learned I was pregnant, when I begged you to help me confront him, you said I was making up stories to conceal the real father's identity.

Did you know that I went to see him on my own? I was so terrified I thought I'd throw up, but I did it. I told him he was the baby's father. He knew I'd been a virgin, knew what he'd done to me. But none of that mattered. He just laughed, said that's what happens when you play with fire. Then he told me I couldn't prove it, anyway. Said I'd better get an abortion or I'd ruin "my cute little figure."

Sweet Jesus, I've had so much therapy I can't remember my own name, but there's one thing I've never forgotten, and that's the way he breathed all over me, held my mouth shut while he forced himself inside me. How inconvenient it must have been for you to acknowledge, even to yourself, that one of your friends raped your daughter.

Well, I'm tired of the hypocrisy, tired of living with these memories, tired of waiting for the justice that never comes. Maybe after this you'll realize just how much I lost that day—and what you've lost, too. I've decided that after yesterday there's no other way.

Look after Dallas. I love her so much, but I could never show her. Every time I wanted to tell her, I felt as though I was betraying the child I abandoned. She'll be better off without me.

I'm a terrible mother, anyway. I gave away my baby. I'll never forget his first little cry, then that nurse taking him away when all I ever wanted— still want—is to hold him in my arms. Not one day goes by that I don't think about him, wonder what he's become, what he looks like. Sometimes I walk in the airport or the mall and see a man about his age and wonder if it isn't him. Every day I think of what life might have been if I'd been allowed to keep him.

Now I just want to go to sleep and never wake up. That's the only way this nightmare will finally end. But there's still something you can do. What I want from you is justice, Mother, the justice you refused me before, the justice owed me and the son I never knew. If you ever loved me, Mother, make Drew Chandler pay for what he did to me.

Grant's fingers shook and the hand holding the letter fell to his knee, blind rage seeping through him. Now he knew why Drew Chandler had seemed so familiar. The man was his father. It was obvious now. Should have been obvious from the beginning. Maybe it was to others. He stared again at his mother's words. They were desperate, the passionate last pleas of a woman who could stand the pain no longer.

As though drawn by some invisible magnet, he sought Rowena's face above the mantel. Their eyes met, hers steady and powerful. So this was why she'd called out to him, why she'd lured him back to the place of his conception. To see that justice was done.

All at once the picture that for the past month and a half had been nothing but a hazy blur loomed before him, clear down to the finest detail. She had handed him his legacy. His complete legacy. Now it was up to him to erase the stain.

"Okay, that's done." Dallas came back into the room and smiled at him. "Hey, you look sick," she said suddenly, stopping short and staring at him.

"Dallas, I think you'd better sit down. I need to show you something."

"What is it?" She quirked a brow, then hastened to the couch and sat next to him, intrigued.

"This. I think you've seen it before." He handed her the note, saw her face turn ashen, hoped he'd done the right thing. But she had a right to know the truth. Like him, she had too many unanswered questions.

"Read it," he said, squeezing her knee. "I need your take."

Slowly Dallas read the note. Time stood still and she traveled to that life-changing moment when she'd entered her mother's bedroom and discovered her limp body, head lolling against the cushion in the pretty pink chintz armchair.

"Oh, God," she whispered, her mouth suddenly dry

with pain and fear, the words swimming before her eyes. There it was, the name she'd forgotten, the name she'd tried so often to remember, but that for some inexplicable reason had erased itself from her memory, or perhaps she hadn't read the letter to the end.

"It's him," she uttered, voice shaking. "Oh, Grandma." Her eyes filled with tears. "I remember now. She came in just as I'd picked up the note and had begun reading it. She grabbed it from me and I hated her for it. Oh, God." Dallas dropped her hands in her lap and let out a shaky sigh. "All this time I've misjudged her, Grant, thought she was trying to hide something she'd done to Mom, when what she really wanted was to spare me the pain of learning the truth." Dallas buried her face in her hands. "I remember everything now. She made me hand it over, told me to forget whatever I'd read. And the crazy thing is, I did. Until now. How could that be?" She looked up, eyes overflowing with confusion.

"Because your subconscious took over. You needed to forget." He reached out, opened his arms and she fell into them. "You'd been through enough as it is."

"But why didn't she tell me when I grew up? I raised the subject several times. She just cut me off, wouldn't continue the conversation. That's when I really began hating her. I was so sure she was to blame."

"We carry a number of misconceptions with us," he said dryly, thinking of his own life. "The important thing now is to see where this is going. For some reason, which will probably remain a mystery, Rowena didn't take her own revenge on Drew Chandler."

"Actually, in her own way, I think she probably did," Dallas said, sniffing, accepting Grant's proffered hankie. "She's just left the coup de grâce for us."

"What do you mean?" he asked, frowning.

"Well, I remember this conversation I overheard a few years back. Right here, as a matter of fact. Senator Hathaway and Grandma were talking about Chandler. I wasn't paying much attention." Her brows drew together.

"Go on."

"The senator was saying that, given Drew's connections—apparently he comes from a wealthy traditional family with big land holdings throughout Georgia—it was surprising he never quite achieved what was expected of him. Apparently, whatever projects he attempted or offices he sought always ended up falling through."

"And?"

"Grandma went silent for a moment, and then she said something like, *And probably never will. Some people's misdeeds catch up with them.* Or something like that. I don't remember anything else."

"The senator, huh? Do you think he knows anything about this?"

"No. I'm certain Grandma didn't tell anyone the truth. If she'd decided to do that, she would have had a public showdown."

"You're probably right," he said upon reflection. He wouldn't think it was Rowena's style to do things by halves. "Instead, she took a calculated risk and bet on us."

"You," she said with a trembling smile.

"No. I think she knew that I'd share this with you. She expected us to deal with him together. She knew you couldn't do it alone. She wanted you protected. Hence the trust and all the provisos. That and the relatives."

"I guess. But really, what can we do? I mean, we

could get a hold of him and tell we know the truth. And then what? He denies it or doesn't give a shit, anyway." She shrugged, despondent. "I wish Grandma had just fucked him up when she had the chance."

"From what you've just mentioned, maybe she did. I'll bet she had a hand in making sure his projects never came to fruition. Whatever he tried, she made sure he failed."

"Yep, that sounds like Grandma. People didn't like to get on her bad side because rumor had it she'd get some voodoo priestess to put a curse on you."

"So she took her revenge indirectly, but left the final blowup to us—the ones who'd been hurt the most by what Chandler did."

"So how do we go about this? Hey," she considered, eyes sparkling with vengeance, "you know anyone who can put a contract on the guy? Blow him away so he can rot in hell? I want revenge."

"No, I don't," he replied witheringly, "and it's not revenge we want, Dallas. It's justice."

"Call it whatever you like, the guy's gotta pay," she said, jumping up.

"I think this could be conducted in a more subtle manner." Grant leaned back on the couch and rested one ankle on his knee, expression hard and thoughtful.

"How?" she said impatiently. "He needs to be publicly shamed."

"As you've just pointed out, that might be hard to swing after all these years. But I can think of ways to make him regret his actions."

"Regret isn't good enough," she said bitterly. "Look at all the harm he's caused. He deserves to be shot."

"I agree. But that's not going to happen," he said

matter-of-factly. "But there are other ways of destroying a man."

She glanced up, shocked at the cold calculation in his expression. She shivered. "God, Grant, you look lethal."

"I plan to be. We owe it to Rowena. And to Mom," he said, pronouncing the word with an effort. It was the first time he'd said the word out loud. The first time he'd thought of Isabel as his real mother.

She gazed at him, eyes filled with a plethora of mixed emotions. Getting up, Grant put an arm firmly around her shoulders and held her close. "You're never going to be alone or frightened again, Dallas. I give you my word on that. And I'm going to make damned sure that bastard gets his comeuppance. If you don't want to be a part of it, I understand." Brother and sister locked in a hug, the embryonic bond that had formed between them only weeks earlier cemented by the knowledge that together they must avenge their parent.

"I'll be there. I won't let you down," she whispered, looking up at him, a smile quivering on her lips.

"That's my girl. Now, let's get to work."

"I don't like it one little bit," Miss Mabella mumbled as she studied the petals of the wilting white rose she'd placed on her altar two days earlier. "There's gonna be big trouble before long, mark my words," she muttered to Melchior, her live blackbird that she'd brought in from the yard. The bird sat perched on the arm of a wide chair in the corner, head cocked at an inquiring angle. "Ain't no stoppin' it," she muttered, peering at the vial of water next to the rose, where she noticed slight turbulence. "She be wantin' justice. Won't rest until she got it." She sighed, then closed her eyes, intoning her incantations while the bird continued to stare, its beady eyes tracking her movement.

Miss Mabella rocked back and forth, her body swaying harmoniously, guided by some mystic rhythm that only she could hear. Forces, uncontrollable powerful forces, were gaining momentum. She could feel the swirl, their might plowing forward like a conquering army. She shuddered, held up her hands, palms raised, and let out a long, deep sigh. Destiny was a powerful force, and strong as Mother Earth herself. There was no stopping it now.

When she'd been unable to find Grant at the Ballastone, Meredith had suddenly known where she needed to go next. Now, as she walked down the gravel path of the cemetery to the graveside, her steps slowed. She gazed down at the grave and her head swam as she recalled the funeral, the coffin being lowered by Tom's best pals into the earth. The final goodbye.

Crouching next to the headstone, Meredith set down the flowers she'd picked up at the stall on her way, as though visiting Tom without them would be sacrilegious. Yet he would have been the first to laugh at her, say she was wasting good flowers on him, that she should have them at home where she could enjoy them. A tiny smile quivered. "Oh, Tom," she whispered, laying her hand on the granite. Her finger traced his name, the dates of his life cut short so abruptly, so mercilessly. He, who'd always thought of others, was always so generous and kind. "Why did it have to be this way?" she whispered. "Why couldn't it have gone on the way we planned it?"

Leaning back on her heels, she closed her eyes. "My

best, my dearest friend," she whispered, tears seeping below her lashes. "I could always tell you everything and I must now."

She swallowed, sat cross-legged next to the grave and pictured Tom before her, handsome and laughing, remembering his kind smile and straightforward manner.

Then all at once she experienced a strange tingle.

"Tom?" She stiffened, as though sensing his presence. Then, realizing she was being foolish, she let her thoughts flow, as though she was talking to him.

"I know this is crazy and that I've always loved you ever since I can remember. And nothing will ever change that. But this is different, Tommy. It's not like us. We were secure, happy, knew the rules, played by them. I don't know how this happened. I didn't see it coming. At first, even though I was attracted to him, I despised him. Then things happened and I realized he's not the man I thought he was—he's so much more. Suddenly he's changing everything, the way he does business, the way he is as a person. He's giving so much of himself.

"But I'm scared, Tommy. Real scared. For the kids, for us, for everything. Part of me wants to love again. Not like you and me. It has nothing to do with us. What we lived and loved will be with me as long as I live. Nothing can change that. And I just need to know it's okay."

Taking a deep breath, Meredith opened her eyes, unclasped her hands and rose. As she looked up, sunshine burst from behind the clouds that had darkened the sky all day. The gravestone sparkled, and she drew in her breath as a warm, tingling energy coursed through her.

"Oh, my God." She reached out as though trying to

touch him. Then the moment was gone, the sun hid once more behind the fast-moving cloud, and she bit her lip, standing perfectly still, yet suddenly feeling light. The devastating sense of despair, the weight she'd carried since Tom's death, had lifted.

"Thank you," she whispered at last, smiling through her tears. "Thanks for trusting me."

Turning, she made her way slowly back toward the gates, a new sense of purpose in her step. It wasn't the end, merely the closing of a chapter, one that she would always cherish.

But now she was ready to face the rest of her life.

24

It wasn't that Dallas wanted her family together at Christmas, for, after all, she didn't really consider such people as Joanna and Charles family. But a party was merely the perfect excuse to get Meredith and Grant back together again whether they liked it or not. She was sure there must have been a misunderstanding. You only had to see them together to know they were perfect for each other. So it was up to her, she reasoned as she jotted down all the guests' phone numbers, to organize a Christmas party that no one would refuse for fear of hurting *her* feelings.

Dallas giggled and curled her legs under her on her grandmother's love seat. She'd invite Mer's family, too. With a satisfied sigh, Dallas set about calling Rodrigo in Miami. No Christmas dinner would work out without him at the helm organizing the details for her. She needed a chef. She'd have to use all her ingenuity to find someone really good at this stage. Everyone was probably booked. But she'd manage. Somehow.

And, she assured herself, getting into the spirit of things, it would be as good as any party Rowena had ever given.

Spreading the newspaper and magazine cuttings over the dining table, Drew Chandler shook his head. "Son of a gun," he muttered, studying the picture of Grant in *Fortune* magazine. He read the fawning article over again. His boy. He should have guessed that any child of his would prove exceptional. Now, at last, life was giving him a chance at a legacy, an opportunity to forge a relationship with the man who would carry the Chandler genes into the next generation. What a pity they'd had to wait until now.

Banishing the uncomfortable realization of exactly why the wait had been so long, Drew concentrated on the positive. He could see himself in the young man. Same gait, same shoulders. In fact, their resemblance was such that it was hard to imagine that people hadn't already figured out the obvious. That it was he who'd fathered Isabel's child.

Isabel.

He could still remember how she'd look that night, so young and lovely, so tempting, laughing with her friends and looking shyly at him. Of course, he'd known it was an act, just one of her tricks for looking innocent while driving a man almost insane with lust. She'd seemed nervous when he'd invited her outside with him. He believed that it was another act, one calculated to inflame his passions. What had happened after that he didn't recall too clearly, although he dimly remembered his surprise when he realized that she was a virgin.

And then she'd come to tell him she was pregnant.

He'd told her that if she hadn't thrown herself at him, she wouldn't be in this predicament. Not that he really believed the child to be his—she'd probably slept with any number of other guys after him. Once she'd had a taste of what he'd given her, he smirked, she probably hadn't been able to stop herself from wanting more.

He returned his gaze to the clippings, to the evidence of the incredible success his own son had achieved. A flash of regret at his own lack of accomplishment hovered. But he set it aside. Once people knew Grant was his son, he would be viewed by his peers in a different light. They would admire him, see the father's strength and resolve in the son.

A smile hovered on his face as he imagined the doors Grant could open for him. If he could get closer to his son, get to know him more intimately, maybe they'd have a chance to connect. Even do business together. He could imagine how successful that would be. Maybe he could persuade Grant to throw some money into politics, enough to get his name off the damned subcommittee waiting list and out for confirmation.

With a sigh, he gathered up the clippings and returned them to the file. He'd just have to hope for the right opportunity. It would turn up, he felt sure, when the time was right.

That moment came when he received an invitation from Dallas Thornton to attend a Christmas party at Rowena Carstairs's mansion.

The house shone in all its former glory, Drew realized as he entered the shimmering hall, seeing Dallas and Grant standing side by side, receiving guests. What a handsome couple they made. He watched

Grant carefully, filled with paternal pride. It wasn't just the power he wielded or the success he'd achieved—though of course that made up a big part of it—but the respect with which people treated him. He'd only been in Savannah a short while, but already he commanded the scene. Thinking of the power he could wield through Grant, Drew smiled confidently.

He'd known the moment he'd seen him, of course. He'd been on edge ever since that lunch with Ross and the others at the club when the subject was first mentioned. The dates, the circumstances, they all fitted. Watching the handsome, charming man across the room, he wondered in retrospect what he would have done if he'd known that this was how the child would turn out? Who could say? It was hardly his fault that he'd avoided that particular responsibility. He'd assumed Isabel would get an abortion, had never dreamed she'd have the child, much less go to the effort of having him adopted.

All at once he wondered if she'd confided in Rowena, a flash of unease coursing through him. But no. That was impossible. Rowena would have raised all hell. No, thank God, that was all in the past. There was no reason it should color his future relationship with his son. Especially now that Rowena was safely six feet under.

"Good evening."

Dallas welcomed him, looking gorgeous in a diaphanous pale pink dress with a slit up the thigh. He felt a surge of sexual desire. Young women did this to him. The thought that she was Isabel's daughter was somehow doubly enticing.

"Good evening, my dear. You look gorgeous, as well you know," he added in a low, intimate tone.

"Oh, you shouldn't say things like that," she replied coyly, slipping her arm through his and drawing him over to where her brother stood.

"Grant, look who's here."

Grant excused himself to the guests he'd been talking to and turned. "Good evening. We're so glad you could come." He reached out his hand.

Drew gripped it. Their eyes met. *My God.* He gulped, seeing himself reflected in the smile. Then, clearing his throat, he made a pretense of studying the dazzling living room. Elaborate yet tasteful flower arrangements adorned the antique furniture, sterling candelabras illuminated the niches. Waiters circulated with silver trays of canapés and champagne.

"She would have approved," he said as they entered the drawing room, and his eyes fell upon Rowena's portrait, reigning majestically above the fireplace. He did a double take, shuddered. He could have sworn her eyes and that enigmatic smile mocked him. Just a play of light, he realized, smiling down at Dallas. "Lovely little sister you have here, Grant." He smiled, squeezing her arm. "If I were thirty years younger, I'd be flirting with her myself." He patted her hand benignly, oblivious to the flash of steel in Grant's eyes.

"Champagne?" Dallas retrieved a glass from a roving tray and handed him the flute. "Oh, there's the senator and Elm, I'll go and say hi." She disengaged herself, leaving Drew facing his son.

"Glad you're here," Grant said, taking a sip of champagne. "I've been hoping to renew our acquaintance."

"Enjoying Savannah?" Drew asked, swelling with pride.

"Very much. In fact, I'm considering spending more

time here," he murmured, glancing across the room at Meredith's back.

"Good. We'll have to get you over to the club and introduce you to more people."

"I'd like that. Actually, I'm considering investing in the area."

"Really? Anything specific?"

"No. Not yet. I would like to be better informed by people in the know. I was hoping you might be able to give me advice on where to focus my attentions."

"Why, it'd be my pleasure." Drew puffed out his chest, another rush of newfound paternal instinct surfacing. "We should get together and discuss it. I can think of a couple areas you might be interested in. How about politics?" he said casually.

"Never dabbled. Plus I'm not American."

"Of course not. But still, you should think about contributing to the party. It can be mighty useful to have powerful friends in D.C."

"Undoubtedly," he drawled, looking across the room to where Meredith had just turned around. "Look, why don't we set up a date for lunch and discuss this. I'd love to talk further, but right now, I'm afraid I have to attend to my guests."

"Why, of course. Tell you what, I'm free tomorrow."

"So am I."

"Then how about you lunching with me at the Chatham Club? We'll have to put your name up for membership. It'll be a good chance to meet the power brokers in the club. Of course, Hathaway and I will back you."

"Very kind. It would be a pleasure. One o'clock?"

"Perfect."

The two men smiled and Grant moved off across the room.

Drew's daydream was interrupted by Senator Hathaway.

"'Evening, Drew. Saw you chatting to Gallagher. Fine young fellow, isn't he? Quite a track record. A real business dynamo."

"You'd be astonished to know how successful he's been," Drew confided, wishing he could tell someone, anyone, that this man they all admired so much was his son, his flesh and blood. He sighed. There would be time enough for that. Right now, he needed to decide how he was going to tell Grant the truth about himself. Watching him cross the room with that confident air of success, Drew wondered again if he'd already guessed. After all, they were so alike. He must have felt the bond, just as he had.

For the first time in his life, Grant was consciously thankful for the iron control he'd developed over the years.

"Lunch tomorrow at the Chatham," he murmured as he passed Dallas. He smiled at her reassuringly, then moved among the guests, eyes pinned on the scooped back of the pearl silk cocktail dress that subtly emphasized the curves of Meredith's figure. He remembered that body well, the way she'd moved under him, the feel of her lying in his arms after they'd made love.

"Good evening."

She spun round, her cheeks flushed, eyes bright. "Grant. Hi. You look…good. You remember Jeff and Melanie?"

"Of course, good evening." He shook hands with Meredith's brother and dropped a casual peck on Melanie's cheek.

"Hope you'll be able to make our wedding," Jeff said with a proud, happy glance at Melanie, who flushed charmingly. Grant glanced quizzically at Meredith, noted the fixed smile on her lips and cleared his throat. "Congratulations. I wish you all the best. When's the date?"

"Probably late April or early May. There's so much to prepare," Melanie said, exchanging an intimate look with her fiancé.

"Well, anything I can do—" Grant raised his palms and grinned. "You're welcome to my yacht for the honeymoon. She's moored in Monte Carlo."

"Really, Grant, you shouldn't be giving them ideas," Clarice, chicly attired in a smart mauve silk sheath, stepped into the group and exchanged a warm look with him. "Glad to see you've decided to stick around," she whispered as she kissed his cheek.

Grant pulled back, surprised, then smiled broadly. "Why not? The crew sits idle as it is. You'd be doing me a favor," he said to Jeff.

Meredith gulped champagne and pretended to follow the conversation. She was certain she must be entering cardiac arrest. She could barely breathe. And to make it worse, Grant was ignoring her. And what did he mean by offering her brother his yacht? He hadn't invited her on it, had he? She'd prepared a speech. A well-thought-out, articulate manifestation of her feelings. Now as she stood next to him, the words fled and all she could think of was the scent of his aftershave, the feel of him so close to her it hurt, the unexpressed and intense desire to have him hold her.

At that moment the band struck up and the parquet floor was cleared for the dancers.

"Shall we?" Grant held out his hand to Meredith.

She swallowed. He seemed so distant, so different to the Grant she'd become close to. This supremely elegant sophisticated being left her insecure, unsure of where she was treading. Maybe that was because he had changed his mind about them.

She stepped onto the floor, her heart sinking as she placed her hands on his shoulders. Grant laced his around her waist. It took her exactly ten seconds to realize he was the best dancer she'd ever danced with. Was there anything the man didn't do right?

Soon other couples were twirling around the room, Dallas and John Rowland, Clarice and the senator. Strange, Grant reflected as he forced himself to keep his hands in check, that these people whom he barely knew had become an integral part of his life. There was Elm, gathered in her husband's arms, smiling up at him and lifting a brow invitingly at some presumably off-color suggestion.

He glanced down nostalgically at the top of Meredith's head; she was staring doggedly at the lapel of his tux. It was tempting to pull her closer, feel her body against his, let his arms close tighter around her. Instead he kept a suitable distance between them. She'd made her point. Made it clear she didn't want more than what they'd had. So he'd ignored the messages she'd left at the inn before he'd moved in with Dallas at Rowena's, knowing they would merely be covering old ground. He wasn't about to insist. He had his pride. He knew when to retreat. Still, he reflected, breathing in the scent of her so close and so tempting, a man could hardly be faulted for having one last try, could he?

Guiding her discreetly toward the French windows, he led her onto the terrace.

Meredith looked up, suddenly aware that instead of the stucco ceiling of Rowena's drawing room, she was staring into Grant's face and beyond that, the stars. She swallowed.

"I'm sorry," he said, his expression anything but apologetic, "but I couldn't resist. We'll go back if you'd rather." He dropped his hands from her shoulders.

"No. Grant, we have to talk."

"Meredith, just because I was tempted to spend a few moments with you alone doesn't mean you have to justify yourself."

"Look. I need to explain."

"No, you don't."

"Yes, I do," she insisted, wishing he would be less obtuse.

"Meredith, this is not a case and I am not a client. I don't need to have things outlined. I understand perfectly."

"No, you don't," she said, surprising herself by stamping her foot in irritation. "If you'd just listen for two damn seconds, I could tell you how I—what I—" She cut off, let out a huff and looked away, not seeing the arrested look in his eyes.

"What, Mer?" he said in a softer voice, eyes never leaving her flushed face.

"I made a mistake. Well, not a mistake, exactly," she said, twisting her hair nervously. "It's just that when we talked the other day, I wasn't ready, I didn't think I would be—"

"And now you are?" He took a step forward, his mouth dry and his pulse leaping.

"Well, it's like this—" Meredith, who had been the leader of her debating group at Yale, could think of no words with which to express the feelings churning inside. "I guess the simplest way would be to show you," she whispered at last, taking a step forward, palms touching the front of his tux.

"Am I to understand that you've had a change of heart?" he asked, wondering if he was dreaming. "Meredith, please, speak plainly, I don't think I could take it if I misunderstood you this time around."

Lifting her head, she slipped her hand behind his neck and pulled him toward her. "Just kiss me, Grant."

"Good Lord." Lowering his head, he gave way to desire. When their lips touched, he discovered a new lingering sensation. When his hands gripped the small of her back, pressing her to him, he knew he would never let her go.

Her head spun and her limbs felt weak as she responded.

"Now, don't go fainting on me," he said, drawing back.

"I've never fainted in my life," she murmured, a smile hovering, "but this sure comes close."

"Then, before you collapse, can I just get a clear-cut answer out of you, Madam Counselor?"

Her eyes met his and she bit her lip.

"Will you marry me? Yes or no."

"Yes," she responded, threading her fingers through his hair. "Yes, yes, a hundred times yes."

"Thank God for that," he muttered, before proceeding to kiss her very thoroughly, wishing he could carry her upstairs and finish what they'd begun.

But that, he realized, intoxicated with happiness, would simply have to wait.

25

"You sure you'll be okay?" Dallas looked anxiously at her brother as she pulled the Mustang in front of the club entrance.

"I'll be fine. Don't worry."

Dallas nodded silently, hands gripping the wheel, lips set. "Call me as soon as it's over."

"I'll come back to the house."

"I'm glad you moved in, Grant. It all feels so much better with you around. I'm really excited about you and Mer, too. Why are you keeping it a secret?" She cocked her head, her face softening for a moment.

"Because I want all this out of my life first." He motioned toward the club and all it implied. "Mer and her kids deserve my full attention. I don't want any interference." His expression turned hard, and Dallas sighed. It would be lovely, she reflected wistfully, to have a man care for her as much as Grant obviously cared for Meredith.

"Right. Let's get this show on the road." He smiled absently, caught up in what he had to do. He opened the car door, then, leaning back across the seat, dropped a kiss on her brow.

She nodded. "I'll be waiting. Good luck."

With a curt nod, Grant ducked under the awning and into the lobby, where he headed for the elevator.

As he traveled to the top floor, he geared himself as he always did when the games began. At this point, he'd detached himself emotionally, assessed his adversary, analyzed a favorable approach and left himself a margin for collateral damage.

The elegant lobby of the club hummed with luncheon guests. He peered into the bar, but there was no sign of Drew Chandler.

"Good day, sir. Can I help you?" The head waiter smiled politely.

"I'm lunching with Mr. Chandler."

"Of course. Follow me, please."

As he followed the waiter, a sudden flash of his mother's picture followed by the childish writing in the suicide note caused him to take a deep breath. No emotion, he reminded himself, seeing Chandler rise to greet him. No damned emotion. If ever he needed to be cold-blooded, the time was now. What was it Dallas had said in the restaurant in Miami? He'd need ice water in his veins.

"Good to see you." Chandler shook hands firmly. "What'll you have?"

"Just a mineral water." He was damned if he'd drink with the man.

"Very well, sir." The waiter disappeared and the men took their seats.

Chandler seemed comfortable, at ease, Grant reflected. Well, that wouldn't last long. "That was one great party," the older man remarked, shaking his handsome head.

"Glad you could make it."

"Always enjoyed Rowena's company," he said, heaving a nostalgic sigh. "Rowena was one hell of a woman. She gave some great parties in her time. That was a few years back now, of course. Just goes to show you that none of us is getting any younger."

"No. Time does fly by. Makes one prioritize."

"You're young to be thinking in such terms," Chandler said, with a smile and a laugh. "Not to mention that you've already achieved so much. You must be proud of yourself."

Grant shrugged. "I was lucky. I worked hard and played hard."

"I envy you a bit, you know. Reaching one's goals, surpassing every measure of success at an early age. It must be satisfying," Drew murmured.

Grant caught the whiff of longing and pricked up his ears. "You must be satisfied yourself. I know very little about your business and your life, but I would imagine that a man of your age and stature would be thinking of retiring, of enjoying life." He leaned back, sipped his mineral water and studied his quarry.

"Retire? Why, not at all. I feel I'm finally reaching my prime. In fact, I got some good news this morning."

"Really?" Grant's expression was one of sympathetic interest.

"Yes. You may have heard that I've been nominated for a diplomatic post—ambassador to Argentina," he said confidingly. "A very prestigious posting. Well, the appointment is finally out of the subcommittee. I'm to get approval from the Senate Foreign Relations Committee next week."

"Congratulations. I gather you're very pleased?"

"Very." Drew nodded, satisfied. "All my life I've dreamed of this, but things never quite came together before. I suppose it's rather late to be fulfilling a life-long ambition, but there it is." He shrugged, smiled, radiating satisfaction.

"I'm very glad for you." Grant hesitated, watched as Chandler's brows joined over the bridge of the aquiline nose he himself had inherited.

"Is something troubling you?" Drew said at last, noting Grant's silence.

"Not troubling, exactly. It's just that—" He cut off, took a deep breath as though making a major decision. "Look, maybe I'm crazy, but ever since we've met I've had this impression that you and I are in some way related." He cleared his throat, giving an excellent impression of embarrassment.

"You do? You feel that, too?" Drew laid down his glass on the table with a snap. "I've been wanting to speak to you. Wasn't sure how to approach the subject," he said hesitantly.

"You're my father, aren't you?" Grant said with simple candor.

Drew swallowed. Their eyes met, the gazes held. Grant watched as the other man's eyes watered. "Yes, Grant, I am," he said slowly, head bowing. After a moment, he lifted his eyes once more, speaking quickly now. "I could hardly believe it when I met you that night at Montalba. But the moment I saw you—" He raised his hand, let it drop. "I knew. I just knew."

"Me, too," Grant responded quietly. "As you can imagine, I've been asking myself a number of questions since." *Like why the hell you raped my mother, you bastard.*

"Of course you have. Not surprising. You must wonder what happened, why I've not been a part of your life."

"Yes, I have."

"Not through any wish of mine," Drew said, a bitter edge to his voice. "Had I known, had I been given the least inkling of your existence, I never would have allowed them to do that to you."

"You mean you weren't aware that my mother was pregnant?" Grant asked with faked innocence.

"No. Isabel and I had a short affair. Nobody knew about it at the time. One of those things that just happens. She was young. A bit of a flirt, if I may say so. She liked the boys and the boys liked her. It was rather hard to resist her. She was so determined, so insistent. I told her at the time that it shouldn't be, that I was far too old for her, that she would regret it. But would she listen?" He shook his head sadly. "No way. Isabel was as headstrong as she was beautiful."

"You mean my mother seduced you?" Grant quirked a brow.

"I guess you could say that." Drew smiled apologetically. "You know how it is, how some women can be irresistible. Isabel was one of them. I'm afraid I gave way to temptation. Then of course she moved on to the next one." He sighed. "We never spoke again."

"So she never told you she was expecting a baby, that the child was yours?"

"Frankly, Grant, though I hate to tell you this, I doubt she knew herself."

Grant resisted the urge to plant his fist in Chandler's arrogant, smirking face. "I see," he responded soberly. "That puts a very different light on matters."

"I'm afraid it does. But don't feel badly about it. She

was young and reckless, and I guess she thought this was the best way out. What I don't understand is Rowena. She must've known something?"

"Not that I'm aware of," he lied. "Maybe my mother went off to Europe and dealt with the situation herself."

"That could be," Drew agreed. "I remember when she left. She was very different when she came back, very sober. From all reports, she didn't do much with her life, kind of lived like a recluse for a few years."

"Didn't you wonder what had happened?"

"Sure I wondered, we all did. But then, like everything else, life just moved on. She met Doug Thornton and got married and nobody thought anymore about the past."

"So you never saw her again, never thought of finding out what might have happened to her?"

"No, I figured she'd soured on all her friends in Savannah and didn't want anything to do with us. Actually, come to think of it, I did see her once," he said, frowning. "It was a few days before she died. I saw her strolling with her daughter downtown and I walked over to say hello."

"And?"

"She was all smiles, looked like she'd gotten on with her life. Wished me well."

"And then you went on your way."

"Yes. I moved on and didn't think any more about it until I read the obituary in the *Savannah News*. She was young to have a heart attack. Though they say that women have them more than one imagines. A pity. She was still a beautiful woman, despite the drink." Drew cleared his throat.

"Well," Grant said at last, trying to swallow the bile

threatening to fill his throat, "at least now I know the truth about myself. Thirty-odd years of wondering who my father is, and now the mystery's solved."

"Look, it wasn't my fault." Drew reached out and touched Grant's arm. "I would much rather it was a prettier story. But I can tell from the kind of man you are that you'd rather know the truth. There have been too many lies already."

"Absolutely." Grant's piercing gaze allowed no room for faltering. "It's all in the past, anyway. No point in reopening old wounds. Now we can move on." He smiled matter-of-factly.

Drew experienced a moment's frustration. There was none of the awed emotion he'd visualized so clearly.

"That's right," he murmured. Grant noticed that his glass was empty. "How about another Scotch?"

"I could do with one. All these emotions are a lot for a man of my age. When I think of all the time we've missed, it makes me want to—" He hesitated, looked down and shook his head.

"Don't feel that way." Grant's conciliatory tone made Drew look up once more. "Things happen as they do for a purpose. You could almost say this is fate. A closing of the circle, so to speak."

"I guess." Drew's eyes wavered an instant, then he smiled. "What matters is that we've finally found each other. I hope we can make a new start together—perhaps you can come and visit me at my new posting. We could get to know each other as we should have years ago, and I'd be very proud to introduce you to my friends—acknowledge you as my son."

"I would like that very much." Grant sighed with nostalgic longing meant to touch the heart of any errant parent. "At least, through her will, Rowena put us on the same path."

"Yes. Amazingly, she did."

Grant studied Chandler's face and read anticipation, wonder, pride. Fatherly feelings, he realized ironically. Exactly what he'd hoped for. The guy was good, Grant had to admit as they gave the waiter their orders, really good. Perhaps by now he even believed his own lies. He was having a hard time not demonstrating the disdain and disgust the man caused him, but sheer force of habit kept his emotions in check.

His father. He would rather a sewer rat had sired him than this despicable creature.

"You know, I was just thinking here as we were ordering, perhaps you'd like to come up to D.C. with me. I have to meet with the congressional committee on Tuesday—right before they break for the holiday. It's basically a formality, but they're the ones who certify the president's appointment. It'd be a wonderful thing to have you there," he said, his smile filled with tentative hope. "This could help make up for all those missing years, all the times that we've been deprived of."

His enthusiasm was pathetic. "I should think that might be arranged."

"You do?" Drew's eyes betrayed a triumphant gleam.

"It would be a pleasure," Grant assured him. "Just give me the time and place and I'll be there."

The waiter placed the dishes before them. Grant looked at his food, revolted at the thought of breaking bread with the creature who'd spawned him. Then, knowing he was only in the first stages of battle in a war he planned to win he lifted his knife and cut the meat decisively. It was too soon to strike the death blow, but unwittingly Drew had done exactly what Grant had intended: handed him the trump card he needed.

For a while they ate in companionable silence. Grant noted Chandler's relaxed air of complacent satisfaction. It strengthened his resolve. Let him wallow in it, roll in it. Let him believe he'd finally overcome the past and was on a winning streak. Let him bask in a few days of blissful oblivion.

It would make his fall, when it came, all the harder.

26

How was she supposed to tell them, Meredith asked herself over and over. Should she consult a psychologist, read a book, get counseling herself? She'd been thinking of little else since accepting Grant's proposal, and now she'd spent the better part of an hour in her mother's kitchen discussing it all over again with Clarice.

Meredith sipped the tea her mother had made for her. Grant was expecting her to tell the kids today, and he was coming over for dinner soon. "I guess I'd better go call them," she said at last. "It's time to leave. Thanks for picking them up, Mom."

"Remember. Just keep it simple." Clarice rose and reached for the mugs. "I'll go get the boys." She smiled, slipped an arm around Meredith's shoulders and gave her a hug. "Go for it," she whispered before disappearing out the back door. "Zack, Mick, your mother's here. Get your stuff together."

She would wait until they reached home, then sit them down in the living room and explain the situation to them clearly, giving them a chance to voice their opinions. Meredith's stomach lurched. If they hated the idea she'd just have to tell Grant that it couldn't be. She pinched the bridge of her nose, trying to ignore the kids bickering in the back.

"It's my kite," Zack said, taking firm possession of the tail.

"Keep your stupid kite, I don't care." Mick gave him a superior glance and turned his back on his brother. "Mom, I want to go fishing on Saturday with Grandpa and Grant."

"I'm not sure if he'll be available."

"Why? He said it was okay."

"He did?"

"Yeah. He's ordered some special flies from Scotland. He's having them shipped here." Mick's tone told her he was impressed. "He said he'd take us fishing in Scotland, too. Salmon fishing," he added proudly.

"I get to go, too," Zack chipped in, wiggling his front tooth. He didn't want to tell Mick he still believed in the tooth fairy, but he hoped there would be five bucks under his pillow, anyway. "He said we could all go. I guess he wouldn't mind if you came along, too," he added graciously.

Meredith swerved in traffic, nearly braking accidentally. The car behind her honked. She waved apologetically.

"You don't know how to fish," Mick was saying with a disparaging sniff.

"That's not true." Zack's chin quivered.

Meredith took a deep breath. "Boys, no quarrelling. Nobody's going anywhere."

"Why not?" they cried, united in opposition.

"Because Scotland is a long way off," she said lamely, dragging a frustrated hand through her hair. This was all going far too fast.

"Grant said we'd fly there in his plane," Mick said, dismissing technical details. "Mom, why do you want to spoil it?" he pouted. "He said we could go for part of the summer vacation."

"We'll have to see."

"I told him how you love to ski and he said we'd go to Colorado," Zack piped up. Meredith glanced in the rearview mirror, saw Zack's head tilt and sighed.

"Guys, I have something I was planning to talk to you about once we get home," she said, her mouth dry.

"Is it about the vacation? Can we go?"

"Not exactly. It's—it's about Grant."

"Are you going to marry him, Mom?" Mick inquired. "Zack, did you take my baseball out of my pack?"

The Jeep swerved once more.

"No, I didn't. You know that'd be neat, Mom. If you married Grant then he could live with us at home," Zack pointed out, nodding. "It's more fun when Grant's around. We can tie flies together."

"I will not have hooks stuck in the carpet. Someone could get hurt. Oh, Jesus," Meredith exclaimed, realizing what she'd just said.

"That's no problem. Grant said he has a house with a big shed in the yard. He said we could fix it up as a fishing room."

"He did, did he?" Meredith let out a huff. She could hardly keep up.

"Mom, you didn't answer. Are you going to marry Grant?"

"Uh, I'm thinking about it," she blabbered. Here she'd been terrified of hurting her kids, and instead they were one step ahead of her.

"Good. We like him, don't we, Mick?" Zack turned his freckled face toward his brother, seeking endorsement.

"Yep. Go for it, Mom."

Was this real? "You wouldn't mind?" She peered again in the rearview mirror, amazed to see them giggling. "What is it, guys?"

"You're in love with him, Mom, anyone can see that. Come on, admit it."

Meredith flushed, caught her breath. "Really, Mick, I—" She could hardly continue when she turned into their street. She did a double take when she saw the shiny Porsche that Grant had exchanged the Jag for parked in full view of the house.

"Look, there he is. Tell him now, Mom, then he can stay for dinner," Zack pointed out practically.

"Yeah! And what *is* for dinner, Mom? Not that left-over meat loaf, I hope," Mick said, waving at Grant.

"Chinese, I guess," she said absently, realizing she'd completely forgotten dinner.

"Cool."

The car slowed as she prepared to turn into the driveway. Grant stood leaning on the hood of the Porsche. He waved a friendly hello. Meredith wished things would go slower. It felt as if everything was spiraling out of her control. Somehow it was all meant to be far more serious than this, more complex. She parked the Jeep in the driveway, watched the boys jump out and run over to Grant and the car. Excited questions involving carburetors and horse-power ensued.

Meredith picked up the forgotten backpacks and watched them. Grant seemed totally at ease with the kids, she reflected, her heart melting. As though sensing her gaze, he looked up and their eyes met over the children's bent heads. She couldn't help smiling. It all seemed so surprisingly right. So natural.

"Okay, guys," she said, blinking away sudden tears, "time for homework."

"Aw, Mom. Grant just said he'd take us for a ride," Mick complained.

"Afterward. Do as your mother says." Grant's tone left them in no doubt that he meant what he said.

Without argument they picked up their backpacks and went inside.

Meredith blinked. Why hadn't there been the usual whining? "How did you do that?" she asked, turning to Grant, amazed.

"It's a natural talent I'm cultivating," he said smugly. "And after spending several afternoons with them after school at their grandmother's without their mother's knowledge, I'm becoming an expert."

"Why, the little rascals. They never told me," she exclaimed.

"Ah! A wise decision. Men stick together when it comes to that sort of thing," he murmured, eyes twinkling. Then, slipping his arm around her, he held her close and together they entered the house.

There was no need to be nervous, Drew told himself. Things were pretty much decided by this stage of the proceedings. He'd already filled out all manner of forms, answered an unbelievable list of questions and was confident that the information would bolster his nomination. This meeting before the Senate panel was nothing but a formality, he assured himself as he walked down the corridor of the Hart Building. He'd shaken hands with Senators Morgan and Tremaine, whom he'd made a point of meeting personally in their home bases. Trips, he was certain, that had been well worthwhile. And as luck would have it, his old friend George Hathaway was presiding. It was unfortunate that he hadn't been able to arrange an interview with Senator Blythe. But, hey, that was a detail. Blythe would toe the line with the others. George had made that clear over drinks last Sunday in Savannah.

Sitting down, Drew took out his notes and the glasses from his breast pocket, then glanced at his watch. They would begin in five minutes. After the long process the nomination had entailed—seven long months, to be exact—he was pleased to have reached this final phase.

Drew watched carefully as the senators entered, shook hands, then took their places on the elevated dais, settling in front of the placards that listed their names. As he took his place at the center of the panel, Hathaway sent him an encouraging smile. Drew returned it, confident that his dreams were at long last within his grasp.

Glancing over his shoulder, he saw Grant entering the room. Dallas accompanied him. Odd, that. Why had he brought the girl along? He'd imagined him coming alone. But never mind. The important thing was that he'd come. He smiled, nodded. Grant acknowledged him with a brief wave. They sat in the second row of chairs and Drew turned back toward the panel.

"Gentleman," the gray-suited, gray-haired Senator Gray from Arizona began, "this meeting is to establish the suitability of Mr. Chandler to represent our nation as ambassador of the United States to the Argentine Republic."

Drew smothered a smile. Argentina. A big posting. He'd been thrilled when he'd finally gotten the word; he'd expected Caracas or Quito.

"Mr. Chandler, my colleague Senator Blythe has a couple questions we'd like you to answer before making our final determination."

"Of course. I'm at your disposal." Drew smiled as he watched Senator Blythe review his notes.

"Mr. Chandler, in the question form you submitted, you were asked if there was anything regarding your personal integrity that might be an issue in the committee's consideration of your nomination." He paused, glanced at Drew.

"That's correct."

"Then perhaps you could clarify your involvement with the Mogeechee water plant." Drew looked up, surprised, and swallowed hard. He hadn't expected this. Hadn't prepared for it. "It appears," the senator persisted determinedly, "that a number of discrepancies were never brought to light. I gather you were on the board of Congressman MacBride's company? The one that was implicated with that Miami drug cartel?"

Drew saw George Hathaway frown as he read the report Blythe had handed him. He swallowed again nervously. He hadn't anticipated any probing questions. What the hell was going on here? "I did sit on the board of one of the MacBride companies, yes. But I resigned the moment the truth was exposed."

"I see. Then you deny having any personal involvement with the Miami cartel?"

"Of course I had no involvement," Drew exclaimed,

pulse racing. A cold sweat broke on his brow and his breath came fast.

"Are you certain about that?" Blythe scrutinized him over the rim of his glasses. "You aren't under oath, but I would remind you that any false statement could seriously injure your cause."

"Naturally, I'm certain," he responded, edgy.

"Mr. Chandler, I'm afraid we have specific information to the contrary," Blythe said, consulting his notes. "You were seen in Miami leaving Mr. Ramirez's residence on Star Island and seen again in his company at a restaurant in South Beach—Osteria del Teatro to be precise—the same evening of—" he verified his notes again "—May twelfth. You also met with Congressman MacBride in the Cayman Islands shortly before he returned to Savannah and kidnapped his wife. We'd like to know why?"

"Why, it was a pure coincidence. I happened to be in Cayman scuba diving and came across MacBride. Had I known what his intentions were, I would have attempted to stop him." Sweat broke out on his brow, his palms.

"Mr. Chandler, MacBride's troubles were already all over the press. You must have been aware."

"No. I assure you. I had no idea." He adjusted the knot of his tie. How in God's name had they managed to unearth this information?

"Other disturbing matters have come to our attention," the man continued while two of the senators leaned over and murmured to each other. George Hathaway's countenance looked bleak.

"What are you insinuating? I have nothing to hide."

"Certain parties have made the committee aware of the results of a full-scale investigation into your financial transactions over the past five years. It appears you omitted to declare a significant number of foreign investments made by your family's holding company in Bolivia."

What parties? Who the hell had done this? "I assure you, I declared everything that was required of me. I—"

"The information has been handed to the proper authorities. I'm sure if all is in order you will have no problem explaining the details to them. Now, one more thing, Mr. Chandler, something that I must admit disturbs me personally even more than the other matters discussed here today, as it raises real questions about your suitability to represent the United States in any capacity." Blythe displayed a piece of notepaper, then proceeded to hand copies of it to his colleagues. "Gentlemen, this was brought to my attention in the past few days. Perhaps, Mr. Chandler, you'd like to clarify." He leaned forward, steely-eyed, and handed Drew the piece of paper.

He took it numbly. The handwritten words swam before his eyes. He adjusted his glasses. But as he read, as the words sank in, his hand shook. Nausea gripped him and his head spun. Not this. Not now.

"I know nothing. This is a blasphemous lie," he blustered. "Someone wants to frame me."

"I don't think so. It was submitted to us from an entirely reliable source, and backed up by a number of other documents substantiating the veracity of the information."

Drew was about to protest again when all at once he was seized by a horrible apprehension. Surely not. Surely this couldn't be. Could he have made a gross misjudgment? Jerking his head round, he met Grant's unflinching gaze. In the ensuing seconds years rolled back, dreams withered and the dreadful truth hit home.

"Isabel." As he whispered her name the full impact of that foolish night's escapade crashed down on him. His chest tightened. He experienced a sharp, stabbing pain, and he gasped.

Chandler looked like a hewn statue, hand raised as though he were reaching out. His face sagged. His open lips emitted no sound.

For an interminable instant their eyes locked, and his life, his mother's ordeal and Rowena's determination flashed before him. And then Grant knew it was over. As the expressions on the senators' faces came into focus, relief hit. His objective had been reached. The blade had fallen.

Rising, Grant took Dallas's arm. Turning his back on the proceedings, he guided her toward the door. There was no point in remaining. Their job was done.

As they walked out the door, he experienced no electrifying satisfaction, no gloating fulfillment. Only the inner peace of closure. At last, justice had been served, their mother's memory avenged, Rowena's mission accomplished.

27

"It looks wonderful," Meredith exclaimed, looking about her, enchanted by the fairy-tale atmosphere Dallas had created.

"Like it?" Dallas's eyes sparkled as she admired her own handiwork.

"You have her touch. Rowena would have been proud," Meredith murmured, taking in the tasteful Christmas ivy curling amid wrought-iron and crystal angels winding up the staircase, the immense tree dominating the hall, trimmed in silver and gold, subtly illuminated by a host of twinkling fairy lights shimmering under the glistening chandelier.

"It's truly beautiful," she sighed, trying to catch Grant's voice in the murmur coming from the living room. "What's that delicious scent?" she asked, sniffing.

"It's a French herbal atomizer I found among Grandma's Christmas boxes in the attic. By the way, where are the kids?" Dallas demanded. The boys and she had established an immediate connection.

"Coming with Mom and Dad," Meredith replied, removing her coat and admiring Dallas's outfit. She looked sensational in a white satin designer tuxedo, an extravagant diamond necklace clasped around her milky throat.

Meredith's brows shot up in surprise as an unexpected yelp emanated from the kitchen, and the door burst open. "Oh, my God!" she exclaimed, laughing at the two bright red poodles scuttling toward her, "what are they doing here?" she asked, surprised to see Rodrigo in his usual uniform, following them.

"Good evening, *señora*." He executed a little bow.

"Good evening, Rodrigo," she said, smiling. "I didn't know you were coming to Savannah. How nice to see you."

"Miss Dallas called me here for Christmas," he replied, his dark features crinkling with pleasure.

"We decided we needed the whole family here," Dallas murmured, avoiding the dogs yapping at her ankles. "Down, guys, I don't want you dirtying my pants." She brushed them off, laughing.

"Was dying them red your idea, Dallas?"

"Oh, no, madam," Rodrigo answered soberly. "It is the custom. Señora Rowena always had them died red for Christmas. She had a specific tint, Russian Red, sent specially from a shop in Paris."

"We felt it was only appropriate that they should be a part of the Christmas festivities," Dallas added, winking. "Grandma would have liked that, don't you think?"

"She sure would," Meredith agreed, a wave of nostalgia gripping her. "All that's missing here tonight is Rowena herself."

"I wish I'd been less mean to her," Dallas murmured

as Rodrigo retrieved the dogs and led them back into the kitchen. "I feel bad now that I know that she was trying to shield me. I was blind and stupid."

"No, Dallas, you were young and hurt. You mustn't beat up on yourself. Rowena understood all that. She knew that one day you would, too. She loved you very much."

"I know. I just wish I'd—" She hesitated, letting out a long sigh. "You're right." She flipped her palms and sighed. "I guess all we can do is carry out her wishes."

"Exactly," Meredith replied, smiling reassuringly, then slipped a hand over Dallas's and squeezed. "She would have loved the idea of you all celebrating Christmas together. Say, who's all here?" she asked, curious. "Grant said you were having *everybody* over."

"See for yourself." Dallas drew her to the arch leading to the drawing room.

"Oh, Lord. He really did mean it," Meredith murmured, seeing Joanna in luminous scarlet silk tottering toward them in matching high heels. Craig was sipping champagne by the fire, looking handsome in a dark gray suit and festive tie, while Sally was chatting to a very attractive woman who was unfamiliar to her. "Who's that?" she whispered.

"You won't believe it, but Charles has dumped Marcy."

"You're kidding."

"Nope. Two weeks ago. Says he doesn't care if he has to downscale, he'd rather live a simpler life and be with Charlotte. He's so much more relaxed. Almost likable." Dallas grimaced comically.

"What about Patricia and Ward?"

"Oh, they're on their way. Mary Chris insisted on going to every Christmas service she could get her pious butt into." Dallas rolled her eyes. "I warned Grant how it would be. But that brother of mine is something else. Once he makes his mind up, there's no altering it. You've been warned," she muttered darkly.

"Point taken." Meredith laughed, radiating happiness. As she watched Grant circulate among his relatives with a bottle of champagne, she wondered if he'd come to a decision regarding Rowena's fortune.

They'd had so much to talk about of their own the past few days, they'd barely touched on the subject.

As she advanced into the room, she thought of Rowena and Drew Chandler and everything Grant and Dallas had told her. It must have been so hard for them to accept. Yet by the same token, now that Drew, having suffered a mild heart attack, was in the hospital, his nomination summarily withdrawn and an investigation pending, Rowena's wishes had finally been granted and justice done. Watching them here tonight, at home in Rowena's house, inviting their relatives to celebrate Christmas with them, Meredith recalled that first meeting in Miami, thought back on Dallas's truculence, Grant's determined reluctance to concede. They'd come a long way since then, she realized fondly.

Taking a deep breath, determined not to get sappy and sentimental, she advanced into the room.

"Darling." Grant moved toward her, happiness written all over him. "Merry Christmas." Dropping a kiss on her lips, he handed her a champagne flute. "Where are the boys?"

"On their way over with Mom, Dad, Jeff and Melanie."

"Wonderful. I have a surprise for them."

"Grant, not another one," she protested, laughing.

"Honey, you're spoiling them rotten. I'll never be able to get them under control again."

"We," he reminded her, eyes twinkling, "we will get them back under control. Plus I'm enjoying myself," he murmured close to her ear, "more than I ever believed possible."

"Why, Meredith." Joanna rustled up to them, eyes glued on Meredith's engagement finger. "Oh, my God," she cooed, lifting Meredith's hand and inspecting the perfect cluster of diamonds warily. "That is something else. Grant, you never do things by halves, do you? Harry Winston, I suppose? Does this mean that you two are getting married?" Her eyes flew warily from one to the other.

"Your judgment is unerring as always, Joanna. Yes, we are getting married."

"Why weren't we told?" she muttered, twiddling her glass nervously as she thought of Meredith getting her hands on all those millions. "And why hasn't anything been resolved yet regarding our affairs?" she queried, voice rising. "I guess you've been too busy feathering your own nest." She cast Meredith a look of loathing.

"Joanna, hold your horses," Grant interrupted. "You won't be disappointed." He winked at her.

"You mean—" Joanna cut off midsentence, eyes arrested.

"Everything comes to she who waits," he whispered mischievously in her ear, causing a smile to dawn.

"Well, I just hope I don't have to wait too long. May you two be very happy," she said in a more gracious tone. She didn't want to spoil it if Grant had made decisions in her favor. "You've heard about Charles and Charlotte, of course," she murmured, lowering her voice. "Incredible. I never thought he'd leave Marcia. Not while she holds the purse strings. But he says he doesn't care about the money anymore. Just wants to be happy. I thought he was crazy," she sighed, deciding on a new pitch, "but I have to say, I've never seen him this content." She frowned. "Maybe he's right. Maybe the money's not that important after all."

"Joanna, are you sure you're okay?" Dallas quirked an amused brow at her cousin, leaned on Grant's arm and laughed.

"Oh, fine. But seeing Charles looking so happy makes me wonder if I shouldn't consider that nice company director from California I met on that Caribbean cruise last spring. He keeps sending me flowers and e-mails. I never considered him seriously as he's not in my league. Still, he was a really nice man, and so handsome." She let out a sigh, then shrugged, raised her glass and turned to Rowena's portrait. "You sure took us for a mighty fine ride," she said, taking a sip. "Grant, I still can't believe you're considering the poodle foundation," she said, fishing for information. "Surely you could send some of that lovely money our way?" she pouted.

"As you remarked earlier, Joanna, I never do things by halves," he answered, shaking his head sadly. He and Dallas exchanged a quick, complicit look.

"Well, at least there's the trust," Joanna conceded, deciding it was time to back off. "My broker tells me that all the investment changes you've made will increase the income by at least a third," she added more cheerfully.

"As your trustee, it's my obligation to see the trust generates as much income as possible."

"I'll drink to that," Joanna agreed with feeling. She

glanced disparagingly at the poodles yelping excitedly around the hall, tugging mercilessly at the lower branches of the Christmas tree. "Will somebody do something about those infernal creatures?" she exclaimed, waving her champagne flute toward them.

"Dallas, control the damn dogs," Grant ordered.

"Control them yourself," she said, tossing her gorgeous blond mane rebelliously. "*I* wasn't the one who insisted they be dyed that ridiculous color. I bet it rubs off on all the furniture," she added, escaping toward Craig and Sally.

"That girl needs taking in hand," Grant muttered as Dallas sauntered sexily back into the living room. "She should find herself a husband. One who can hold her in check."

"She will, in good time. Or he'll find her." Seeing him react in such a possessive manner left the ghost of a smile hovering on Meredith's lips. He was unused to being flouted, she realized tenderly. Handsome, at times impossible, always generous and, oh, so tender. That was her Grant.

"Ah, there they are." Grant smiled as he stepped forward to receive the Rowland contingent now pouring in. The boys, excited to be part of such a grown-up party, were dressed in the blue-and-red Ralph Lauren sweaters Tracy had given them for Christmas.

"Mom, look at this new game." Zack shoved the DVD at her.

"Hi, guys." Jeff and Melanie had their arms piled with presents, which Mick helped them stack under the tree.

Soon they were assembled in the drawing room. Clarice sat next to Charlotte on the settee, while Joanna flirted with all the men in the group.

Dallas pattered busily back and forth, making sure

the kitchen staff hired for the occasion were on the ball.
The kids followed her around like faithful puppies.

"Okay," she said, coming back into the room. "Dinner is served."

"Oh, wonderful." Joanna flapped her eyelashes at John Rowland, who gallantly offered her his arm.

"Clarice?" Grant offered to escort his future mother-in-law and proceeded into the dining room with the others trailing in their wake.

"Oh, my goodness," Joanna exclaimed, stopping in the doorway to admire the room, a catch in her voice. "I remember it looking like this when I was a little girl."

"So do I," Ward agreed.

"It's exquisite," Clarice murmured, glancing affectionately at her future son-in-law.

"We have Dallas to thank for that," he said, looking over at her proudly.

"Dallas indeed," Patricia said waspishly, her lips pursed. "I thought you were only interested in horses and young men, not table settings." She sniffed at the polished mahogany of Rowena's George III dining table, which she'd always secretly coveted. It was superbly decked with crisp white linen and Rowena's eighteenth-century buffed sterling. Baccarat crystal and Royal Doulton sparkled in the glow of two gleaming candelabras.

"Mother," Mary Chris muttered, turning beet-red and blinking behind her thick lenses, "that was unchristian."

"Unworthy of you, Patricia," Charles agreed, shaking his head. "Let's enjoy Dallas and Grant's generous hospitality. Charlotte, I believe you're here," he said, peering at the place cards.

"What's this?" Joanna reached for an envelope that

was placed in the middle of her place setting. Her name was scribbled on it in black ink. She turned it over as John pulled out her chair.

"Oh! I have one, too," Mary Chris murmured, picking hers up.

"Hey, so do I." Ward held his up for the company to see.

Charles looked down at his plate, frowning. "Perhaps we should open them."

Joanna took her knife and slit the top of the envelope while Grant and the others took their seats.

"Oh, jeepers!" Joanna stared at the cashier's check in awe. Her fingers shook. Could she be reading right? Zeros swam before her eyes. "Is this serious?" she squeaked, staring openmouthed at Grant.

"Don't thank me. Thank Rowena. And Dallas. She was a big part of the decision to split all the money fairly between you."

Charles cleared his throat. "This is extremely generous," he said at last. "I'd given up any hope. I—" He glanced at Charlotte, eyes tender. "Thanks," he said at last, turning to Grant.

"It's yours by right. I'm sure this was what Rowena intended."

"Maybe I could get a fishing lodge now," Ward said dreamily.

"Mary Chris, if you give more than five hundred dollars of this to the church, I'll make Grant take it all back," Dallas threatened.

"Oh, no, you won't." Mary Chris clutched her check, tears gathering. "Think of all the good work that can be done with this, Mother," she whispered, turning to Patricia.

"Yes, dear, but for the moment I think you should

leave it with me." Patricia, having recovered her usual sugary attitude, deftly plucked the check from her daughter's fingers and slipped it into her purse. "Much safer this way. You, too, Ward," she said peremptorily, reaching across the table.

"No." Ward held the check out of reach.

The whole table fell silent at the firmness of his tone.

"Ward," Patricia repeated, steel hovering just below the surface.

"I won't give it to you," he said, face flushing. "Grant, you gave the money to *me*, didn't you?" he asked, turning toward the end of the table for support. "I don't have to give it to anyone."

"Absolutely not," Grant agreed smoothly.

"There." Ward stared at his mother, surprised at his own daring.

Patricia opened her mouth, then closed it. Never had Ward spoken to her in such a tone.

Meredith laid her hand on Ward's arm. "You can put it in the bank, Ward, and Grant can help you invest it," she said kindly.

"Yes." His face lit up. "I'd like that. I don't know anything about investing. Would you mind?" He turned his innocent gaze upon his cousin.

"It'd be my pleasure, Ward."

"Maybe you could come fishing with us," Zack piped up. "We're going to fish in Scotland with Grant. It'd be okay if he came, too, wouldn't it, Grant?"

Meredith smiled and exchanged a look with her mother. A week earlier she never could have imagined this.

Joanna was still gloating over her check. She smoothed it tenderly. "At last," she whispered.

Then an interruption occurred as the door to the

kitchen opened and Rodrigo entered, triumphantly carrying a huge decorated turkey reposing on a vast silver salver. The kitchen staff followed with the trimmings.

After a satisfying meal, which lasted an hour and a half, the company repaired to the living room, where they dropped into Rowena's ample couches and armchairs, more champagne was served and presents were opened.

"Boy, I've eaten so much, I'll burst out of my Dolce pants," Dallas exclaimed, pouting at her waist.

"Well, before you do that I'd like to give you this." Grant leaned over from his perch on the sofa arm and handed her a festive flat package.

"What is it?" Dallas asked, curious, sitting up straighter.

"Open it and see," Mick urged, leaning perilously over the back of the couch where Dallas was seated.

Everyone watched as Dallas wrestled with the bright red ribbon and discarded wrapping paper about her, which Meredith picked up. "Oh, my God!" she squealed, her hand covering her mouth. "Oh, Grant, I don't believe it." She jumped up and threw her arms around him. "You are the best brother anyone could ever wish for," she exclaimed in a quivering voice. "Guys, look, look what he's given me." She held up the picture of a stallion in one hand and waved the horse's papers in the other.

"I thought you'd like Someday Soon as the stud for your breeding program," Grant said, his voice laced with satisfaction as he slipped his arm around her and squeezed. "He's at Johnny Graney's place in Ireland right now, but you can go and pick him up in the New Year."

"It's a horse," Mick said excitedly, taking the picture

from Dallas's weak clutch and showing his brother and the other members in the room.

"And not just any horse," Dallas murmured, gazing up at her brother, then at Meredith, her eyes filled with tears. "This is too wonderful. This and knowing that you two are really going to be together," she said reaching for their hands and turning toward Rowena's portrait, gazing down at them with her half smile from above the mantelpiece. "I hate to have to say this," she murmured, swallowing, "but you knew exactly what you were doing, Grandma. God bless you."

There was a moment's silence as everybody's eyes turned toward the picture. Then an enthusiastic "hear, hear" resounded throughout the room.

"To Rowena," Charles said, raising his glass.

"To Rowena," everyone present answered.

And raising their glasses in unison, they drank.

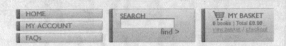